All We Hold Dear

Kelly Cheek

Cover and book design by Kelly Cheek

ISBN: 978-0-9909982-7-3

Printed in the United States of America

KELLY CHEEK LITERARY ADVENTURES
CENTENNIAL, CO

Author's Note

When researching the historical aspects of this story, I put forth great effort to remain accurate. All information pertaining to the Trail of Tears and the events leading up to it is, to the best of my knowledge, true and accurate. By the same token, I attempted to describe Manitou Springs in a way that was faithful to the time.

However, there were a few instances when the information available to me was a bit lacking. For example, at the time that Isadora Byrnes arrives at Manitou Springs, the only people living there were, as the story relates, Native Americans and the occasional French trapper, neither of whom, unfortunately, left a written record.

Also, there were a couple of occasions when the information available was contradictory. This being a novel, it is primarily a work of fiction. Therefore, at these times, I used whichever source worked for the story – as an author, I'm allowed to do that.

I won't say what these points are. If you don't know, it shouldn't spoil the story for you, and if you do, hopefully they're small enough points that the story will still provide a little enjoyment for you.

Besides, the one I chose to use could have been the correct one anyway.

Thank you for reading.

Kelly

Also by Kelly Cheek

Trial by Fire

The Lost Colony

JackSimile and the Phantom Fury

We are now about to take our leave and kind farewell to our native land, the country that the Great Spirit gave our Fathers. We are on the eve of leaving that country that gave us birth. It is with sorrow we are forced by the white man to quit the scenes of our childhood. We bid farewell to it and all we hold dear.

Attributed to Charles Renatus Hicks, Second Principal Chief of the Cherokee Nation

few diehard cicadas continued chirring in the trees, their raucous sound blending now with the crickets and frogs. The sun had set an hour before and the summer heat was becoming more bearable. The massive bulk of Pikes Peak rose to the west, and a mild, cool breeze was languishing down the mountainside.

Near the base, and appearing only a little less imposing than the mountain, stood a gargantuan log house. A stream slipped melodiously past, attracting the wildlife. A mule deer and her fawn emerged from the deep shadows of the forest at the back of the yard, attracted to the stream for one last drink before retiring. Now completely illuminated by the full moon, the doe was cautious, but she ignored the raccoon that was also indulging.

The night birds were about as well. An owl dipped noiselessly through the air, alighting on the branch of a linden tree, and carefully examined the lawn for movement. Cicadas in the immediate vicinity of his perch ceased their call for a few moments, then started up again, although with a little less spirit, as if they were ready to bed down for the night.

The distant scratching sound of tires on pavement gradually grew in volume and the animals looked up at the approaching lights of a car. Turning off the road, the car pulled up to the front of the house, where the driveway expanded into a larger parking area. The doe was particularly cautious, ready for flight on a moment's notice, and kept watching until the car door opened and an elderly woman slowly pulled herself out. The animals resumed their drinking after the woman laboriously made her way up the steps to the front porch.

The woman turned her key and entered the front door, as the beam of a flashlight played across the inside of a second story window.

Finn Gallagher sighed and folded the flaps back down on the box he had been looking through. He was getting discouraged. There were stacks of boxes in this room, but it seemed like they held nothing but papers and receipts; useless junk.

He pushed the box aside and shined his flashlight at the next one, opening the flaps. He put the flashlight down with the beam aimed at the top of the box. Some of his friends were proponents of small, easily concealed flashlights, but Finn still preferred his big club of a torch and the wide beam it provided.

"Who are you?" came a woman's voice from behind him, and Finn quickly snatched up the flashlight, gripping it tightly as the overhead light switched on. He turned and saw an elderly woman standing in the doorway.

"Oh, darlin'," he said with a prominent Irish accent, "sure and you weren't supposed to be here tonight."

"I asked who you are! What are you doing here?"

Finn stepped toward the woman, but stopped when she raised her right hand. It was holding a revolver, pointed at him.

"Where is it, dear?" he asked. "Don't you think enough people have died?"

"I don't know what you're talking about," the woman replied.

"Come on, lady," Finn said, exasperated. "Let's end this."

"I accept," she said. She raised her other hand, and Finn saw that she was holding her phone. She looked down at it to press 911, and in that moment, Finn rushed her. Startled, she squeezed the trigger, but the bullet smashed harmlessly through the front window. In the same instant, Finn hit her on the head with his flashlight and the woman crumpled into a heap on the floor.

Finn glanced at the broken window. Even though the houses in this area were spaced far apart, he knew that the sound of the gun-shot and shattered glass might attract neighbors. He sighed and started to go out the door, but he hesitated as he looked down at the woman. He knelt and placed a finger on the side of her neck. He could find no pulse.

"Shite!" He stood up. "Stupid old woman!"

He shook his head, then ran down the stairs and out the front door.

The emergency vehicles pulled away from the curb, leaving Dora Baskin standing on the sidewalk, sweltering in the afternoon sun. Her client, Anthony Jones, lay strapped to the gurney in the ambulance, but it had driven away without the lights or siren.

Anthony was dead. The case was closed.

Dora took a deep breath and looked down at her feet, trying not to think about the blood that had seeped into her left shoe, but with each step she took, she could feel it. She climbed into her 1995 Corolla, started it up and turned on the air conditioner, sighing as the summer heat slowly dissipated.

Oh, God, I can't do this anymore, she thought.

She put the car in gear and headed north on Santa Fe Boulevard toward downtown Denver. Occasionally she glanced at the South Platte River rushing by on her left, but she knew that doing that was only a distraction at best. She was still surrounded by poverty. At each intersection, she saw at least one homeless person holding a cardboard sign. Some of them she recognized, and each one made her feel like a failure.

She continued north, passing the enormous hulk of the old Gates Rubber Company, ugly and empty for as long as she could remember. After passing through a few other industrial neighborhoods, she eventually entered the Santa Fe Arts District, and she appreciated the renovations that had resuscitated the area. The art galleries and community theaters that now lined the street were popular destinations for the trend setters and trend followers of the area. But just a block or two behind these businesses lay residential neighborhoods, mostly Hispanic, which were still struggling. Gentrification had raised property values in the area, but it also ran out the lower income residents who could no longer afford to live there.

As an inner city social worker for a small struggling firm called "Looking Up," Dora attempted to intercede for the underprivileged in the area, so she was especially sensitive to poverty. She herself had used up what savings she had, and gone into debt besides, caring for her mother toward the end. Now, she lived paycheck to paycheck, but at least she *got* a paycheck. It was the condition of those living in abject poverty that really troubled her.

Her primary responsibility was to match her clients with government sponsored programs that could help them turn their lives around. But all too often, inadequate funding for the programs left Dora feeling angry at the abundant injustice in the world and discouraged over her own inability to help.

Frequently, though, her clients were just too deeply entrenched in old habits and patterns to stay on "the straight and narrow."

Anthony was the latest case in point. As a poor young African American, he was practically a poster child for victims of the system. Raised by a single mother who managed to find money for drugs and alcohol, but little else, his own destitution was almost inevitable. His mother died of an overdose five years before when he was twelve, and thus began his life on the street. Lately, in the summer months, he had been sleeping beside the Platte River under the Mississippi Avenue overpass, and panhandling at the intersection during the day.

He had been referred to Dora last year and she had worked tirelessly to get him into government-funded programs that would provide some education and even help him get a job. He stuck with it for a while, but eventually it became too hard for him to keep up the effort, to make meaningful changes. Life on the street, though difficult, was familiar.

Dora hadn't seen him in several weeks, but when the police called her this afternoon, they said that Anthony had given them her name. She rushed to the scene to find Anthony bleeding, being treated by the EMTs.

He had been conscious when the police arrived and he gave a brief statement. Apparently he had gotten into an altercation with a young white man who had called him a 'lazy nigger.' Shortly after that, he was stabbed. The white man was nowhere to be found.

Careful to stay out of the emergency workers' way, Dora had gotten down on one knee and placed her hand on Anthony's forehead. He stirred briefly, just enough to cough, sending a bloody froth onto her foot. His breathing gurgled in his throat, then stopped altogether.

After a brief attempt to revive him, the EMTs decided that his injuries were just too severe.

Dora was shaken. She had never watched someone die before and she could not purge the image of Anthony's face from her mind. She turned on the stereo and listened as the old cassette player started playing Handel's *Water Music*. Though she liked all kinds, she found that baroque music helped her relax when she had had a trying day.

She had been playing Handel a lot lately.

Within a few minutes, Dora turned right on 14th Avenue, driving a few blocks past the attorney's offices and bail bond agencies, finally pulling up in front of a nondescript brick building. She looked at the faded sign above the door that said, "Looking Up – Helping Coloradans get back on their feet."

Dora picked up her purse from the seat beside her and got out of her car, almost instantly melting in the summer heat. She made her way to the door and went into the relative coolness inside and saw Madeline, her supervisor, talking to the receptionist. Madeline looked at Dora's face, then at the splash of crimson on her shoe.

"What the hell happened to you?" she asked.

Dora just shook her head and moved down the hall toward her little cubicle of an office. Madeline fell into step beside her.

"Anthony's dead," Dora said. "He died just after I got there."

"Oh my god," Madeline replied. "What happened?"

"He got in a fight. Stabbed in the gut." Entering her office, Dora fell back into her chair. Madeline followed her in and closed the door behind her. "I know you wanted me to drop him a while back. I guess it's time now, huh?"

"Yeah," said Madeline, "and now you can throw yourself heart and soul into another case." Dora caught the sarcasm in Madeline's voice.

"We're supposed to care about these people, right?"

"Yes, we care, but we can't lose ourselves trying to help them." Madeline paused. "Honey, we've talked about this before. Failure is a part of what we do. But you can't view them as *your* failures. Some of these people are just in too deep. Even with our help, they still have to do their part, and we have no control over that."

"I know, Maddie."

"All we can do is make programs available and encourage them to take advantage of them. At the risk of sounding cold and heartless, it's just a job."

"I don't know how to think of it as just a job. I didn't get into this just to bring home a paycheck." Dora looked at the folders on her desk. She picked up the one that was on top. It was Anthony's. "These aren't just cases, they're people."

"Well, considering how common the so-called failures are, you better figure out how to see it that way, or it's going to eat you up." Madeline paused, then looked at Dora through narrowed eyes. "You know what you need? You need to get laid." Dora rolled her eyes and looked up at Madeline with a disgusted expression. "I'm not talking about romance. You just need to relieve some pressure."

"Maddie, you know I'm not into meaningless sex. I'm not a one-night-stand kind of person."

16

"I know, Isadora," Madeline acknowledged. "And I'm not recommending this as your boss, but as your friend."

"I appreciate that, but it's just not me. And you know I hate the name Isadora."

"I'm sorry. But what is 'you'?" Madeline asked, obviously frustrated. "A long string of romances that don't go anywhere?"

"That's not fair."

"You have to admit you've ended more relationships than most women your age."

"I haven't ended all of them," Dora protested.

"No, some you just overanalyzed and cross-examined until the guys had enough and left of their own volition." Dora looked at her, crestfallen. Madeline's face softened as she seemed to realize that she had gone too far. "I'm sorry. That was out of line. I didn't mean to upset you."

Dora silently nodded her head. Madeline stood and went to the side of Dora's desk, giving her shoulder a squeeze.

"I've got a report to finish," Madeline said. "How about after that, we go have a drink?"

"Sure, Maddie, that'll be nice." Dora gave a half-hearted smile as Madeline left.

Dora spent a few minutes composing a brief addendum to Anthony's file, then placed the folder in her "Out" box. Case closed. Simple as that.

She neatened up the other items on her desk and was gathering her things when her cell phone rang. It was a number she didn't recognize.

"Hello?"

"Hello, is this Isadora Baskin?" asked an unfamiliar voice. She cringed again at the name.

"Yes, it is."

"Ms. Baskin, I'm Sergeant Jerry Devlin of the Manitou Springs Police Department." He paused for a moment. "Ms. Baskin, I'm very sorry to have to tell you this, but your grandmother is dead.

17

As we could find no information concerning the location of your father, it seems you are her next of kin."

Anthony's death still fresh in her mind, her eyes instantly filled with tears as a sob escaped her lips. She bit her lip and took a deep breath to regain her composure.

"I'm so sorry, Ms. Baskin."

"Please, call me Dora," she said.

"Of course, Dora."

"What happened?"

"Well, I'm afraid she was killed late last night during the course of an attempted robbery."

"Oh my God!" She had prepared herself to hear that her grandmother had died of a stroke or a heart attack, but murdered? She couldn't imagine her sweet little grandmother suffering a violent end, but she struggled to focus her attention on what Devlin was saying.

"Fortunately, we caught a break. Well, in a way. A local man doing a neighborhood watch patrol happened to be passing by at the time, heard a noise and saw the perpetrator running from her house. The man on patrol was armed and he shouted for the intruder to stop, but when he didn't, he shot him."

Dora pulled a tissue from the box she kept on her desk for clients and wiped her eyes. She could picture the scene, could see the neighborhood and her grandmother's house. But she couldn't reconcile the peaceful scene with the idea of her grandmother being murdered.

"There were signs of a forced entry," Devlin continued. "He came in through the front door, and based on the clues at the scene, it appears your grandmother was the victim of a botched robbery attempt." Dora could hear the sound of pages being turned and assumed Devlin was looking through his notes. "Do you know anyone named Finn Gallagher?"

"No, why?"

"That was the name of the assailant."

"Did he get away with anything?"

"No, it doesn't look like it," said Devlin. "We think your grandmother surprised him before he had found anything he wanted. We don't know if he meant to kill her or if it was an accident, but either way, it was committed during the commission of a felony."

Dora sighed and put her head in her hand.

"Again," Devlin continued, "I'm very sorry."

ora was packing a couple of bags for a few days down in Manitou Springs. Yesterday Madeline took Dora's cases and ordered her to take a week off. Dora resisted at first, but realized that it would likely do her some good to get away, even under these circumstances. Eric Benson, her grandmother's lawyer, had called while Dora was packing, and she made arrangements to meet with him as soon as she arrived.

She looked at herself in the mirror on the wall of her bedroom. She was a "Hodges Hottie." At least, that's the way her grandmother's family had referred to their features, the characteristic golden hair, deep brown eyes and naturally tanned skin. Her grandmother's maiden name was Hodges, and these features had been passed down through generations of that line. Dora's hair was shoulder length and her features, she had been told many times, had an attractive, almost exotic look, even without makeup, which she seldom wore. Though this morning, she opted for a little concealer when she saw the circles under her eyes.

She carried her bags to her car and climbed in after them. Within minutes, she left behind her dumpy little apartment in the historic Capitol Hill neighborhood near downtown Denver. After a short drive west on Colfax, she got on I-25 south. As she made her way out of Denver, she frequently glanced at the mountains to the west. She'd been so focused on the cases and problems in front of her that she hadn't bothered to really look around in a while. She felt herself relaxing the farther she drove from   Denver, and the closer she got to Manitou Springs.

The springs from which the town takes its name were discovered by white men in the early nineteenth century, though they had been used by Native Americans long before that. Even now, the springs pumped their water into various receptacles around downtown Manitou Springs, at several historic markers, some still producing their characteristic chugging sound, and tourists enjoyed tasting the fabled mineral water.

The town was old with narrow streets winding around irregular blocks built on the mountain. There was also a quaint downtown area that featured stores and businesses with Victorian-styled storefronts, and the ice cream and candy shops. As a child, she had loved going to museums, book stores, and other attractions with her grandmother, who took her out for ice cream or fudge afterwards, making her promise not to tell her parents.

And she loved the huge log house that her grandmother had lived in all alone. The house that Dora herself now owned. According to the attorney, Eric Benson, the bulk of the estate was the old house.

Dora loved her grandmother, but had not had any real contact with her for a while. In fact she was ashamed to realize that it had been years, her relationship with her grandmother one of the many casualties of her parents' failed marriage. Her parents, embarrassed by their increasingly sucky marriage, and tired of explaining it to family, or of trying to tell a believable lie, had gradually started keeping to themselves. Family reunions went on without them.

Dora's thoughts drifted to her difficult life with her parents. Her mother had been a beautiful woman. She was an artist in her vital years, and made decent money from art shows and commissions, until depression made it difficult for her to work. The debts piled up, compounding with interest, as her father's pay was barely enough for groceries and rent, and they moved every few months into cheaper and cheaper apartments. Seven years ago, Dora's father cashed his last paycheck and quietly slipped away. Her mother, already prone to depression and racked with unhappiness, descended even deeper.

Dora paid her mother's debts using her own meager savings, and started searching for a decent but inexpensive apartment for her. She also paid for doctor's visits and prescriptions, since her mother had no insurance, and began investigating welfare programs for which her mother might qualify.

After a year on anti-depressants and other prescription drugs, her mother got in the bathtub and cut her wrists. Dora had been the one to find her. After all these years, Dora was still haunted by the image burned into her memory, of her mother's emaciated form in the bloody water.

When it got particularly bad, Dora leaned on her suicide survivor support group. It helped, but it was still hard for her to open up. Old habits were hard to break.

With her mother gone, Dora had more time on her hands, so she immersed herself in her job and continued the isolation to which she had become accustomed. What had started as her parents' dysfunction continued as Dora's way of life. As Madeline had reminded her last night, it affected her love life as well. Having witnessed her parents' miserable marriage for so many years, and the pitiful way it ended, when Dora *did* enter a romantic relationship, she was often overly cautious. She meticulously analyzed every little thing that was done or said, attempting to divine the meaning or motivation, until the man *du jour* tired of it and left. The last one had left several months ago.

For the first time in her life, Dora finally conceded that she was lonely.

Dora smiled as the terrain changed. The hills and buttes that became common between Castle Rock and Colorado Springs caused a nostalgic shiver down her spine. She used to love going down to Gramma Izzy's house to visit when she was a child, and the rugged landscape was a pleasant reminder of those times.

The topography changed again as she rolled into northwestern Colorado Springs, the looming bulk of Pikes Peak serving as a backdrop to the city's urban sprawl. She could see the red rocks of Garden of the Gods on her right and knew that she was getting close to her turnoff.

Her first stop was the attorney's office, where she signed the paperwork that made her grandmother's house officially hers. With the paperwork beside her in a folder emblazoned with the "Taylor, Benson and Schulmann" logo, Dora felt ready to see her inheritance. In addition to the house, there was some cash, stocks and bonds. What had not been willed to charity amounted to a few hundred thousand dollars, more money than Dora ever dreamed she'd have.

On the way, she stopped at the Manitou Springs Police Department, but there was nothing new about Gramma Izzy's case. It was essentially closed, though not filed just yet. The neighbor who had shot the intruder stated that he may have seen a couple more people in the shadows around the house, but couldn't be certain. Sergeant Devlin had said that they had found no evidence of other people in the house, but in light of the neighbor's testimony, he assured Dora that they would be patrolling the area for the next few days.

Memories came flooding back as she drove through the little town at the foot of Pikes Peak. Gramma and Grampa had lived in a fairly secluded area outside of town, as Highway 24 climbed northwestward up the side of the mountain. After just a short time, Dora exited from the highway and headed south. Over the years, a neighborhood had been hewn from the rocks and forest, but even after all this time, the neighbors were widely spaced, allowing a feeling of isolation.

And there ahead of her stood Gramma Izzy's house. She pulled up the driveway and onto the gravel parking area, next to a tan Impala, and for the briefest moment, she thought that Gramma Izzy was home.

To Dora, the house had an almost magical look. It was a huge structure, constructed of smooth, golden logs perched on a large base of river rock. It had been added on to at least a couple of times since its construction, but the additions had been faithful to the original structure. The high front porch, about four or five feet off the ground, wrapped all the way around the house, widening into a sizable deck on the south side. The house seemed, on the exterior at least, to be in very good shape, aside from a broken window on the second floor.

What the hell am I going to do with a place like this?

Dora turned her car off and sat for a bit, just looking at the enormous house. Her breath caught in her chest for a moment as she felt a flood of nostalgia. She remembered family reunions spent here in summers as a child. The house had been full of relatives, but with at least six bedrooms on the second floor, plus a couple of small intriguing rooms on the third floor, there had been plenty of room for all of them.

She shook her head and sighed, then got out of the car and approached the front door. There were still lengths of crime scene tape in places, but Sergeant Devlin had assured her that they were finished and that she could enter, so she pulled them down and wadded them up.

Keys in hand, she unlocked the hand-carved door and walked inside. There were gouges in the door frame where a crowbar had been used to force the door open, but the doorknob and the deadbolt still worked, so she locked the door behind her. A chill of apprehension slithered down her spine, not only because of what had happened here two nights ago, but also because she had never been here by herself. She didn't believe in ghosts, but if ever there was a place still firmly entrenched in the past, this would be it.

The entryway was a room unto itself. There was a large bench and coat rack combination along the wall to the left and two chairs and a small table on the right, but aside from these things, it seemed rather bare and empty. A fine powder dusted the tables and doorframes, no doubt from the crime scene investigators' search for fingerprints.

Dora walked slowly into the living room, smiling at the comforting feeling that washed over her. She remembered the beautiful antique furniture from her childhood and despite her previous misgivings at entering the house, she started to feel more at home. The other rooms on the lower floor were furnished similarly.

Absently fingering the smooth varnished yellow pine handrail and balusters, she leisurely climbed the stairs while surveying the oil paintings that ascended with her, portraits of people long dead.

The second floor was, like the first, also full of quality antiques, though a couple of the bedrooms were unused and unfurnished. Boxes and other items were strewn haphazardly in them and Dora figured that they had probably been used for storage. It was in the second of these rooms that Gramma Izzy had been killed, and it was messier, as if the burglar had been looking in the boxes when he was interrupted. The only sign that remained of the violence was the broken window that she had seen from the outside. There was no blood. The police said that Gramma had been struck in the head and that the cause of death was blunt force trauma.

Dora went into Gramma Izzy's bedroom and looked around. The bed was unmade, and it appeared that things had been disturbed in this room as well, and again, the surfaces were covered with fingerprint dust.

She walked around the room, looking at family photographs, many of which she had seen several times growing up, and most of which were grouped on a small table near the bed. There were a couple of photographs of Dora, a few of her father at various ages, and some of other relatives that she only vaguely remembered from her childhood. Then there were pictures of people, like the portraits ascending the stairs, who remained unknown to Dora. But one photograph, a picture of Gramma and Grampa, brought tears to her eyes. Grampa had died several years ago, and now Gramma was gone, too. But Dora looked at Gramma's eyes in the photograph, always smiling and warm. Even at times when her face wore a stern expression, there was still a mischievous twinkle in her eyes.

I'm sorry I wasn't around more, Gramma.

Dora put the photograph down and wiped her eyes. She wandered up the narrow staircase to the third floor and looked around, having only a slight recollection of the place from when she had played up there as a little girl. It was a little different than she remembered, as it seemed to be used only for storage now, with a few pieces of unused furniture, stacked boxes and trunks, and a hodge-podge of miscellaneous items spilling out of drawers and crates.

Feeling a grumbling in her belly, she realized that it was after noon, so she went back down to the first floor to look around the kitchen. She first went through the refrigerator and threw out some things that appeared to be older and going bad. From what was left, she put together a sandwich and a small plate of cheese and crackers.

From the counter where she was working, she looked out the back window at the large yard with scattered flower gardens lining a path leading down to the creek just to the south of the house. Roses of various colors lined the back fence, and cosmos were growing in almost every flower bed. Along one side of the property was a forty foot long hedge of lilac bushes, forming a twelve foot high barrier.

Again, she experienced a feeling of nostalgia. Gramma had always had such a green thumb. Dora remembered how she used to love being outside in Gramma and Grampa's garden when she was a little girl. The assorted flowers always attracted honeybees and a variety of butterflies.

Dora carried her lunch outside and made herself comfortable in a chaise lounge under a linden tree. She had barely finished her sandwich when, lulled by the murmuring of the creek, and by a head full of disquieting thoughts, she fell fast asleep.

Dora awoke to the rumbling of a gathering storm. She rushed inside just before the rain started. Being all alone in this enormous empty house, made her feel on edge, and as the lightning flashed and the rain fell in darkening sheets outside, Dora tried to ignore the uneasiness she felt. She had to focus her mind on something else.

She had imagined a big cleaning project, but as it turned out, it wasn't as bad as she thought. Other than the disorder from the burglary, and the ensuing investigation, the house was in pretty good shape. She spent about three hours cleaning, and as she was doing this, she found a phone book, and flipping through the pages, she located a glass company and arranged for the repair of the upstairs window.

Just out of curiosity, she turned to "Estate – Appraisals and Liquidation." She found several listings and scanned through them. Then, feeling a pang of guilt at thinking about selling the house, she sighed and closed the book, shoving it back in the cubbyhole where Gramma kept it.

She decided to go through the boxes and trunks on the second and third floors, throw out the inevitable junk, sort things that could be sold or donated, and see if there was anything worth keeping.

The sun had gone behind Pikes Peak, so Dora switched on the entryway light. Starting up the stairs, she again looked at the portraits. Wondering if perhaps they were relatives, she examined them more closely. She didn't recognize anybody in the paintings, but in the bright overhead light, she noticed the contrast of a dull spot on one of them. She leaned over to look more closely at it, and she smiled. Apparently at some time in the past, a hole in the canvas had been mended with thread as if it were a piece of clothing.

It was a portrait of a beautiful woman, apparently a Native American, though she was dressed in the clothing of a white woman from about two hundred years ago. Her fine-featured face bore a serene expression with just a hint of a smile, as she sat in a red tufted chair. Her long black hair fell casually around her shoulders, as if she were simply relaxing at home, perfectly at ease.

Another painting appeared to be a family portrait, a handsome Native American man sitting in a chair with a pretty white woman standing behind him, her hands resting on his right shoulder. Around her neck hung a gold pendant, and while the painting didn't show much detail, it looked as if there might have been some kind of design on the face of the pendant. A blonde girl of perhaps two years old, a good-natured smile on her face, sat on the man's lap.

Yet another painting was of an older couple, both with silver hair. The painting was done in a style similar to the others. It looked much like other nineteenth century portraits, except for the uncharacteristically garish dress the woman was wearing.

Not finding any clues as to their identities, though, or of the other portraits lining the staircase, Dora continued up to the second floor and began looking through boxes in the two unused bedrooms. There was a plethora of mundane items – receipts and other papers, the necessity of which had expired years ago. After a few hours, Dora had cleared out several boxes of trash. During that time, the man from the glass company had come and repaired the window.

By now, it was dark outside. Dora stretched and sighed. She was satisfied with what she had accomplished in such a short time, but there was still a lot of junk on the third floor. Still, she had not learned anything more about Gramma Izzy, other than a possible pack rat tendency.

Having put in a good day's work in the house, Dora was tired. She chose the bedroom next to Gramma's room and, after making sure that doors and windows were locked, she went to bed.

ora woke up to bright sunshine and the singing of birds outside her window. She luxuriated for a few minutes, listening to the birdsongs, before she stretched and sat up, dangling her feet off the side of the bed. She looked around the room, appreciating the homey décor, and she smiled at the comfort she felt.

She went downstairs to the kitchen, since coffee was her first order of business, and as it brewed, she walked around the house. She felt good about the work she had done the day before, but today, she felt aimless.

The coffee maker beeped when it was finished brewing and Dora went back to the kitchen and poured a cup. Again, she saw the phone book in its cubbyhole.

What am I going to do with a place this big? she thought in response to the returning guilt. She shook her head. She knew she wasn't being cold and callous, simply practical. She pulled out the book and opened it again to "Estate – Appraisals and Liquidation." Unsure of how to choose a company to help her sell the house, she picked one with a catchy name and dialed the number.

"Estate of Mind, Shawn speaking," said a voice on the other end.

"Hello, my name is Dora Baskin. I've just inherited my grandmother's estate and am trying to decide what to do with it. Without obligating myself just yet, can you tell me what's involved in liquidating an estate?"

"Well," replied Shawn, "the first step would be for me to come over and see what you've got. I'll make some notes and take some pictures, and then I can work up an appraisal of the approximate value."

"Okay." Again, Dora felt guilty but she pushed it aside. "When could you do that?"

"Actually, I've had a cancellation," he said. "I could be there at 11:00. Would that work for you?"

"Perfect." They briefly discussed fees, and she gave him the address.

"Great," he said. "I'll see you at 11:00." She put her phone down and tried to ignore the scolding she felt from her grandmother. But Dora knew the scolding was actually coming from her own conscience. She felt as if she were betraying Gramma Izzy.

Dora heard a car pull up in front and she went to the living room window. She saw a royal blue Chevy Malibu convertible, circa 1965, with the top down. Behind the wheel was a man of about thirty-five, who was gathering some items from off the passenger seat.

Dora watched appreciatively as the man got out of his car and casually pushed his sandy hair back into place. She noticed the easy way he moved, and aside from the clipboard in his hand and the camera around his neck, she thought he looked more like a surfer than an estate appraiser.

He climbed the steps to the porch and pressed the doorbell. Dora didn't want it to seem as if she had been watching him, so she waited a few seconds before opening the door.

"Hi. Shawn Murphy, Estate of Mind," he said, extending his right hand.

"Dora Baskin. Come in." She shook his hand as he stepped through the door, and Shawn held her gaze before realizing the ongoing nature of their handshake.

"Sorry," he said as he let go of Dora's hand. "You can have that back."

Dora smiled and closed the door behind him.

"Beautiful place," Shawn said, looking around the foyer.

"Yes, it is," Dora agreed. "It's just a little too much for me." He nodded.

To start with, Dora led him down to the basement, a dark, unfinished area, punctuated occasionally by a few pine logs as support columns. The basement was expansive, barely illuminated by a couple of dim, overhead bulbs.

At the foot of the stairs, to their left was a washer and dryer, and a line was strung over the laundry area with a couple of items of clothing still draped over it. Directly ahead, a few dusty pieces of broken furniture were arranged beside a workbench, doubtless repair projects that Grampa never got to before he died. On the right, a wine rack lined the wall with a fairly respectable collection of wine. And in between these three main areas, a few scattered cardboard boxes sat crumbling in musty arrangements.

Shawn took a few photographs, then they went back upstairs.

"Obviously the rest of the house is much nicer than the basement," Dora said.

"Good to get that out of the way," Shawn smiled. "But it's a huge area. Great potential for more living space."

Dora led him through the sunroom, a bright cheerful room which had been added on to the back of the house, then through the kitchen, dining room and living room, before leading him upstairs. In each room, Shawn jotted down notes on his clipboard and snapped pictures.

"So you said this was your grandmother's house?" Shawn asked, coincidentally as they came to the room where she had been killed.

"Yes, she died a couple of days ago."

"I'm very sorry to hear that," he said sympathetically as he continued scribbling notes. "Do you want to get rid of everything?" Something about that phrase struck a nerve in Dora. Already struggling with her feelings of guilt, she didn't like to think that she was just 'getting rid of everything.' That sounded so detached and heartless. Shawn seemed to pick up on her hesitation. "Are you sure you want to do this?"

"No, I'm not." Dora sighed. "'Getting rid' of my grandmother's things just sounds so cold, though I guess that's what I'm doing."

"Sorry," Shawn said. "Bad choice of words on my part. But it's natural to experience some negative feelings about this."

"I'm sure it is," Dora said absently. "She was killed just the night before last, so I honestly haven't given a lot of thought to this yet, beyond calling you."

"Did you say she was killed?" he asked.

"Yes, she surprised a burglar. Right there, as a matter of fact," she said, pointing to the floor where her grandmother's body had been found.

"Wow." Shawn glanced at the floor, then looked back at Dora, looking deeply into her eyes. "Well, listen. Why don't you just show me the rest of the place so I can work up an initial appraisal, and then you can decide what you want to do. No obligation at all."

As they went through the rest of the house, Shawn took copious notes and snapped several more pictures. Then Dora led him up the narrow staircase to the third floor.

"I've always loved attic rooms," Shawn said with a wistful smile as he looked around. "Such interesting shapes." Dora smiled in response as she turned to appreciate the room herself. When she turned back toward Shawn, he was looking at her, but her attention seemed to break his gaze and his face flushed. "I'm sorry, I don't mean to stare." Dora shook her head and smiled at his embarrassment.

He hastily turned his attention to the boxes and trunks in the room. "Do you mind?" he asked, motioning toward them.

"No, not at all."

Shawn lifted the lid of one of the trunks and looked inside.

"These look like personal things," Shawn said.

"Isn't everything in someone's house personal?" Dora asked.

34

"Well, yes," he said, attempting to regain his composure. "But I meant that, unlike furnishings, some of these items look like things that may only have value to you. Like family heirlooms."

"I haven't really had a chance to look through those yet," Dora admitted.

He nodded silently and made some more notes before descending the stairs toward the front door.

"You know," Dora said as she hesitated at the foot of the stairs, "maybe I *should* wait a while and take some time to go through this stuff. I don't know what's wrong with me, doing all this back and forth shit."

"You're in an emotional upheaval after the violent death of a family member," Shawn replied. "It's perfectly normal."

"Oh, now you're a psychotherapist?" Dora teased.

"I've just seen it several times," Shawn smiled.

"Yeah, well I feel like I've dragged you out here for nothing."

"Well, I suppose you could make it up to me," he said.

"How's that?"

"Come and have lunch with me."

The Sahara Café on Manitou Avenue, the main street through town, was a popular lunch spot. Dora and Shawn didn't have to wait long, and they had their hummus and Mediterranean samplers in very short order. They had already been talking about her grandmother's estate for a few minutes, and Dora was feeling more relaxed.

"Estate of Mind?" Dora asked teasingly.

"I know," Shawn replied with a little good-natured embarrassment. "Manitou Springs is kind of a new age, metaphysical town, and 'Estate of Mind' seemed catchy. And I admit that I thought the name might generate business based on the creativity factor. But I guess people usually aren't looking for creativity when a loved one dies."

"It caught *my* eye."

35

"Yeah, well you're an exception. Seriously, though, I think you should wait, look through your grandmother's things, spend some time with them. You might find you want to keep the house after all."

"You're really not very good at your job, are you?" Dora asked with a smile.

"Oh, you noticed," he smiled. "Actually, when I was a kid, I wanted to be an archaeologist. Even before I knew about Indiana Jones. Maybe it's kind of nerdy, but I love history." Dora smiled as he shrugged his shoulders. "I just really enjoy learning about people in other times, the things they went through."

"So, why aren't you an archaeologist?"

"My family was poor. We couldn't afford anything beyond junior college, and I just went to work right after that. I don't know. I guess estate liquidation is kind of about history." He laughed. "If you apply a really loose definition."

"Well, I appreciate you not being upset with me. I feel like I've been kind of wishy-washy about this. But I think I *will* wait a bit."

"I think that might be wise," Shawn confirmed. "Take the time to look through some of the things in those boxes and trunks. You might find yourself reconnecting with them."

The sky was a bright, piercing blue as Dora got out of Shawn's Malibu. They had spent the afternoon together at the restaurant and being back outside now, Dora felt wilted in the heat, as a police car rolled past on the road behind them.

"Thank you," she said. "I had a nice time."

"I enjoyed it too. Give me a call if I can do anything to help with your grandmother's estate."

Dora waved as he backed out of the driveway. She waited for his car to disappear before going into the house.

She liked Shawn and was glad, on a personal level, that she had met him. But she was also inspired by what he said about looking through Gramma Izzy's things. Over the years, first her parents, then Dora herself had put up numerous walls, and she had been content being inside them. While she didn't think she felt ambitious enough to start tearing them down yet, she thought she might like to at least peek over them and see what was on the other side.

So Dora went up to her room and changed into some sweats, ready to get busy, then climbed the stairs to the third floor. The floor was divided into two small rooms built up against the slope of the roof, with dormers pushed out on either side. The irregular shape of the rooms cast deep shadows in the approaching twilight. Looking around the dark space, Dora wondered where to start. The boxes, some marked, some not, seemed to be stacked and arranged without any real design.

She decided to start with a very heavy box near one of the windows. It contained books, old leather-bound first editions, almost all of them in excellent condition.

She pushed the box aside and noticed an old wooden trunk decorated with faded Native American designs. It was all by itself, as if it held a special position among these things. Then again, maybe Gramma Izzy had just wanted it to be easily accessible.

Lifting the top, Dora peered inside and saw several things that she would not have immediately associated with her grandparents. First was a set of distinctly Native American nesting baskets. They appeared to be old and delicate. Dora carefully removed them from the trunk and set them aside.

There was an old arrow with black and white striped feathers. The glue and sinew attaching them to the shaft were obviously quite old, and she removed it carefully from the trunk. There was clothing, some made of deerskin or other animal hide, some of woven material, all with Native American designs, as well as old and yellowed handwritten documents, including, to Dora's dismay, what looked to be a bill of sale for slaves.

There was jewelry made of beads, stones and feathers; some kind of animal's tail hung from a stiff thong of rawhide; a carefully folded length of cloth with a red and blue stripe pattern; a beautiful comb carved from a single piece of iridescent mother-of-pearl. Though a couple of teeth were broken off, Dora appreciated the workmanship and caressed the delicate carving of a rose on its surface.

At the bottom of the trunk lay an old and cracking black leather satchel. Dora thought that was all there was, but when she moved it, she saw a small box of black leather. Opening it, she found a necklace with a gold pendant. The pendant had a silver design etched into its surface, an intricate carving of the letters "A" and "I," and as she examined it, she saw that it was actually a locket. She opened it to reveal two old, faded portraits. One was a pretty woman with blonde hair, the other was a handsome Native American man. She recognized the couple from the family portrait on the stairs. This locket was probably the pendant hanging from the woman's neck in the painting.

She returned to the box that contained the documents and books, wondering if they would tell her anything about the people in the painting. The books were mainly novels and volumes of poetry, all from the eighteenth or nineteenth century. Some were recognizable classics – Herman Melville's *Moby-Dick*, James Fenimore Cooper's *Last of the Mohicans,* Daniel DeFoe's *Robinson Crusoe*. Then there were others that Dora had never heard of – Frances Burney's *Cecelia*, and Horace Walpole's *The Castle of Otranto: A Gothic Story*. One book, though, had no markings on the spine.

Dora slipped the book out of its place in the box. There were no markings on the front cover either. She opened the book and heard a soft creaking sound from the binding. The smell that emanated from the open book was, not quite musty, but definitely old, recalling to Dora's mind the comforting memory of visiting a used book store with Gramma. She gingerly turned the pages, examining the yellowed paper and ink that had faded to brown long ago. The handwriting was feminine, almost ornate, but perfectly legible. Skimming through the script, Dora saw that it was relating the personal experiences of a nineteenth century English-woman.

Now this could be interesting! she thought.

She took it downstairs with her and into the kitchen. Unable to think about preparing anything for dinner, she skimmed through the yellow pages and ordered Chinese food, opened a bottle of Cabernet that she had chosen from the basement, and poured herself a glass. Then, perched on the stool that Gramma Izzy kept by the counter, she carefully opened the old book and started reading.

"One can never predict with any degree of accuracy what the future may hold." I could certainly agree with that little pearl of wisdom from my mother who, dear woman that she was, admittedly tended toward adages teetering on the precipice of being cliché. "One never truly appreciates what one has until after one has lost it."

Looking back, now, as I begin to record this account, so many years have passed, yet it is etched so vividly in my memory as if it happened only yesterday. The happiness and the losses pour forth in a deluge as they emerge from my pen.

My name is Isadora Byrnes. Having visited London on a few occasions, I knew that life offered more excitement than my quiet little existence in Liverpool of 1829 afforded me, though even London seemed a bit stuffy for my taste. As a child, my family life had been happy, but as I matured, I found that I longed for more amusement. My parents and my younger sister, Emily, often encouraged me to marry a good man and bear children. While a good man did offer a certain appeal, I was surprised, and somewhat disconcerted, to find myself more attracted to men of lesser character.

I was, if I may say so, a pretty girl of diminutive stature, from a quiet family of little means. My blonde hair, fair skin and sky-blue eyes were, I was told, the envy of many girls, and when I was young, I was trivial enough to think that such things mattered. My comely countenance meant that I was never lacking for interested suitors, but I found that they offered no enticement.

41

My parents had disapproved when I introduced my fiancé, Liam O'Riordan, a young man of questionable background and occupation. That I had come to know such a person without their knowledge, and then to accept his proposal without their consent was, I am certain, a matter of some embarrassment. My mother was accustomed to indulging her daughters to the extent that our limited means allowed, but my father was more outspoken and conscious of our position in society. While I think my mother hoped that I would eventually come to see the young man for the rascal that he was, my father simply forbade me to see Liam. To their disappointment, and ultimately, my shame, their disfavour only seemed to increase the attraction.

Our modest stone house stood near the crest of a hill near the outskirts of town. It was summertime and I, as usual, was thinking about Liam. Sixteen year old Emily and I had been in town purchasing piece goods. Liam met me as we came out of the shop. We were slowly walking home through town, Emily now lagging a few steps behind by design, as Liam and I spoke quietly between ourselves.

"I don't know how to break it to you, lass, but they won't let you marry me," Liam said, his Irish brogue thick on his tongue. "You know that, don't you?" Coppery highlights in his dark hair blazed in the sunlight as he looked down toward me.

"You don't seem terribly disturbed by that," I responded with a mischievous smile, attempting to be coquettish. I flipped my blonde hair over my shoulder, affecting a façade of indifference. "I'm nearly 19 years old. I can marry without their permission."

"You could, but would you?" Liam asked, his eyes narrowed as if he did not quite believe me. This caused my façade to begin crumbling.

"Well, of course I would," I said indignantly. "I love you."

"I know you love me, dear," he replied easily, "and I love you. I can't think of any other girl that suits me more than yourself. But

we come from different worlds." He continued picking apart my attempted apathy with a maddeningly casual cheerfulness. "Imagine the looks you'd get from your friends and neighbours if I was to show up at one of your fancy society parties."

"We don't have fancy parties, Liam. Despite what you seem to think, we're not 'upper crust'."

"I'm sure your parties are fancier than what I'm accustomed to." He smiled, knowing he was aggravating me. "Still, it might be fun to drop in and see your friends' reaction to me wearin' me Sunday best."

My façade of indifference totally destroyed now, I exclaimed, "I'm so tired of these old conventions of behaviour! Why can't people who love each other simply marry without having to be concerned about the disapproval of others?" I almost stamped my foot but decided that that might be carrying it too far. Liam smiled and took my hand, casting a quick glance back toward my sister.

I looked at our hands and felt my annoyance melt away. "Even if my family does eventually give us their blessing," I said, "they are not rich by any means. I have no dowry to offer you. Do you mind that we'll be poor?"

Liam smiled again. "We'll be fine. I've got some interests of me own that will be paying off handsomely very soon. Don't you worry."

I sighed at this, feeling a familiar tension. I did not know Liam's occupation, and Liam had not been forthcoming about it. I had the distinct impression that what he did was not fitting. As the values of proper society would have it, I was admittedly quite wary about it, but at the same time it seemed to appeal to my desire for excitement. Pondering our intertwined fingers, I leaned closer to Liam, putting my head on his shoulder, not knowing or caring if my sister was watching. Letting go of my hand, Liam wrapped his arm round my shoulders and lightly kissed my forehead.

"My ship will be coming in soon, and when it does, we'll jump on it and sail it away to America."

"Is it really as wonderful as your brother has said?" I asked, looking up at him excitedly.

"Danny's not one given to embellishment. America's a new, wild country with more space than anybody could ever need. He writes to me about plains of grass stretching out beyond the horizon, their surface darkened with enormous herds of massive buffalo. Of mountains that tower so high they disappear in the clouds. He says there are still areas that white people have never seen, let alone settled. Aye, girl, we'll get over there and make a new life for ourselves."

"But when?"

Liam glanced back toward Emily again and leaned closer to me with a mischievous smile, lowering his voice to a conspiratorial whisper.

"Is tonight soon enough for you, lass?"

"Oh, Liam, do you mean it?"

"Our ship sails at midnight. Meet me at the Salthouse Dock at 11:30."

"I shall be there."

"Very good. I'll see you at the dock."

Liam kissed my forehead, let go of my hand and walked away. After he left us, Emily caught up with me and walked alongside, carrying our purchases. I looked at my reluctant chaperone with some apprehension.

"Remember your promise," I said.

"I know, Isadora," she said grumpily. "I'll not tell Papa you saw Liam."

"Or Mama, either." I reached over and relieved her of one of the packages, and she managed a slight smile.

The rest of our walk home was quiet, but my mind was jumbled as I thought about my meeting with Liam tonight. We had talked often of running away to America and starting a new life, but it had always seemed like an out-of-reach dream. I could scarcely believe that we were actually going to do it.

44

At the same time, I felt a pang of guilt planning this clandestine escape, for though I loved my family, I felt a growing need to get away from my annoyingly tedious life. I craved adventure, and Liam O'Riordan was the man who was going to provide it.

"I thought I made myself clear. You are not to see Liam O'Riordan." Papa was stern as the four of us were gathered in the parlour. Mama was busy with mending and Emily was glancing half-heartedly through a book, but Papa's attention was fully on me.

"I know, Papa."

"And yet you met with him today!" I glared angrily toward Emily who refused to meet my eyes. I looked back toward Papa, casting about for a defence.

"I know you and Mama don't like Liam, but I love him. I see who he is on the inside."

"What he is is a good for nothing bounder!"

"That's not true, Papa."

"Nobody even knows what he does. If his activities were legal and moral, then why does he refuse to speak of them?"

"I don't know."

"Your mother and I only want what's best for you, so don't fight us on this."

"You always say you want what's best for me," I said, feeling the tears starting to come. "But I don't agree with what you think is best."

"It's not my concern if you agree, girl. You'll do as you're told as long as you're living under my roof. Although that could be changing soon." I looked up at him, fearful that Emily might have overheard Liam and me discussing our plans for that night, but I said nothing, waiting to hear what he meant. Mama seemed to fidget.

"Mr. Longerman, my employer, has expressed an interest in you for his son," Papa said and my heart fell. He looked away,

45

and I thought that I saw his lip quiver slightly, but he remained stern.

"I am sorry, Papa," I said, regaining some conviction, "but I will not marry him."

"You ungrateful chit!" he growled as his apparent distress was quickly replaced with anger. "We do not have the luxury of flitting through life without a care to our associates."

"Liam and I love each other."

"You may grow to love Avery Longerman in time. In any case, our status is too fragile to risk it on an alliance with a criminal."

"I care nothing about our status! Our neighbours are nothing more than a collection of meddling busybodies."

"I know it may not seem like it," Mama contributed, "but we also care about your happiness and well-being."

"Of course that's important to me, Mama," I replied, softened by her calm manner, "but if you really cared about me, you would not suggest I marry someone I do not love simply to elevate our status. I will not marry Avery Longerman. I am in love with Liam and I mean to marry him."

"Go to your room!" Papa said.

"I am not a child, Papa!"

"I said go to your room, girl. And if you keep bandying about with me, you can also go without your supper."

I went upstairs, angry and more resolved than ever to make my escape.

I packed lightly, carrying only a single bag. My anger had eased, and as I crept down the stairs just after eleven o'clock, I knew that I would miss my family. But I was convinced of my love for Liam and determined that I would not marry Avery Longerman, so I left a goodbye note on the mantle and slipped quietly out the door.

I had never been out of doors by myself in the middle of the night, and I felt a tingle of excitement as I made my way along the

46

streets of the town I had known all my life. There was a half moon and many stars overhead, and they illuminated my journey west toward the Mersey, but it was still dark enough that it rendered the streets strangely unfamiliar to me. I breathed a bit easier as I came closer to the docks, lit somewhat more brightly than the narrow streets I had just navigated.

When I reached the Salthouse Dock, I could see sailors busily readying the ship for sailing, but Liam was not in sight. I admit that I was a bit timid being alone on the dock at night, but the only people I saw were those who were busily working, and they had no time to interfere with me.

Time passed and I could tell by the increased activity that the ship was nearly ready to set sail. I was becoming nervous that Liam would not arrive in time, and I began to wonder if he meant that I was to meet him on the ship. But after a few more minutes, I finally saw him running toward me. I sighed with relief and smiled until I saw his face. He carried one bag, an old leather valise, swung low and steady in his hand as if it were heavy, and he wore an expression of urgency as he looked from me to the sailors on the ship.

"Have you been waiting long?" he asked. Then, without waiting for a response, he said, "Get on the ship, love. It's about to leave," and he ushered me toward a ramp up to the vessel.

"Liam, what's wrong?" I asked, sensing distress under his hurried manner.

"Nothing, dear," he replied. He endeavoured to smile but did not quite accomplish his goal. "We simply need to hurry."

A sailor on the deck was motioning for us to board, so I started up the ramp. I did not hear Liam's footsteps accompanying me and I turned to look for him. He seemed to be distracted by something behind us. He turned to me and handed me the valise that he carried, and I was surprised by the weight of it.

"Take this, love," he said. "The sailors can show you to your quarters. I'll try to get back before you leave, but if I don't make

47

it in time, I'll catch up with you in America." He pushed me up the ramp amid my protests as the sailor at the top gestured for me to hurry. Then, Liam was gone, hurrying along the dock below as the shadows of men gave chase.

"Come on, miss," the sailor said as I reached the top of the ramp. He took my hand and helped to steady me on the deck. "We can't wait no longer."

I ignored him and walked toward the back of the ship, looking down at the dock in the direction that Liam and his pursuers had run. Straining to see into the dark, I could see Liam, his back against a stack of crates, as the other men approached him. I could not hear what was said, but I could see Liam shaking his head, and he lunged at one of the men. The man struck back, and soon all of them were upon Liam, hitting him savagely. My heart nearly stopped when I saw the flash of a knife blade in one of their hands. The blade swung several times as it was sunk into Liam's flesh, and I watched in horror as Liam slipped down onto the dock, un-moving.

Tears streamed down my cheeks as Liam and his now dispersing attackers grew smaller. It was only then that I realised that the ship had pulled away from the dock. As I could no longer see Liam, I turned toward the ship that was bearing me away. The sailors were busily working on the rigging and sails, and I assumed that nobody else onboard had seen the horrible spectacle that I had witnessed. I knew then that Liam would not be catching up with me in America.

I spent nearly a week in my dismal cabin, more alone than I had ever been. Having left my family behind, I had also lost the love of my life, and I had never felt so low. Tossing with the waves, I shed tears seemingly without end, clutching Liam's valise to my chest, knowing that it was all I had left of him.

After the first week, I finally felt strong enough to open Liam's valise. Alone in my cabin, I gingerly fingered the clasp, unbuckled *the strap and opened the case. My astonished eyes beheld several bundled stacks of gold coins inside. I had never seen so much money in my life! There was also some sort of silver block. The surface of this artifact was etched with beautiful ornate patterns, apparently some form of artistic sculpture.*

Along with the gold and the silver artifact were several letters from Danny O'Riordan, Liam's brother in America, along with maps and numerous other documents, all apparently with the design of getting Liam and me to the New World. Liam had indeed been making good on his promise. Knowing his poor background, and seeing all the gold and the silver artifact in the valise, I knew that he had done it by means of dishonourable enterprise. But I could not find it in my heart to fault him now, having lost him forever.

I spent not a little time in my cramped cabin studying the letters and documents. From them, I discovered that Danny was in the far western frontier of America, in a rugged mountainous portion of what he called the Louisiana Purchase. It was a rough area, full of wild beasts and wild natives. It sounded terrifying and wonderful.

I allowed myself to entertain a notion of finding Danny to tell him personally of Liam's death, though I realised, based on the apparent vastness of the land depicted on the maps, that the chances of being successful in this endeavour were miniscule. Having read the letters in the valise, I knew that Danny had taken up trapping and trading and apparently tended to move around in a largely uncharted area known as the Rocky Mountains. But just the thought of going to live in this young, wild land breathed new life into me.

The oceanic crossing was fairly long but ultimately uneventful. Having had a little time to mourn Liam and to devise a plan of action, it was with excitement and anticipation that I came up on deck early one morning in September, struggling under the weight of my luggage. The air was warm and the sky was cluttered with all manner of clouds, but they did little to diminish the sun's persistent shine.

Now docked in the harbour of Charleston, South Carolina, I could see the excitement and activity taking place in this large seaport, and I felt a sudden disquietude, struck with the anxiety of being a lone woman, barely nineteen years old, traveling to an unfamiliar country and not knowing a soul. The enormity of what I had undertaken now weighed quite heavily upon me. I had become acquainted with the few other passengers on the ship, but we would soon be going our separate ways. I would have to strike out on my own.

Therefore, tightening my grip on the bags I carried, and fortifying myself with a deep breath of fresh, seaside air, I made my way down to the pier and immersed myself in the people of this new land.

It did not take me long to find someone willing to provide directions, and I quickly purchased a seat on a coach heading west. The coach was going to Georgia on the first leg of my journey toward the Rocky Mountains. I watched with a little amusement as a man loaded my luggage on top of the coach, for he seemed surprised by the weight of Liam's valise.

One other passenger shared the coach with me on this first part of my journey, a young woman about my age. She was very pretty, with a dark complexion and long, straight black hair, worn down about her shoulders. Her face was noble, with high cheekbones and eyes that were as black as night.

From her appearance, I understood her to be an Indian, the natives of which many frightful stories had been related, though she was dressed in modern clothing with the addition of colourful beads and ribbons. Her manner seemed so gentle and friendly, I found it difficult to attribute to her such a savage nature.

As the coach pulled away and we began our journey, I attempted to converse with my traveling companion.

"My name is Isadora," I said as she settled into the seat across from me. She looked at me with an inscrutable expression, then looked away.

"Noya," she said to the window.

Perhaps not so friendly after all.

"Noya? Are you an Indian?" I asked, losing my grip on propriety.

"I am Ani-Yun'wiya," she said coldly, "or as you people call us, Cherokee."

"People were talking about Indians on the ship," I continued. "I must say, you are not what I was expecting."

"I'm sorry I've disappointed you."

"Oh, I am not disappointed. They described Indians as fearsome naked savages wearing paint on their faces and jabbering unintelligibly. I am quite happy to find that they were wrong."

Noya looked at me for a moment before responding.

"We 'Indians' are expected to learn your ways and to be integrated into white society."

"Expected by whom?"

Noya sighed, seeming irritated.

"White people." Then she seemed exasperated, but continued. "To be fair, it is not just you white people who want this but also some of my own people. In their defence, many of my people feel that this is the best way for us and our ways to survive. Those who have not cooperated in this way have often suffered much indignity, and even death."

"Oh my heavens," I said. "I had no idea."

"You have not have heard of this?"

"No, I have only just arrived from England."

She looked at me for a moment, then looked away, settling back in her seat in an attempt to ignore me and to sleep. I directed my attention to the passing scenery out the window.

I was in the coach for most of three days, with overnight stops at inns. It was tedious and uncomfortable, the monotony broken only by the addition or subtraction of a passenger. Noya remained. By the third day, she seemed willing to converse.

"Why do you English keep coming here?" she finally asked with some irritation.

I was taken aback by her directness but recovered quickly.

"I cannot speak for all English who come here," I said. "I was coming with Liam, my fiancé, to start a new life together."

"So where is he?"

"He was killed as we were about to leave." She seemed surprised at my response, her features softening.

"I'm sorry. Where are you going now?"

"The Rocky Mountains."

"Why?"

"Liam's brother is out there somewhere. From his letters, it sounds wonderful!" I responded. I do not know whether it was simply my imagination, but she seemed to regard me with just a bit more admiration.

"And you know nobody here?"

"Only you," I said with a smile. She seemed confused, as if she did not know how to feel about this silly English girl in front of her. "Tell me about yourself and your people."

"We are being crushed," she said, her expression suddenly fierce.

"I do not understand."

"White people have been coming to this land for many years. The greater their numbers, the more of our land they take. For a long time, we lived peacefully together, but the white people keep increasing.

"As far back as the time of the first American president, George Washington, white people hoped to 'civilise' us, trying to get us to abandon our ways and customs. For the most part, we Cherokee no longer live in traditional villages but have been convinced to live in isolated, fenced-in farmsteads like the white people. They have educated us, taught us to dress as they do, to live as they do,

52

to talk as they do. And yet, even though we are now much like them, we are still not accepted. Our rights are ignored, our land is taken to be settled by more white people, and those who try to fight are beaten or killed."

I noticed that Noya had stopped grouping me with the 'white people,' but had begun saying 'they' and 'them.' Given her strong feelings against her persecutors, I appreciated this small kindness. I also noticed that, as her emotions rose, she moved her hands as she spoke, not in the familiar emphatic gestures common to white people, but in almost descriptive movements that I found to be very beautiful.

As the time passed, Noya continued talking about her people and of the contemptuous treatment that they had endured. Truth be told, I found it difficult to believe that modern, civilised people could be that cruel.

"And now, gold has been found in northern Georgia," she continued, "and while the Cherokee are forbidden to look for gold, even more white people are going there and trespassing upon my people's land."

"Is that where you live, in Georgia?" I asked.

"Yes, in Gainesville."

"Then you live in a settled area. Can the authorities do nothing in the face of this lawlessness?" I asked.

"The authorities will do nothing," she replied resentfully. "Our ancestral land has, for the most part, been taken over by Georgia, and the American government supports them in this decision. The current president, Andrew Jackson, has said that negotiating with the Indians is 'an absurdity.' Better to just take what they want and be done with it.

"We are a sovereign nation, with a government. A couple of years ago, we adopted a constitution. We can even send a deputy to Congress. And the United States has, in the past, recognized that standing. Now we are finding that the white people do not honour their agreements."

I wondered what I had gotten myself into. The government, consisting of men who only a half century ago were British subjects, was confiscating the property of these gentle people? Of course, I was only hearing one side of the story. While Noya seemed well-versed on these topics, I decided that her emotions must be clouding her perception of events, and while I expressed sympathy, I determined to reserve judgment until I was certain that I had all of the information.

Noya fell silent and, for some time, there was no sound but for the rattling of the coach over the dusty and rocky track. While we had shared the coach with others along the way, Noya and I now had it to ourselves.

We were a few hours from Gainesville, Georgia, when the coach started slowing down. Curious, I looked out the window and spotted a thick column of smoke ahead.

"Noya." The words seemed to freeze in my throat. Silently, I pointed out the window.

She followed my gaze and we watched people, dark skinned and terror stricken, running in different directions, some keeping near the road, others running away from it. One young woman was crying, carrying a bloody baby, limp and blue.

The settlement consisted of several small wood-sided cabins, all in flames. By now, the area was deserted save for a young Indian woman wailing pitifully over a young man.

I was nearly in shock, looking at the horrible tableau being enacted before me, when we heard the loud crack of a gunshot followed by a thump up above us on the coach. Without warning, the coach shuddered violently and came to a sudden stop. Noya and I were thrown forward as the coach listed badly to one side. We were picking ourselves up when the door was yanked open by a young Indian man armed with a musket and a pistol. He trained the pistol on us and angrily spoke a few indecipherable words. Noya instructed me to get out of the coach and stepped out behind me.

Our driver appeared to be dead, sprawled on his back in front of the coach where he had been thrown, a widening river of scarlet flowing from his chest. One of the wheels of the coach was lying on its side with many broken spokes and a tree branch stuck through it, apparently thrown into it by a second young Indian man.

Noya spoke to the men in their native tongue. Emotions ran high as the conversation ensued, with many pointed looks in my direction, but eventually they seemed to reach an agreement and the men began unhitching the horses.

As they did this, Noya approached me and explained.

"A band of white men destroyed their village and stole their livestock. These men killed our driver out of anger, and were going to kill you too, but I convinced them that this would accomplish nothing."

I admit that I was nearly hysterical as she told me this. "Why would they kill me?"

"Your skin is white," she responded. "Some in the Cherokee nation, and other nations too, refuse to submit to the unfair treatment from the white man. They advocate war, even though the odds are against us."

I could think of no response to that, as the fear was still coursing through my body.

"These men are each taking a horse," she replied, "in hopes of finding the men who did this and exacting revenge. But they are outnumbered and will likely end up dead."

"But the coach cannot be driven like this," I said. "What are we to do?"

"We will take the other two horses and ride to my home. That is all we can do."

With that, Noya climbed up on top of the coach and tossed down our luggage. She decided that the best way to accomplish our goal would be for both of us to ride one horse, and use the other as a packhorse, tying our luggage to his back.

55

"You have ridden a horse, haven't you?" she asked, seeing me fidget nervously.

"Indeed I have, although not bareback, and never astride."

"After tonight, you won't be able to say that."

The two Cherokee men finished unhitching the first two horses and rode away into the dusk, leaving Noya and me alone. Noya climbed down from the top of the coach and tied our bags to one of the remaining horses. After this, she pulled her skirt almost up to her hips and almost effortlessly swung up onto the other horse's back. I am quite sure that I blushed, not only from seeing her so casually bare her legs, but also from the knowledge that I would have to follow suit. My only consolations were that it was getting dark and that there was no longer anybody nearby to witness the spectacle.

Casting a glance around, I sighed and pulled my skirts up as Noya had done. She braced herself and offered her left foot and hand for me. Somehow I understood the wordless instructions. Lifting my skirts up as she had done, I took her left hand and stepped onto her foot, pulling myself up behind her. She took the reins of the packhorse and we were on our way almost before I had settled on the horse. I tried to pull my skirt down over my thighs but finally realised the futility of my attempts at modesty.

We were still some distance from Noya's home, but as it was now dark and there was no moon, we could not ride as fast as she would have liked. Therefore, our ride was rather long and, for me at least, uncomfortable.

We were well into the night, the raven sky pierced by innumerable points of starlight, when we arrived at a brick house surrounded by stately oak trees. Noya brought the horse to a halt and I climbed down and self-consciously arranged my skirts.

We gathered our luggage from the back of our packhorse as the front door of the house opened and a man and woman emerged. The man carried a lantern, and in its yellow light, I could see the anxiety etched upon their attractive faces. They greeted

56

Noya with relieved hugs and kisses, while glancing at me with a guarded expression.

"We were expecting you last evening," her mother said. "What happened?"

Noya briefly related to them the account of the village east of town. Then she turned to me.

"This is Isadora Byrnes. She has recently arrived from England and I have invited her to stay with us. Isadora, this is my mother Mahaley and my father Yansa."

"Yancey," her father corrected as he extended his hand. "I prefer Yancey. Yancey Franklin. Please come in. We are sorry you have had to endure these hardships as an introduction to our country."

He directed us into the house while he took our luggage and carried it in behind us. A young Negro man had appeared, apparently woken from sleep and hastily arranging his clothing. Noya's father instructed him to take the horses to the barn and feed them.

"It is after three o'clock in the morning," Mahaley said. "I am sure you are exhausted. Get some sleep and we can talk when you are rested."

Noya led me up the stairs, and at the upper landing, I paused to appreciate a large, beautiful portrait of Mahaley. Noya smiled, then led me to a room at the back of the house as her father carried our bags up behind us. After depositing my luggage in my room, they both left me to collapse on the bed in utter fatigue.

The next morning dawned warm and cloudless, a beautiful day after the hardships of the previous. I had managed to sleep despite the violent images in my mind of the destruction of the Indian village. I found Noya and her family eating breakfast downstairs. They greeted me with smiles.

"We thought you should sleep as long as possible," Noya said. "I hope you do not mind that we started our breakfast without you."

"Certainly not." I took the seat that she offered next to her.

"Did you sleep well, Miss Byrnes?" Mahaley asked.

"Isadora, please," I said. "I slept very well. Thank you." An elderly Negro woman, whose name I later learned was Dorcas, placed a plate before me laden with eggs, biscuits and gravy, ham, and grits. There was also coffee, which I had decided over my previous days in America that I did not care for.

"This looks delicious," I said. "Thank you."

"Is there anything else I can get for you, ma'am?" Dorcas asked.

"Do you have tea?" I asked hopefully.

"No, we don't, ma'am," she said. "I'm sorry."

"That's all right." I hoped my disappointment did not show. I was desperate for a cup of tea.

"Tea is available in some places," Noya explained, "but not as readily as it had been before our war with England. And often,

those who do have access to it, still consider it unpatriotic to drink it."

"I hope that I shall be able to survive in such a barbaric land," I said only half facetiously. "Thank you anyway. And thank you Yansa for your warm hospitality."

"Yancey," he said irritably.

"I'm sorry," I said. "I did not mean to cause offence."

"I am not offended," he said, shaking his head and waving his hand as if brushing aside the notion. "I simply prefer the name Yancey."

"Yansa is his Cherokee name," Noya said. "It means Buffalo. Yancey is a white name. My father is not as proud of his heritage as other Cherokee." Yancey bristled at this.

"My heritage is twofold," he replied in a reprimanding tone. Turning to me, he explained. "My mother was full Cherokee. My father was a white soldier. I do not feel that I can live by both sides of my heritage at the same time. In view of the difficult times in which we live, and the lessons of our recent history, I think it is important to choose sides carefully. I am not taking sides against the Cherokee, but I do see the benefit of making friends with the white man."

"To what lessons are you referring?" I asked.

"The lessons of our political affiliations."

"During the war of the Americans against England," Noya explained, "the Cherokee sided with the British. We had already been trading with them. Many of the supplies we were making use of came from the British. England seemed like the stronger opponent, but besides that, we were fighting for our own land. Our own livelihood."

"And we made bitter enemies in the process," Yancey continued. "The Americans gradually began to recognise the Cherokee as a sovereign nation, but not without a fight. Even now, the Cherokee nation fights for its land and rights, but loses ground on a daily basis."

60

"We have done well," Noya said. *It seemed to me as if her dark cheeks flushed with shame.*

"We have," Yancey said sternly to Noya. *"Because I have done what I must to take care of my family."* Turning to me, he sighed and lowered his voice again. *"I am associated with a number of men who are working for the good of all. Men who are trying to forge a diplomatic agreement between the Cherokee and the whites. Cherokees must live peacefully with the whites or be wiped out."*

"We are living peacefully with the whites, and we are still being wiped out," Noya protested.

"Which is why diplomacy is also required. Major Ridge and his son John are working for a diplomatic settlement with the whites."

"Major Ridge?" I asked.

"He is a chief of the Cherokee nation," Yancey explained. *"He and his son John are trying to smooth relations between the whites and the Indians. Major Ridge is one who has chosen his allies wisely. He fought alongside Andrew Jackson in the wars against the Creeks and the Seminoles."*

"And look what it has gotten us," Noya said. *"Jackson is president and does not care at all about us. And you are not working with the Ridges. To my knowledge, you've never even met them. Besides, Major Ridge, as you said, is a chief, he is not the Principal Chief, nor is his son, John."* She turned to me. *"John Ross, on the other hand, is Principal Chief of the Cherokee Nation, and he is trying to convince the American government to let us keep our land and stay here."*

Yancey looked at me and smiled apologetically. *"I am sorry, Miss Byrnes – Isadora. I am afraid we are not being very hospitable. Please forgive our argument. I fear it is one we have often. My daughter is, like myself, one who holds very strong opinions, and we hold them tightly. Sometimes our opinions differ and, to my wife's dismay, our disagreements become heated."* I looked at

61

Mahaley. Her face remained impassive, though she did offer a slight smile in my direction.

"That's all right," I said. "I am only now becoming acquainted with the situation as it stands. Frankly, I must admit that I am utterly appalled at the horrid treatment that the white people have apparently leveled against the Cherokee. Until coming here to America, I fear I had remained quite embarrassingly ignorant of the issues."

"You are not like most other white people," Noya said. "I appreciate your sympathy to our plight."

"My daughter and I do agree on that, at least," Yancey said with a smile.

After breakfast, Noya invited me to accompany her on a walk. Outside, I was able to see her home more clearly in the morning light. The red brick house was quite roomy, as I had begun to guess from seeing the inside. The property surrounding the house was expansive as well, with a large oak-lined lawn in front, and plentiful flower and vegetable gardens in the back. A densely wooded forest closed in on the eastern side. Across a river that bisected the plot of land were generous cotton fields, recently harvested, punctuated by the dark heads of a few Negroes who were still working in them.

"Do the Cherokee own slaves, then?" I asked Noya.

"Some of the richer Cherokee do, particularly those who have tried to emulate the white man. I am afraid my father is one who wants to be a rich white man."

"Was his father a rich white man?"

"I do not know if he is rich, but he is white," Noya said. "However, the story is not quite as nice and civilised as he implied. His father was a young soldier assigned to the area where his mother lived. She was about 17 years old at the time and was very beautiful. The soldier, Thomas Franklin, was infatuated with her but she expressed no interest in him. After some time, Franklin could not take the rejection any longer and took her forcibly."

"Oh, Noya. How perfectly awful."

"Yes. She became pregnant after that."

I was somewhat taken aback by how easily she spoke of this. Good society in England did not speak so freely or openly of such things. But I recognised that this was a different country and many of its customs were quite different from those to which I was accustomed back home. I was also a little embarrassed when I realised that I was taking offence because of some of the very conventions that had disenchanted me in the first place about life in England.

"So, your father . . ." I started.

"Yes, my father is a bastard, and the child of a rapist." She said it without hesitation, but did seem embarrassed by the fact. "He did not learn of this until a few years ago. He had been raised by his mother, and later, his stepfather, and thought of himself as a Cherokee. She told him his father was dead. But before she died, she decided he should know his true history, even if it was a dark one. She told him about Thomas Franklin and about what he did to her. And strangely, that is the side of his heritage he chose to embrace."

"Perhaps," I ventured, "he is trying to 'choose his allies wisely,' as he said."

"Perhaps," Noya allowed. "But I tend to think that he is more attracted to the gold he can acquire. At breakfast, he spoke of Major Ridge and his son, John."

"Yes," I said, "I remember you speaking of them at breakfast. What is it that they promote that your father agrees with and that you do not?"

"Major Ridge and his people, or the Treaty Party as some are beginning to call them, are too willing to accept the white people's proposals for the Cherokee. While John Ross is fighting to keep our land, Major Ridge thinks that we should accept the government's payment and leave our homeland."

"Where would you go?"

63

"The government is 'granting' us some land hundreds of miles away, west of the Mississippi River, which they are calling the Indian Territory.

"While I do not always agree with the things that Major Ridge and his associates promote, I do know that they think it is for the good of our people. But some of my father's pursuits seem indisputably for his own gain and cannot be considered good for the Cherokee, even when looked upon with the most liberal viewpoint."

"I am sorry, Noya."

"I do not like thinking such things of my father," she sighed, "but I'm afraid there is just too much evidence to ignore this possibility."

We arrived at a small building and Noya led me inside. Our wanderings had not been random after all. The building, I discovered, housed a mission and was divided into several rooms including a classroom and a small medical clinic. Leading me to the clinic in the back, Noya introduced me to a fair haired, soft-spoken young man named Edward Hodges. The man was rather plain in appearance but had a becoming smile, one which, I soon found, came easily.

"Edward is a doctor," Noya told me with a hint of pride in her voice.

"How do you do?" I said as I curtsied.

"Very nice to meet you, Miss Byrnes," he said. "You're English, aren't you?"

"Yes I am. I only just arrived in America a few days ago. And you, Dr Hodges? Are you a native of this area?"

"I am, though my family came to America from England almost two hundred years ago, by way of Jamestown. We journeyed south and scattered a bit, into Georgia and the Carolinas."

"Isadora is on a journey of her own, on her way to the Rocky Mountains," Noya informed him. "She is staying with my family during her time here."

64

Edward was about to respond when we were interrupted by the entrance of an Indian family. The man, supported on each side by his wife and son, was holding a bloody cloth to the side of his head.

"Tooantuh," Edward addressed the man. "What happened?"

"We were attacked by the Neenoskuskee," he said.

I looked at Noya, puzzled. She explained. "Neenoskuskee means 'robbers.' Georgia has called them 'The Pony Club,' which makes them sound more benevolent and less threatening." She narrowed her eyes in an expression of disbelief. "They are bands of white men who use violence to forcibly take what belongs to the Cherokee. I do not know if they are organised or if they are separate groups, but they are intent on taking our possessions. They were likely the ones who attacked the village yesterday."

Edward had begun cleaning and examining the man's wound. "Noya," he said, "could you assist me?" She went to his side and helped him as he stitched the gash on the side of Tooantuh's head.

During the time we were at the clinic, two of Tooantuh's neighbours came in, apparently victims of the same attack. Thankfully none of the injuries were too serious and the people all left after their treatments.

Keeping myself out of their way, I watched with amazement as Noya assisted Edward. She was not bothered by the blood and was equally at ease stitching cuts and speaking soothingly to the patients. She seemed to anticipate Edward's needs, the two working deftly as a single unit.

At about midday, we started back toward home.

"Where did you learn to do all of that?" I asked.

"I learned right there," she replied. "I admire the work they do and wanted to help, so a couple of years ago, I volunteered. Edward has helped me a great deal and now I am comfortable helping out with most of his work. I go there two or three days a week."

"I am impressed," I said. "I was astonished watching the two of you work together. You are really quite accomplished."

"Edward is a very good teacher," she said with a smile.

"You fancy him, don't you?"

Noya's smile was distant. "He cares so much about people. And the colour of their skin does not matter at all to him. He is as comfortable among the Cherokee as he is with his people. He wants nothing more than to help, and he is truly sympathetic to the plight of my people." She hesitated, then narrowed her eyes against the sunlight. "I do like him, but I cannot be sure of his feelings for me. He never speaks of it."

"I would not lay too much store in that," I replied. "He does seem to admire you greatly. Perhaps he is shy and cannot bring himself to speak of his feelings for you."

She smiled and we walked quietly home.

ora closed the book and put it down on the countertop. Having been so immersed in Isadora's world, it was almost a shock to find herself back in the present, in Gramma's house. After reading about Isadora Byrnes' journey to America, Dora felt a little embarrassed about the qualms she had felt earlier about being alone here. What a wimp!

It was now dark outside and she looked at the clock on the stove. It was nearly nine o'clock. She hesitated for a moment, then picked up her phone.

"Hello?" said Shawn.

"I hope I'm not calling too late," Dora said.

"No, not at all. Have you already decided what to do about your grandmother's house?"

"Actually I'm calling about something else. I remember you saying that you were a history nerd. I thought you might be interested in some of the things I've found here." She hesitated for a moment, then forged ahead. "Would you be able to come over tomorrow?"

"I have an appointment tomorrow afternoon, but I suppose I could swing by there in the morning. Care to tell me what this is all about?"

"Just some things I found in the trunks upstairs. I'll show you when you get here."

After she hung up, she exhaled in relief.

"Well, Madeline, I think you'll be proud of me," she said to herself. "This is me being impulsive."

Feeling a little self-satisfied with her initiative, and tired after a busy day, Dora went upstairs and got ready for bed.

Dora had overslept and was rushing now. She had meant to be finished with breakfast when Shawn came over at ten o'clock, but she heard his car pull up in front of the house as she came downstairs, her hair still wet from the shower.

"Come in," she said, pushing the door open for him. "Apparently, I underestimated the tranquilizing effect of nights in a small town. I just got up a few minutes ago."

Shawn smiled and waved it off. Dora led him into the dining room.

"Take a look at what I found," Dora said excitedly. She had arranged some of the items she had found in the trunk on the dining room table. Shawn looked at the baskets, the arrow, the jewelry, the old leather valise, bending to get a closer look without touching them.

"Nice," he said appreciatively. "Do you know anything about them?"

"So far, just a little." Dora picked up the locket and opened it. "These people are in a family portrait over the stairs. And although I'm not sure yet, from the description I've read, I think this woman may be Isadora Byrnes, an Englishwoman who came to America in 1829."

Shawn looked up from the items on the table. "A description you read?

Dora produced the book and handed it to him.

"It's a journal that Isadora Byrnes wrote about when she came to America. My full name is Isadora. I was named after my grandmother, and I think she was named after Isadora Byrnes. Also, my grandmother's maiden name was Hodges, and I've already found a doctor in the first chapter named Hodges who must be an early ancestor."

"Well, how fun is that!" Shawn said.

68

"If you're interested, go ahead and get started," Dora said, handing him the book. "I've already read the first couple of chapters, so you have some catching up to do."

Shawn didn't respond but was already engrossed in the first page. Dora went into the kitchen and started making coffee. She remembered seeing some cereal in one of the cabinets, so she poured herself some corn flakes and quickly ate it while the coffee brewed.

By the time she brought two steaming mugs of coffee back to the dining room, Shawn was immersed in Isadora's account.

I had never really decided to stay in Gainesville. I had simply pro-crastinated in leaving. During the past year, Noya and I had be-come such good friends that I was loathe to abandon her to con-tinue towards an unknown destination.

I began volunteering beside her at the mission and found gen-uine satisfaction in helping those less fortunate than I. I found the Cherokee to be wonderful people, polite and appreciative, and I looked forward to my time at the clinic.

Noya had persuaded me to stay with her family. As there was sufficient space in the house, and since they all assured me that it would not be an inconvenience, I finally assented.

I had spent only a few gold coins since arriving in America, and kept the greater portion wrapped tightly in cloth within the valise. The valise remained hidden at the bottom of the wardrobe in my bedroom. Thus my 'fortune' remained intact.

Occasionally, I would withdraw the mysterious silver artifact from the valise and study it, drawn to it beyond reason. I did not display it, although the etched ornamentation on its surface was quite artistic, a beautiful pattern of interlocking Celtic knots. I in-stead kept it concealed within the valise and hidden at the bottom of the wardrobe.

Ultimately, my intention was to go farther west and search for Danny O'Riordan, but for now, I had no specific plan for achiev-ing that goal. Each day was an adventure in my new home, alt-hough not always a pleasant one. A good cup of tea was still elu-sive to me, and I hated the coffee that they served here, although I

71

found that adding cream and sugar, as I took my tea, did make it a bit more palatable.

An even more serious issue than the tea situation, northern Georgia at that time was a lawless place. Violence against the Indians was becoming a common occurrence, and Noya and I spent many days tending to wounds inflicted by angry settlers. And while there were occasions when the Indians perpetrated violence against whites, usually it was the Indians who were the victims. I must admit that even when the Indians were the attackers, I sympathised with their plight and tended to forgive them. But in the main, the Cherokee behaved in an exemplary manner and gained my admiration on a daily basis.

One of the more reprehensible events in this debacle had taken place in May of 1830 when Congress passed and President Jackson signed into law the Indian Removal Act which took away all the land from the Indians who had lived in the southern states since time immemorial. I found it appalling that these new 'settlers' believed they actually had the right to do this. More and more, I was becoming disgusted by the arrogance of my race.

Already, the Choctaw Indians had been obliged to sign over the last of their land to the white Americans, and were preparing to move to the so-called Indian Territory that the white people had granted them west of the Mississippi River. Officials of the Cherokee nation were working tirelessly to allow their brothers to keep their land and homes. Most people agreed that their efforts seemed to be, for the most part, in vain.

Noya was a regular reader of the Phoenix, *a newspaper which was printed in both English and Cherokee. The publisher was a young Cherokee named Elias Boudinot who was a member of the Ridge Party. His writing often reflected the views of Major and John Ridge concerning Cherokee relocation, and Noya always read his articles thoughtfully, though they sometimes made her angry.*

72

I had a difficult time deciding which side was right in the debate. I felt that the Cherokee should be allowed to live on the land that they had occupied for centuries, so in this way, I agreed with Chief John Ross and his party. But I also knew that if the Cherokee continued being killed, eventually there would be no Cherokee nation. Since the survival of the nation depended on the survival of its individuals, I agreed with Major Ridge and his party that the Cherokee should accept the monetary offers, meagre though they were, of the United States government and move to the "Indian Territory." I suppose that, like Noya, I agreed most with John Ross.

While I did hold opinions on the issue, I usually opted for lighter reading material. Yancey had assembled a modest but well-stocked library which I often browsed. He had a number of volumes of English literature, but I found that I tended to favour American works. In the library, I had found a new novel called Last of the Mohicans by an American author named James Fenimore Cooper. It was a fascinating account of battles which took place before and leading up to the American war against England, and about the growing tensions and relationships among northern Indians and white people. Given the current state of affairs, I was particularly touched by a statement near the end of the book: "The pale-faces are masters of the earth, and the time of the red-men has not yet come again." I felt obliged to admit that it did not look very promising now either.

One chilly evening in October, 1830, we were all in the parlour. While Noya was reading the Phoenix, *I sat opposite her, finishing* Last of the Mohicans. *Deep in thought, I quietly closed the book. I looked up at Noya and smiled at the furrow that had appeared between her eyebrows, a common sight when she read the* Phoenix. *Then I glanced over at Yancey and Mahaley who were on the other side of the room, nearer the fireplace. Yancey had a book in his hand but I had yet to see him open it. Mahaley was busy with her mending.*

73

"I do not understand," Mahaley said quietly. "Why is there a problem with our money?"

Yancey sighed. "They did not pay me as much for my cotton this year."

"Because we are Cherokee?" Mahaley asked, though it sounded more like a statement.

"Apparently. Then I also needed money for supplies and maintenance."

"But we have always had enough money to cover these expenses."

"Yes, but prices have gone up," he responded with a note of irritation in his voice. "Some things are harder to get now."

"You told me that we could live for years on the money that we had in the bank. Why is there not enough money for our regular expenses now?"

Yancey noticed me looking at them and turned away, seemingly embarrassed. I felt my face flush as I realised that I had been eavesdropping. I stood to return the book to the library.

The weather had warmed again, and Noya and I were sitting on the front porch, relaxing in the mild heat of the afternoon. Yancey had some business in town and was standing at the top of the steps adjusting his coat when his foreman, Sam, a young Cherokee with an authoritative air, came up the steps, holding something in his outstretched hand.

Yancey looked at what the man was holding. "What is it Sam?" He picked up the thing between his thumb and forefinger, holding it up in the light, and his eyes grew larger as he looked at the small yellow nugget sparkling in the bright sunlight. "Where did you find this?"

"Down by the river," Sam replied. "Right at the edge of the woods."

"Does anybody else know about this?"

"No."

Yancey hesitated. Then he walked down the steps with Sam fol-
lowing closely behind.

They had just disappeared around the side of the house when
Mahaley, driving a buggy, turned off the road and smiled up at us
as she came to a stop in front of the house. A servant came running
from the direction of the barn and took the reins from her as she
climbed down and gathered the things she had gotten in town.

"You received a letter, Isadora," she said.

"From my father?"

"No, I'm sorry. Still no word from them."

I had written to my family in England over a year ago, to reas-
sure them of my health and general well-being. I did not know how
long it took for letters to find their way across the Atlantic, but I
had begun to despair of ever hearing back from them.

Mahaley flipped through the mail and found the letter. "It's
from Beatrice Ferngood." I was puzzled as she handed it to me.

"That's my aunt, my father's sister. She lives in Birkenhead,
across the Mersey from Liverpool." I feared that my family had
not forgiven me for leaving. The realisation of my fears, it turned
out, would have been preferable to the facts.

After a brief introduction and an expression of relief at my
safety, Aunt Beatrice came to the point:

> *According to various neighbours, only a few*
> *days after your departure, three men of rough*
> *background and coarse demeanour appeared at*
> *the door of your family's house, under cover of*
> *night. While there were gaps in the various tes-*
> *timonies given by the neighbours, the police*
> *were able to piece together a fair picture of*
> *what happened.*
>
> *The facts discovered in the investigation in-*
> *dicated that the men were members of* Fian
> Rúnda *and were looking for valuables which*

had been taken from them by one of their own. It was determined, I am very sorry to say, that your Liam was the thief, and the scoundrels had succeeded in tracking his movements to your home in Liverpool. Your father claimed to know nothing of the things for which they searched, which apparently angered the men even more.

There was some shouting, and as you may recall, some of your neighbours were a nosy lot, so the policemen were able to reconstruct a general idea of what happened. Still, little is known of the events that followed save for the fact that your father, your mother and your sister were all killed.

I can assure you that the testimony of a few witnesses and a thorough investigation led to the arrest, conviction and subsequent hanging of the individual perpetrators of this heinous crime, although that knowledge admittedly does little to undo the pain and suffering already inflicted.

It also did little to assuage the grief which quickly overcame me. I vaguely remember swooning and being helped inside by Noya and Mahaley. I kept to my bed for two days after that, but Noya was nearly always there, comforting me, providing for my needs and comfort.

Besides the sorrow, guilt weighed so heavily upon my heart that I could scarcely catch my breath. There was no way that I could deny that the ruffians were after the money which I had in my possession here in America. Was my family dead because of me and my actions? Had I stayed there, had the money been readily at hand, would they still be alive? Or would I have ended up being a victim as well?

"According to traditional Cherokee beliefs," Mahaley said, "blood revenge must be done to restore the balance between the physical world and the spirit world." Sitting in the window seat of the parlour, she was holding me in her arms and gently stroking my hair. Warmed by her body and by the sunlight on my back through the window, I found her soft but unwavering voice to be very soothing. "This was usually done by the closest male blood relative of the victim, but I believe that the balance can be found even when done by the English government. Their murders having been avenged, your family is now able to pass peacefully from this world into the next."

I sighed and closed my eyes.

"Of course," she continued, and I could hear a smile appear in her words, "the white man's preachers have done much to enlighten us about the soul of man."

I sat up and kissed her on the cheek. She continued to smile gently.

"Do you know that I had another daughter?" she asked.

"No I didn't," I replied.

"She was born a little more than a year after Noya. She would be about your age now. But it was a hard pregnancy and there were complications." She spoke with a wistful sadness, of a pain dulled by time but still keenly felt.

"Yancey and I were poor then. We lived in a small, rough cabin a few miles north of here. My mother still lives there. It was a cold winter, and food and firewood were scarce. I gave birth during the day when Yancey was out. My mother helped me but it was very painful, much more than with Noya. I gradually recovered but my baby did not. She died a few days after she was born."

"Mahaley, I'm so sorry. I had no idea."

She smiled at me and brushed a strand of hair from my face.

"I wanted to give my husband more children but I never could after that."

77

I settled back into her arms and felt them wrap around me again.

"I know that I am not your mother," she said as she laid her cheek against the top of my head, "but I am very happy to have another daughter now."

Once again, the tears came, and I held Mahaley tightly.

"Oh, how I wish I had a cup of tea," I said.

Noya and I had gone for a walk. It was about a week after I had received the accursed letter and, continuing in the role she had taken on while I was confined, she felt obligated to make me feel better. Indeed my spirits were somewhat lighter after our stroll.

"Have you noticed that my father has been acting strangely?" Noya asked on our way back.

"He has been going down to the river with Sam when he is not needed elsewhere," I replied.

"I'm beginning to suspect that he is mining for gold."

"Yes," I said, "that thought has occurred to me too. I hope that nobody else has taken notice of it." As Noya had indicated in our discussions shortly after we met, the state of Georgia had made it illegal for Indians to mine for gold, even on their own property.

We opened the door and entered a quiet house.

"Father must be out back again," Noya said.

"Yes, but where are your mother and Dorcas?"

"I don't know." Suddenly we heard pounding on a door at the back of the house. "That's the door to the basement," Noya said.

Rushing down the hall, we found a wooden chair wedged under the door knob. When we removed it and opened the door, Mahaley and Dorcas emerged.

"Are they still here?" Mahaley asked fearfully.

"Who?" Noya's face expressed alarm.

"There were two men, white men, and they spoke strangely. Similar to your accent," she said to me, "but different. They were asking about 'the silver pyxis'."

"Pyxis? What's a pyxis?" Noya asked looking puzzled.

"I don't know." We all looked to the ceiling as footsteps sounded upstairs. Noya went to a cabinet in the hallway and pulled out one of Yancey's pistols.

"Go out back and find father," she instructed. Mahaley and Dorcas went out the back door but, unwilling to allow Noya to confront two men alone, I insisted on staying with her. She crept toward the foot of the stairs and started up the staircase. I was horrified at the prospect of coming face to face with a pair of thieves, but I stayed close behind her. When I stepped on a creaky tread, heavy footsteps sounded on the floor above and a man appeared at the top of the stairs.

"Willie!" the man called out with an Irish accent. "Come 'ere, lad." The other man joined him and they looked down at us. "What should we do, eh?"

"It's only a couple o' women," the second man said with a crooked smile. He reached into the pocket of his jacket and Noya cocked the hammer on her pistol. The man stopped and pulled his hand back out. At that moment, I recognized the sound of the back door being thrown open and we heard heavy boot steps running toward us. The intruders heard it too, and wasted no time in hurtling down the stairs past us. Caught completely by surprise, we were unable to stop them as they rushed out the front door.

By the time Yancey and Sam appeared, the intruders were gone.

After we had calmed down, we did a careful search of the house. Yancey and Mahaley's room was a mess, but as they cleaned it up, they could not determine that anything had been taken. The door to Noya's room was standing open and it appeared to have been disturbed too, but nothing seemed to be missing from there either.

Apparently they had not yet gotten to my room when their nefarious activities were interrupted.

ora turned her head and stretched her neck. She and Shawn had been sitting at a corner of the dining room table, Dora on the side and Shawn at the head, craning their necks to read the pages together.

"I wonder what those Irishmen were after," Shawn said. He pulled his phone from his pocket, opened a dictionary app and typed in the word "pyxis." When it displayed the definition, he read it aloud.

"Pyxis – a small box used by ancient Greeks and Romans, usually to hold medicines, etc."

"That silver artifact she mentioned," Dora said. "That must be the pyxis. Except she described it as a block."

"Yeah, you're probably right," Shawn agreed.

"You know, I think we're *both* a couple of nerds," Dora said. Shawn looked at her with a puzzled expression on his face. "It's a beautiful sunny day in a beautiful town in the Rocky Mountains," Dora continued, "and we're sitting inside reading a two hundred year old journal."

"We could go outside and read," Shawn suggested, only half jokingly.

Dora shook her head and smiled. "Hopeless nerds," she said. They stood up and Dora led him to the back door and onto the deck at the south side of the house.

"Although technically, it's not a journal," Shawn said as if their conversation had continued uninterrupted.

"What do you mean?"

"Well, a journal is like a diary, something with daily entries, lots of mundane stuff. 'This morning I had ham and grits for breakfast. Again. Noya is my BFF! OMG! Yancey is being a real a-hole today.' Stuff like that." Dora grinned. "This is more like an eyewitness account of a historical event."

"What event?"

"The Trail of Tears."

"Trail of Tears," Dora said as she opened the big umbrella over the outdoor furniture, angling it toward the sun. "That phrase sounds familiar, but I can't think of what it refers to."

"It was the forced removal of the Cherokee from their ancestral homeland," Shawn explained. "All the things that Noya talked about in the first couple of chapters, and some of the things that Isadora mentioned in this chapter were precursors to the Trail of Tears."

"Of course," Dora said. "You know, after all this time, and all the history lessons, I can still hardly believe that we could do that to them."

"It's one of the darkest blots on American history. And it's not like the Cherokee were the only ones. We did the same thing to several Indian nations before and after them. In fact, you have a painting of it. I noticed it yesterday. The western scene on your stairway wall of the Native Americans is a picture of the Trail of Tears."

Dora shook her head. "You know, as a social worker, I deal with injustice and inequality every day. Now, being reminded of this as a part of my own personal history, I can understand what Isadora said." Leafing back through the pages they had just read, she found the passage she was looking for. "Disgusted by the arrogance of my race," she read out loud.

Shawn nodded thoughtfully. "Well, you shouldn't come down too hard on yourself. You weren't *entirely* to blame for it." And he looked over at her with a grin. Dora smiled and swatted his arm, surprised by how natural the contact felt.

"Do you remember anything about Irishmen coming after the Cherokee?" Dora asked.

"No." Shawn's expression was puzzled. "Just the southern Americans. They wanted the land occupied by the Indians."

"They mentioned 'the pyxis,'" Dora said. "So that must have been unrelated to the Indian conflict."

"In the trunk where you found all that stuff, did you see anything that matched Isadora's description of that artifact?"

"Nothing even close."

"Maybe the Irishmen finally succeeded in getting their hands on it."

Spring had become my favourite time of year in Gainesville. It was a new town, only a few years old, and the residents took great pride in beautifying their surroundings. At the end of April, 1831, in Mahaley's flower garden behind the house, Noya and Edward were married. He had finally expressed his affection for her, though it was only after I insisted that Noya pursue the matter. Hardly considered proper where I came from, or here either for that matter, but I had seen enough evidence of his feelings for her that I thought such impertinence might be forgiven. I am happy to say that I was correct in this assumption.

They went to Savannah for their honeymoon. While they were gone, I helped out more around the house. With Yancey's financial troubles, the cause of which was still apparently not entirely clear, he had sold several of the slaves, keeping only Dorcas and a couple of the field slaves. This meant that there was more work for Mahaley to do around the property, and I lent a hand wherever I could.

I had just finished my morning chores and was preparing to leave for town when Mahaley, missing Noya I think, stopped what she was doing and held me in her arms. I relished the thought of being her "golden-haired daughter."

I was spending more time at the mission clinic when Edward and Noya were away. I think it helped me to cope, not only with my loneliness for Noya, but also with the loss of my family. I came to know a few of the Indians personally, particularly those with recurring health problems, or those with children who often seemed to pass illness back and forth between them. Often they would specifically ask for me to help them.

While Edward was away, I worked more closely with the minister, Reverend Parkin. He was an older gentleman with a wild mane of white hair and a stern countenance that belied his fondness for people in general and Indians in particular. He did possess some medical experience, but was not trained to the extent that Edward was.

I had acquired a fair amount of experience myself, working with Edward and Noya, and was becoming adept at administering treatments for many common injuries and illnesses.

On this one particular day in April, my life was about to change.

The door burst open and a number of people rushed in, all of them Indians, some assisted or carried by others. One of the men who had been laid on a cot before me was a handsome green-eyed Indian with reddish-gold highlights in his hair. Despite his somewhat European features, he was dressed, not in the clothing of the whites, but in skins and moccasins, and a headdress that I can only describe as a sort of turban, usually worn only by the older, more traditional Cherokee.

The young man was only partially conscious but was obviously in pain as his left arm was bent at an unnatural angle and with a point of bone protruding.

He lost consciousness as I set, splinted and bandaged his fractured arm, dabbing away the spatters of blood on his face. I had removed the cloth from his head and was feeling for other wounds, and had in fact found quite a large, rather nasty oozing bump on the back of his head, when his eyes opened and, for the first time since his arrival, he seemed to see clearly. I cannot say the same for myself, for I seemed to see him through a gentle mist. I regret to descend to the use of such trite romanticism, but I know of no other way to express it.

After several awkward seconds, I found my voice.

"Do you hurt anywhere besides your arm and your head?"

He shook his head and I realised that I was still holding it in my hands. I lowered his head gently to the pillow, our gazes locked upon each other.

"What is your name?" I asked.

"Atsila," he responded, and I found myself silently trying out the word in my mouth.

"What is your last name?"

"I have no last name. My father did not take a Christian name. I suppose my last name could be 'son of Da-yunisi'."

"I am Isadora Byrnes." My focus was broken long enough to notice that Reverend Parkin seemed spent. I directed my attention back to Atsila. "I must help with the others, but I shall return to check on you later."

He nodded and I reluctantly left his cot to help Reverend Parkin treat the other injuries. I later learned that these casualties were the result of yet another conflict between the whites and Indians. There were, I am afraid, two fatalities, but most of the other injuries were relatively minor. There were three gunshot wounds, but none of them were life-threatening. Aside from that, two broken arms, some bruised ribs and several cuts requiring stitches.

Nobody seemed to know, or rather they were unwilling to express, who was to blame. But after a few hours, the activity died down a bit, and I returned to Atsila's cot.

"How are you feeling?" I asked him.

"I am well," he said, though I knew he must be in pain. I remembered the bump on the back of his head and prepared a dressing for it.

"What happened today?"

He looked away, but only for a moment. "We were fighting against the white men."

"What white men?" He looked at me for a few moments before replying.

"The Georgia Guard."

*"You were fighting the Georgia Guard?" I asked incredu-
lously. Up until a few months ago, federal troops were in the area,
and had been for some time, charged with trying to keep the peace
between whites and Indians, but confrontations were still frequent
and often bloody. The state of Georgia did not like having the federal troops there, as they wanted sovereignty over the area without
interference from the federal government, especially since gold
had been discovered and white people were swarming over Cherokee land. A few months ago, Georgia facilitated this by forming
a militia force called the Georgia Guard. Informed of this, President Jackson, eager to wash his hands of the situation, withdrew
the federal troops. The Georgia Guard was a brutal group of men,
sanctioned by the Georgia government, and becoming widely
known for their harsh and violent treatment of the Cherokee. And
this handful of Indians had battled them?*

*"Not the whole Guard," Atsila said. "Only three of them. Our
chiefs are weak," he said bitterly. "We should not give up our ancestral land so you white people can spread out."*

*I was momentarily taken aback. "I assure you, Atsila," I said,
struggling to keep my anger in check, "I do not agree with what
the government is doing. White people should not be taking your
land except as tenants, and even then, only with your permission."
I held his gaze. His green eyes blazed with an intensity I had not
seen for some time. Then, that intensity softened a bit. His eyes
narrowed slightly but never left mine and he smiled ever so
slightly.*

*I smiled in response and left him to rest while I helped Reverend
Parkin deal with the two dead men and their family members who
had arrived to take away the bodies.*

*"My dear," said Reverend Parkin when things had calmed
down, "I am so glad you were here today. I don't think I could
have handled all of this on my own." He eased himself tiredly into
a chair and sighed. I sat down next to him and smiled.*

"I am glad too," I responded.

"If only Edward had been here. Maybe he could have saved those two," the minister said, regretfully looking at the recently vacated cots.

"Their wounds were too grave," I said, placing my hand gently on his arm. "They were already beyond help when they arrived."

His stern face softened. "That's good of you to say. Still, it is always sad to lose one."

"Yes, it is," I agreed.

I got up, poured a glass of water and handed it to him, then poured another for myself. The next few minutes were passed in silence as I imagined that it was a delicious cup of tea.

"Well my dear," he finally said, "it's getting late. Why don't you run on home?"

Looking at the clock on the wall, I saw that it was nearing six o'clock in the evening. I was torn. I knew I was expected home for dinner, but there were still three injured people in the clinic who needed care. They were resting peacefully now, but as the night progressed, they would almost definitely be in more pain, and I did not want to leave Reverend Parkin alone to care for them.

I also realised that I wanted to be here for Atsila, although my attraction to him was irrational. I hardly knew him, the affinity I felt for him based solely on his handsome countenance. But I rationalised that he seemed to feel a similar attraction, and in the end, my heart won out over my rational mind.

"I will go home," I finally said. "Dinner will be ready soon, but I will return afterwards and will bring some food for you as well."

"Oh, you don't have to do that," he protested. I held up a hand as if to brook no further objection. He smiled. "You're a sweet girl, Izzy."

I felt a brief pang as I remembered how often Liam uttered a similar phrase, and I quickly went out the back door.

Yancey had granted me the regular use of a carriage, and it was tied up behind the clinic. The ride home took only a matter of minutes. Dinner was ready when I arrived, and Mahaley and Yancey were already sitting at the table. I briefly explained to Mahaley what had happened at the clinic and that I planned to return. Yancey was irritated by the news of the battle.

"Indians like those are not making the process any easier," he said. "If they keep that up, things are not going to go well for the Cherokee."

"Things are already not going well for the Cherokee," I said. I fear I had acquired Noya's outspokenness, at least where her father was concerned. "These people are simply fighting for what is theirs."

"This war will not be won by bloodshed but by diplomacy."

"I agree it would be wonderful if diplomacy alone resolved the issue," I replied with a bit more force than I should have. "But in the meantime, people are being mistreated. They're being beaten and killed. They are desperate, and some respond by striking out like cornered animals. Right or wrong, I cannot fault them for such a response."

He fell quiet at that. Lately Yancey's arguments had diminished to little more than the utterance of platitudes. There was almost no passion or heart behind his statements. I did not know what to make of it, but it did make it easier for a thinking person to win an argument with him.

Reverend Parkin was asleep on a cot, having thoroughly enjoyed the fried chicken that Dorcas had sent for him. Everyone else was sleeping peacefully too, but Atsila had woken shortly after midnight, and we had been talking quietly for an hour.

"My mother is Scottish," Atsila said. That explained the reddish-gold sheen in his hair and his green eyes. "Her father was a goldmith who came to America when she was a baby. They gradually worked their way to Augusta, Georgia, where they settled. He opened a shop selling silver and gold articles. He was an experienced artisan but he was not much of a businessman. The shop *was not very profitable, but it did attract my father who appreci-ated beautiful workmanship.*

"He met the smith's daughter and they fell in love. The court-ship was rocky. Her parents were wary of Indians, but my father eventually won them over. After a couple of years, they married."

"So your father is a Cherokee?" I asked.

"He was. He was killed by the Guard two weeks ago."

"I am terribly sorry," I said.

"He was a peaceable man who never wished ill for others." Atsila spoke with the bitterness of a fresh wound.

"What happened?" I asked quietly.

He paused, then took a deep breath, as if to steel himself for a difficult telling. *"Some white men showed up on the edge of our property one day and were digging in the ground. My father went outside to find out what they were doing. They said they were look-ing for gold. Some friends of theirs had found gold in a field next to us. I knew the people who lived there, but they had moved away months before. It was a widow and her two children. Her husband had been killed by a white man and they were afraid to stay any longer. So the house was empty and the land was no longer being worked.*

"We had seen white men over there for a few days before this but my father did not want trouble. I told you my father was a peaceful man. He was not threatening at all. But now that they were on our property, my father simply asked them if they would please move. They didn't care. It was only when I came outside with a musket that they left.

"The Georgia Guard arrived that evening. I had gone hunting and did not get back until late. I found my mother bruised and naked on the floor and my father dead. There were three of them, my mother later told me. One of them held her while the other two beat my father with their muskets. After he stopped moving, they took turns raping my mother while she sobbed." Atsila paused, shaking his head as he took a deep breath.

91

"My father lay there dead – my mother could see his bloody face a few feet away from hers. Apparently their attackers tired of her crying and struggling as they violated her, and finally knocked her out. I don't know how long she lay there, naked and beaten, before I got home."

I could not speak as tears spilled down my face. I struggled to keep quiet to avoid waking the other patients. My body was shaking uncontrollably, but not from cold. Anger filled me at the thought of the vicious attack on Atsila's family. Atsila, seemingly touched by my emotion, pressed his hand on mine as I gathered my composure.

"My parents and my sister were killed nearly two years ago," I finally said, "also over gold. I understand your pain." The anger seemed to melt from Atsila's face.

I took a deep breath and squared my shoulders, hoping to relieve the pall of melancholy that had settled over us. After a busy and stressful day, the late hour was taking its toll. I suppressed a yawn, though not very effectively.

"I promised to wake Reverend Parkin at one o'clock so he could check on the patients," I said, "and so that I can rest. You should rest, too."

Atsila agreed, holding my gaze. Finally, I stood and went over to Reverend Parkin's cot and gently shook him awake.

I slept fitfully, my dreams populated with alternating images of inhumane violence and uncommon beauty.

Reverend Parkin was asleep when I awoke the next morning, though he was sitting upright in a chair. The other patients had done well during the night, and in fact, one had left in the early hours.

I found Atsila awake but drowsy. He smiled when he saw me and my heart leapt.

"How are you?" I inquired.

"I have pain in my arm and in my head, but I reckon that's to be expected," he smiled. "Actually my head feels much better."

"Wonderful," I replied. "Is your mother aware of what happened, and of your condition?"

"No," he said. "I sent her away after my father was killed. She is staying with her father near Augusta. I would prefer that she not know until my wounds have had time to heal."

"I understand." I looked up and saw that Reverend Parkin had woken and was following up on the remaining patient who was also waking now. I was running out of excuses to stay by Atsila's side. When he saw me, Reverend Parkin approached me with a tired smile.

"I think I can handle things this morning," he said. "Go on home, dear. Mahaley is probably worried about you."

I looked down as Atsila started to sit up.

"I will be leaving too," he said.

"Are you sure you feel well enough to ride?" I asked.

"I will not be riding. My horse was killed in the fight. But I can walk. My home is only three miles north of town."

"My home is on the way. I will give you a ride. My carriage is in back."

Reverend Parkin's face displayed surprise, but I smiled at him as I gently guided Atsila out the back door.

"Is anybody waiting for you at your home?" I asked once we were in the carriage.

"No," Atsila replied. "It is just me now."

"Then we will stop at my home and you can have breakfast." I said it with enough firmness and determination that Atsila did not argue.

On the way, I explained my living situation, so he was not expecting to be among white people. I do not know if that had an effect on his decision to agree to breakfast. My young heart was much lighter on the short ride home.

As I had hoped, breakfast was just being served when we arrived at the house. Mahaley was gracious and welcomed Atsila. Yancey, however, was cold and a bit surly. Having heard the story

93

of the skirmish that had taken place, he knew the identity of this young Indian. Atsila seemed reserved toward Yancey as well.

Yancey hurriedly finished his breakfast and excused himself. Atsila watched him leave, then glanced at me and continued eating his breakfast while Mahaley engaged him in friendly conversation, much of it involving Atsila's history. Atsila was amiable and respectful toward Mahaley and the rest of our time at the breakfast table was quite enjoyable.

After breakfast, as I took Atsila home, I asked him about the silent exchange that took place between himself and Yancey.

"It is nothing," he replied, looking forward.

"Atsila," I persisted, "when two people have known each other for as long as you and I have, one cannot keep secrets from the other." I looked askance at him and smirked at my little joke.

He allowed the hint of a smile to soften his countenance, then leaned toward me and spoke quietly, as if someone might overhear.

"After my father was killed two weeks ago, I vowed, as the next male blood relative, to avenge his death. It was not my intention to declare war on the entire Georgia Guard, though they are little more than vigilantes and bullies, and I would not be unhappy to see them gone. But I was determined to find out which individuals were responsible for my father's death and my mother's rape.

"So I watched them, followed them, listened to conversations when I was able. That's how we chose who to attack yesterday. And the three that I was after are now dead." He glanced over at me and paused. "But as I was tracking them, I saw Yancey Franklin meeting with two of them, William Dawes and Elijah Parsons. I do not know what he was up to, but money was exchanged and they seemed to be on good terms."

"Well, Yancey is a businessman," I said. "He conducts business with many people in the area, including white people." As I was saying it, I could hear the lack of resolve in my voice and realised that I was merely casting about for an excuse. The fact

94

was that I could not think of any good reason why Yancey would be doing business with the Georgia Guard, given their treatment of his countrymen.

We came to a stop in front of Atsila's house. He climbed down from the carriage, carefully cradling his broken arm. Once on the ground, he took my hand and kissed it after the fashion of the white people, and he smiled the sweetest smile I have ever seen.

"Goodbye, Isadora Byrnes," he said. "Thank you for everything you have done for me, and for my people."

"Goodbye, Atsila," I replied. "Get some rest. I will check on you in a day or so." That was not the policy of the mission clinic, but neither was it the policy of the clinic to form an infatuation with one of its patients.

"He is not welcome in this house!" Yancey said angrily. "He is offensive to me and to the survival of the Cherokee people."

We were in the parlour after I had returned from Atsila's house. Mahaley was there as well, sitting at her little writing desk ostensibly answering correspondence.

"Atsila is as much Cherokee as you are," I spat back at him, "and he cares about the survival of the Cherokee." I knew I was on shaky ground arguing with Yancey about who is allowed in his house, but I was angry too. Atsila had introduced certain doubts into my mind about Yancey's loyalty. In hindsight, I realised that the evidence had been there for some time. I had simply disregarded it, for the sake of peace, and for the sake of Noya and Mahaley.

"I will not allow a rebel and an outlaw to be seen frequenting my home." Yancey's voice was steady. He had managed to recall the passion that he once had. If only that passion had been accompanied by honour and loyalty to the Cherokee.

"What business do you have with William Dawes and Elijah Parsons?" I asked, and the shaky ground upon which I was standing began to tremble.

Yancey looked at me through narrowed eyes. From the corner of my eye, I saw Mahaley look up toward us.

"What do you know about them?" he asked.

"I know they are members of the Georgia Guard." I thought it best to not indicate that I knew they were now dead, so as not to implicate Atsila. "I know you were doing some sort of business with them." His face suddenly seemed almost as pale as my own. "What business would a Cherokee man have with a militia group known for their hatred and brutality against Cherokees?"

"My business is none of yours," he said weakly.

I ignored him.

"Then I remembered that you are only half Cherokee." The colour flooded back into his face, but I impetuously continued under a momentum I felt powerless to resist. "I know that you seem determined to be a rich white man, but I can assure you that most of the white people with whom you do business will only see the Indian in you. When it no longer benefits them, you will be just another savage to them." And then that trembling ground opened up to swallow me.

"Get out of my sight!" Yancey shouted, his eyes blazing. He moved toward me, but Mahaley was on her feet and stepped between us. Yancey stopped, his chest heaving with emotion, and I went upstairs to my room in a similar condition.

Sitting on my bed, trying to catch my breath, I pondered what to do. Yancey was beyond angry with me and would likely not let me stay, even after he had regained his composure. Mahaley would provide a voice of reason – I knew that she wanted me here – but I doubted that even she would be able to overcome Yancey's fury.

But did I even want to stay, knowing what I now knew about Yancey, not only his business dealings, but also his angry outburst? At the same time, I realised that I was at least partly responsible. Why had I insisted on pushing him? Why could I not keep my mouth shut?

Opening the doors of the wardrobe, I retrieved my luggage, although I had no idea where I might go. As I fingered the valise that Liam had given me, I noticed it felt light. Shaking it, I heard a muffled yet perceptible jingling sound. When I opened it, two of the stacks of coins were missing, and the cloth wrapping the remaining one was loose, allowing the coins inside to move about.

I sat down again, remembering another oft-repeated pearl of wisdom from my mother: "Don't keep all your eggs in one basket." After learning about the death of my family and my subsequent "adoption" by Mahaley, and deciding that I would stay in Gainesville, it was the memory of that old chestnut that moved me to divide the six stacks of gold coins, placing half of the money in the local bank. I had left three stacks of coins in the valise for easy access. Now, less than one stack remained, along with some silver. I had hidden the letters, documents and the decorated silver artifact under a loose board at the bottom of the wardrobe. I pulled the rest of my possessions out of the wardrobe and checked under the board. Thankfully, they were still there.

I sat back down on the bed, thinking of Yancey's financial troubles. Could it be that he had found my money and seen it as a way out of his troubles? He was the only one I could bring myself to suspect. I trusted Noya and Mahaley completely, and nobody else had had access to my room.

Carrying the valise, I opened my door and started downstairs, intent on confronting Yancey. As I descended, I heard his voice raised once again in anger. My first thought was that it was directed at Mahaley, but then I realised that there was more than one voice, and they were outside. As I reached the first floor, I could see the front door standing open. Mahaley was on the porch with Yancey, who was holding a musket, and there were three men on horseback, also armed with muskets.

I came up behind Mahaley. "What is happening?" I asked quietly. She turned to me with an expression of worry on her face.

"It's the Georgia Guard. Somebody reported to them that Yancey was mining for gold."

"This is my land!" Yancey shouted at them. "What I do here is my business. I am not hurting anyone."

"The Cherokee ain't allowed to mine for gold," responded the man in front, evidently the spokesman for the trio. "That's the law." I'm afraid that was true – despite the unfairness of it, the

99

Cherokee were prohibited from mining for gold, even on their own property.

"We haven't even found any gold," Yancey argued.

"Ain't exactly the point, now is it?"

"How am I supposed to support my family?" Yancey asked.

"That ain't none o' our concern," the man responded. "You are to cease any and all mining operations!"

"You will not tell me what I will or will not do on my land!" Yancey shouted.

"We are tellin' you," the leader said, lowering his voice but speaking with cold menace, "and you will do what we say."

Yancey took a step toward them and raised his musket, but one of the men did not wait to see his intention. Yancey fell dead, shot through the heart. The next few seconds were something of a blur. I was aware of Mahaley screaming and falling down over Yancey. The next thing I was aware of was the approach of the three men, now on foot. Yancey's musket was somehow in my hands. I pointed it at the men, hoping that I did not need to use it. I had never fired a gun in my life.

The men hesitated, glancing at each other, doubtless trying to decide if the woman before them was a threat. I tried to hold the musket convincingly, but apparently I was not successful, as they started forward once again, stopping only as Sam, the foreman, rounded the side of the house. He also had a musket.

"Alright," the spokesman said, raising his hands in what he meant to be a non-threatening gesture, "we don't want no more trouble." They backed up and mounted their horses. "Just remember what we said. No mining for gold."

They turned and rode away.

I knelt beside Mahaley and held her, as Sam carried Yancey's body inside.

Shawn closed the book and put it on the table as Dora rotated the umbrella, repositioning the shade as the sun made its slow march across the sky.

"Are you finding this as fascinating as I am?" Shawn asked.

Dora nodded. "I never really knew anything about the Trail of Tears. And to be brutally honest, I haven't really been that interested in Native American history." She sat back down and scooted her chair to take better advantage of the shade.

"History textbooks I remember from school didn't exactly go out of their way to make it interesting," Shawn affirmed.

"When I was a little girl, Gramma enjoyed taking me to museums, and I always enjoyed it myself. But at the time, it didn't really sink in what it was all about. Even that was kind of unreal to me. The exhibits were just dusty, crumbling artifacts. I never realized that it was about real people."

"It's difficult for a child to connect with history," Shawn agreed, "or with museum displays. Even *I* didn't start becoming a history nerd until my early teens."

"Yeah, it always seemed so far removed from reality, from anything I was familiar with," Dora said. "But this isn't just dry history. It's like having someone who was there tell you their story personally."

"In your case, it's a relative telling you."

"Before, when I thought about Indians, it was usually in reference to the 'Old West.' I never really thought about how long of a struggle they had."

"Sure. Most people are more familiar with the stories about cowboys and Indians in the old west, in the late nineteenth century. But I've seen that era referred to as simply a 'mopping up.' Most of the damage had already been done. The few Indians who had not yet been put in reservations were just fighting for their own survival."

"I feel like John Wayne lied to me," Dora said with a bitter smile.

Shawn thought for a moment, then tapped the book. "I noticed another reference to that silver artifact."

"Yeah, me too. You know, I've been thinking – maybe we should go upstairs and see if we can find it. I haven't looked in all the boxes up there. Maybe Gramma kept it somewhere else."

"I'm game," Shawn agreed.

They got up and went inside. Dora placed the book on the kitchen counter as they walked through, then led Shawn up the stairs and into the attic room.

The trunk with the Native American designs stood open, with a few of the items still strewn on the floor around it.

"That's where the items on the dining room table came from," Dora said, pointing at the trunk, "and that box is where I got Isadora's book."

"Okay," Shawn said. He looked at the other arrangements of boxes as he sized up the room. "How about I start with this box and you take that one, and we meet in the middle?"

Several boxes contained clothing, some of it outdated by a century or more; others contained old documents; and while they found all of it interesting, none of it related to what they were looking for. They pushed them aside and moved on. A little over an hour later, they had eliminated all of the remaining cartons and had found nothing resembling Isadora's description of that etched silver artifact.

Dora went back to the trunk and glanced at the papers she had pulled out of it before. The bill of sale for the slaves was still on top. There were old handwritten receipts and other documents, but none of them gave any indication of what they were looking for.

Disappointed, they went back downstairs and out onto the deck to read more of Isadora's account.

With bowed head and a sorrowful glance toward Mahaley, Reverend Parkin turned and nodded to two men with shovels, who started pushing dirt into the grave. I had my left arm around Mahaley who stood at the graveside sniffing back the tears. On my right was Noya, her hand in mine. Edward stood loyally at her side. The couple had arrived home only hours after Yancey had been killed, the joy and happiness of their marriage and honeymoon instantly turned to sorrow.

Others were there for the funeral as well, mostly Indians, but there were a few white people who either knew and liked Yancey and Mahaley or who knew Noya and me from our work at the mission.

As we all turned to go home, I noticed Atsila standing at a distance beside a large magnolia tree, its cheerful white flowers completely out of place on this day. Atsila's arm, of course, was still in a sling, but the bandage on his head had been replaced by the colourful striped turban he had been wearing when we first met. I let go of Noya's hand, guiding Mahaley toward her, as I went to see Atsila.

"How are you doing?" he asked as I approached.

"I'm doing fairly well," I replied, "although it was quite a shock. Of course, Mahaley and Noya are taking it much harder. How are you feeling?"

"Much better," he said. It had been two days since I last saw him, and I was pleased that his injuries were healing well. "What will you and Mahaley do now?"

"I will stay with her. She cannot afford to keep the three re-maining slaves, nor will she be able to work the land. As it hap-pens, Yancey had run up numerous bills and gambling debts, and they were being called in by the lenders. I have paid the debts, so she needn't worry about them, but she is going to sell much of the property."

"Even the house?" he asked.

"The house is too large for the two of us," I admitted, "but I have suggested that we take in lodgers to support ourselves."

"A very good idea," Atsila agreed.

I felt comfortable in his company, and we started walking to-ward the carriage. Mahaley, Noya and Edward were still talking with friends and well-wishers, so we walked slowly.

"You were right about Yancey," I said. "After his death, I found a number of people who were willing to talk to me about him. I am afraid that much of what I heard was not very savoury. Besides the gambling, Yancey had entered into agreements to be-tray his fellow countrymen. Debt collections, foreclosures, Yancey would turn the information over to the whites, and of course, they would treat the Indians worse than they would treat white people in similar conditions."

"Why would he do that?" Atsila asked.

"Money. He probably hoped that it would put him in good stead with the white men, and offset his debt, but unfortunately, that had gotten much too deep."

"Does Mahaley know?"

"Not the worst of it. I don't think she needs to know." I turned to Atsila. "What about you? What will you do now?"

"My mother is afraid to come back here. I have encouraged her to stay with her father. He is old and can use her help."

"But you did not answer my question," I persisted. "What about you, Atsila?" His hesitation was conspicuous. I stopped in my tracks, and he turned to look at me. He seemed embarrassed to continue but finally he began speaking.

"The men who started digging for gold on our property have come back, and there are more of them. They have taken over my house. I am outnumbered, and of course, the Georgia Guard is supporting them."

"You have nowhere to go?" I understood how difficult it was for him to admit this defeat, and I struggled to suppress the anger I felt toward the white people who had taken his home away from him.

"I will be alright," he said. "I can do many jobs with my hands. I will find someone who will take me in."

"You already have," I replied. "Come with me." I led him over to the carriage where Mahaley, Noya and Edward were preparing to climb in.

"Mahaley," I said, "we need a caretaker at our boarding house, do we not?"

She looked at me, pondering what I was saying. "Yes, I suppose we will."

"Could we give Atsila a room in exchange for jobs around the property?"

She looked at Atsila, then back to me. "You paid Yancey's debts, including a mortgage on our house," she said. "The house is more yours than mine."

"No," I said, "the house is still yours. We are partners in this venture and will make decisions together concerning it."

"Dear Isadora," she said, taking my hand, her face beaming with gratitude. "Yes, he is welcome in our home." I smiled and turned to Atsila.

"There you have it," I said. "And your first assignment will be to teach me how to shoot."

Despite the loss of Yancey, settling in to our new life at the Gainesville Boarding House was surprisingly easy. Mahaley and I were so fond of each other that working together was a joy. My fondness for Atsila was also, I am sure, another factor.

As land ownership was somewhat complicated where the Cherokee were concerned – it was a new concept introduced to them by the white man – I let Mahaley make the arrangements concerning the acres of property behind the house. In the end, one of our Cherokee neighbours acquired the land as it already adjoined his property. On the subject of gold on the property, apparently Yancey's statement to the Georgia Guard had been correct: he and Sam had not found any more. That one nugget that Sam found had evidently been an anomaly.

When we were ready to start taking in boarders, I placed handwritten notices around town advertising our vacancies. Noya, Edward and Reverend Parkin also provided endorsements in their contact with people through the mission, particularly the Cherokee. Many Cherokee had their homes taken from them, and while some were moving west, some decided to stay in the area. We did not need much, so I suggested we charge reduced rent, and Mahaley agreed. As a result, in the first month, we had no more vacancies.

I kept my room at the back of the house. Mahaley moved out of the room that she had occupied with Yancey and into the room next to mine. The room she moved out of was the largest bedroom in the house, and it was now occupied by a mother and her 8 year old daughter, Talu'tsi and Tala respectively, more victims of white oppression. Noya and Edward had taken a small house in town, nearer the mission, so Noya's former room now housed an elderly Cherokee man named Nayu who had outlived his family and was no longer able to work his land. The two remaining rooms upstairs were home to Helen Garrity, a young widow of Welsh descent, and Tsuganotsi, a man who, due to a beating at the hands of a gang of white men, was now blind. He had a rather surly disposition, but due to his condition, and the reason behind it, I was inclined to forgive this.

In the basement of the house were the former slave quarters. Atsila occupied the largest of these, and though I suggested that he take one of the lighter upstairs rooms, he seemed to like his room, and indeed it was quite cozy. Another basement room was taken by Ganasita, a motherly type with a very kind face and a disposition to match. The remaining basement rooms we intentionally left vacant to use for storage, but which would be available in case of an emergency situation.

Mahaley, it turns out, was a great repository of Cherokee lore, and I often noticed her sharing these stories with Tala. She would take the little girl upon her lap and relate to her the story of the first strawberries, or why the rabbit has a short tail, or the legend of the cedar tree. I enjoyed hearing these tales at least as much as Tala did, and I found joy in observing the pleasure that Mahaley derived from telling them.

Running the boarding house necessitated a reduction in the time I spent at the mission clinic, but I felt that my time was still well-spent in caring for our various duties at home, in service of our tenants.

Atsila had fulfilled his first assignment: by the end of this first month, I could hit a 12-inch target with a pistol from a distance of twenty yards, and with a musket from ninety. He seemed impressed by my prowess, and I admit to feeling a glow of pride at his compliments. More than that, though, I now felt better able to defend myself and my loved ones.

During the course of my training, Atsila and I grew closer, greatly enjoying each other's company. Despite the side of him that could calmly track and investigate the men who had attacked his parents, and then cunningly ambush and kill them, to all of his fellow residents in the boarding house, he was warm and caring. He had a likable temperament that attracted people to him. Of those, I freely admit I was foremost.

The garden in back of the house was producing well and on a hot afternoon in July of 1831, I was picking okra. It was a strange vegetable that I had never seen nor eaten before coming to America. I had come to love it, but did not enjoy picking it. The prickly *leaves made my arms itch so, despite the heat, I was wearing a light jacket with long sleeves.*

I had been in the garden for what seemed like all afternoon, but in reality was probably closer to half an hour, when Atsila appeared at the end of the row, holding a glass of lemonade. At that moment, his smiling face was almost as welcome as the cool beverage. His arm had healed well, and though it was still tender at times, he was an industrious worker and managed to carry out his tasks to good advantage.

I smiled as I accepted the glass from his hand and began drinking the cool liquid with greedy abandon. I lowered the half-empty glass with a sigh.

"Thank you, Atsila," I said. "You are a welcome sight."

He smiled, and I stood there for a few moments catching my breath before finishing the lemonade. He took the empty glass and went back into the house, leaving me to wonder at his silence. I was not left to wonder for very long.

Having finished picking the okra, I carried the basket into the kitchen and placed it on the work table. Mahaley was there with a strange expression on her face.

"Atsila seems to think of me as your mother," she said.

"That's not very surprising," I said lightheartedly. "That's the way I think of you too." I kissed her on the cheek.

"He asked my permission to court you." I quickly pushed her away to look at her face. She was serious.

"Why did he not ask me?"

"It is the Cherokee way, and Atsila is very traditional," she answered. "The mother is the one who often arranges the marriage, or who gives permission." It made sense. Cherokee children belong to the mother's clan, and a person's heritage, including hereditary leadership and property, were passed through the mother's line. The Cherokee mother was essentially the head of the household. It was therefore logical that Atsila would approach Mahaley for permission to court me.

"How did you answer him?" I asked breathlessly.

"I was not certain of your feelings." She looked intently at me, the beginning of a smile creeping onto her lips, but she asked me anyway. "Is Atsila someone you want?"

"Yes!" I said without hesitation. She took me into her arms and held me tightly.

A few hours later I found a basket filled with meat outside the door to my room. Puzzled, I took it to Mahaley and inquired about it. She smiled.

"He has asked you," she said. "When a Cherokee man wants a woman, he will kill a deer and bring its meat to the woman he desires. If she wants the man, she will let him know by cooking the meat for him." I pondered this for a moment. So many parts of Cherokee life were imbued with rich symbolism. I looked down at the meat in the basket, then back at Mahaley.

"I hope you realise," I said with a smile, "that our dinner menu has changed."

In August of 1831, almost exactly two years after my departure from England, Atsila and I gathered with friends and family near the shore of a picturesque lake, at a remote area in the woods behind the home of Kanasdatsi, an old Cherokee priest. As Noya and Mahaley were now my only family, I was happy to have them there with me.

Mahaley stood near me during the ceremony. Although I was not officially a Cherokee benefiting from their clan system, she considered me her daughter and an honourary member of Aniwaya, or the Wolf Clan.

Atsila's mother, Fiona was there too, and I was happy to meet this woman who hailed from Scotland, not far from my childhood home. I could tell that when she was younger, her hair had been bright red. Now, with white and grey hair mixed with it, it gave the impression of a pinkish halo around her face. Her green eyes were still bright, and while I know she was happy for Atsila, her face seemed drawn and sad, a result, I am sure, of the ordeal she had endured only a few months before.

Her brother, Atsila's uncle, was present as well, and later provided music on the bagpipes, which the Indians seemed not to care for.

As I wanted to honour Atsila's culture, I agreed to a traditional Cherokee wedding. Atsila looked very handsome indeed wearing a blue shirt decorated with red ribbons and tied about the waist with a wide red sash. He wore deer skin moccasins and a red and blue striped turban wrapped about his head.

According to tradition, Atsila and I each had blue blankets wrapped around us as we listened to songs sung in Cherokee, only parts of which I understood. Kanasdatsi spoke for a bit, partly in Cherokee and partly, for my benefit, in English. He spoke of Kanadi and Selu, the first man and woman according to Cherokee tradition, then verbally painted a beautiful picture of our future together.

Following this, Atsila and I exchanged baskets. He gave me a basket filled with meats indicating his vow to always provide for our household, and I gave him a basket filled with bread and corn which demonstrated my willingness to prepare the food and provide nourishment for our family.

Kanasdatsi then removed the two blue blankets from our shoulders and covered us both together with one white blanket, symbolising the beginning of our new life together. He handed us the wedding vase, a beautifully decorated clay vessel with two spouts, from which Atsila and I drank simultaneously.

Feasting, dancing and singing continued late into the evening, but Atsila and I tired of it before our friends and family. As yet another dance commenced, he caught my eye. Without a word, we slipped away into the dark forest. I followed his lead through the woods, until we came to the shore of the lake. Here, Atsila guided me to a canoe which he rowed to the island where friends had prepared a small cabin for our wedding night. Paneled with smooth boards of yellow pine and embellished with Indian décor, the little cabin was welcoming, as the wedding feast continued across the water.

My heart was pounding as Atsila led me inside and we were truly alone for the first time. We did not need to light any lamps or candles. The interior was illuminated just enough by the distant fire of the merrymakers across the lake.

Atsila took me in his arms and kissed me, fumbling with my unfamiliar clothing. I helped him with the fastenings, blushing the whole time, until I stood naked before him, breathing so hard I was certain that I must surely faint. But my shyness was quickly overcome by the appreciative expression on my new husband's face.

He quickly removed his own clothing and again held me close, this time with nothing between us, and I trembled as his hands softly caressed my body in ways I had never imagined. He guided me to the bed and we lay down together, exploring each other's bodies with a tender hunger that almost brought me to tears.

Propriety prevents me from going into detail, but suffice to say that, after a brief initial pain, the next hour or so was the most exquisite time I had ever spent with a man. Despite our mutual hunger for each other, Atsila was always considerate, a true gentleman, and we fell asleep in each other's arms.

I awoke to silence, or rather to a lack of human sounds. It was dark, and the nocturnal creatures were about. I stood up and looked out the window, but it was dark in the distance where the wedding feast had taken place. My stirring woke Atsila and he stood behind me, wrapping a blanket around us.

We stood there listening for a while, picking out individual sounds. Ducks quietly muttered near the shore. Crickets conducted a symphony in the woods behind our cabin, and in the shallows to the west, I could hear the raucous croaking of bullfrogs. Through it all, there was a beautiful bird song, a trill that rose in pitch at the end. Atsila noticed me tilting my head to hear it, and as I looked up at him with a puzzled expression on my face, he smiled.

"Whippoorwill."

"What a beautiful song," I said.

"There are some who believe that the call of the whippoorwill is an omen of death."

"That lovely song?" I asked. "I don't believe it."

Atsila smiled again. "I don't either."

I turned around so that we were facing each other, pressed together with his arms around me. Standing in front of the window, his face was dimly illuminated by the light of a nearly full moon. I kissed him. He held me tightly and sighed.

"I wish you could have met my father," he said. "He could tell you the name of every bird by its song. I can name a lot of them, but I know of no one who is as able, or as quick, as my father was." He looked out the window, a pained expression on his face. "In this time when the Cherokee are blending in with the white people, my father held tightly to our traditions, and stayed close to the earth and its creatures." His voice was wistful.

"My father could tell what part of England a person came from by hearing only four or five words from his mouth," I said quite seriously. But then I smiled. "Perhaps not quite as useful a talent as your father's."

Atsila looked down at me and smiled.

I laid my face against his chest and held him tightly, delighting in the warmth of his naked body pressed against mine. He kissed the top of my head and I lifted my face so that I could kiss his mouth. I felt a now familiar heat, a stirring deep inside me. Evidently we both had had our fill of the natural world outdoors, as we went back to bed and made love again.

"I think I could learn to enjoy this," I said playfully.

We stayed in the little cabin on the island for four wonderful days, after which we returned to our home at the boarding house. I moved into Atsila's large quarters, and while I had been hesitant to move into the basement, the room was actually quite comfortable. The windows, though high and small, faced south, rendering it not bleak but rather very cheerful. Within a week, my old room was rented to James Smith who, despite the name, was an old Cherokee who had fought alongside the English in the American Revolution.

We all settled into a comfortable life and, though we were aware of the news concerning the Cherokee, it did not directly affect us, until one cold evening in early December. Atsila had just *finished his chores outside when he came in the front door followed closely by another man.*

"Isadora," he said, "I'd like you to meet John Ross."

"John Ross? Principal Chief of the Cherokee Nation?" I had heard the name so many times since I had become friends of the Cherokee, that the man had attained almost godlike status in my mind. I quickly gathered my wits and extended my hand. "I'm so very pleased to meet you."

"And I am very pleased to meet you," he said with a soft, sweet voice. He was not what I had expected. Handsome, with blue eyes and brown hair, he appeared to be about forty years old. I later learned that he was only one-eighth Cherokee, and while he had the appearance of a white man, he did have some Indian features. He was soft-spoken and respectful, and I found him to be a most agreeable person.

"Mr. Ross is on his way north but he wanted to stop and meet you," Atsila said with a hint of a smile.

"Meet me?" I asked. "How would he – " Remembering that the man was standing in front of me, I was embarrassed at having spoken of him as if he weren't there. Instead, I addressed the question to him rather than to Atsila. "Forgive me. How would you know anything about me?"

"My home is not that far from here, in Rome," he said with a gentle smile. "I've heard plenty of talk about the white woman in Gainesville who is a friend of the Cherokee. Some go so far as to call you an angel."

I felt uneasy with this comparison, and I knew from the warmth in my cheeks that my face was flushed. "I can assure you, sir, that I am only a woman."

"Well, ma'am" he said, "in my life so far, I have not encountered a single person who turned out to be a real angel. However, I can say that what matters most is how other people come to view you. Your work at the mission, and now here where the majority of your tenants are Cherokee, has elevated you in the eyes of my

people. You may not be a 'real' angel, but you are that kind of person."

While flattered by the remarks, I was eager to deflect this praise. "Perhaps you should meet Reverend Parkin and Dr Hodges," I said.

"Yes, both very fine men," he replied. "I just came from the mission. They are also spoken of very highly by the Cherokee people in this area. In fact, they are the ones who gave me directions to your boarding house." Seeing my discomfort, he quickly changed his tone. "I did not mean to embarrass you. I simply want to thank you for your help. The Cherokee have few friends in Georgia and that number seems to be decreasing all the time. It's good to know that you and others like you are on our side."

"Well Mr Ross, I do not like to see injustice of any kind. What I do for the Cherokee, I would do for anyone."

"Which is what makes you that kind of person," he said.

"Will you stay for dinner?" I asked him. He hesitated, and I continued. "I do not wish to keep you from your business, but you do need to eat."

"That's a mighty kind offer, ma'am," he said. "Most of my evening is free, and I admit that I am feeling a bit peckish."

There were thirteen people gathered around the dinner table that night as Noya and Edward joined us. Everyone expressed appreciation as Mahaley and I brought out a feast of ham with mashed potatoes and red-eye gravy.

A happy clamour reigned as if the tenants were celebrating the visit of a dignitary. Some of the Cherokee initially displayed reverence toward John Ross, but they were quickly disarmed by his quiet, good-natured disposition, and soon all were relaxed and enjoying themselves. Eventually, the light-hearted talk turned to more serious conversation.

"Mr Ross, as you can see, I'm not a Cherokee," said Helen Garrity in her soft, birdlike voice. Her blonde hair was even lighter than mine and her skin more fair. "So I have no personal stake in the outcome of your battle, aside from concern for my friends." She smiled at those sitting around the table. "But I'm curious: given the likelihood of things not turning out your way, why don't you encourage the Cherokee to move to the Indian Territory? Wouldn't it be better for all of you?"

"Why would that be better than being allowed to stay in the home we inherited from our ancestors?" he asked.

"Well, I was just thinking that it might be more secure, where you're not surrounded by people who don't like you." She said this with some embarrassment.

"That is the reasoning that the Ridges employ," he responded. "And I will readily admit that there may be some merit to it. But I am certain that there is no place of security for us. I have no confidence that the United States will be more just and faithful towards us in the barren prairies of the west, than they have been when we occupied the soil that we inherited from the Great Author of our existence." This was followed by a general grunt of approval around the table, primarily from the Cherokees in attendance.

"We should band together and drive the white man from our land," growled Tsuganotsi, the blind Indian. "They are trespassers and bullies."

"I understand your feelings," said Mr Ross, "but we cannot win this war with weapons. The white men are too numerous and strong. You know that, Mr Smith," he said, turning to the elderly Indian who had fought alongside the English against the Americans in their revolution. "We must fight this injustice without violence. Our might in battle is not enough any longer. We must prove the strength of our character."

Atsila fidgeted in his seat a bit, likely from the memory of the act of vengeance he carried out against the murderers of his father. I did not know how John Ross would now view the Cherokee belief concerning blood revenge, but for Atsila's sake, I was not going to ask.

"Should we just lie down and let them trample us?" asked Noya. "Or force us out of our ancestral home?"

"Certainly not," said Mr Ross. "We must resist. We must fight. But we must do it by their rules, in their courts of law."

"In the meantime, many of our people continue to die," said Tsuganotsi.

"And likely many more will die before this is over. Just a few days ago, I myself was nearly the victim of a plot devised by the Pony Club." Several expressed surprise as no one had heard about this. "Yes, it's true," he continued.

"My brother Andrew and I were visiting with Major Ridge at his home when there was a knock on his door. A white man named Mr Harris launched into a rather elaborate tale to determine if Mr John Ross was there.

"Well, apparently his curiosity was satisfied, for even though he left at that time, he and some of his cronies appeared later when we were on our way home. He said, 'I have been for a long time wanting to kill you and I'll be damned if I don't now do it,' – begging your pardon, ladies – and he raised a gun, meaning to do me harm.

"But we wheeled our horses around and galloped away. I was able to avoid the assassin's bullet and my brother and I made good our escape."

"Oh my goodness," I said. "How awful!"

"Mmm," he nodded in agreement. Then, noticing the clock on the wall, "Well, I see from the time that I must make another escape." He pushed back his chair and stood up. He said good-bye to everyone at the table, then turned to me. "Isadora, thank you for your kind hospitality."

I took his arm and walked him toward the front of the house. At the door, he bent at the waist and kissed my hand. "Thank you again for your kindness. It is appreciated by many Cherokee in the area, and I am certain you will receive the ultimate reward for your compassion."

"It was wonderful to meet you," I replied. "May God bless your efforts to make this right."

He smiled at me with gratitude in his eyes, and was gone.

ell, I hate to interrupt this," Shawn said, looking at his watch, "but I have to go. I have an appointment with a client."

"What? You mean somebody else was actually taken in by your über-clever name?" Dora joked.

Shawn smiled. "Don't read any more without me."

"No problem," Dora agreed. "I need to get some groceries anyway. I'll make dinner when you get back."

They stood up from the table and followed the deck around to the front of the house. Shawn turned and looked at Dora.

"It shouldn't take too long. I'll be back as soon as I can." She smiled as he walked down the steps and got into his car. After he drove away, she went in the front door, left Isadora's book, and picked up her purse.

She remembered passing a Safeway on Highway 24 on the way to the house, so she had to drive only a few minutes. Selecting things that she knew she would need for the week, she also passed by the meat department and found two thick steaks and decided to grill them for dinner tonight.

Dora returned home as afternoon clouds rolled in from the mountains and the rain began. She had the groceries put away when Shawn returned, hunched over to protect an armful of library books from the rain.

"Planning on being bored?" Dora joked.

"These are books about the Trail of Tears, smartass," he said.

"You do remember we already have one, right?"

"Just background material," he smiled. "It's been a while since I studied anything about it. I just need a refresher course."

Dora had made a pitcher of white wine sangria, and she poured two glasses which they took to the sunroom at the back of the house. Decorated with white wicker furniture and plush, colorful cushions, it was a comfortable and cozy room to relax in and watch the thunderstorm.

"Did you find anything interesting?" Dora asked, looking at the books that Shawn had brought with him.

"I haven't had much time to look into them yet," he said, selecting a book, "but I did look up the Georgia Guard since I didn't really remember anything about them. I haven't found much, but apparently Isadora was right on the money. Some have said that the Georgia Guard was even more violent and brutal than the Ku Klux Klan would later become. In time, Cherokee leaders actually fled to neighboring states to hold meetings, out of fear of the Guard."

They sat for a few quiet moments.

"I can't imagine living under that kind of fear," Dora said. "We take our freedom too much for granted."

"Yeah," Shawn agreed, "especially when you realize that our freedom was built on the defeat and subjugation of others. I mean, I know that sounds kind of preachy and moralistic, but look at our history."

The storm eventually wore itself out and the sun burned through the clouds as they drank their sangria. Dora suggested that they fire up the grill and start preparing the steaks. They could hardly wait to sit down to dinner and resume their reading.

Near the end of January of 1832, Noya and Edward welcomed an infant son, Peter, into their home. The boy had Edward's fair hair, but his olive skin seemed a combination of their colouring. Named after Edward's father, Peter was a welcome addition to their family.

Mahaley was the proudest of grandmothers. She was irritated during this time by only one thing: that she had to spend so much time tending to her duties at the boarding house. I was happy to do some of her chores when I was able so that she could spend time with Noya and the baby, although she was missed by Tala who had come to enjoy her storytelling sessions.

It was about this time that I discovered that I myself was with child.

Atsila was in town for supplies, expected to be home around dusk, and I was anxious to tell him the news. Mahaley had gone upstairs for something, and it seemed almost as if I had the house to myself. As the light of day began to fade, I made my way around the main floor lighting the lamps. I was in the parlour when I heard hoof beats. Thinking that Atsila was coming home, I looked out the window and saw four armed men on horses. They did not appear to be friendly.

A musket and a pistol were kept at the ready in a small cabinet near the front door, and I quickly seized the musket as a shiver rattled my body and my breath caught in my chest. Heavy boot steps pounded over the porch, and then a fist banged several times on the door.

125

"We know there's Injuns in there," called out a loud voice. The words sounded a bit slurred, as if the speaker had been drinking. "Why don't you make this easy and c'mon out? We got business to discuss!"

My stomach threatened to turn flips, my heart pounding so hard I was sure it was audible, as I pressed my back against the wall beside the door.

"What the hell's a white woman doin' consortin' with savages?" the apparent leader yelled, accompanied by laughter from his cohorts. "Next thing you know, you'll be wearin' war paint and ridin' bareback!" His words elicited cackles and imitated war whoops from his men.

I shrank back from the door, hoping that Atsila would not return until after these ruffians had gone. Suddenly, a door swung open upstairs and Tsuganotsi began coming down the stairs, feeling his way down the banister with one hand, and holding a pistol in the other.

As he carefully neared the bottom of the staircase a few feet ahead of where I stood frozen in fear, I whispered, "Tsuganotsi, I think it's the Pony Club! Be very quiet!" I hated to think what would happen to him if he were seen holding a gun.

No sooner had I thought this, the door crashed open. Hidden behind the now open door, I watched in horror as Tsuganotsi pointed his gun toward the men, but the leader of the gang saw him and fired first. Tsuganotsi fell down the remaining steps, blood already pooling under his head.

What happened next happened very quickly, much faster than I can here describe it. The leader was now inside where I could see him past the door, and I quickly raised my musket and shot him. He fell with a lead ball in his chest, his gun clattering on the floor in front of him. In the instant that I shot him, I was aware of movement at the top of the stairs and I saw Mahaley with a pistol in her hands. She fired it before the leader hit the floor and the man directly behind him dropped, and in his death spasm, he squeezed

126

the trigger, his shot missing Mahaley by only a few inches and embedding itself in the wall at the top of the stairs, after passing through the large portrait of her that hung there.

"Get out!" I screamed angrily, as I reached for Tsuganotsi's pistol at my feet.

I was half aware of approaching hoof beats as the two remaining men turned at the sound of my voice. My pistol was already raised, but I knew I could only shoot one of the men. They both raised their guns. I fired, shooting the one nearest me through the eye. At the same time, another shot rang out. I closed my eyes, preparing for the pain of the bullet. Instead, the fourth man fell dead, shot by some unseen assailant.

Mahaley was at the bottom of the stairs now, carefully stepping around Tsuganotsi's body. Together, with mounting apprehension, we peeked around the door to see Atsila bounding up the steps from his hastily abandoned buckboard.

I fell into his arms. He held me so tightly I thought I would faint from lack of breath, but I did not care. When he let go of me, I looked at Mahaley. She was looking somberly at the bodies, particularly Tsuganotsi's, her breathing heavy as tears glistened on her cheeks.

Helen Garrity had heard the racket and came to the entryway. She was in tears herself as she looked at the dead bodies, and Mahaley quickly regained her composure.

"Helen," she said, "would you please help me finish preparing dinner?" Mahaley put her arms around Helen's shoulders and guided her away with a glance over her shoulder at us.

"Should we report this attack?" I asked Atsila.

"No!" Atsila replied adamantly. "Four dead white men in a house full of Cherokee? There would be no white people on our side."

"What are we going to do with the bodies?" I asked with mounting apprehension.

Atsila thought for a few minutes, pacing back and forth.

"We prepare Tsuganotsi for burial. I will contact Reverend Parkin about him. These four," he said, shifting his attention to the outlaws, "I will put in the river."

"The river?" I asked. I thought about the river that served as the property line since selling the cotton fields.

"Yes," Atsila said. "Just downstream from us are the rapids, which will quickly carry the bodies away. About a mile farther downstream is the falls, with jagged rocks at the bottom. With any luck, the bodies will be unrecognisable by the time they get past there. It is several miles before the river slows. We will remove anything that could identify them and that, combined with the current, will hopefully keep suspicion far removed from us."

The next half hour or so was spent wrapping Tsuganotsi's body and stripping the other four men. After unloading the supplies from the buckboard, Atsila and I carried the bodies out to the wagon.

"I will dump the bodies in the river," he said, "and then go to the mission and tell Reverend Parkin that Tsuganotsi's gun went off when he was cleaning it."

I set off to get some cleaning supplies. There was a considerable amount of blood, and I was hoping to get it cleaned up before the others arrived for dinner.

It was a mournful group gathered round the dinner table that evening. Those who were aware of what happened said nothing. Those who were not, still knew that Tsuganotsi was dead.

"Reverend Parkin will make arrangements for Tsuganotsi's burial," Atsila said that night as I perched gloomily on the side of the bed. "He sends his sympathies." I nodded.

"And the bodies?"

"They were swept away quickly, just as I expected," he replied. "In the rapids, with the whole night ahead, they should be far away before anybody discovers them." I sighed but did not respond. "Are you alright?" he asked. I looked up at him.

"I killed two people." Atsila sat beside me and put his arm around my shoulders.

"Yes," he said. "It is a grave responsibility to take someone's life. But think about how many lives you saved. They would have likely killed more than just Tsuganotsi if they had not been stopped."

"I know," I said. The men were heavily armed. Besides each having a musket, we also found three pistols and four knives on them, now added to our own artillery.

I lay in bed, in turns weeping silently and shivering with anger. Atsila held me close to him as my mind finally relaxed enough that I was able to get a few hours of fitful sleep. I awoke tired, and lingered in bed after Atsila rose and started dressing. I remembered the news I had wanted to share with him last night.

"What names do you like?" I asked him.

"What names?" he echoed, looking puzzled.

"There is no rush," I continued. "We do have a few months to decide." My meaning gradually became clear, and I could see his eyes widening with excitement.

"Are you going to have a child?" he asked. I smiled and nodded. He was instantly at my side, sitting on the edge of the bed and holding me tightly. The happiness of the moment was a stark contrast to the grim emotion of the night before.

During the following days, since none of us knew of anybody who could repair damaged artwork, I took it upon myself to attempt a repair of Mahaley's portrait. I found that, fortunately, the bullet had passed through the background. I was able to obscure the damage by means of some careful mending, blending the threads with the canvas. When I was finished, we were all happy to find that the hole could not even be seen if one was not aware of it in advance.

1832 was an eventful year for us and for the Cherokee in general. In March, a Supreme Court ruling was handed down that

129

stated that the Cherokee nation was sovereign and that Georgia law no longer applied to them. Following this happy outcome, President Jackson and the state of Georgia proceeded to ignore the ruling. So despite the positive decision, nothing really changed for the Cherokee. At least not until later in the year.

In early September, our darling Clara was born. I wanted to give her a Cherokee name, but Atsila insisted we name her after my mother, and I was unable to refuse. She had a fuzz of blonde hair and a happy disposition. I knew that babies' eyes often change colour after a while, but hers remained dark, a deep warm brown which proved to be a beautiful combination with her golden hair.

Atsila had fallen in love all over again, this time with little Clara. To see him holding her so gently, gazing at her for long periods of time, was an absolute joy. There were many times when I would look up at him and see him silently smiling at her. Even if I had given him a son, I could not imagine him being any more proud.

Noya, Edward and Peter were doing well. They settled into family life relatively easily, although Edward was necessarily busier than usual since the time that Noya and I could spend at the mission clinic was greatly reduced.

Noya had for some time been complaining about the slant of the writing in the Cherokee Phoenix. The newspaper seemed to be pushing more than ever for removal of the Cherokee to the new Indian Territory west of the Mississippi, and in 1832 the editor, Elias Boudinot, himself a Cherokee, resigned under pressure from John Ross.

In October, the state of Georgia continued its mistreatment of the Cherokee by holding a lottery to award parcels of Indian land to white people. This lottery continued into 1833. Our boarding house narrowly missed being forfeited in this way, though our former cotton fields across the river were taken from their new owner.

Needless to say, this lottery resulted in the further displacement of many innocent Cherokee. Some gave up and voluntarily made the move to the west, but some stayed, hoping that John Ross and his party would finally be successful in their efforts to hold on to Cherokee land.

Early in the year, we heard news in town about four men who had gone missing, but eventually this was replaced by fresh gossip. Apparently these men had never been found and there was never any evidence that pointed an incriminating finger at us. They were known around town to be rather worthless, good-for-nothing men and, in time, the general public lost interest in them.

Some people knew that I was the one who had paid Yancey's debts and mortgage. Even though the boarding house was officially owned by Mahaley and was occupied mostly by Cherokee, many thought of me as the owner. Eventually Mahaley decided to actually transfer the deed to me, in hopes that this would protect the property from new white settlers. Being a white woman, I believe this served to save us from at least a few of the problems common to many Cherokee. However, this was not always to be the case.

Dora and Shawn stood on the stairs examining the portrait with the mended area. Having just read about the confrontation that resulted in a bullet hole through the painting, they looked at it now with a renewed interest.

"So that's Mahaley," said Dora.

"Pretty lady," Shawn said. "And brave."

Dora nodded in agreement.

They had finished their dinner a little while earlier as they continued reading. The steaks were perfect. Shawn had volunteered to grill them, saying that he needed to renew his "man license" after being such a history nerd. But that didn't stop him from leafing through his library books to find more information concerning the Supreme Court case about which Isadora had written, and about Andrew Jackson's reaction to it.

"Though nobody can prove it," he related, "it's rumored that President Jackson said that 'Chief Justice John Marshall has made his decision; now let him enforce it!' Whether he actually said it or not, that's the attitude he took."

"You know," Dora responded thoughtfully, "these people we learned about in school, the founding fathers, I think we sometimes tend to deify them a little. But this account we've been reading tells me that, well, they were just men. They may have done some amazing things, but they also made some phenomenal blunders!"

"I know," Shawn agreed. "History is full of accounts of great people doing not-so-great things."

They turned and, going down the steps, went back out on the deck to finish their drinks. The sun had slipped discreetly behind the mountains about an hour before, and as the temperature cooled, the grinding sound of the cicadas started dying down. They walked to the back of the deck and leaned casually against the pine railing, looking down toward the creek.

"So, Shawn Murphy," Dora said, "what's your history?"

"Oh, nothing too exciting. Dabbled in a few different things before my brother and I started our estate liquidation business. Not rich, but doing okay. One marriage, one divorce, no kids."

"And one library card," said Dora.

"Right," Shawn smiled.

"All very neatly summed up."

"Yeah, well, like I said, nothing too exciting. I've had an okay life, my parents are still alive and well down in Pueblo. My brother, Colin, lives here with his wife and two kids. And our business makes enough money for us to live on. But if it helps, I also enjoy reading, horseback riding and long walks on the beach." They both smiled. "What about you? Any more like you back home?"

"No," Dora said quickly. "Only child of unhappy parents. Mother dead, father gone, probably dead. No relationships."

"I'm sorry." Shawn seemed uncomfortable and attempted to cover it with humor. "No library card?" Dora snickered and glanced at him.

"I've never summed up my life that neatly before. It's not much, is it?"

"I'm sure there's more to Dora Baskin than just that brief summary."

"I'm a failed social worker with no time for other people. I've always buried myself in my work, dealing with other people's problems. According to my boss, I do that so I don't have to address my own problems."

"Why do you say 'failed social worker'?" Shawn asked.

"Well, maybe failed is too harsh. I throw myself into my cases and almost never seem to make a difference."

"I'll bet you make more of a difference than you think."

"I do try, but it seems like I'm seldom able to get them back on their feet."

"Isn't that ultimately up to them?"

Dora scoffed. "You sound like my boss."

"Besides," said Shawn, "even if you accomplish absolutely nothing else, at least for a while, they know that someone cared about them."

After a moment of silence, Dora smiled and looked at Shawn. "How come you're such a nice guy?"

"Can't help it," he shrugged. "I come by it naturally." Dora rolled her eyes.

"Do you want another drink?" she asked.

"No thanks," he said. "I should get going. Don't want to overstay my welcome."

"You haven't yet," she said softly.

"Well good," he said. "Tomorrow's Sunday. I'm free all day if you want to delve back into Isadora's writings together."

"I do."

They walked back through the house and Shawn picked up his blazer. A few minutes later, he was gone. Dora put the few dishes they had used into the dishwasher, then wandered aimlessly through the house for a few minutes.

Standing at the front window, she detected some movement, and she leaned closer to the glass, peering out. The headlights of a passing police car illuminated the front yard and a pedestrian walking down the road.

Dora thought that the pedestrian looked up at her a couple of times as he passed. She fought back a paranoid shiver as she realized that she would have been very noticeable from outside, back-lit by the lights of the house. It would have been natural for someone's eyes to be drawn toward her.

She yawned and realized how tired she was, so she made sure all the doors were locked and went to bed. She fell asleep looking forward to Shawn's return the next morning.

Life has a way of changing in gradual, almost imperceptible ways. Everything seems the same for so long, but one day, you realise that everything is different. That was the way it was in 1833. Not much happened that really affected us in a lasting way at the boarding house.

Negotiations were still ongoing between the Cherokee and the United States government. The differences between John Ross and John Ridge and their respective parties widened, with each criticising the others' viewpoints about how best to settle the issue. John Ridge thought that it would be best if the Indians moved away as the government wanted. John Ross was still hoping against hope that the government could be convinced to allow the Indians to stay in their ancestral home.

As an ominous footnote to this episode, we heard talk about Indian Removal Forts being built at various locations throughout Georgia, though there was little specific information about their actual purpose.

At our home in Gainesville, we had new neighbours in back, across the river. A white family had won and taken over the parcel of land that used to be our cotton fields. They built a nice home there, but they usually left us alone, and when we did have dealings with them, they were pleasant enough.

Talu'tsi and Tala, the mother and daughter, still lived in their room upstairs. Even though Mahaley was spending time with Peter and Clara, she still made time for Tala and their story time. In fact, it had become such a common occurrence that often, when

Mahaley was relating stories to her, Tala often finished her sentences as she memorised the stories herself.

Ganasita still lived in the boarding house, though she moved from her room in the basement to the room that Tsuganotsi had been in. In the end, this worked out well because Atsila and I took over her former room as a nursery for Clara who, by her first birthday, was clearly going to be a real beauty, if I may be forgiven a mother's bias.

On the anniversary of our marriage, Atsila presented me with a beautiful locket, a gold pendant with the letters "A" and "I" etched in silver on its surface. Opening the locket revealed a miniature painting of each of us. He had commissioned the simple portraits from a local Indian who was known for his artistic ability, and I was quite impressed since they were good likenesses, even though I had not sat for the painting. The locket hung round my neck ever since.

Nayu, the elderly Cherokee upstairs did not show up for breakfast one morning in April. Upon investigation, we found that he had passed away peacefully in his sleep. James Smith was still there, as was Helen Garrity, though by the year's end that changed. Helen had an older sister in Maryland who became ill, and in November Helen moved out of the boarding house to care for her.

In time, we took in two new boarders. One was a young red-headed boy named Timothy Spaar. He was a pleasant type, with an easy smile, but kept to himself a great deal.

The other boarder, who had moved in more recently, was Joseph Ellington, a sullen man with a ruddy complexion but not much hair. He was very quiet, but when he did speak, I sometimes caught just a bit of an accent, as if he were trying to cover it, or perhaps he had just been in America for a long time and was gradually losing the accent. At any rate he, like Timothy, kept to himself and was very private, so aside from providing income for their rooms, they made little impact on our group.

But there was not much violence to speak of, at least none that affected us directly. So when these aforementioned changes happened, they caused a bit of a ripple at the moment, but we quickly settled back into our regular routine. By the end of 1833, seemingly not much had changed until we thought about how our lives had been the year before. Reflecting back on the violence of January 1832, this had been a peaceful year. And peace, or at least a lack of violence, has a way of making one relax and let down one's guard.

"She's so adorable," said Timothy Spaar with a smile. The sunlight shining through the window burnished his red hair to a bright sheen and illuminated a spray of freckles across his face. He appeared to be around twenty years old and was quite shy. He had been something of a loner to start with, but toward the end of 1833, he had started spending a little more time with the rest of us. It seemed to require some effort on his part, but as it turned out, he was a very amiable person. He was now watching Clara playing on the floor of the parlour, and she seemed to like him too. I simply smiled as a response to his statement and continued my knitting.

"How do you feel about all o' the violence against the Indians?" he asked.

I paused in my knitting and looked up at him curiously. "Well, I hate to see anyone suffering, especially when it is un-deserved." He appeared to be weighing my answer thoughtfully. It took several seconds for him to respond.

"What if they did deserve it? I mean, not the Cherokee, but anyone." I could not tell if this was just an awkward attempt at conversation, or if he had a deeper agenda.

"On an intellectual level, I don't think anyone should be made to suffer needlessly. That is not to say that I do not believe in just punishment for crimes, but the punishment should not be excessive. However I admit that, like most of us, there is a side of me

139

that longs to be able to see evil people suffer as they have made others suffer, especially when it affects me personally."

"Does this affect you personally?" he asked.

"Well, as you know, it is not directed against me specifically, since I am English," I said, still wondering where this was going. "But I am married to a Cherokee. Of course, Clara is one quarter Cherokee."

She looked up at me at the mention of her name. She smiled and blew a bubble, a recent skill she had acquired and honed to perfection.

"Mahaley and Noya are my best friends and they are Cherokee," I continued. "Most of the tenants here are Cherokee, and they are my friends too, so obviously it affects me greatly. Why do you ask?"

"Oh, no reason really," he responded, trying to shrug it off. "It just seems to surround us every day, and yet here in this area, and especially in the boardin' house, it don't seem to touch us much." If only he had seen what happened here a little over a year ago.

"Yes, we have been fortunate," I said.

"What would you do if the violence came around to us?" he asked.

"Timothy, do you know something?" I was becoming alarmed by the direction of this conversation.

"No," he replied quickly. "No, I just – never mind. I was just curious." And he stood up and left the room, leaving me as confused and apprehensive as ever.

I sat there for a couple of minutes before putting down my knitting. I picked up Clara and went out on the front porch where Atsila was mending a support on the railing.

"How much do you know about Timothy?" I asked.

"Not much," he replied with a serious and reflective expression on his face. "I know he works as a clerk in a small office in town, but I don't know what the business is. I know he came here from Augusta, but I don't know if that's where he's from originally. And

I know that he is infatuated with you." Now he was displaying a teasing smile.

"What?" I asked. I had been concentrating on the other details Atsila had provided and was not sure that I had heard the last part correctly.

"How can you blame him?" Atsila asked mockingly. "Your appeal is obvious."

"Stop it," I said. "I'm serious. We really know very little about him."

"That's true," he said. "I think the same could be said for the other tenants too, when they were new."

"Yes, but Timothy has been here for nearly a year."

"Is something bothering you?" he asked. In reply, I related to him the puzzling conversation I had just had with Timothy in the parlour.

"Maybe he is just not very good at making conversation," he said.

"Yes, I thought of that too," I agreed. "I hope that is all it is. But I have to admit that I am worried that he knows something that he is not telling us."

"Well, don't get too worked up about it. We'll keep an eye on him. And the next time I'm in town, I'll quietly ask around to see if anybody knows any more about him."

"All right, that's a good idea." I was hoping that Atsila might have thought of some action that could be taken, but I admit that, not knowing what the whole conversation was even about, there was not really anything that could be done.

"Don't worry about it," he said with a smile. "I think he's harmless."

On a warm day in April, 1834, I was busy washing bed linens. Since the weather was so fine, I was in back of the boarding house spreading the laundry out to dry. Clara, of course, was with me and, at a year and a half old, she kept me quite busy keeping her

141

out of trouble. At this time, she was busily playing near the back door.

I pulled another sheet out of the basket, shook it open and began spreading it out, and I looked over toward the back door. Not seeing Clara, I assumed she had toddled back into the house. I finished spreading out the sheet to dry, then went to the door, but did not see Clara anywhere. Turning, I looked around the back lawn, but knew she could not have gone far without being seen. I went into the kitchen where Mahaley was working on lunch for us.

"Did Clara come in here?" I asked.

"No, I have not seen her." Mahaley discerned the apprehension I was suddenly feeling, and we spread out to try to find her. The door to the basement was still firmly closed, so we concentrated our attention on the main floor. After we had searched the whole first floor, Mahaley headed upstairs while I, in a growing panic, went back outside. There were short privet hedges on either side of the back door, and I reached my arms in, peering inside, but to no avail. I was certain that there was no way Clara could have made it past me and down to the river in the short time that my back was turned, but I could not think of where else she could have gone.

Snowmelt in the mountains due to the warm weather meant that the river was running high and fast. I can barely recall the emotions I felt while looking at the rushing water and not seeing my baby anywhere around, and I could feel the tears coming. By this time, Mahaley had joined me and put her hands on my shoulders. Turning me to face her, she focused my attention on her face.

"Where did you last see her?"

"She was right by the door," I pointed, explaining through the sobs. "I only turned to spread out a sheet and then she was gone." She looked carefully around the property, and focusing on the rear of the house, she started back.

I felt helpless, and I followed Mahaley as she backtracked toward the back door. As we got nearer the house, something

142

seemed to catch Mahaley's attention at the farthest end of the eastern-most hedge. I followed her to see what she saw. There was a small broken branch, leaning down toward the ground. Bending over, Mahaley examined the twig.

"This is a fresh break," she explained. It was still moist where the branch had been broken. "And look," she said, pointing to the ground. There were a couple of gouges in the ground and the grass was flattened. Even as we were looking at it, a few blades of grass were just starting to stand back up.

Mahaley straightened back up and continued looking at the ground, following tracks that I could not see in the grass around to the side of the house. On the eastern side of the house, there was a patch of spruce trees, and grass had never grown under them. This was where Mahaley found footprints which even I could see. Three clearly defined prints of a man's boots.

"The edges of these footprints are still sharp," she said. "The tracks are fresh."

We continued toward the front of the house, and nobody was there, but again, Mahaley did point out fresh boot and horse tracks at the side of the front porch. She tried to follow the tracks from there, but the ground was hard and rocky.

"Atsila has not yet returned from town, has he?" she asked.

"No," I replied.

"Go find him," she said. "Someone has taken Clara." I took off at a run toward the barn and as quickly as I could, got the carriage ready. Knowing Atsila's plans for the day, it did not take long to find him, though I could sense the minutes ticking away, taking Clara farther from us. By the time we got back home, it had been nearly two hours since she had been taken.

Atsila examined the tracks and agreed with Mahaley's assessment. The person had apparently grabbed Clara and hidden behind the hedge until I had given him an opportunity to make his way around the side of the house. Atsila pointed at the tracks by the side of the porch and his interpretation of them was that the

143

kidnapper had experienced some difficulty. He did not simply come to the horse, mount it and ride away, but the tracks seemed, in a couple of areas, as if he were almost stumbling. Atsila thought that the person may have been grappling with something – perhaps Clara was struggling and squirming, and trying to get away from him.

"Do you remember hearing anything?" he asked, turning to me. I struggled to remember any sensations of the moment but could not recall anything out of the ordinary. But suddenly I was reminded of the unnerving conversation I had had with Timothy Spaar a few days before.

"Atsila, it was Timothy!" The moment I said it, I could see the realisation in his eyes as he seemed to recall the incident as well. He immediately ran into the house and upstairs into Timothy's room, with Mahaley and me following closely.

The room was neat and tidy, but Timothy was not there. We looked around for anything that could provide any clues to his whereabouts or why he would take Clara, but we could find nothing incriminating. Atsila began opening drawers, and he found a couple of letters addressed to Timothy. Both letters were a few years old and were from someone named U'ta-na'kata and Tsisqua.

"They're his parents," Atsila said, looking at the letters. "They are Cherokee."

"They cannot be his blood parents," I said, remembering his red hair and freckles.

"No," he said as he continued to peruse the letters. "I found out about them in town when I was asking about Timothy. His parents died when he was young and he had no other relatives. U'ta-na'kata and Tsisqua were friends and raised him as their own." He angrily threw down the letters. "Nothing!" he hissed, and continued looking around the room. I saw a small slip of paper sticking out the top of a book on a shelf and I pulled it out. It was the stub from a paycheck.

"Gainesville Gold," I said, reading the company name.

"It's a mine surveying company in town," Atsila said.

"Maybe he's there," I said, but realised as soon as I had how unlikely that was.

"If he took Clara, he would not have taken her to work with him," Atsila said.

He ran back downstairs and gathered a musket, a pistol and ammunition. "Can you and Mahaley unload the wagon?" he asked. He had gotten some supplies but nothing too large, so we readily agreed. He ran to the barn, saddled a horse and rode to the front porch where I was waiting, nearly in shock.

"Don't worry," he said, placing his hand gently on the side of my face. "I'll get her back."

Mahaley emerged from the front door and handed him a quickly assembled parcel of food. He thanked her and set off, slowly at first as he examined what tracks there were. I don't know if he actually saw where the tracks went or if it was merely a guess, but soon he reached the road and, with a quick glance back at me, he took off toward the east.

The hours dragged by slowly as if they had nothing better to do than to torment me. Mahaley tried to focus my attention on dinner and other responsibilities, and when I was able to do so, it did help the time to pass more quickly. Unfortunately I fear I was little help to her. I spent the day worrying about my little Clara, and now for Atsila as well, since I did not yet know the level of Timothy's desperation.

After all this time in America, I felt I needed a cup of tea to calm my nerves.

As evening approached, the tenants trickled in, and they immediately sensed that something was wrong. Mahaley repeatedly took them aside to tell what we knew, so they would not bother me about it.

I later learned what happened after Atsila left. He had seen one or two tracks which, to his practised eye, stood out from the others, but on the rock-strewn road, proved difficult to follow. His progress was slow, and he lost the trail often and would have to circle back until he was able to pick it up again. Eventually the tracks went off the road, to the north, at which point the trail became easier to follow as it went through woods and over soft ground.

It was not long before he reached the river, and the tracks turned back to the east, but he had lost so much time in getting started and in keeping track of the trail on the road that it was already starting to get dark. He continued for as long as he could see the trail, and was about to stop for the night when he saw the dim glow of a small fire ahead. He dismounted and tied the horse to a tree branch, and with his pistol stuck through his belt and his musket in his hands, he quietly crept ahead on foot.

As he approached the campfire, he could see Timothy's red hair, but try as he might, he could not see Clara. His first thought was that Timothy had thrown her in the river, and he very nearly shot him in anger, but not wanting to forfeit any certain information about her, he held back.

With the musket leveled at Timothy's head, he walked into the circle of firelight. Timothy jumped as his face registered first surprise, and then relief when he saw who it was. But that relief turned to confused apprehension when Atsila did not lower the musket. Timothy raised his hands, keeping them in view.

"Where is she?" Atsila demanded.

"Where is who?" Timothy asked.

"I will kill you right now!" Atsila said. "Where is Clara?"

"Clara?" he asked, clearly bewildered. "I ain't seen Clara since breakfast."

Atsila was beginning to feel confused himself as he could see that Timothy genuinely did not know about what had happened. "What are you doing out here?" he finally asked. Timothy hesitated to say at first, but the sight of the musket still pointing at his head loosened his tongue.

"I'm after Joseph," he said. "Atsila, please! You know I would never do nothin' to hurt Clara. Or you or Isadora, for that matter." Atsila did know that, and he lowered the musket and sat down opposite Timothy, though he remained on guard. Timothy breathed a sigh of relief and put his hands down.

"My father," he began, "or rather, he's like my father – he's Cherokee. He fought bravely with Major Ridge and Andrew Jackson in the war against the Creeks. In appreciation for his service, he was presented with a pair o' pistols, and when he died, he left 'em to me." Atsila was getting impatient, and could not see how any of this related to Clara, or to Joseph either. But he waited, allowing the story to unfold.

"I was in my room a few days ago and was puttin' the case with the pistols away in my chest of drawers, when I noticed that my door was ajar. I saw Joseph in the hallway, and he walked away and I didn't think nothin' of it at the time. But the next day, when the pistols disappeared, I remembered seein' him watchin' me put 'em away and knew that he was the only one who could have taken 'em.

"There had been other things, too, that I thought I had mis-placed, but now I was suspicious that he had taken those things too. But the pistols were the most important things to me. So I watched him. The location of his room across the hall from mine made it easy to see when he came and went, without him seeing me.

"Well a couple o' days ago, I saw when he left and I went to look around in his room, but I never found none of my things. When I was in there, though, I found some notes from some local folks that I knew was no good. And I saw one that mentioned Miss Isadora. So I was watching Joseph real close, 'cause I like you folks and don't want nothin' bad to happen to you." This ex-plained his quizzical questioning a couple of days before.

"So this mornin' after breakfast, I decided to follow him. Jo-seph went into town first and met with two men I didn't know. I couldn't hear nothin' that was said – I didn't want to get close enough to be recognised, but after a few minutes, he started back. I stayed in the cover of the woods when I could, and when he turned off the road to go home, I decided to wait. I figured if he came back out in a while, I could see where he went and maybe find where my things are, and maybe even find out what he's plot-tin' against you folks.

"Well, I wasn't waiting but about a half hour, when he comes tearin' out at a gallop, and he's carrying some kind of bag in front of him. I figured he must have took something else, but I couldn't tell what. I start followin', but I lose him at first since he's riding so fast, 'cause I have to keep enough distance between us so I

149

won't be seen. But I finally find where he went off the road, and that makes it easier 'cause I can see his tracks better.

"I been followin' him since then but I lost his trail a ways back when it was gettin' dark. I'm sure he'll stick to the river, but I don't know for how long, so I figured I better stop for the night and see if I can pick up his trail in the mornin'."

Atsila pondered what Timothy had said and realised that he believed him. He told Timothy that Clara had been taken, and Timothy was eager to find her. After Atsila brought his horse closer to camp, he and Timothy ate a quick dinner and went to sleep, hoping to be refreshed and able to find Joseph and Clara in the morning.

After a sleepless night, dawn arrived at the boarding house, but ominously, the sun did not shine. It was cloudy and threatening rain, and while that seemed appropriate to my mood, I feared what rain might mean for Atsila's ability to find Clara. It was gloomy inside as well, since everyone knew that Clara was missing and that Timothy had kidnapped her. Joseph had never come home last night either, and nobody knew why.

Early that morning, a short note was affixed to the front door:

> Your wee one will be returned to you un-
> harmed when you give back our property. You
> will be notified where to take it. If you do not
> abide by our rules, the child will be killed.

The note was handwritten and unsigned, and although it looked like the work of a novice criminal, it only served to fray my already ragged nerves. What property did I have that they could possibly want? I felt helpless and wished that I was able to do something constructive, something that would help Atsila. I was beginning to see from the note that there were more involved in this than just Timothy, and I feared for Atsila's safety if he did catch up to those responsible.

I was heartened a short time later, however, when four men, all Cherokee, rode up to the boarding house.

"We heard about your child," said Tooantuh, a man I knew from the clinic. "We want to help Atsila find her."

"Thank you," I said gratefully, with tears in my eyes. "I cannot tell you much except that Atsila went east from here. And it was many hours ago."

"The trail may be cold, but we will find it." And with that, they rode away.

As the tale was told to me later, Atsila and Timothy woke up at first light and were immediately back on the trail, although it was harder to find and follow. But it did help having two sets of eyes looking for the signs.

Shortly after getting started, Atsila spotted something in the water at the edge of the river. He quickly dismounted and disentangled a pink ribbon from the branch on which it was clinging. He recognised it as one which I often tied in Clara's hair. With mounting anxiety, he looked all around for her, hoping to see her nearby, yet hoping at the same time that she had not just been abandoned at the mercy of the elements.

After a couple of hours, it started raining. At first it was just sprinkling, but it turned into a hard rain, large rampaging drops which beat the new leaves off the trees above them to cover or wash away any signs of the trail that might have survived the night. Atsila was distraught, not wanting to give up the search, but knowing it would be useless to try to find a trail now.

At that moment, Timothy silently pointed ahead through the trees. There, near the bank of the rushing cataract, now swollen from the deluge, was a cabin. It was a rough little structure, but there was light in the window. On the far side of the cabin, huddling beneath the overhang of the roof but getting soaked anyway, was a chestnut mare. She was Joseph's.

Atsila and Timothy climbed down off their horses, tied them up and quietly made their way on foot. They both had been trying to

151

keep their guns and powder dry during the continuing downpour, but had not been very successful. Timothy was   hoping he would not need to use his gun against Joseph, but he had it ready. Atsila had a large knife in his hand, not wanting to trust that his powder would be dry enough to ignite.

There was a door on the side of the cabin facing them and they crept toward it. Through the window beside the door, Atsila could see Joseph inside, staring into the fireplace. He seemed to be alone.

There was a simple latch on the door and Atsila put his hand on it as Timothy raised his pistol. Atsila pressed the latch down and then quickly threw his shoulder against the door, but it did not budge. He cursed himself for not trying it first, as Joseph, alerted by the noise, let loose with a shot that splintered through the door. Fragments of wood sprayed against Atsila's face leaving a gash near his right eye.

Atsila cursed himself again for not taking more time to examine the cabin as he saw, through the window, that there was another door on the other side. Joseph ran out that door to his horse. Atsila and Timothy quickly tried to intercept him, but the sodden ground was so slippery that they could not move fast enough. Joseph was already riding away when they arrived at that side of the cabin. Timothy raised his pistol, hoping to wound him, but the hammer only made a mocking soggy tap against a wet cap.

Certain that they had lost him, they watched him ride away along the river, but his horse, losing her footing on the soggy ground, stumbled and fell. Atsila and Timothy started running toward him again as the horse regained her feet and ran away in fear.

Joseph was immediately up and, in a panic, was attempting to turn and run. Only inches from the riverbank, he slipped and fell, sliding downward into the water. Scrambling to grab hold of the rocks, the overflowing river finally swept him away. Atsila and Timothy could only stand there helplessly, watching Joseph being carried away from them. Before he disappeared from view, they saw him plunge under, and he never came back up.

Angered more than sorrowful at his loss, Atsila quickly turned and ran back toward the cabin, hoping to find Clara inside, but the dirty little structure was empty. He stood there dispirited, as Timothy closed the door behind them.

"Well," said Timothy, "at least we have a warm shelter until the rain lets up." Atsila began searching the cabin for any clues to Clara's whereabouts. Timothy followed suit and very quickly found the box containing the set of pistols from his father, as well as a few jewelry items that he had missed.

Atsila was not as successful. However, he did find some discarded scraps of paper, some of which seemed to be early drafts of a ransom note, others of which were written in a foreign language. Feeling completely discouraged, he threw himself down in a chair by the fire and listened as the rain continued to pound the roof.

About an hour later, the clouds parted and the sun peeked through. Without the rain pelting the roof, they could hear the rushing river. Then they heard horses nickering, and they looked warily at each other as they reached for their guns.

Atsila pressed his back against the wall and quickly glanced out the window. He recognised four Indians on horses, soaked through from the rain, advancing toward the cabin. Opening the door, he went outside to greet them.

"Atsila," said Tooantuh, "you are well?"

"I am," Atsila replied.

"Have you found your child?"

"I have not."

"We have come to help."

"Thank you, my brother," said Atsila. "How did you find us? The rain must have washed away our tracks."

Tooantuh was looking suspiciously at Timothy but then directed his attention back to Atsila.

"We were following your trail along the river when the rain started. We just hoped that you continued on that path, or else we might have missed you. What have you found?"

"Not much," said Atsila. "Joseph, the man who took her, was here in this cabin, but he was washed away by the river. And Clara was not here." Tooantuh looked at the other three men with him and indicated that they should spread out.

While looking around the area, it was noticed that the path along the river ended there, with the forest closing in right up to the bank of the river on the east side of the cabin. But there was a wide trail heading south from the cabin. While any recognisable tracks had been washed away by the downpour, it was obviously a well-used trail, and seemed to be the only other way to or from the cabin.

Atsila and Timothy gathered their belongings, mounted their horses and joined Tooantuh and his men. The trail was exceedingly muddy, steam rising from the soggy ground, and the men rode slowly in an effort to prevent their horses slipping on the wet leaves. It was not long before they arrived at another cabin, similar to the one they left, just east of the trail. They dismounted and cautiously approached on foot, but found the cabin empty.

They rode on for a few more minutes and eventually arrived at another cabin, but this one had four horses tied up to a crude porch railing.

Again, they dismounted and Atsila mounted the porch and knocked on the door, Timothy close behind him. The four Indians stayed back but remained visible to the occupants. The door was opened by a crusty looking white man. His eyes went wide as he appeared to recognise Atsila, and he quickly raised a pistol and pointed it at him. Before Atsila could react, Timothy fired and the man fell back inside the door. There was a sudden bustle of activity inside the cabin and a shot rang out as everyone scrambled for cover. One of Tooantuh's companions, too slow in finding concealment, fell dead.

Being in the bright sunlight, it was difficult to see inside the cabin, but when another shot was fired, Atsila saw the flash and aimed his musket toward it. He heard a thud and knew that he had hit his mark. He did not take time to reload but pulled out his pistol, prepared to fire again at the first sign of an assailant. Apparently seeing a man through a window, one of the Indians behind Atsila fired and was rewarded with another hit.

Suddenly Atsila heard running boot steps on the wooden floor of the cabin and a crash of glass. He knew then that the fourth man had escaped through a window in the back. Four horses, he thought, equal four men, so he jumped up on the porch and flattened himself against the wall beside the door. He was prepared for the sound of another shot, but it never came. He did hear a quiet shuffling inside, though, and raised his pistol as he peeked through the door. There was a woman, leaning over a box, reaching inside.

"Stop!" Atsila shouted. The woman froze and looked over her shoulder, slowly raising her hands. Timothy and the three Indians filed through the doorway behind Atsila, their guns drawn. "Move over there," Atsila ordered, motioning to the other side of the room.

The box rocked slightly as something inside moved. Atsila went towards it and looked inside. Lying on a pile of rags was Clara, dirty and pale, but alive. There were crusty marks that tears had made through the dirt down the side of her face as if she had been crying for some time. Now hoarse and weak, she was only able to manage pitiful and exhausted whimpers. Atsila slipped the pistol through his belt and picked her up. She was shivering and burning with fever.

The others kept their guns trained on the woman as Atsila quickly went out the door. "Leave her," he said. They reluctantly followed him.

"We should not leave her alive," Tooantuh said. "We will not be safe."

155

"We ain't safe anyway," Timothy said. "One man already got away."

"You can take her to the Federal Marshal," Atsila said, "if you can find him, and if you think he will give you justice. I need to get Clara home." He climbed on his horse and, holding Clara tightly, rode off toward the boarding house. Eventually Timothy and the Indians left the woman and followed Atsila.

Dora had gotten the idea of making a southern-style breakfast like those Isadora had described. After making an early run back to the grocery store, she prepared ham, homemade biscuits and gravy, grits, eggs and cornbread. Although Isadora, in her account, had not yet fulfilled her desire for a good cup of tea, Dora served English Breakfast Tea with cream and sugar, feeling a bit guilty for Isadora's sake at the ease with which she was able to do so. It had been a while since she had taken the time to cook an actual meal, but she found that it came back fairly easily.

The morning was already very warm and they had opted to eat at a small table in the shade of a tree in the backyard. Both of them had anticipated the heat and had dressed casually in shorts. Dora, having found a feather in the trunk, marked her place in the book with it and closed it.

"Life back then certainly was different from today," Shawn said. "I mean, I'm not even talking about the technological differences. Just the way of life – every day was literally a life and death struggle. We certainly don't have to contend with that today."

"No, we don't," Dora said distractedly, as she remembered the sight of Anthony lying dead at her feet.

"You know, I've had this idea developing in my head as we've been reading." Shawn drank the last swallow of tea from his cup and placed it on the table. "I know you've said that this place is too big for you, and I agree." Looking up at the house, he shook his head. "I don't know how your grandmother managed it for so long. But what if it was not just your home, but also your job?"

"What do you mean?" Dora asked.

"What if you turned it into an inn, like your namesake?"

"An inn?"

"A bed and breakfast. Think about it – it's perfect. It's in a beautiful location. The house is in great condition. Most of the rooms already have bathrooms." He motioned toward the dishes on the table before them. "And you've demonstrated the kind of spread you can put out."

"You're crazy," she scoffed. She stood up and as she stretched her back and her shorts rose a bit, Shawn appreciated the curve of her brown thighs. She looked up at the house and, while the thought was not altogether crazy, as she had said, it did seem a bit overwhelming. "Do you realize how much work that would be?"

"Of course there would be work involved," he replied, "but it's just work that you would be doing for yourself anyway – just a little more of it. I mean sure, that's a simplified way of looking at it, but wouldn't that be cool, to be able to stay home and do the same kind of work as Isadora Byrnes?"

"Yeah, I guess it would," she admitted. "But I don't know if I'm cut out for that."

"Just a thought."

The sun was setting in the west but the air was still hazy from the mist that had been rising since the sun had come out. I had helped Mahaley prepare dinner but I was not hungry, so as the tenants sat down to their meal, I sat on the front porch. I could give little attention to anything but Clara and Atsila. It had been almost a day and a half since she was taken and I was beside myself with worry for them both.

Noya and Edward had come over with little Peter, now two years old, and Noya was sitting with me on the front porch. She knew that there was nothing that could be said that would make the situation better, so she just sat silently with me. I sighed, wiped away another tear, and looked up just as a nebulous rider appeared through the mist. As he came closer, I suddenly realised that it was Atsila!

He stopped in front of the porch and jumped down off of his horse, holding my little Clara in his arms. I had never known a feeling of such intense relief as I experienced at that moment. It was short lived, though, when I saw the grim expression on his face.

"She is alive, but she is ill," Atsila said, and rushed her into the house. Noya and I followed right behind him, and others gathered from the dining room when they heard the commotion. Laying her down on the divan in the parlour, he stepped back so that Edward could take a look at her. The poor child was whimpering and shivering, and her arms and neck were red with what looked to be some sort of rash. I wanted so desperately to hold here and

159

comfort her. Edward examined her carefully, as Atsila held me in his arms.

I heard more people behind us, and I turned to see Timothy entering the house with three Cherokee men. I stiffened with anger and broke free from Atsila's grip. I picked up one of the pistols that we had been keeping within easy reach and pointed it at Timothy, but Atsila grabbed my arm and took the gun from me.

"Timothy did not take her," he said. "Joseph did. Timothy helped me find Clara. And he saved my life." I looked from Atsila back to Timothy and, having held the notion for so long that Timothy had been the kidnapper, it took a few moments for the truth to sink in.

"Timothy, I am so sorry," I said.

"Nothin' to be sorry about, ma'am," he said. "I just hope Clara's all right."

Edward took a blanket that Noya handed to him and wrapped it around Clara. He stood up and looked at me. "It's hard to say at this time," he said. "The fever and the rash could be scarlet fever, but the rash doesn't look quite right. Also, it may be too soon for scarlet fever symptoms to occur unless she was exposed to it before she was kidnapped. And I'm not aware of any cases in the area. Atsila, what were the conditions where you found her?"

"It was dirty," Atsila said bitterly, "and they kept her in a box full of rags."

"In that case, it's possible she just has a cold and a skin irritation from the dirty rags. But in the meantime, keep everyone who hasn't had scarlet fever away, just in case. Keep her warm and watch that rash. If it gets worse or starts to blister, let me know. We may need to bleed her." Having had scarlet fever as a child, I rushed to Clara and held her in my arms. As an afterthought, Edward said, "You might want to wash her, too. She'll be more comfortable when she's clean, and see if that helps the irritation."

"Of course," I said. "Thank you, Edward!" He nodded with an encouraging smile and turned to Noya who had already gathered

up Peter in preparation for leaving, as neither of them had had scarlet fever. Others were making their way out of the room as well.

After I bathed the dirt from her skin, dressed her warmly and wrapped her in a blanket, Clara slept soundly. I stayed with her in the nursery, sitting by her side, until exhaustion took me and I too sank into a deep sleep. By morning, I awoke to find that the rash was fading and her golden hair clung in damp ringlets to her face as the fever broke.

Mahaley prepared breakfast herself to let me sleep. Everyone was still eating when I came upstairs with Clara, and all were quite happy to see her apparently feeling so well. She was still fussy and uncomfortable, but much improved from her state of the night before.

After the table was cleared, Atsila lingered behind. I had the feeling he did not want to leave Clara and me. We heard hoof beats approaching the house in front and we looked at each other with apprehension. After looking out the window, Atsila opened the door to Tooantuh and his two companions.

"Is the child well?" he asked.

"Yes, she is much better," Atsila said.

"That is good." Tooantuh glanced over his shoulder at his friends. "We have heard of white men's plans. We are in danger."

"Because of killing those people at the cabin yesterday?" Atsila asked. "They know who we are?"

"Yes," Tooantuh nodded. "They know our names." Atsila had related to me the events of the previous day at the kidnappers' cabin. I looked up at him as he thought about what Tooantuh said.

"I will stay," Atsila finally said. Tooantuh seemed surprised.

"Here, you will not live long," he said.

"I will not leave my family." Atsila looked down at Clara and me, then back at Tooantuh. "They are my responsibility. I cannot abandon them. And I will not make them flee with me."

161

Tooantuh looked at him with admiration. "You are a true Cherokee," he said. "We are proud to know you. Your bravery and honour will be spoken of wherever we go."

Atsila smiled and nodded. He raised his hand and waved as the Indians turned and rode away.

"Are you sure you should stay here?" I asked him as I closed the door. "It won't be safe. We could go someplace else with you."

"No," he shook his head. "This is our home. We will stay."

Atsila kissed me, then he went upstairs. Timothy had gone back to his room after breakfast, and Atsila related to him what Tooantuh had said. When Atsila told him that he was staying, Timothy agreed. He was staying too. I was very happy that my husband was going to stay with us, yet at the same time, I was terribly worried for him, and for Timothy. So when five horsemen arrived in front of the house shortly before noon, I insisted that Atsila and Timothy stay hidden.

I gathered four pistols and placed them on a table within easy reach and opened the door with a musket in my hands. Knowing what these men were likely here for, I freely admit that I almost hoped they would give me an excuse to shoot them.

"Where's the Injun?" one of them asked.

"What 'Injun'?" I mocked.

"At-see-lah," he said.

"He's gone."

"Where'd 'e go?"

"I don't know."

"Listen, little lady," he said as he shifted in his saddle to climb down off his horse. I raised the musket toward him and cocked the hammer. He stopped and looked at me, then eased back down into the saddle.

"There is no need to dismount," I said. "You will not be staying."

"At-see-lah and this Timothy fella killed some white men. They gotta pay for their crime."

162

"Perhaps you were not listening. As I have already told you, they have both gone," I said firmly.

"You think you're gonna defend yourself with one musket?" he asked with a smirk. His friends seemed to think that his comment was funny. At that moment, Mahaley stepped into view beside me, also holding a musket, and with a pistol stuck through her belt. The man and his friends stopped snickering. I gathered all the steel I could muster into my eyes – considering the heated emotions I was feeling, I did not find that task to be out of my reach.

"Leave," I said coldly, "or I shill happily kill you."

They looked at each other, whispered, then turned and rode away, but I saw them split up at the road. Two went west and three went east, and I assumed they were concealing themselves in various positions along the road to watch the house, although I noticed that one of them was examining the ground, probably looking for tracks. Mahaley and I exchanged glances that conveyed a combination of fear and anger, and we went inside, closing and locking the door behind us. Atsila was waiting there for me and looked at me with such affection that my heart nearly melted.

"If you and Timothy are determined to stay here," I said, "you must remain concealed."

"Yes," Mahaley agreed, "you have to stay out of sight."

"I'm not worried," Atsila said, seemingly unconcerned. "We have two brave women to protect us." I knew he was only joking, but I could feel the fear rising again, chilling my heart.

"Atsila, please! I know the pain of losing parents. And so do you. I do not want that for Clara." His expression became more serious at that.

"We will stay hidden," he said, and he looked at Timothy. When Timothy nodded his response, Atsila looked back at me and kissed my forehead.

We had barely finished our conversation when we heard a carriage approach.

"What now?" I asked in exasperation.

We all went into the parlour and looked out the window. A woman, about fifty years of age, was struggling to get down from the carriage. She was a large woman, not obese but tall and unwieldy, with pewter-coloured hair piled in an elaborate coiffure upon her head. While she was well-dressed, she seemed more attired for a society ball than for a carriage ride in the country. The low-cut dress of bright blue taffeta barely confined her ample bosom. After the anxiety of the last couple of days, I admit that watching her provided some welcome amusement.

Exchanging curious looks among the four of us, I motioned for Atsila and Timothy to go downstairs. After they were safely hidden, I went to the door and opened it as she was climbing up the steps of the porch.

"Oh, good afternoon dear," she said with an unhurried delivery and a voice of unexpected volume.

"Good afternoon," I replied. "May I help you?"

"Well, yes, I'm hoping you can." She finally reached the door and she pressed a hand to her bosom, taking a moment to catch her breath after the effort. "My name is Elizabeth Forsythe and I need a place to live." I glanced at Mahaley, and I could see that she seemed as puzzled as I was. Elizabeth Forsythe did not look like our usual tenant.

"We actually do have a room coming available," I responded. "May I ask how you heard about our place?"

"Oh, well who hasn't heard of your place?" she said expansively. "You're a rather famous personage in this area, young lady," she said. "'The white angel of Gainesville' is how some describe you." I was flattered, yet given my husband's increasing notoriety of late, I would have preferred to not be quite so famous.

"Well, thank you," I replied hesitantly. I realised I had not yet introduced Mahaley and quickly rectified that oversight.

"So nice to meet you, Mahaley," she said. She heaved a deep breath into her chest, causing her generous breasts to separate momentarily and then to almost completely engulf the pendant that

164

was dangling between them. It required a force of will to not watch in fascination.

"Won't you come in?" I asked.

"Why, yes," she smiled. "Thank you." She noticed the pistols that were still arranged on the table beside the door but said nothing about them. I directed her into the parlour where we sat down.

"Have you just recently arrived in the area?" Mahaley asked.

"Oh heavens, no. I'm originally from Richmond, Virginia, but I've been in Georgia for many years. My husband died a few months ago and I've found that our house is just too big for me to be rattling around in by myself."

"I am very sorry about your husband," I said. "But would you not be happier if you just purchased a smaller house?"

"I don't think so," she said straightforwardly. "When my husband died, I found myself lonely, not just for him but for friends. I found that my friends were actually my husband's friends. When he died, they stopped coming around, and if I went to visit them, they seemed impatient to be rid of me. I've tried making new friends, but without much success."

She examined her nails as she hesitated. Then, with a sigh, she looked up at us and continued.

"I understand that I'm not the picture of gentility. I actually come from a humble family of little means. I used to be a pretty young thing, and when I caught the eye of a wealthy young lumber baron, I found myself in a whole new world. But even after all this time, I've found that it's not my world. I was only in it because of my husband, and now that he's gone, all I have are the things he left me."

"I am so sorry," I said. "And do you think that you would be happy here?"

"You know, dear," she said, "I think I would. I've heard about how you help the Cherokee so much, and that's just wonderful. I think it's just dreadful the way they are being treated. After all, they were here first."

I smiled as I found myself inexplicably liking this odd woman. "And do you like the Cherokee? I only ask because most of the people who live here are Cherokee."

"Oh, I adore them!" she said. Coming from anybody else, that statement would have sounded like an exaggeration, but from Mrs Elizabeth Forsythe, it sounded perfectly natural.

In the afternoon, following Elizabeth Forsythe's departure, James Smith, the old Cherokee who had fought in the Revolution, passed away in his bed. I drove my carriage into town to notify Reverend Parkin. I made certain my musket was visible as I passed one of the five horsemen from earlier in the day. He did not bother to hide himself. After I passed, he fell into line behind me, following me into town, as if he thought that I might be stupid enough to meet Atsila in public.

Reverend Parkin assured me that he would take care of the funeral arrangements.

After I returned, after the other tenants came home, we gathered them all together and explained the situation concerning Atsila and Timothy. We made certain to impress upon them how very important it was that nobody knows of their whereabouts. Everyone to a person expressed their understanding and agreed.

We cleared out Joseph Ellington's room and cleaned it in preparation for Elizabeth's moving in. She was going to sell numerous things, including her large house, and move into our boarding house in a few days time. Initially, I doubted her ability to sell a large property such as hers in such a short period of time, but she proved me wrong. She explained that she did not care if she received the full value of the house. She already had more money than she could spend, and she just wanted to quickly move on to her new life.

Periodically, we saw one or two men riding by, watching the house, apparently hoping to catch a glimpse of Atsila or Timothy so they could fall upon them and deliver "justice," but they were ultimately disappointed. We saw them more frequently on one day in May, when Elizabeth moved in. The increased activity seemed to attract their attention, but Atsila and Timothy made good on their promises to remain hidden.

That year, as an anniversary present for Atsila, I commissioned a family portrait from the same Cherokee who had painted the miniatures in my locket. The man was very personable and was quite happy to see that I wore the locket with his paintings inside them. While I was with him, he did some sketches of Clara and me, and he still had the sketches he had done of Atsila. Even though I had already seen his work on the locket miniatures, I was not prepared for the quality of the final canvas that he presented to me. He had captured our likenesses almost perfectly, and Atsila seemed overwhelmed. The portrait was hung over the fireplace in the parlour.

I must say that Elizabeth made quite an impression on the tenants. Tala, the little Cherokee girl, now eleven years old, was enamoured with the colourful outfits that Elizabeth regularly wore, even though they were often held together with clasps that were made for a less strenuous task. And while Timothy still seemed to be infatuated with me – I became more aware of it after Atsila mentioned it – he was utterly taken with Elizabeth, or "Betsy," as she preferred.

It was almost comical to see them together. She was not at all unattractive, but she was twice his age and towered over him by at least three inches. She moved from place to place with the grace of a rockslide, and if Timothy was around, he was often following in her wake.

Shortly after she moved in, I visited Betsy in her room and was astonished to see how crowded it was. As it turns out, she had not gotten rid of as many things as I was originally given to believe. As a result, the perimeter of her room was lined with stacks of boxes, crates and pieces of furniture. There was barely enough space amid all of her possessions to make a path through the room from the door to her bed.

"Betsy, I've just this moment been struck with an idea," I said as I gazed about in amazement. "I told you that a tenant, an elderly Indian, died shortly after your first visit."

"Yes, you did, dear," she replied with an expression of pity. "Poor man."

"Yes, well his room was right over here, next to yours. Would you be willing to pay a higher rent if we were to put a door through this wall and create a larger suite for you? You might have room for all of your things to spread out more comfortably." As I was disclosing the idea, her face was expressing a glow of excitement seldom seen in a person past childhood.

"I would be delighted," she said, "to pay, not only for both rooms, but also for the carpentry work that it would require!" With that, she wrapped her arms around me and squeezed. Fortunately, I had just enough time to turn my head so as to avoid suffocation, but which had the effect of pressing my left eye firmly against the bulge of her prodigious bosom.

Once her display of affection was complete, she released me and, oblivious to my embarrassment, began looking around at her things and determining where she would place them. I took my leave from her and went downstairs to discuss the matter with Mahaley and Atsila. They both agreed with me that it was a splendid idea and Atsila, having done carpentry work on numerous occasions, assured us that it would not be too difficult a task.

So in a few weeks, Atsila was able to get started on the construction. I acquired the materials gradually, as I thought it best not to arouse suspicion in those watching the house – to all outward observers, we were now a houseful of women. But once we had the needed materials, he got to work.

Betsy spent little time alone. If anyone was home, she was likely to be in their company which sometimes meant that she was in the way, but she was always willing to lend a hand in whatever we were doing. So it was that, in late June, as Atsila worked upstairs, Betsy was busily washing dishes while I dried them. Clara was in the kitchen with us, playing with a doll, and I noticed that Betsy frequently watched her.

"I just realised," I said, "that I've never asked if you have children."

Her face glowed with pride. "Oh, yes I do. Robert and Rebecca. They're both grown and married now. Robert has two children of his own and Rebecca has one on the way."

"Do they live nearby?"

"No," she said, her smile turning sad. "Robert lives in Raleigh, North Carolina and Rebecca is in New York. I do miss them, and my grandbabies. Anne Marie is two years old now," and she glanced again at Clara who was very nearly that age. Behind Clara, Atsila entered the kitchen.

"Your suite is finished," he said to Betsy. With a sharp intake of breath, Betsy's hands were up and reaching for a towel, slinging soapy water on the dishes I had just dried. She rushed out of the kitchen as I picked up Clara who was momentarily startled by the sudden activity. As Betsy pounded up the stairs, Atsila and I followed behind her.

She went into her room, still crowded with her things, and looked at the door that adjoined her room with the next. She opened the door and looked into the other room, and the joy was visible on her face. As she turned to express her thanks, I noticed that Atsila was keeping himself positioned a little bit behind me, and I could not quite conceal a grin at his bravery.

ooks like you were right about that family portrait," Shawn said as they stood on the stairway once again, looking at the painting. "It *is* Isadora, Atsila and Clara."

"Yes," Dora replied. She studied the faces for a moment before turning toward Shawn. "And you were right yesterday – this *is* fun. Finding out about my ancestors, how they lived, what they went through. I mean, there's not a lot of detail about the Hodges, but still, it *is* interesting background information."

"You've never done a family tree?"

"No. My family never really talked about our ancestry. We got together with other relatives when I was younger, but if anything was said about our history, I never heard it. Or was not interested enough to pay any attention until now. Have you? Done your family tree, I mean."

"I've messed around with it a little, nothing too serious."

"What's your ethnicity?"

"I'm a mutt, actually. Mostly Irish and English, a little German. A little Cherokee even, or so I'm told."

"Really? Maybe we're related," Dora joked.

"Could be," he smiled. "But I admit it's very easy to lose myself for a few hours at a time when researching my family tree. I managed to trace a couple of relatives who were in Jamestown in the 1600s."

"Very cool!"

"You're pretty lucky," Shawn said. "Not many people I know have an already assembled family history in their attic."

Dora had never considered herself lucky, but she was beginning to recognize certain areas of her life where she did have it pretty good, especially now, thanks to Gramma Izzy. She felt herself relaxing a little and thinking that maybe she really *was* lucky.

We finished the year of 1834 fairly happily. That is not to say that things went well for the Cherokee. Negotiations continued between John Ross' National Party, Major Ridge's Treaty Party and the United States government, but without any real success. Tempers were flaring and violence was breaking out even between the two Cherokee factions. While there was still plenty of Cherokee blood being spilled by whites, we were chagrined to hear stories of Cherokees being beaten or killed by other Cherokees from opposing parties.

The state of Georgia was still confiscating Cherokee land for its white settlers. In fact, in the spring of 1834, despite being Principal Chief of the Cherokee Nation, John Ross returned from a session in Washington to find that his own home and property had been taken from him. But in our little corner of Georgia, it went well.

Betsy was firmly established in the boarding house and loved everyone there. We had no further encounters with the men who were hoping to avenge the deaths of Clara's kidnappers. Sadly, though, we did hear that one of Tooantuh's companions had been found and killed. There were occasions when I would happen to see one of those men, or watchers, as we came to refer to them, riding past, looking at our house. For this reason, Atsila and Timothy continued to remain concealed inside, or at least in hidden areas outside.

Since they understandably sometimes felt restless due to their confinement, the rest of us did our best to help them cope. As a

173

result, though they were practically under the noses of those who had been searching for them, they remained safe.

I am also happy to report that I believe I had gone for nearly a year without thinking longingly about a cup of tea. Or at least without feeling desperate for one.

In February, we discovered that we had a new neighbour who had moved into the property next to us, to the east. A gentleman named Quentin Fairfax purchased the house and acreage, and moved in soon afterwards. Mahaley and I decided to go over and introduce ourselves, and welcome him to the neighbourhood. Betsy insisted that she wanted to accompany us.

So, dressed warmly against the winter chill, the three of us marched to his home, bearing baked goods as a welcoming gift. Given the size of the properties, it was nearly a ten minute walk, and Betsy was winded by the time we arrived and knocked at the door. A handsome, well-dressed Negro with beautifully clear skin the colour of nutmeg, opened the door.

"Good afternoon," I said. "We live next door and wanted to welcome Mr. Fairfax to the neighbourhood." The Negro smiled and stepped aside, inviting us to enter, after which he went to fetch Mr. Fairfax.

Soon afterwards, we heard uneven footsteps and looked up to meet the new owner. He was a tall man, around sixty years old, with hair that shined like polished silver. His eyes were a warm brown with creases in the corners which indicated to me that he smiled often, which he almost immediately demonstrated. His clothing, as well as the furnishings and appointments of his home, indicated that he was quite well-to-do. He walked with a limp, but the effect was lessened somewhat by his agile use of a gold-headed walking stick.

"Hello ladies," he said with a smile, and with a voice as smooth and sweet as honey. He spoke with the relaxed accent of most of the people in this area, and I was becoming quite adept at under-standing it.

174

"Good afternoon," we said simultaneously. "We live down the road," I said, motioning toward the west. "My name is Isadora, this is Mahaley and Betsy, and we wanted to welcome you and your family to the neighbourhood."

"Thank you very much," he crooned. "I'm Quentin Fairfax. I don't have a family, though. My wife passed on a few years ago, but I certainly appreciate the welcome."

"I'm so sorry to hear about your wife," said Betsy as she oozed around us and closer to Mr Fairfax.

"Well thank you," he replied to her with a gracious smile. Then, directing his attention to the rest of us again, he asked, "Would you ladies like some coffee?"

I was about to say no thank you, as this needed to be a short visit. We needed to return and finish preparing dinner, but I fear Betsy was too fast for me. "Oh, I would love some. Thank you." Mr Fairfax looked at Mahaley and me at which point we both assented.

"Jimmy," he called, and the handsome Negro appeared again. "Would you prepare some coffee for us, please?" I was impressed by how politely he spoke to a slave, so different from many others in the area.

Jimmy bowed his head in a respectful nod, then turned and left.

Mr Fairfax motioned us into a sitting room off the entryway and we made ourselves comfortable, presenting him with the food that we had brought. After a few minutes, Jimmy brought a tray bearing the coffee and cups, and set it down on a table, and Mr Fairfax offered us some of the cakes that we had just given him. I put a generous portion of cream and sugar into my coffee and pretended to enjoy it.

"What is it you do, Mr Fairfax?" Betsy asked.

"Call me Quentin," he said. "I'm a retired Federal Marshal. I lived and worked most of my life in Athens. But I took some time to care for my wife, Susannah, while she was ill."

"What was she like?" Mahaley asked.

175

Quentin looked off into the distance for a moment. "Susannah was the kind of person who always looked for the best in people, and she usually found it. She could see someone in sore straits and would immediately want to help them and then would find a way to do it. She was a real Good Samaritan."

"You must have loved her very much," I said.

"Yes, I did," he reflected. "And I think I inherited her philanthropy. Because seeing her do that inspired me so that I'm the same way now. I like to help people whenever I can."

"That is very commendable," I said.

"I went back to work after she passed away," he continued, "but then when I was shot by a fugitive just last year, I decided that it was time to retire and move to the country, so here I am."

"Oh, I hope it was nothing too serious," Betsy said.

"Just serious enough to put a stump in my step," he said, patting his right leg. "But what about you ladies? I understand you're all widows," and his face affected an expression of sympathy.

"Oh, no," said Betsy. Knowing the awkward situations she sometimes caused, I saw the need to jump in before she thoughtlessly said too much about Atsila.

"My husband is alive but he had to go into hiding," I interrupted, and I briefly related what led up to it, though I purposely left out the fact that he was hiding in our house.

"I hear your place is a boarding house for Cherokees."

"Not specifically," Mahaley replied. "It just worked out that most of our tenants are Cherokee."

"Well good for you," he said with a smile. "I think they're getting the dirty end of the stick. I'm happy to say that not   everybody is in favour of Jackson's Indian Removal Act. I know the Quakers as a group are against it. I've been hearing about a young politician named Lincoln, up in Illinois, who is speaking out against it. Davy Crocket up in Tennessee is opposed to it. Why, I even heard about a bunch of ladies in Ohio who drew up a petition against it. So the Indians may come out ahead eventually."

176

"We hope so," I said. His optimism was refreshing, but I'm afraid that, having witnessed so many instances of injustice against the Indians, I admit that I could not be quite so positive about the outcome.

"You're obviously not from around here," Quentin said, directing his attention to me. "You're English, aren't you?"

"Yes, I am," I responded. "I moved here about five and a half years ago."

"She has been such a blessing," Mahaley said, and I felt my face flush with the compliment. "She was a tremendous help to me after my husband was killed. It's only because of her that I still have the house. Now, not only does she help me run the boarding house, but she also volunteers at the mission clinic in town, to help the Cherokee."

"I only do what anybody else would do," I said.

"Well, ma'am," said Quentin, "I hope you'll forgive me for disagreeing with you, but I have to say that that's just not true. I've heard some terrible stories about what's been done to the Indians. In fact, working at the clinic, I'm sure you've seen enough proof of that yourself."

"Yes, I suppose you're right," I said, casting about for a way to change the subject. "But it's no different from what I would do for anyone else in their position."

"Hmm," Quentin smiled, "just like Susannah."

"You have a lovely home," cooed Betsy. "I didn't realise that being a Marshal was so lucrative." Despite the crudeness of the comment, I was happy that the conversation changed to a different topic.

"Oh, I'm afraid it's not," laughed Quentin. "I got an inheritance from my father when he died. That's how I got these things," he said motioning to the décor. "I was able to do some traveling with Susannah and we brought back some nice things from a few different places in the world. I can't take all the credit, though. She picked out most of these things."

In time, Jimmy returned, along with a lovely young Negro girl, and the two of them began gathering up the coffee service, as well as the food that we had brought over.

"You ladies have already met Jimmy," Quentin said. "And I'd like to introduce you to Alice."

"How d'you do?" she said with a curtsy and a becoming smile.

Seeing Quentin's polite and humane treatment of Jimmy, and now Alice, I liked him all the more. My family had not ever owned slaves in England, and I had never liked the idea of slavery in general, though I knew that, in this locale at least, I was in the minority.

"I am very impressed with your treatment of them," I said after they had left.

"They're the children of a slave my father owned," he replied. "But my father's views on slavery gradually changed in his later years. He wanted to set them free, but I'm afraid that Georgia's laws on manumission are pretty limiting. Seems the government feels that folks would probably only set 'unproductive' slaves free, and then society would have to bear the burden of caring for them. And then, of course, all slaves would become unproductive.

"Old Ben, the slave, actually died before my father did. But he still owned Jimmy and Alice, and the law wouldn't allow him to grant manumission in his will. When my father died, ownership transferred to me.

"Well, I don't like slavery any more than he did," he continued, but he lowered his voice as if he feared someone else might hear, "so I've granted Jimmy and Alice their freedom. But since I can't do it legally, they still live here and work for me. In return, I provide them room and board and I even pay them for their services.

"But someday, I hope to be able to legally free them so they can go where they please. In the meantime, they seem to be happy enough here."

"Quentin Fairfax, I swear," said Betsy, "you are an absolute inspiration!"

"Well thank you, ma'am. I reckon it's good to be an inspiration to others." Then turning to me, he said, "Mahaley mentioned that you volunteer at a mission. Tell me about that."

"Well," I said, "it's run by Reverend Parkin. I help out in the medical clinic along with Noya, Mahaley's daughter, and her husband Edward."

"Does it keep you pretty busy?"

"It is often fairly busy. There is a tremendous amount of violence that white people level at the Cherokee, so there are usually cuts to stitch or bones to set. Although lately, we have had to turn the less serious illnesses and injuries away, due to dwindling funds."

"I'm sorry to hear that," he replied, with a sympathetic look that quickly brightened. "What can I do to help?" Catching me off guard, I had to ponder for a moment.

"Well, I suppose you should talk to Reverend Parkin about that."

"Good!" he said, slapping his knee. "I'll do that. Sounds like a good cause."

Quentin did just that. Within a few weeks, not only had he donated cash to help with operating expenses, he also acquired medicines to restock the diminishing stores at the clinic, and was planning an addition to the building to enlarge the clinic and classrooms. He began referring to it as the Susannah Fairfax wing.

I was amazed at how quickly he got things going. He was a commanding figure himself, but he also seemed to have some powerful connections in town and in the state, which helped to cut through the formalities and impediments, and to quickly get positive action started. As a result, by April, materials had been acquired for the addition and work began in May.

The Indians were astonished that a white man would be so willing to help so much, and some even seemed suspicious of him and his intentions, but Quentin's sincere kindness and esteem quickly

179

won them over. Several Cherokee volunteered to help with the construction, and soon there were more than enough workers.

Not everyone was so pleased with this, though. There were often white townspeople who looked disapprovingly on the work as they passed by. After only a couple of days of work, the new construction was damaged one night, obviously the work of vandals. Quentin made certain that guards were posted after construction ended each night thereafter.

During 1835, there were other disturbing things happening as well, as the United States went to war with Indians in Florida. While it did not affect our lives in Gainesville, Georgia, many Cherokee saw it as a dire omen of things to come. This seemed to fan the flames of patriotism in many of the white settlers and to incite them against the Cherokee, so that soon, more violence was being inflicted on the Indians.

We implemented certain safeguards in our household. For instance, we continued keeping guns primed and loaded in various convenient locations throughout the house, especially near doors and windows. Also, none of us would go into town alone. We always went in pairs, and always armed.

We were all frequently invited to Quentin's home for meals, and we often invited him to ours. We all came to like and trust him early on, so I revealed to him that Atsila and Timothy were still living in hiding in our home. I admit this was partly at Atsila's insistence, as he had been hearing about this white man who was doing so much to help the Cherokee that he wanted to meet Quentin himself.

The poor man was in quite a nervous state due to his continued confinement. He spoke sometimes of wanting to face down his accusers and be done with it. This perplexed me greatly, and he always assured me that he would not do it, knowing as he did that undoubtedly it would only attract more white people to our home. But I still worried that he might, in a fit of anxiety, balk at his self-imposed imprisonment and be caught or killed.

I was only too happy to introduce him to Quentin, and accordingly his and Timothy's small circle of friends expanded and provided some welcome relief from our household of women.

In September of 1835, I had a small gathering for Clara on her third birthday. The group was much the same as is always seen at the boarding house. Talu'tsi and Tala were there, as were Ganasita, Betsy and Timothy. Noya, Edward and Peter had come, and so did Quentin, and with Atsila, Mahaley and myself, it was a delightful little party.

I happily watched as Mahaley gathered Tala, Clara and Peter, now almost four years old, close around her, and she began to relate a traditional Cherokee story.

"Long ago, the rabbit had a long bushy tail," she related. "His tail was longer and bushier than the tail of the fox. The rabbit was very proud of his tail and he was constantly bragging to all the other animals about how beautiful it was. One day the fox got so tired of hearing the rabbit boast about his tail that he decided to put an end to his bluster.

"When the weather got colder, it finally became so cold that the waters froze. The fox went down to the lake carrying four fish. When he got to the lake, he cut a hole in the ice and tied the four fish to his tail, then he sat down and waited for the rabbit to come by.

"Soon, the rabbit came hopping over the hill, and the fox quickly reacted, dropping his tail into the cold water. The rabbit hopped up to the fox and asked, 'What are you doing, fox?' The fox answered, 'I'm fishing.' The rabbit asked, 'With your tail?' and the fox replied, 'Of course, that's the very best way to catch fish.'"

The children loved this, as Mahaley made faces and used different voices when quoting the animals.

"The rabbit asked, 'How long have you been fishing?'" Mahaley continued. "The fox said, 'Not long,' and he pulled up his tail, showing the four fish he had tied to it. "I'm going to trade them for some beautiful tail combs in the Cherokee village. There is only one set left, and if I catch enough fish, I know I can get them.' But the rabbit thought, 'If I fished all night long, I would have enough fish by morning to trade at the Cherokee village. Then I could get those tail combs for myself.'

"Then the fox said, 'It's getting late and I'm cold. I think I'll come back and fish some more in the morning.' As soon as the fox had left, the rabbit dropped his tail down into the icy water of the lake. Brrrrr, it was so cold!" and Mahaley did an exaggerated shiver, delighting the children. "But the rabbit wanted those tail combs more than anything. So he sat down on the hole in the ice and fished all night long.

"In the morning, the rabbit found that his tail was frozen in the lake and he couldn't pull it out. When the fox came over the top of the hill, the rabbit called to him. 'F-f-fox, p-p-please help m-m-me!'" and Mahaley performed an overstated stutter and teeth chattering, and the children giggled with joy.

"So the fox happily walked behind the rabbit and gave him a big shove. The rabbit popped out of the hole and slid all the way across to the other side of the lake. But his tail was still stuck in the ice of the lake. And that is why to this day, the rabbit has such a short, little tail."

The children applauded Mahaley's performance and, all smiles, she kissed each one of them. Then she got up to see to the needs of the other guests.

My initial estimation of Clara was turning out to be quite accurate. She was a child possessed of such exquisite physical attractiveness that my heart often swelled with pride when I looked at her. Her hair had become a wonderful tawny gold colour, and combining that with her dark brown eyes and flawless, naturally tanned skin, she displayed an almost unearthly exotic beauty. Her disposition was equally pleasing.

"She's beautiful," Noya said. She had come up beside me and put her arm about my shoulders. "She seems to have inherited the very best features of both of you."

"Thank you," I said, returning the embrace with my arm around her waist. "She does seem like a little angel, doesn't she? She never has a bad mood." Noya smiled, then looked at me.

"I miss you," she said, leaning her head down against mine. "I loved the time we used to spend together here. When I married Edward, I still saw you regularly at the clinic, but now that's only about once a week, if even that much."

"I know," I said. "With my duties here, I can't volunteer as much time as I used to. And when I do, it seems we are seldom scheduled at the same time anymore." We paused as we both watched Peter offer a flower to Clara. Clara accepted the flower and pressed it firmly against her nose, inhaling deeply, and we both smiled. "How do you like the new addition at the clinic?" I asked. Work was completed at the end of August and I had not been there yet.

"It's wonderful!" she said enthusiastically. "It is as if we have finally come into the nineteenth century! I still have to be trained to use some of the new equipment, but it will really help us to provide better care for our patients."

"I'm very happy to hear that," I said. "Quentin is so glad to be able to help."

"Yes, he is a godsend." We both looked at Quentin who was sitting at the table eating a slice of cake. Betsy was beside him, wearing a bright green dress that, like most of them, was straining to conceal her bountiful attributes. Frequently, I saw her lean closer to Quentin, ostensibly to hear something he said, but I think she just wanted to be able to brush her shoulder against his. I also noticed that Timothy was sitting on the other side of Betsy and

185

seemed to be competing for her attention, rather unsuccessfully, I'm afraid.

I felt Noya move slightly and I looked over at her as she was holding something out to me. It was a lovely comb, a lustrous hair ornament made of mother-of-pearl, with a rose carved on its surface. I looked up at her face and she smiled.

"For your long, bushy tail," she said.

Her eyes twinkled with delight at her joke and I laughed. Then I looked back at the comb and took it from her hand.

"I saw this and thought of you," she said. "It's beautiful."

"Is it ever!" I exclaimed. "You are such a dear. Thank you so much."

As I worked the comb into my hair and secured it in place, Noya leaned closer to me and spoke just above a whisper into my ear. "I wanted to tell you first, after Edward and Mother, of course. I am going to have a baby!"

"Noya!" I almost squealed as, ever English, I struggled to keep my composure. But it was not to be. I turned to her and enveloped her in a tight embrace. Releasing her, I looked up at her face and saw the happiness and excitement in her eyes.

"I would like for Peter to have a little sister," she said. "She will be born in the early spring."

"You realise, don't you, that God may decide that Peter needs a brother instead of a sister?" I asked with a smile.

"Of course," she laughed, "and I will be happy with either."

"I suppose Edward is excited."

"Oh, no one could be more so." Edward had taken Peter onto his lap and together they were listening to Clara, who seemed to be expounding on the virtues of the now mangled flower she was still holding. Peter looked as if he were getting bored with her thesis, but Edward patiently listened, affecting all the right facial expressions when expected.

The happy sounds were suddenly cut short by a loud pounding at the front door. I looked over at Atsila. He and Timothy were already up and moving toward the basement stairs, though I noticed the look on Atsila's face that said that he was not happy about hiding again.

I looked out the front window of the parlour and saw a number of armed men, at least two of whom I recognised from my confrontation last year. I went back toward the front door and pulled a pistol out of the cabinet we kept in the entryway for this purpose. I checked to be sure it was loaded and, after making certain that Atsila and Timothy were not in view, I unbolted and opened the door.

"May I help you?" I asked, wearing the coldest, hardest expression I could affect.

"Well, look at this, boys," said their apparent leader, looking at some of the guests who had come up behind me. "We got us a Injun party." His friends seemed to appreciate his humour more than we did. "We come for your husband," he said, coming quickly to the point.

"Don't you think this is getting rather tiresome?" I asked with a bored expression and tone of voice.

"We don't think you been honest with us," he replied. "You say your husband ain't here, but you ain't never seemed too upset about it. Then we hear that someone seen him outside in back o' your house."

I made no response, but continued staring coldly into his eyes. I raised my eyebrows as if waiting for him to make his point.

"I think you're a liar," he finally said.

"Well, I think you're an imbecile, so I suppose we both have things which we must tolerate about the other."

He took a step towards me, but I raised the pistol and he stopped in his tracks.

"I think we better go in there and have a look around for your husband, and while we're at it, maybe we'll take care of this Injun infestation you got there," he said with a sneer.

"You will not step foot in this house."

187

"Look, we don't want to shoot no white woman but – " He abruptly stopped speaking, and I saw his eyes focus on something behind me.

"What's the problem, Tom?" asked Quentin as he shouldered his way through the press of people behind me.

"Mr Fairfax," the leader, Tom, said. "I didn't know you was here."

"Well, I am," Quentin responded. "These people are my friends. We're enjoying a child's birthday party, so state your business so we can get back to it." Suddenly nervous, Tom seemed to have little to say.

"It's nothin' sir. I guess we was given bad information. Sorry to bother you." He and his men made a quick retreat to their horses and rode away. I waited until they were all off the property, then closed and bolted the door.

"Young lady," Quentin said, "you are somethin' else." I smiled weakly at him and exhaled the breath that I belatedly realised that I was holding.

"So, you know them," I said as I put the pistol back in the cabinet.

"Tom and a couple of the others. They work at the lumber mill."

"The lumber mill?" I did not understand the significance.

"I bought the lumber mill a while back. I guess you could say I'm their boss."

We had no more confrontations that year, though there were still instances when we saw men riding past and looking toward the house. We did not always recognise the individuals, but often enough, we did.

In December, a small group of Cherokees gathered at the home of Major Ridge's nephew Elias Boudinot a few miles west of Gainesville. Here, they surreptitiously signed the Treaty of New Echota. After Ridge made his mark, he quietly said, "I have signed *my death warrant." The treaty called for the removal of all Cherokee to the new Indian Territory west of the Mississippi River. There was a provision in the treaty for any Cherokee who so desired to remain and become citizens of the states in which they resided, but this provision was stricken from the treaty by President Jackson.*

The passage of this treaty was significant in that the Principal Chief of the Cherokee Nation, John Ross, and the Cherokee nation in general neither supported nor signed it. In February of 1836, the treaty was overwhelmingly rejected by the Cherokee National Council. But within a few months, it was ratified by the United States Senate and signed into law by the President. The deadline for removal was 1838.

Early in March, Noya experienced severe cramping. Fortunately Edward was at home with her at the time, and he did what he could but when she hemorrhaged, he was unable to stop it. Their little girl was stillborn.

Noya, weak and exhausted from pain and loss of blood, survived but was heartbroken. I am sure that Edward was too, though he put up a valiant effort to remain strong and cheerful for Noya's sake.

In June, federal troops arrived on Cherokee land to 'keep the peace' between the whites and the Indians, but there was little peace to be kept.

"Are you ever going to tell me what this is?" Atsila asked. He was looking at the etched silver artifact, which I had placed on top of the dresser in our bedroom. Clara was asleep and Atsila and I were getting ready for bed.

"I don't know what it is," I responded. "It was in the bag that Liam left with me. I just think it's beautiful."

He picked it up as he had several times before and examined it closely. "It's so heavy," he said. "It must be made from a solid block of silver."

189

"Yes, I reached the same conclusion some years back. But the etching on its surface is what I find so beautiful and intriguing."

Atsila traced the designs with his fingertips. "Do you know anything about the design?" he asked.

"No, not really," I replied. "It looks Irish. Those interlaced designs embedded in the surface of the block are called Celtic knots, but I know nothing of their meaning or history." He replaced the artifact on the dresser and turned to me as we heard a bird call outside. It was familiar, though I could not remember what it was or where I had heard it.

"Whippoorwill," Atsila said, seeing the look on my face.

"Yes, that's right," I said, suddenly remembering. "We heard it on our wedding night." He smiled at the memory, and as I stood before the window, he came up behind me and wrapped his arms around me as he had on that night. We stayed there for several minutes, listening to the haunting call, feeling completely content in our closeness to each other.

As the temperature had risen and the oppressive afternoon sun was burning hotly in the cloudless sky, Dora and Shawn had moved inside, and she turned on the ceiling fan in the living room. Being on the east side of the house, the living room was cooler, and they had made themselves comfortable on the sofa.

"Well, there's another mention of that damn artifact," said Shawn.

"I know," Dora agreed. "It sounds beautiful. I wish I knew where it is."

"If it was solid silver as Atsila said, they may have sold it a long time ago. Cashed it in for a lot of money."

"Yeah, I suppose so. What's a Celtic knot? I've heard the term but I'm not sure what it is."

"There are a lot of different kinds of Celtic knots," Shawn said, as he fingered a chain around his neck. He pulled it out from the collar of his shirt, revealing a small silver pendant on the end. "This is one."

Dora leaned closer to look at the intricate interlocking pattern embossed on the surface of the pendant.

"It's beautiful," she said.

Dora got up and walked into the dining room where she still had things from the trunk arranged on the table, returning a moment later. She had recognized another item described in Isadora's account, and she came back carrying the mother-of-pearl hair ornament.

Shawn smiled when he saw what she was holding. "Isn't it fascinating to think that these things were owned and worn by someone two centuries ago?" he asked.

Dora nodded. "It's even more fascinating to know the stories behind them, and getting to know the person who wore them." She sat back down on the sofa and caressed the textures of the carved edges of the comb. Then she took a handful of hair and pushed it back on one side. She secured it in place with the comb and looked at Shawn.

"Beautiful," he said sincerely. Dora smiled and leaned against him as his arms wrapped around her. He placed a tender kiss on her forehead. At that moment, the thought occurred to him that he was happy.

It was a warm afternoon in July of 1836, and Noya had physically recovered from her miscarriage of four months before, but was still racked with melancholy. Soon after she lost the baby, it was not uncommon for her to start crying in the morning, and then by noon she would be exhausted. She managed to carry out her everyday activities, including caring for Peter, but she did it as an automaton.

As time passed, it got to be a little easier for her, and we all made a point of visiting her and letting her know she was loved. We felt this was especially important since Edward often had to be at the clinic and was not always available for her.

We found that one thing that seemed to help her the most was getting her outside, walking in the sunshine, as I had done with her the day before. After doing this, she seemed much less sad, and at times even managed a smile.

After two years of home incarceration, Atsila had been venturing out of doors more as well. Obviously, I feared for his safety when he did so, especially since we still would occasionally see people who seemed to be watching for him. But I could certainly understand his feelings. He would only go out in the back, where he was concealed to some extent by hedges, trees and by the house itself.

He and Timothy were behind the house playing a game that was popular among the Cherokee, called danah-wah'uwsdi. Using long-handled sticks with a small basket-like apparatus on one end, they would catch and throw a small leather ball back and

193

forth, using the basket on the stick. Atsila was quite accomplished at this. Timothy was learning, but was not nearly as adept.

Mahaley and Betsy had gone into town to visit Noya on this particular day. Ganasita, Talu'tsi and Tala had been gone since after breakfast, and Clara was napping in her room in the basement. I had the house to myself and, though I was working in the kitchen, I was enjoying the quiet.

I should have known better.

I heard the front door crash open, and immediately after this, I heard Atsila shout, "Timothy, get down!" This was followed by a gunshot, and I was torn, wanting to run to Atsila, but knowing I also had an intruder to face in the house. I went toward the back door where I had a pistol, but I was not able to get to it.

"Leave it," said a quiet voice from behind me.

I turned and saw one of the men I had seen on numerous occasions in front of the house. He had a musket aimed at me. "Move over there," he said, pointing toward the work table, away from the door. I did as he said, partly aware of the voices and an additional gunshot coming from the back but struggling to focus on my own situation.

The man moved toward me, leering at me the whole time. He placed his musket on the table beside my pistol, both out of my reach, and came closer to me. I had backed away as far as I could and he was now touching me, putting his hands on my waist. I could smell coffee and tobacco on his breath, and I felt as if I was going to be ill.

"Don't make any noise," he said, "or your squaw-man is dead."

I had no illusions that they might leave us peacefully, but for now, I remained quiet. He kept pressing against me, then reached into the top of my dress, cupping his grimy hand over my breast. Feeling the anger well up inside me, I tried to push him away. My struggling only seemed to amuse him. He smiled as he ripped my bodice apart, then my chemise.

194

"You sure are a purty thing," he said as I continued pressing him away from me. My growing anger seemed to give me strength, but he was still considerably larger than I, and my efforts to push him away were, for the most part, in vain.

One time, when I did manage to repel him, I balled up my hand in a fist and hit him in the face as hard as I could. It probably hurt my hand more than it hurt his face, but I was happy to feel his nose crush under my fist as blood poured from his left nostril. It shocked him momentarily and he stepped back, but then he was angry. He hit me across the face with the back of his hand and I tasted blood on my lip.

I tried to pull the ripped pieces of my clothing together to cover myself, but as he advanced toward me, I had to give up on that as I again tried to push him away. He seemed to be distracted by my exposed breasts, and by the constant motion of my hands trying to shove him away. The movements of my hands seemed to work in my favour. He did not notice when I found the knife on his belt. I pulled it from the scabbard and, before he could react, with a savage grunt, I thrust the point of the blade between his ribs and into his heart. He gasped as his face displayed surprise before he fell dead.

The entire struggle, I am certain, took less than two minutes. I stepped over the dead man and went toward the back door, picking up my pistol and the musket on the way. I ran out the door and saw Timothy standing there, crying and holding a musket at his side. I stepped farther out and saw two men lying on the ground, and was horrified when I realised that one of them was Atsila.

I ran and fell on my knees beside him, picking him up by the shoulders and cradling his head. He was bleeding from a wound in the upper abdomen, but he was still breathing. He looked up at me and smiled weakly, as I caressed his cheek. Then he noticed the blood on my mouth where the man had hit me.

"Are you alright?" he asked.

"Yes, my love," I said. "I'm fine."

"Good," he said quietly. He struggled for a breath, then said, "I know you'll take good care of Clara. I love you both so much." Tears were running down my face as I held him, rocking him back and forth, and with a sickening dread, I knew that this was the end.

"I love you too," I said. "Please don't go – I need you." But it was too late. He stiffened briefly, then went limp in my arms. The anguish that coursed through me prevents me from remembering that moment clearly. I do remember the sound of his last breath leaving his body, and I remember that I let out a scream of despair and desolation at that moment.

Quentin had heard the commotion and hobbled over to our place as quickly as he could, his walking stick in one hand, a musket in the other. He found me still holding Atsila in my arms, still rocking back and forth and sobbing. I was aware of very little besides my grief until some time later. Quentin helped me into the house where I changed into a different dress. He and Timothy carried Atsila inside and dragged the other two men against the back of the house. I was sitting in the parlour when Mahaley and Betsy arrived home.

Quentin intercepted them and told them in private what had happened. They came into the parlour and, sitting on each side of me on the divan, just held me and quietly cried with me. Timothy was sitting silently by himself in a chair on the other side of the room.

When the intruder crashed through the front door, his companion had gone around the back of the house. Atsila had seen him come around the corner with a musket and called out to warn Timothy who was concealed by some trees. That was the warning I had heard. Atsila's gun was not within easy reach. The man had seen Atsila and recognised him as the one they were after, so he fired. Timothy, who was closer to his musket, grabbed it and shot the man, but too late to save Atsila.

I knew that Timothy felt awful, and I knew that Atsila's death was not his fault. I stood and walked over to where he sat. He

196

looked up at me with tears in his eyes, and I knelt before him and wrapped my arms around him, and we both started sobbing anew.

I have only a few random memories of that evening. Clara, knowing something was not right, stayed very close to me. I remember Ganasita, Talu'tsi and Tala touching my arm, my shoulder, my face, and expressing sympathy. Edward, Noya and Peter came over, and Noya held me tightly, and together we wept.

Noya stayed, and she and Mahaley remained close to help me through that first night. Though I did not notice at the time, I realised later that helping me seemed to help Noya. She was much stronger from then on.

I awoke the next morning and slowly climbed the stairs. Noya had slept with me and had taken Clara upstairs that morning when she woke up. I opened the door leading into the main part of the house, where Mahaley was working in the kitchen.

The blood had been cleaned up the night before, and everything set back in place. But I could still see the man in front of me. I could still feel his hands on my body, grabbing my breasts. I could still see him lying dead on the floor, his knife protruding from his chest.

Mahaley came to me, smiling gently, and gave me a hug. Hearing me shuffle in, Noya came too, and they both took me by the hands and led me to the front door. As it was opened, I saw a couple going down the steps of the porch. Hearing the door open, they turned, and I recognised Dosa, a young mother whose child I had treated at the clinic. She came back up and, without a word, wrapped her arms around me and held me for a few moments. Then, just as quietly, they left.

After this, I was able to notice the items on the porch. Apparently, during the night and well into the morning, people had been leaving flowers, fruits and vegetables. There was venison, there were hams, there were fish. Beautifully woven baskets and beadwork, lengths of cotton fabric and ribbons and other woven items.

Articles of clothing and Indian jewelry, pottery, deerskins and furs.

And I cried again.

"Yea, though I walk through the valley of the shadow of death," read Reverend Parkin, *"I will fear no evil, for thou art with me."* I looked at the people standing around the new grave. Fiona, Atsila's mother, had come as soon as she heard about Atsila's death. She stood across from me, looking sadder than ever, dressed in black, her bright hair sticking out incongruously from the black shawl she wore draped over her head.

"Thy rod and thy staff they comfort me." Mahaley and Noya stood on each side of me, holding my hands. And though I could not see them, I knew Quentin and the residents of the boarding house were behind me.

"Thou preparest a table before me in the presence of mine enemies." In the distance, I saw groups of white people, and I was troubled that my first instinct when seeing white people I did not know was now one of suspicion.

"Thou anointest my head with oil; my cup runneth over. Surely goodness and mercy shall follow me all the days of my life, and I will dwell in the house of the Lord for ever." Reverend Parkin, his head bowed, closed his Bible, and there were a few muttered *"amens."*

He came slowly toward me. Dislodging my right hand from Noya's, I offered it to him. *"I'm so sorry, my dear,"* he said, his white mane billowing in the gentle breeze. *"Please take care. Stay close to your friends and family — let them help you. And if there's anything at all that I can do, please don't hesitate to ask."*

"Thank you," I said. *"And thank you for the lovely service."*

Seeing that people were starting to disperse, he nodded to two men who were standing at a distance under a tree, holding shovels. I watched as they began to fill in the grave, covering my husband's coffin. After a while, I turned and saw Fiona waiting at a distance. She approached me and together, we started walking toward our carriages.

"Isadora, dear," she said softly with her prominent Scottish accent, "I just wanted to thank you for giving Atsila so much peace and happiness, if only for a short time. I know he loved you dearly."

Mahaley and Noya fell in behind us, and Edward had Peter and Clara by the hands. "He was a lovely man," I said wistfully. "You should be very proud of the person he became."

"I am," she replied. "And I'm proud of you too. Since I've been here, I've heard nothing but praise for you." We reached the road and she looked down at Clara. "And thank you for giving me such a beautiful granddaughter. She looks like you, but I can see a bit of my boy in her too."

I thought that I had no more tears, but I managed to loose a couple more when she held me tightly in her arms.

"May God be with you," I said and kissed her on the cheek.

"And with you dear," she said, then she turned toward her carriage and was gone.

"I just can't stay here no more," Timothy said. He had taken Atsila's death very hard, and now, a week later, even though I had assured him several times that he was not to blame, I knew he still felt guilty. I also knew that during their time in exile together, they had grown close. His decision to leave did not come as a surprise.

"I understand," I said. "You will be missed. You've been a great friend, not only to Atsila, but to me and everyone else here." His eyes were welling up with tears, and as I pressed my palm to his cheek, they spilled down.

"Thank you, ma'am," he said quietly. "But I ain't done that much."

"You helped Atsila get Clara back. And you saved Atsila's life that same day. Your friendship has done more than you know." He looked down but said nothing. "Do you know where you'll go?"

"I'm feelin' kinda homesick for my family," he said. "I reckon I'll go back to Augusta, to start with anyways. My sister's still there."

"I hope you live a long and happy life," I said sincerely. "And know that you always have friends here." He gave a sad smile. I stepped closer to him with my arms outstretched, and he hugged me fiercely. Then he went upstairs to pack up his things.

With Timothy leaving shortly after Atsila's death, we finished 1836 as a small group of women at the boarding house. Talu'tsi and Tala had talked a few times about moving west to the Indian Territory, but so far, they remained. For a few months, Ganasita felt very fatigued. The dear old woman had aged quite a bit in the recent years, and in December, after a short stay at the clinic, passed away in the night.

Betsy persisted in her sometimes embarrassing behaviour and flamboyant style of dress, though she did, at least, become more aware of it, to the point of frequently apologising to those she flustered. Quentin seemed more amused by her than embarrassed, and I noticed them becoming closer. At times when I saw her leaning close to him, I often saw him leaning back.

Quentin really extended himself to watch over us, and even cut and paved a narrow trail through the woods between our houses, to provide faster and more direct access in case of another emergency.

Sometime in the latter half of 1836, I heard that I had earned a new nickname. Some of the Indians were calling me Unega Ani-Yun'wiya, or the White Cherokee. This was after I had found, among Atsila's things, a choker-style necklace made of red and blue beads. I started wearing it and other items I found, feeling that he was closer to me when I did so.

I also made use of many of the items that were left on the front porch after his death, including several pieces of jewelry of Cherokee workmanship, and cotton fabric woven by the Indians. A few *of the Indians seemed to recognise the items and were pleased to see me wearing them.*

I was not necessarily trying to copy the Indians. I respected them and their ways too much to attempt that. But I missed my Atsila so desperately that I wanted his things close to me. And generally speaking, I found that I identified with the Indians better than I did with most of the white people in the area. Apparently the Indians understood that and, while they still addressed me to my face as Isadora, they spoke of me to others as the White Cherokee.

Before the year was out, I had a large granite headstone erected on Atsila's grave. I knew that it was an extravagance, but I could afford it, and it made me feel good to do it. On its face, I had carved a portion of a poem I knew, by Anne Bradstreet, an Englishwoman who had moved to America two hundred years before me:

> *If ever two were one, then surely we.*
> *If ever man were lov'd by wife, then thee.*
> *My love is such that Rivers cannot quench,*
> *Nor ought but love from thee give recompense.*

Goodbye, my dear husband.

A brief sparkle caught Shawn's attention from the corner of his eye and he looked at Dora. There were tears in her eyes, slipping down her cheeks.

"What's wrong?" he asked.

"Atsila's funeral," she said. "It reminded me, tomorrow's Monday. My grandmother's funeral is tomorrow."

"Oh."

"I feel like such a shit!"

"A shit? Why?" he asked as he put an arm around her shoulders.

"I've hardly even thought about her. I barely knew her any more. I haven't seen her in years, and she leaves me all of this." Dora paused and looked around the room. "I'm going to feel like such a hypocrite showing up at her funeral."

"Oh, honey, she wouldn't want you to feel that way," Shawn said, giving her shoulder a squeeze. "Would you feel better if I went with you tomorrow?"

"Why would you do that?" she asked, looking up at him. "You didn't know her."

"Funerals aren't for the dead, but for the living. I'd go for you."

She looked at him for a moment, then reached up and put her hand on his neck, giving him a brief hug and whispered, "Thank you," in his ear.

As they had eaten such a large breakfast, they had skipped lunch and Shawn decided to take Dora out for an early dinner. Placing a quick call to his brother, arrangements were made to meet at Shawn's favorite pizza place, Hell's Kitchen. It was just off Manitou Avenue, very close to many of the tourist attractions of Manitou Springs. The small interior was somewhat bare bones with old aluminum tables and chairs, but the air conditioning was welcome considering the heat of the afternoon, and the pizza was delicious.

Colin Murphy was a stockier version of Shawn, and about five years older. His wife Robin was a plain woman, pleasant but rather quiet, with fair skin and short black hair. Colin was the more dynamic one of the couple, while Robin was more of an introvert. She tended to fade into the background when he was around, but she didn't seem to mind.

"So he actually talked you out of hiring us?" Colin said with a teasing smile.

"Well, not yet," Dora replied. "I'm still thinking about it. But I have to admit, he did introduce some intriguing ideas."

"Yeah, he does that. Did he tell you 'Estate of Mind' was his idea?"

"Yes, he did, with supporting arguments."

"I thought it would be a shame for her to give up that property," Shawn said. "You should see it! And the history we've been discovering is fascinating!" Shawn and Dora spent the next few minutes telling them what they had learned. Colin and Robin listened with some interest, though clearly not with the enthusiasm shared by Shawn and Dora.

"I have to admit," Dora said, "Shawn's idea of turning the house into a bed and breakfast has got me thinking. I've never considered that kind of enterprise, but it's starting to sound kind of interesting."

"I really think she could make a success of it," Shawn enthused.

"Plus, the link to my ancestors – it would be like a family business."

"That does sound kind of appealing," Colin agreed.

"I just don't know if I can handle it."

"Maybe I could help," Robin meekly volunteered. When everyone looked at her, she continued. "Shelley's in college now and Troy will be leaving in a couple of weeks. I've been trying to think of something to fill my time."

"That's a great idea," Colin said. "She takes care of the business side of Estate of Mind, but that doesn't take much of her time."

"I'll keep that in mind if I decide to follow through on it," Dora promised. Robin smiled in response.

They ordered another pitcher of beer and visited for another hour or so, but Colin had an appointment in the morning that he wanted to prepare for.

"We're going to have to call it a night," he said.

"Again, we're sorry about your grandmother," Robin said, shaking her hand.

"Yes, I hope everything goes well tomorrow."

"Thank you," Dora said.

"Well, Dora, it was very nice meeting you," Colin said as he also shook her hand.

"Very nice to meet you both," she said with a sincere smile. "The people I know in Manitou Springs just increased three hundred percent!"

It was not quite dark yet as they neared Dora's house, but the sun had gone down behind the mountain and was casting a dusky shadow. Shawn pulled up in front of the house and his headlights illuminated a man on the front porch, focusing closely on the doorknob. Apparently alarmed by the sudden light, he quickly ran down the steps and away, disappearing around some hedges.

"Did you see that?" Dora asked with alarm.

"Yes, I did," Shawn replied. Dora had her phone out and was already calling the police, who arrived within a matter of minutes. The door was still locked and Dora, who had waited until the police officer arrived, unlocked it for him.

205

As a precaution, Officer Jenkins entered the house to do a quick walk-through, while Dora and Shawn waited on the porch. Emerging from the house a couple of minutes later, Officer Jenkins declared it safe. "Since the door was still locked, he obviously had not yet gained access. You arrived just in time."

"What could he have been after?" asked Dora.

"Well, your guess is as good as mine, ma'am. But you know this is a very nice, big house, furnished with a lot of expensive antiques. Any local higher-end burglars would consider this a prime target."

"Don't you think it's a little too coincidental? This happened just a few nights after my grandmother interrupted a burglary and was killed."

"It may or may not be a coincidence, ma'am. But the fact is, since he didn't gain access to the house, there's little or no forensic evidence that could help us to determine the identity of the perpetrator, or what he might have been after. But if you want to come down to the station, you could give a statement, and maybe provide a detailed description of the man you saw, look at mug shots."

"We didn't see his face," Shawn said. "He stayed turned away from the light and was gone in a couple of seconds."

"We will continue to patrol the area, keep an eye out for any suspicious activity."

"What if he shows up again?" Dora asked.

"Well," the officer said, "I noticed there's an alarm system installed in the house. Make use of it. Set the alarm once you're inside, and set it when you leave."

Since Dora did not know anything about the alarm, Officer Jenkins offered some assistance. They found a phone number for the alarm company, and with the policeman's verification, they helped Dora with the code and to get it set. With that done, she felt safer when Jenkins left. But she still made a point of closing all the drapes before she and Shawn delved back into Isadora's book.

In January of 1837, after threats of violence from angry Cherokee, about six hundred members of John Ridge's Treaty Party left for the new Indian Territory, paying their own way. In March, Martin Van Buren replaced Jackson as President, but vowed to follow in the footsteps of his predecessor. And that he did. In March, a second group of Cherokee were taken west, the first party to be voluntarily removed at the expense of the American government.

Early in the year, Reverend Parkin was notified by the mission board that sponsorship was being revoked due to the apparently inevitable removal of the Indians. Even so, they lasted longer than most, as several other missions in the region had closed down as many as five years before. Reverend Parkin was reassigned to a parish in Kentucky, but Edward and Noya were initially undecided about what they would do. Convinced of the value of their work, Quentin promised to provide funding himself if they would put out the word for more volunteers, which they did.

Most of the missions, or their spokesmen, saw removal as the only way for the Cherokee to survive as a people. Because of this, many of the Indians began to see missionaries as advocates of removal, and viewed them as associates of Major Ridge's Treaty Party. As a result, fewer Indians were coming to the clinic for treatment, and we heard reports of an increase in the number and severity of illnesses among the local Cherokee, and a rise in the number of deaths.

Edward and Noya tried to combat this trend by speaking out against removal. Noya was the primary voice for this since, as a

207

Cherokee, they felt that she would be more likely to be trusted by the Cherokee people. As they were no longer associated with the mission, some did believe them and made use of their services. Still, the additional volunteers turned out to not be needed.

Strolling through town in the spring used to be a joyful experience for me. Flowers were in bloom, the air was starting to get warmer and fragrant, people were friendly.

Not so anymore. At least, not to me.

In late April of 1837, I noticed a tangible change. I saw fewer Cherokee and more white people. The white people I saw often seemed colder to me, perhaps because of the Indian garments and ornamentation I wore. Overall, there appeared to be a pervading sense of hatred or animosity toward the Cherokee. As I was an obvious sympathiser toward their plight, white settlers directed those feelings toward me as well. Even walking with Clara, which I did on some occasions, did not seem to lighten the mood.

To be fair, though, not all of the white people were against the Cherokee and their situation. Those who had been in the area longer generally felt more sympathy toward them. But the newer settlers often displayed attitudes ranging from indifference to outright hostility.

The mentality and behaviour of the general populace toward the Indians, and toward me, caused me to examine my own feeling of connection to them. Rather than wanting to befriend them, I felt myself drawing away from them. I found that I wanted little to do with them, and even recognised within me a feeling of distrust toward them. They were not the kind of people I wanted as my friends.

Deep inside, I felt bad about that. But anger and sadness overwhelmed me, threatening to crush and smother my feelings toward others. Exceptions to that, of course, were the Indians, mainly the ones I knew from the boarding house and the clinic. Among the white people, Edward, Betsy and Quentin, and a handful of others, received my friendship and goodwill. But for the most part, I wanted little to do with anyone else.

I had not been the object of further violence, though I did continue the practice of being armed and in the company of a second person when in public. This day was no exception. Mahaley and I had come into town to stock up on certain supplies in the general store, and Jed Gilkison, the proprietor, was gathering the things we needed.

He was friendly enough, one of those who had been in this area for many years, and he seemed to be sympathetic toward the Cherokee. Many of them were his customers and had been for years.

A couple of white patrons, however, were quick to move to the other side of the store when we entered, animatedly whispering to one another and casting disapproving glances at us. Feeling disgusted toward them, and making certain they knew it, I stepped outside. I felt as if I needed air.

But the atmosphere outside seemed just as stifling. People who looked at me did so with censuring expressions. I felt like an outcast, like a brigand who had eluded capture for quite some time but whose luck was about to run out. Was my assessment accurate? Had the mood and attitudes really changed that much? Or was I just being overly sensitive?

Mahaley emerged from the store, followed by Jed who was carrying a crate of supplies which he loaded onto the back of the wagon. I climbed up onto the wagon and took the reins, anxious to be on my way, and Mahaley climbed up beside me. We made our way down the road, drawing more deprecating looks from passersby. I felt suffocated, as if the leering gazes of those people were a weight that was pressing down upon me.

I saw the bank up ahead and, on a sudden impulse, pulled the wagon over.

"What's wrong?" Mahaley asked.

"I don't know," I replied. "I just suddenly had the notion to withdraw my money and close my account."

Mahaley looked at me with a quizzical expression. I shook my head.

"It's not anything that I can explain. I don't trust these people any longer. I want to have my possessions with me, not locked in some white man's vault."

Mahaley sat quietly as I climbed down from the wagon and went in the bank.

"Is there a problem?" asked Mr. Thompson, the bank president, after he had been told of my intention. He was a rather small man in spectacles, whose smooth skin and white hair made him seem prematurely old.

"No, there is no problem," I replied. I could not explain to him the intense feelings permeating my being, nor could I justify this action based on those feelings. "I just need to get my money and close my account."

"Well, I just want you to be sure about this. Your money is always safer in the bank."

"I am sure. According to my records, I should have just over $900. I would like it in gold coin, please."

"Isadora, I hope you're not going to go and do anything silly." He said this with a condescending tone, the way he might speak to a child. Or an Indian.

"Mr. Thompson, I am in a bit of a hurry, so if you could run along and get my money for me, I would appreciate it." Comprehending my patronising tone of voice, he pressed his lips tightly together and went to a teller to process the withdrawal.

Again, I could not explain it, but I felt better having my gold with me again.

Two weeks later, in May, a major monetary crisis started in New York, the effects of which were eventually felt elsewhere in the country. Financial experts would go on to argue the cause of the panic, but many blamed it on the increased release of banknotes which did not have the backing of gold reserves. Banks

210

closed around the country and the losses soared into the hundreds of millions of dollars. In a successive chain of events, prices rose, jobs were lost, and the resulting depression would last for several years after that.

Mr. Thompson's bank was among those that failed, and I considered myself extremely fortunate to have closed my account just two weeks before.

In the following months, the boarding house became more of an inn, as tenants came and went rather quickly. The decrease in the number of available jobs, and the overwhelming prejudice against the Cherokee, meant that many of them were becoming destitute. For those in dire situations, we charged little or no rent. Many left after weeks or days, to pursue opportunities elsewhere, or to surrender to the pressure and prejudice, and move to the Indian Territory.

Talu'tsi and Tala were among those who finally moved west. Tala, now a pretty young lady of fourteen, had grown quite close to Mahaley and me, and Clara was very fond of her as well. It was a very emotional day in October when they packed their meagre possessions into four bags and loaded them onto the wagon for the ride into town. They had been with us from the time we opened, and had been our friends and companions for six years.

The fast turnover of tenants, though I did not recognise it at the time, was a good thing for me. I admit that I had become something of a hermit after Atsila's death, and as noted earlier, had developed a certain distrust, in fact almost a loathing of white people in general. I tended to prefer to stay at home and not venture out among the general populace of the town. Our many tenants provided human interaction that I would not have had otherwise. The fact that they were Cherokee was significant, as I enjoyed visiting with them rather than considering it something to be endured.

It also meant more work for Mahaley and me. Betsy often pitched in, and while this sometimes resulted in even more work

211

for us, usually it was a great help. The extra work kept us preoc-
cupied to an extent, and time passed more quickly.

Thus we were somewhat busy and distracted when 1837 ended
and 1838 began.

It was a beautiful warm day in mid-June, 1838. It had not rained in a while, but for us, the dryness was only a minor inconvenience. We carried water from the river behind the house to water the vegetable garden, which was not that uncommon anyway, but aside from that, it affected us very little.

I was sitting on the front porch with Clara who was playing with a doll that Tala had given her when they left. Having just finished cleaning the rooms that had been vacated that day, I was taking a moment to rest.

Birds were singing in the trees, and bees were actively visiting each flower in the flower beds around the porch. The sky was a beautiful cloudless blue, and the day was giving every indication that it was going to be a good one.

When will I ever learn to not trust outward appearances?

The first indication of trouble was the sound of distant hoof beats. Many horses were approaching, though I could not yet see them past the trees lining the road. Though I had no idea who was coming, I had learned not to take chances. I quickly took Clara's hand and took her inside where I called to Mahaley. She came from the direction of the kitchen, wiping her hands on a towel.

"Take Clara, please," I said urgently. Mahaley seemed puzzled at first but took her hand. By then, the sound of the approaching horses could be heard from inside the house, and I quickly selected a musket and went back out on the porch, closing the door behind me. The horses were visible now as they turned off the road and approached the house. It was a detachment of federal soldiers in

213

their blue uniforms. They stopped in front of the house and, dis-mounting, approached me with muskets in hand.

"Step out of the way, please," said the officer in charge, a man of about thirty, with bushy sideburns and eyebrows.

"What business do you have here at my home?" I asked defiantly.

"I understand this home is owned by a Cherokee," he said.

"I'm afraid your understanding is inaccurate," I replied. "This is my house."

He seemed momentarily confused, but recovered quickly as he looked at a paper in his hand. "Well I'm sorry, ma'am. We have orders to round up Indians for removal."

"Removal?" I asked disgustedly. "Sir, you speak of removing these people as casually as if you were talking of taking out the refuse."

"Again, I apologise." He looked back at the paper in his hand. "We're here to enforce the Indian Removal Act. The deadline has come and gone, and any who have not already complied have to be removed forcibly. According to this information compiled by the Georgia Guard, there are Cherokees living here."

He turned slightly and nodded to a soldier on his right. At that, soldiers started up the steps and I made a movement to level my musket toward them. "Ma'am," the officer said, seeing what I was about to do, "this will only end up worse than it already is if you try to interfere."

Hopelessly outnumbered, I knew he was right, and I stood there helplessly as the soldiers swarmed past me and into the house. I heard Clara scream and I rushed inside. Mahaley was being forced outside by two soldiers with bayonets affixed to their muskets. Another soldier was holding Clara's hand and I rushed over and took her from him. We had one Cherokee tenant who was in her room that day, a young widow, and she came down the stairs, a look of terror on her face, with more soldiers behind her. Betsy came down after them, yelling incoherently at the soldiers.

Following them outside, I now saw a soldier seated on a wagon that had stopped on the road, behind the horses that were milling about on the front lawn. Mahaley and the young widow were forced up onto the wagon, where three other Cherokee already sat, and as the rest of the soldiers reassembled and mounted their horses, the officer did the same. He casually gripped the brim of his hat with his thumb and forefinger and nodded slightly in my direction.

"Very sorry to disturb your activities, ma'am," he said. "I hope you and your little girl have a good day." With that, he wheeled his horse around, and they all followed him away to their next stop.

"Wait!" I called. "Where are you taking them?" But nobody heard me.

Mahaley sat in the back of the wagon, watching me sadly, fearfully, until they passed behind the next stand of trees and disappeared.

Taking Clara, I rushed back inside the house and saw Betsy, agitated and watching through the door.

"Betsy, will you please watch Clara?" I asked with a note of urgency.

"Of course, honey," she said breathlessly. "But what are you going to do?"

"I have to find out where they are taking them." Realising that Betsy and Clara were the last people in the house, I stopped. "Why don't you take Clara and go to Quentin's place. You will both be safe there."

"Yes, of course," she said again distractedly as I handed her my musket. With a brief brush of my hand against Clara's cheek, I ran out to the barn and started hitching up the carriage. Once finished, I drove it to the front of the house where I could see Betsy, having gathered up a few necessary items to take with her, now leading Clara down the trail through the woods toward Quentin's house.

215

I watched until they were out of sight, then I ran inside to gather a musket, a pistol and ammunition, then back to the carriage. I had lost precious time hitching the horse and carriage and gathering the guns, and I hoped that the contingent of soldiers was staying on the main road or I might not be able to find them again.

I passed the turn to Quentin's house, but knowing there were no Cherokee there, I continued on. I drove slowly, turning to look toward other houses off the road, not wanting to miss them, and finally, within an hour of leaving home, I caught up with them. The wagon was full and there were two more Cherokee walking behind it, all surrounded by the mounted soldiers.

Mahaley seemed to be comforting others crowded on the wagon. She saw me and smiled sadly, then turned her attention back to a young Indian girl who was crying.

After a while, as we continued our journey down the road, I saw what seemed to be the destination ahead: a very large stockade made of logs sunk vertically into the ground, apparently one of the Cherokee Removal Forts about which we had been hearing rumours for several years.

Large gates were swung open and the soldiers and wagon went inside. One of the men at the gate saw me approaching and directed the attention of an officer toward me. He was an old man, probably somewhere in his sixties though he seemed older, with the tired look of a man who had seen too much in his life. He slowly walked toward me, as if he were carrying a heavy burden on his shoulders.

"You don't need to be here, ma'am," he said.

"How long are you going to hold these people here?" I asked, ignoring his statement.

"Until we have enough for the next group going west," he answered.

I looked past him into the stockade and was repulsed by the squalid conditions. The stockade was open to the sky, so there was no shelter for those inside. We were experiencing a drought and there was little relief from the summer heat. I saw a few small tents scattered around, but everywhere, Indians and a few Negroes were sitting or lying on the ground. And occasionally, the turn of a breeze would bring the acrid odour of old urine and feces to my nose.

"My friend was brought here with nothing but the clothes she was wearing," I said. "Surely you don't mean to keep these people here without shelter." I was close enough that I could see a sympathetic spark in his eyes.

"I know the accommodations are not good, ma'am," he said. "We will try to provide them every comfort we can, but if you want to bring some items from home to ease her stay, you may certainly do that."

"Thank you," I said. "I will not be able to make it back here until tomorrow. Will they be moved before then?"

"No ma'am," he said.

"May I see my friend?"

He regarded me as he considered my question. Finally, after a short hesitation, he said, "Yes ma'am." He helped to steady me as I climbed down from the carriage, and he led me through the gates, glancing over at me with what I interpreted be a look of embarrassment.

I can barely express what I saw. Besides what I had seen earlier through the gates, I could now see that many of the people on the ground were ill. Those who were not sick still bore the look of a people who had lost hope, and my heavy heart went out to them.

I was led to where the wagon stood, now empty. Among those milling about, I could see Mahaley, looking lost, and my eyes filled with tears. She saw me as I approached, and we held each other tightly.

"I can't stay," I said, "but this officer has said I can bring some things for you. I will be back tomorrow. Is there anything you want?"

"Yes," she said immediately. "Can you find out about Noya?"

"Of course," I said. In the immediate confusion of the roundup at our home, I had not even thought of Noya. "I will check on her before I go home."

"Thank you," she said, and for the first time, the tears tumbled down her cheeks.

The old officer touched my arm. "This is really no place for a lady," he said. "And they're about to close the gates. You should go now."

Mahaley and I hugged each other again and I reluctantly pulled away.

"I will return tomorrow morning," I assured her. She nodded her head and looking over my shoulder, it nearly broke my heart to see her sadly watching me leave.

The officer led me back toward the gates, past the poor, suffering Indians. Several of them were coughing, some painfully. There was also the smell of diarrhea, and I knew that severe illness was rampaging through the stockade.

"Isadora!" I heard someone call, and I turned to see Noya coming toward me, her feet kicking up plumes of dust.

"Noya! Are you alright?"

"Yes," she said as she reached me, and we embraced. "But I know Edward will be worried. He was working at the clinic when they came for me. I was able to leave Peter with Rebecca, our neighbour next door, but I was not able to get any information to Edward."

"I will tell him," I said. "And your mother is here." I pointed to where I had just spoken with Mahaley, and Noya started scanning the faces anxiously. "I have to leave now, but I will be back in the morning." She looked at me again and the fear was plainly visible on her face.

"I love you," she said as she hugged me tightly, and I could feel her tears on the side of my face.

"I love you too," I replied, and I pulled away from her as she went to seek out Mahaley.

The officer resumed leading me to the gate. As he did so, we walked within a few feet of some of the sick Indians.

"These people need medical treatment," I implored. The old officer nodded with a sad resignation.

"I know," he replied as we passed through the gates. "But I'm afraid we can't do anything for them."

"I can help," I said as a thought occurred to me. "Her husband is a doctor," motioning behind me toward Noya. "He works at the mission clinic in Gainesville, and I assist him there myself. I will try to help them when I return tomorrow. Will that be all right?"

I did not know the extent of fellow-feeling that existed in this place, but this officer seemed to possess it. He looked at me with a brief twinkle in his eye.

"Young lady, I admire your spirit. If you want to be here and help, you're welcome to."

"Thank you," I said. "Are you in charge here?"

"Yes ma'am," he replied. "Colonel Thomas Franklin. If anybody interferes with you tomorrow, you just direct them to me."

"Thomas Franklin?" I asked as he helped me up onto the carriage.

"Yes ma'am. Goodbye now." He turned and walked back into the stockade and the gates swung closed.

I was able to drive faster on the way back, and I passed the turn to my house and continued into town. I was thankful that the horses could see where they were going, because I could barely see through the tears. As I got closer to town, I was shocked to see soldiers digging up a grave, but I did not take the time to stop. I drove directly to the clinic. Nobody was there, and the doors were locked.

Next, I went to Noya and Edward's house, and there I found Edward taking Peter home from their neighbour.

"Isadora, they've taken Noya," he said, with a note of panic in his voice.

"I know," I replied. "They've taken Mahaley as well."

"But I don't know where she is."

"I do. I've been there." I told him about what I had seen at the stockade. "The soldiers are keeping them like animals in that horrible place. I'm going to gather some things for Mahaley and go back in the morning. You do the same for Noya. And what about medicine? There are some very sick people there."

"Yes, of course," he said. "I'll go back to the clinic. Do you know what's needed?"

"I did not actually examine anyone, but I heard a lot of severe coughing. There was also the overwhelming smell of diarrhea and vomit."

"Could be whooping cough, dysentery, cholera," he said.

"It's so horrible there, Edward." I could feel the tears coming again, but fought to hold them back. I did not want emotion to get in the way of helping Noya and Mahaley.

"All right, I'll gather what I can" he replied, his voice cracking with emotion.

"Yes, do," I said. "And clothing and blankets. They have absolutely no shelter within the walls of the stockade. Meet me at the boarding house in the morning and we can make the journey together."

It was getting late and would be dark in a couple of hours. I rushed home so I could gather the things I planned to take to the stockade the next morning, but first I stopped at Quentin's house. He heard my carriage approach and the door was open as I came to a stop in front.

"Good Lord, Isadora," he said, "what's happened to you?" Looking down at myself, I realised that my shoes and the bottom of my skirt were covered with filth from the stockade.

"Oh Quentin," I replied tiredly, "it's awful. They are rounding up all the Indians to force them out west. They're holding them in filthy stockades like so much livestock. Mahaley and Noya are there. I will be going back there tomorrow to take them some clothing and blankets." I briefly described the conditions at the

220

stockade again, and I noticed that it never became more believable with the retelling. "How can they treat other people like this?"

"I don't know, dear," he said. "I've seen a lot of bad things in my years as a marshal, and I could never understand what drives some people to do the things they do."

Betsy came down the stairs and displayed relief at seeing me. "Oh honey," she said, "are you alright?"

"Yes, I'm fine Betsy. Thank you. And thank you for watching Clara. Where is she?"

"I just put her to bed. She's asleep."

I glanced at Quentin and he nodded his head. "She can spend the night. In fact you all can. I have plenty of room."

"Thank you so much, Quentin," I said. "I need to gather some things to take to Mahaley and Noya tomorrow, and then I'll be back."

As I went down the front steps and pulled myself up into the carriage, I realised how fatigued I was, physically and emotionally. The ride home was thankfully short, but it was still a chore to unhitch the horse, give her a quick brushing and feed her, along with the other horses.

Then, gathering up the guns, I went to the house, where I noticed that the front door had been broken in. It was getting dark, but I could see candle light flickering against a wall through the door from the library. Creeping quietly to the doorway, I peeked into the room. There stood a white man, his back to me, picking through Mahaley's decorations, glancing at books, and I noticed that he had gathered some things into a pile in one central location, presumably to take with him.

Feeling hatred welling up, I stuck the pistol through my belt and leveled the musket at his back. "Get out of my house," I said firmly. He spun around and seemed startled, first at hearing someone speak, and secondly at seeing a musket pointed at him.

"Hold on there, miss," he said nervously, putting his hands out in front of him. "I thought this house was empty."

221

"Get out of my house," I repeated.

"All right," he said consolingly, as if he were trying to calm me down. "I'll get out. Don't worry." I could see him looking me up and down. "My, you sure are a purty little Indian." He snickered and started inching toward the pile of things he had gathered. "A purty little blonde Indian."

I noticed that there were guns in the pile at the very moment he reached for one. I shot him in the chest.

The moment the shot rang out, I put the musket down and pulled the pistol from my belt, listening for the sound of anyone else in the house. I stood there for at least a minute, my ears straining to hear any sound that did not belong, but thankfully, I heard nothing else.

I pulled myself up the stairs and started gathering blankets, as many as I could carry, even stripping them from the beds. I carried them downstairs and into the library where the intruder had already started making a pile of supplies.

I glanced at the dead man, noticing that I felt nothing, then turned and went back upstairs to Mahaley's room to get some additional clothing for her. I also wanted to provide some shelter for her, but knew we had no tents. I remembered some canvas tarpaulins in the barn, and I went out there, found them, and loaded them onto the back of the wagon.

The exhaustion, and the thought of what had happened that day, remembering Mahaley's and Noya's faces, and the horrible place where they were being kept, made me suddenly feel overwhelmed. I sank down on the ground with my back to the wagon wheel, and I cried. How could these awful things be happening to my friends, my family? How can people be so cold and uncaring about others? There were so few people that I truly cared about any more, and two of them had now been taken from me and placed in horrible, inhuman conditions. I could feel the dark moods descending over me again and I fought desperately against them.

I heard footsteps approaching the barn and I quickly wiped the tears away. Pulling the pistol from my belt, I pointed it at the door, trying to stifle the sobs still racking my body. The barn door was pulled open and Quentin looked in at me.

"Isadora, it's me!" he said, ducking back. I exhaled and lowered the gun, my arms feeling like iron, and I resumed sobbing. Quentin hobbled over to me and held me. "It's all right, honey," he said. "We'll get this figured out. We'll get them back home." I was not sure I believed that any longer, but it felt good to be held and comforted.

"What are you doing here?" I asked when I could speak again.

"Well, Betsy thought she heard a gunshot, but she thought it came from east of us. I didn't hear it at all, so I thought nothing more of it for a minute or two. But then, knowing you were over here alone, I decided to make sure you were all right. I went to the house first and saw the front door was busted in, and I saw the dead man in the library. When I didn't find you in the house, I came out here."

I leaned my head back against the wheel, feeling the exhaustion again. Quentin seemed to notice how I felt, and he pulled himself up.

"You need to get some rest, honey," he said, as he started hitching up horses to the wagon. "We'll load up the stuff you've gathered and take it over to my place where it will be safer overnight, and you can start out tomorrow from there."

He worked quickly, then helped me up onto the wagon, driving it toward the front of the house.

He told me to stay on the wagon while he carried everything out, but I would not allow this partially lame old man to gather it all, so I stubbornly climbed down and helped him. By the time we had finished, the wagon was nearly full of blankets, clothes, and all the guns and ammunition we had. Quentin did not want Betsy, Clara and me living here alone, so we gathered things for us as well.

223

I made one more trip back down to my room. I opened my wardrobe and pulled out the valise that held my gold coins. I picked up the silver artifact from the dresser, remembering the last time Atsila and I had examined it together, and I placed it in the valise, then packed clothing around it. As I got back downstairs, Quentin was placing a note on the door, directing Edward to meet me next door in the morning.

Betsy met me at the door as we arrived back at Quentin's house, and while he drove the wagon around back to tend to the horses, Betsy helped me to bed. I was asleep before she left the room.

Edward arrived early and transferred the things he had brought into my larger wagon. On the way to the stockade I saw, like yesterday, another group of soldiers digging on someone's property, apparently a grave, and I pointed them out to Edward.

"Yes," he said, "someone told me yesterday that the soldiers have been instructed to dig up Cherokee graves to take the silver pendants and other valuables from the corpses."

"Oh, how awful," I said. I experienced a brief moment of wanting to take my guns and open fire on the group of soldiers desecrating the Indians' graves. Fortunately, it passed. We drove the rest of the way in silence.

We arrived at the stockade but the gates were closed. A smaller door opened next to the gate and a young soldier ambled toward us, eyeing us curiously.

"You have business here?" he asked.

"Yes," I replied. "Colonel Franklin said that we could return today to help some of the sick Cherokee."

"Wait here," he said and disappeared back through the door.

A few moments later, the gates were pulled open and we were allowed to enter. Again, the sights and smells assaulted my senses, and I could see that Edward was affected similarly.

"Good God," was all he said.

Once inside the gates, I quickly examined the faces in the crowd, peering through the dusty haze, ooking for familiar features. In a few moments, I located Mahaley. We slowly drove the wagon near the wall of the stockade, around the Indians' camps, and as we approached, Mahaley and Noya saw us and waved. We had barely alighted on the ground and Noya was in Edward's arms and Mahaley in mine.

We exchanged greetings and expressions of concern about their welfare, then went to the back of the wagon to unload the supplies. We left some changes of clothing with Mahaley, as well as the blankets and tarpaulins and some pans and utensils.

"We also brought medicine," Edward said. "Isadora told me how sick some of the people are, and she wanted to help them."

"I do too," said Noya, and she accompanied us, guiding us to some that she knew were especially ill.

"Have you seen the man in charge of this place?" I asked her as we were walking.

"I think so," she said. "There is an older man who seems to have some authority here. The man who was leading you out last night."

"Yes," I replied. "His name is Colonel Thomas Franklin."

"Thomas Franklin?" Noya stopped and grabbed my arm, turning me to look at her. "My grandfather? He's in charge of all this?"

"Well, he is not happy about it." I remembered the sympathy and the embarrassment he displayed as he led me among the wretched prisoners. "I had the impression that he really wanted nothing to do with this. He's the one who granted me permission to come back and help the sick."

At that moment, as Noya was mulling over what I had said about him, I saw Franklin heading toward us.

"So you really came back," he said.

"Yes, Colonel, thank you." I directed his attention to Edward and Noya. "This is Dr. Edward Hodges, and his wife, Noya."

"Pleased to meet you," he said, shaking hands with Edward. "Ma'am," he said with what looked like an expression of shame. He seemed as if it was difficult to meet her eyes. "I used to know someone named Noya."

226

"I was named for my grandmother," she replied. "My grandfather was a young soldier named Thomas Franklin."

He had a sharp intake of breath and looked as if someone had suddenly struck him. He stood frozen in place for a few moments, then turned.

"Excuse me. I'm sorry," he muttered as he quickly walked away.

After exchanging some awkward glances, the three of us started tending to the sick. The suffering of those people was almost more than I could bear. We did very little to help them, aside from providing blankets to those who had none. Those who had cholera or dysentery were often so advanced as to be outside the realm of relief, except for those who finally succumbed to the illness.

There were at least three of those, an old man and two children. They passed away while we were there, but I know they were not isolated incidents. Shortly after we arrived that morning, I observed a couple, under guard, carrying their dead child outside the gates to bury it. Upon closer inspection, I noticed that there were numerous graves outside the stockade.

Seeing that young couple laying their dead child in a shallow grave, among so many other unmarked mounds of earth, touched my heart, and I cried for them.

"I don't know if I was assigned to this post because they knew I would conscientiously try to care for the Indians, or if they did it just to keep me out of the way."

Colonel Franklin had composed himself and come back out, and he seemed to be opening up. Mahaley was also with me, as were Edward and Noya.

"I've seen so much injustice over the years, and I've tried to speak out against it when I can. Unfortunately, most people don't want to hear it, particularly my superiors. I think I've become something of an irritant to them."

He sighed, then turned and looked directly at Noya.

"I was a very young soldier, barely seventeen years old, when I met your grandmother. She was so beautiful, and to an impressionable young boy like me, very exotic."

He smiled and looked off into the distance. For a moment, he was lost in his memories, and I thought he actually looked a little younger then.

"She was such a friendly girl, and she seemed to like me. She was always nearby when I was carrying out my assignments, and was always ready to visit with me.

"In the weeks that followed, we grew very close, and I imagined that we could make a life together. But she didn't share my views. I guess I misinterpreted her friendship for something more." His smile had gradually faded and, once again, Colonel Franklin was an old man.

"I make no excuses for what I did. I was stupid and impetuous, and led by forces and feelings which were not yet fully under my control or understanding. Afterwards, I was so ashamed. I couldn't bear to see her face, to see the resentment in her eyes. To see her looking at me but to not see the friendship anymore, well, I asked for a transfer of assignment after that."

He stared at the ground for a moment, then looked up at Noya.

"Did she and your father have a happy life?"

"Yes, they did," she said. I had the impression that she was deeply touched by Colonel Franklin's story, and by his obvious remorse, and chose to not provide details of the hardships. *"She married a very good Cherokee man who raised my father as his own son."*

"I'm glad," he said. He sat up, straightening his back, and took a deep breath, expelling it loudly as if he were attempting to cleanse his soul.

"I'm retiring in a few weeks. I'm too old to do this. I've seen enough. What we're doing to the Cherokee, and what we did to the Seminoles and the Creeks and the Chickasaws and countless others before them . . . ." He shook his head and sighed again.

228

"I've carried out too many orders that I didn't agree with. I'm just tired of it all."

"The Cherokee removal," I said, "when is it scheduled to take place?"

"It's already taking place," he replied. "The first group was forced out in April, and a few other groups have gone since then. Unfortunately, several Indians have died along the way, and John Ross has asked that the removal be suspended until the weather cools."

"And until then, what?" I asked.

"I will do all I can to provide for the needs of the Cherokee in my care," replied Colonel Franklin.

"Sir, are you implying that these people have to stay in this compound through the summer?" Edward asked with a tone of disbelief.

"Until further notice, yes, I'm afraid that's the way it looks." Seeing the dispirited expressions on Noya's and Mahaley's faces, he quickly looked away, again seeming ashamed.

Before Edward and I left, we erected shelters for Mahaley and Noya, using the canvas tarpaulins that I had brought. I felt as if my heart were being torn apart when Mahaley held me tightly as we were saying goodbye. Noya was weeping in Edward's arms, and I felt divided, as if I should stay here with them. I felt guilty for going back home, to sleep in a comfortable bed while Noya and Mahaley would be sleeping outside on the ground, surrounded by sick and dying people, the odours of death and disease wafting about them.

Several detachments of Cherokee, as Colonel Franklin had told us, had already left for the new Indian Territory. They were sent by boat on the Tennessee River, to the Ohio River, the Mississippi River and finally the Arkansas River which ultimately arrived at the Indian Territory. As the summer progressed, though, water levels lowered considerably due to an unprecedented drought.

In July, in addition to postponing subsequent removals until cooler weather, John Ross, along with the Cherokee National Council, made another request. They asked President Van Buren to allow them to oversee the Cherokee removal themselves, instead of the military doing so. The President agreed and John Ross and his brother Lewis began making preparations. He organised twelve different groups to be supervised by either full-blood Cherokee tribal leaders or educated mixed bloods.

During their forced stay at the stockade in Georgia, Noya and Mahaley were helped a great deal by Colonel Franklin. Conditions were undeniably awful. The food the government provided for the Indians was frequently stolen and sold. In its stead, the Indians were provided spoiled meat and wormy flour and corn meal.

Also, it was not uncommon for girls and young women to be forced into the surrounding woods by soldiers and violated. And of course, diseases wiped out many individuals. But Colonel Franklin took it upon himself to protect Noya and Mahaley, insulating them from some of the worst conditions that he knew existed there.

In late summer, Mahaley and Noya were transferred along with several other Cherokee in the stockade to a fort in eastern Tennessee. As this was over one hundred miles away, this naturally precluded the possibility of driving there regularly to see them and care for the needs of other Cherokee.

Shortly after this, Edward told us goodbye and took Peter up to the new location, intending to accompany Noya and Mahaley on their forced removal. Making himself known to John Ross, it was determined that he would be one of the doctors assigned to whichever group Noya would ultimately be in.

Some were thinking that the removal would resume sometime in September, but nobody really knew for certain. Due to the low levels of the rivers, though, it was decided that the remaining detachments would be moved over land.

During the heart rending pain and sorrow of this time, Quentin and Betsy found some happiness. They were quietly married in a small private ceremony in town. They had been drawing closer to each other for some time, and living in the same house as we had been for the last three months only served to precipitate the inevitable.

In early September, I myself made a momentous decision.

"Are you certain about this, Isadora?" Quentin asked. His face wore a worried expression.

"Mahaley and Noya are the only family I have," I responded. "I can't bear to just stay here while they are forced to march hundreds of miles away from their home."

"Are you prepared to make that kind of journey?"

"Quentin, I am prepared to bear the hardships of this journey myself and to do whatever I can to make my family's journey easier as well."

"Sure, honey, I appreciate your feelings, but are you really aware of what this means?"

"Yes, Quentin, I am fully aware," I said as the tears started trickling down my cheeks. "I cannot just stay here while my mother and my sister are taken away from me again."

He could see my determination and made no further objections. As I wiped away the tears, we finished the business we were conducting. Signing the deed to the boarding house over to him, he paid me $500, a paltry sum for the house and land, but I was happy to get it, to be on my way. He had lost some money when the banks failed the previous year, and I was not going to press for more.

I had already sold most of the horses and purchased two spans of oxen, and Quentin helped me to equip the wagon with bows to support a canvas cover. I had also secured many supplies for the journey, and I wasted no time in loading them into the wagon.

Quentin had very cleverly created some hiding places in the wagon in order for me to conceal guns and other valuables. As I was feeling nervous about taking well over a thousand dollars in gold with me on this excursion, I was happy to be able to have it all tucked away in a secret place.

Clara, now six years old, was eagerly anticipating the journey. To her, it was simply going to be an adventure, and she knew nothing of the hardships that would become a part of our daily lives for the duration of the trip. That innocence reminded me of myself just nine years earlier.

A few days before I had determined to leave, Quentin asked a favour of me.

"You remember, don't you, when we first met, and I explained about Jimmy and Alice?"

"Yes, of course," I replied.

"Would you take them with you?" he asked. "If they could go posing as your slaves, they could get out of Georgia and get their first real taste of freedom."

"Oh, Quentin, that would be wonderful for them. Indeed I would be happy for them to join us."

"Thank you, Isadora. I'll send three horses with them. They can use one as a pack horse, so they won't have to take up space in your wagon." With that, he created a spurious bill of sale in case anyone questioned me about them.

So, having amazed myself at how quickly I could arrange a complete life change, with tears in my eyes, I waved goodbye to Quentin and Betsy. I was leaving, not only the modern conveniences to which I had become accustomed during the past years, but also two good friends and the only home I had known in nearly a decade.

Driving on decent roads most of the distance, we made fairly good time, although I still chafed at the slowness of our travel. Apparently Clara did too, as she kept asking if we were almost there.

Our trip to Tennessee was uneventful, but it took us over a week to get there, and I was afraid that Mahaley and Noya's group

234

might begin their march before I arrived. I needn't have worried, though. By the time I reached the fort where they were being held, their departure date was still uncertain.

They were happy to see us when we arrived. And they were surprised that we were planning to travel the entire distance with them.

"Are you mad?" Noya asked as she grabbed me and hugged me tightly. Mahaley was standing nearby and was smiling, but still considering me as if I were perhaps not quite right.

"We are going west," she said, "toward the Darkening Land." The Cherokee believed that the place of the dead was in the west, toward the setting sun.

"You two are my family," I said. "All of my memories from the last nine years include you. 'Whither thou goest, I will go'," I said, quoting Ruth from the Bible. They both smiled and held me close.

Conditions here were somewhat better, but still horribly offensive. The drought ended and the rainy weather in the early autumn added mud to the conditions inside the forts. Disease continued to be a problem here, and Edward was kept busy tending to sick Cherokee, but they benefitted little since they had to remain in their filthy conditions.

The grounds outside the fort, like the stockade in Georgia, were dotted with numerous Cherokee graves. Edward insisted that Noya not help him, as he did not want to risk her health, so Noya spent her time with Peter and Mahaley. Before they left Georgia, I had brought them some books, so they had some little means of distraction, but the death and mourning surrounding them made these diversions difficult and fleeting.

For the duration of my stay here, I was fortunate to have found and rented a small enclosed field a short distance from the fort. Here the oxen and the one horse I had kept, along with Jimmy and Alice's horses, had a little room to move about and graze. We set up our camp on the edge of this field where we would sleep at night. During the days, I arranged for Peter to come out of the

235

fort, and Jimmy and Alice kindly watched him and Clara when I was with Noya and Mahaley.

Finally, nearly a month after I arrived, the order was given to load up and march. Our group was to be under the supervision of Richard Taylor, a chief of the Cherokee, appointed by John Ross. After the long wait, despite the hardships that I knew awaited us on the march, I was eager to be underway. The sooner an unpleasantness is begun, the sooner it will be over, as my mother might have said.

feel so much better!" Dora said.

"Why? What do you mean?" Shawn asked.

"I saw the bill of sale for two slaves in the trunk upstairs and got a nervous feeling the other day. I'm happy to see that that was just a bogus cover story."

Shawn smiled. "I'd say you and Isadora are both cut from the same cloth."

"I don't know about that. Isadora seems to be a lot more adventurous than I am."

"But you're both humanitarians. You both have the desire to help those less fortunate, and you both follow through on that desire," he persisted.

"Well, I'm flattered by the comparison," Dora said humbly. "But with that, I'm going to have to get to bed." Shawn looked at his watch and saw that it was after ten o'clock.

"You're right," he agreed. "You should get some sleep. Do you want me to sleep on the sofa?"

"You don't have to sleep on the sofa. There are plenty of furnished bedrooms for you to sleep in. But yes, after the attempted break-in this evening, I was going to ask if you would mind staying overnight."

"It's not a problem. So what time do we need to get up for the funeral?"

"Shawn, you really don't have to go to my grandmother's funeral with me," she said.

"I know I don't. So what time should we get up?"

237

Dora smiled and gave him a long hug.

There was a good turnout at the funeral. It was not a crowd, but several older friends of Dora's grandparents came to pay their respects. Some of them, Dora knew from years ago. Others she met for the first time at the funeral home. They were all very happy to see her.

Shawn generally kept quiet and stayed in the background, but he was always at her side to offer support. During the service, Dora leaned against him and slipped her arm through his, and kept it there till the end.

"Thank you," she said when they were on the way home.

"For what?" he asked.

"Just for being there. I didn't have a hard time at the funeral as I thought I might, but still it was nice having a friend there with me. Even a friend I've only had for three days."

"God, is that all?" he said. "It feels like I've known you for at least four and a half."

She smiled as they pulled up in front of her house.

"Are you coming in?" she asked.

"I will if you want me to," he replied easily.

"We have to see what's going on with Isadora."

When we first started out, we very slowly made our way north. This painfully slow initial progress was, I understood, due to efforts to coordinate our movements with those of other groups. And even once we were under way, our progress was often still hindered by the slowness of the detachment ahead of us, led in part by a man named James Wofford who, by at least one account, was a drinker.

Some of the men would, during the course of our journey, stray off the trail to hunt or forage. So as not to tax the natural resources of the area, we tried to keep a good distance behind Wofford's group.

Our group had, besides Edward, another doctor named William Morrow. This man displayed early on that he felt little regard for the Cherokee. He was seldom to be seen in the camp and seemed rather to look for ways and opportunities to be away from them. Almost every night of the journey, he stayed with friends and other white people along the way and did little to attend to the medical needs of the Indians. As a result, Edward was kept quite busy.

There was also a minister, a Reverend Daniel Butrick. He was a controversial figure. Due to his strong stance in favour of the Cherokee, a people to whom he had ministered for about twenty years, and his belief that they were actually the lost tribes of Israel, he formed an unbreakable bond with them. He could often be found visiting individual Cherokees throughout the journey, and displayed a great love and fellow feeling toward them.

The second in command of our group was a Cherokee named Walter Adair. He rode in front, leading our detachment in the direction we were to go. Richard Taylor, the Cherokee chief assigned to oversee our group, brought up the rear. Though I personally had no dealings with him, he seemed a fair man. While he drove our detachment fairly hard, he was never unreasonable. He himself was being driven to get the job done, but on several occasions, he allowed us to camp in one place for longer than one night if the weather or health matters called for it.

The first major operation involved crossing the Tennessee River. This was accomplished in early November by ferry at Vann's Town, and it was a harrowing experience. The ferry was often overloaded and more than once threatened to capsize. This operation took all day, as can be imagined, since our group consisted of over one thousand people, besides animals and a few wagons.

Once across the river, we were able to move somewhat faster. But it was heartbreaking to see these people, many of them already weakened by sickness, grief or old age, or a combination, struggling to walk all day, leaving the only home they had ever known. Their faces were lined with worry and sadness, and I was constantly on the verge of tears on their behalf.

Mahaley continued an activity she had begun in the stockades. When we stopped and camped for the night, she would gather the children who were nearby and relate to them some Cherokee wisdom or folklore. An idea had begun forming in her mind, about which she had spoken to me, of compiling a library of these stories. I encouraged her to this end, and she seemed excited about it. She actually began looking forward to reaching our destination so that she could begin. One evening early on our journey, she related the story of the cedar tree.

"A long time ago, the Cherokee people thought that life would be much better if there was no night, only sunny days. They asked the Creator if he would make it day all the time so there would *never be any darkness." She spoke very easily to the children, in a voice that they found very appealing, and they all paid close attention to her.*

"The Creator listened to them and made the night stop so that it was day all the time. But very soon, the forest grew so thick that it became difficult for them to walk through it and to find their paths. The people had to work much harder in their gardens to keep the weeds pulled from the corn. It got very hot and the people could not sleep, and they became short tempered and argued a lot.

"It did not take them long to realise that this was not a good idea, so the people asked the Creator, 'Please, we have made a mistake. We don't want it to be day all the time. Please make it night all the time instead.' The Creator loved the people and he decided to do as they asked and he made it night all the time.

"So the day ended and night fell upon the earth. Soon, their crops stopped growing and it got very cold. The people could not see to hunt, and with no crops growing, they were soon very cold, weak and hungry, and many of them died."

Looking around, I could see that, not only were the children enthralled with her, but the adults were too.

"Those who were still alive prayed again to the Creator. 'Help us, please. We have made another mistake. You made the day and night perfect from the beginning. Please forgive us and make the day and night as it was before.'

"Again the Creator listened to the people. The day and the night became as it had been in the beginning. Each day was evenly divided between light and darkness. The weather became more pleasant, the crops began to grow again and the hunting was good.

"The people were happy, and they thanked the Creator for their life and for all the food they had to eat. The Creator accepted the thanks of the people and was very glad to see them smiling again.

"However, during the time of the long darkness, many people had died, and the Creator was very sad about that. So he put their

241

spirits in a new tree he made. This tree was named a-tsi-na tlu-gv, the cedar tree.

"So now, when you smell the cedar tree, or when you see it standing in the forest, remember that you are looking upon your ancestors."

A pleasant silence settled over the group and the children smiled. I noticed that the adults smiled too, though their smiles seemed somewhat melancholy. Then one of the children broke the silence.

"But we aren't taking the cedar trees with us," she said with a concerned expression on her face. "Won't our ancestors get lonely here without us?"

Nobody had an answer and a heavy sadness seemed to settle over the group, and eventually, they dispersed to their own camps to get some rest.

Each day was a monotony of weary travel. The scenery slowly changed, as did the company, since some days Mahaley rode with me, other days Noya. Some days, I walked, depending on the terrain, so as not to overtax the animals. Peter often rode in our wagon so that he and Clara could have companionship, playing childish games and bouncing on the cotton-filled mattress that I had brought. But it was heartbreaking to see other individuals stumbling along, ill-clothed for the cold weather. I shared what I could, but soon had little more to spare.

Occasionally we would see white people on the way, and I was happy to see that some of them seemed sympathetic to the plight of the Cherokee. Some, though, were there to prey on them. There were those who set up "whiskey shops" on the way, near the camps. As a result, there were often drunken brawls in the evenings, punctuated by loud oaths, which made a good night's sleep rather elusive.

Others hid their hostility beneath a cloak of charity. At one point, a group of people met us on the way with stacks of blankets

242

as gifts for the Indians. Belatedly we learned that they were used blankets from a hospital that had recently seen a smallpox outbreak.

Whether this contributed to the illness of our company, I cannot say with any positive assurance, but the knowledge of this resulted in our being refused passage through certain towns and villages, which often meant a deviation of several miles.

I was also saddened by the sight of new graves along the way, some from previous groups, but some from our own as well. While there were a few babies born on the trail, our number was reduced by the death of some who finally succumbed to the illnesses that afflicted them, or by old age giving in to the strenuous exertions of the march.

It was at the end of November, after we had passed Nashville, Tennessee, that Noya became ill.

Noya had been riding with Edward on their wagon, wrapped in a blanket against the cold, when she started feeling fatigued. Their wagon was smaller than mine, but there was room for them to unroll some bedding for her to lie down. We stopped to make these arrangements, and I was helping her into the back.

"Noya," I said, feeling her hands, then her forehead, "you feel particularly warm." This caught Edward's attention and he examined her more closely. She had a fever and soreness in her throat, besides feeling very tired. Edward said little, but I could see the worry in the grim set of his face as he helped her into the bed.

"I will ride with her," Mahaley said. "I want to take care of her while we are traveling."

"All right," said Edward. Then he turned to me. "Would you mind taking Peter with you in your wagon?"

"Yes, of course," I replied. "Do you know what it is?"

"Well, she's not coughing yet, so I don't know if it's the beginnings of whooping cough or just the common cold. But of course, in these conditions, even the common cold can be fatal."

243

"Oh dear," I said, as I felt the considerable weight of worry settle upon me. The rest of the detachment continued trudging along past us, and we finished making adjustments to our wagons, tightening the canvas covers to block as much of the frigid wind as possible.

"Keep yourself and the children warm," Edward admonished, as we both climbed back up onto our respective wagons to continue our journey.

That evening, Noya started coughing. In time, her coughing fits led to difficulty breathing and were often so violent that they were followed by vomiting. The poor woman was in terrible distress, but Mahaley was tireless in caring for her, especially when Edward was called upon to look after someone else and could not be with her.

During the first week of December, two children died, one from whooping cough. I remembered that this child had been one that had been in our camp, and had contact with Mahaley and Noya. She was one of the children who enjoyed Mahaley's storytelling sessions, and Mahaley was heartbroken when she heard about her death.

But her grief was lessened a bit when Noya started feeling better. After a few days, Noya could start taking in food without prompting a coughing attack. She was weak and tired, but we were much relieved to see her on the mend.

Then Mahaley started coughing.

Mahaley seemed to have it much worse. In the evenings, during her illness, I would often sit with her and speak about her idea of creating a collection of Cherokee stories. While she was usually unable to contribute to the conversation without coughing, it did seem to cheer her to listen, and to get her mind off of her discomfort.

Unfortunately, her discomfort only worsened. Her coughing attacks became so hard that she would be doubled up in bed, grasping her sides in pain. These fits would be followed by vomiting and gasping for breath. After a while, she could not even eat without coughing and vomiting it back up, and this went on for about three weeks. The dear woman suffered so much that when she finally died at the end of December, we knew it was a relief.

She died in the afternoon, as we were still traveling. I suddenly heard Noya wailing in the back of their wagon. Edward pulled off the trail and stopped, and I followed suit. I jumped down from my wagon and ran to theirs and looked inside. Edward was holding Noya in his arms and trying to comfort her. Mahaley lay there on the bedding, very small and still, her body emaciated after her extended illness. I looked at her face, now gaunt and ashen, but still possessing a touch of her former beauty. I left Edward and Noya to themselves and stepped back outside, where my tears broke loose.

I leaned against the wagon and buried my head in my arms and sobbed, feeling the darkness descending over me again. I had now lost my second mother and felt an incomprehensible agony deep inside. I don't know how long I stood there thus, but the thought of Clara entered my mind, and I knew I had to be strong for her. And for Noya.

I wiped my eyes on the blanket that was draped about me, and I turned around, leaning my back against the wagon, but the sobs were still coming.

The detachment continued filing past as the sound of Noya's crying could be heard by all, and their faces, though etched with their own worries, expressed sympathy for our family. Finally, at the rear of the column, I could see Richard Taylor riding closer. He had heard the sound many times before and, though he did not stop, he sadly removed his hat and bowed his head as he passed.

In a few minutes, needing to stay with our detachment, we got under way again. The rest of that day, I could hear occasional sobs from Noya in the back of their wagon. I tried not to cry myself as I attempted to answer the questions that kept coming from Clara and Peter about what was wrong.

We were in Kentucky, approaching the Ohio River, and when we stopped for the evening, Edward, Jimmy and I, assisted by two Cherokee men whose names I'm afraid I failed to ask, scraped a hole through the snow and the frozen ground as deep as we could manage. There, we gently deposited Mahaley's body and covered it up.

A few other Indians gathered with our family around the new grave, some who had been friends in Georgia, and some we had met on the trail and who had enjoyed Mahaley's storytelling. Few words were spoken, but a couple of them started singing Amazing Grace, *a song that had become an anthem of sorts for the Cherokee while on this march. Everybody joined in, those of us who did not know the Cherokee lyrics singing in English, and by the time the song was complete, most of us were in tears.*

Noya was inconsolable and cried for hours after Mahaley's death. The next day, we had come to a stop a few miles from the Ohio River with another detachment ahead of us. Nobody could move because of the snow and the frigid cold. Due to ice in the river, the ferry could not run, so we were stranded where we were for the indefinite future.

Wrapped in two blankets, I was sitting on a rock before a fire that struggled to remain burning in the cold wind. The wind brought tears to my eyes, as did my thoughts. I had been contemplating the last nine years, and I found myself weeping anew at the loved ones I had lost during that time. Liam, my mother, my father, my sister, Atsila, and now Mahaley. I sighed and shook my head, hoping to clear some of the sadness from my mind, though I knew that this was a hopeless endeavour.

Never before until now had I been ashamed of the colour of my skin. The cruelty being leveled against these people by the white man would have been difficult to believe had I not witnessed it myself. Knowing that, despite my skin colour, many of them considered me a friend was a source of pride to me now.

I poked the fire which caused it to flare up a little and, in so doing provided a bit more heat for a second or two. Sitting with my back against the wagon wheel, I pulled my blankets tighter around myself. Tilting my head to the side, I listened, waiting for a lull in the wind. When it came, and the rushing sound of the wind through the rocks and bare-limbed trees died down, I was able to hear the people around me.

I could hear the sounds of mourning Indians, but I was pleased to notice that those sounds were not coming from   Edward and Noya's wagon. At that moment, Edward came down from their wagon and stretched. He saw me sitting before my fire and walked over to join me.

"Edward," I said, "I don't think I can take any more."

"Well, I'll tell you this," he replied with a tired smile, "I've never known a stronger woman than you, Isadora Byrnes."

"Strong? I feel so empty and drained of strength."

"I think it's because of you, Isadora, that Noya is still alive. After she lost the baby, she was in such a deep melancholy that I feared that she would do herself harm. But your efforts in cheering her finally brought her back." I scoffed at his statement and shook my head.

"It wasn't just me, Edward."

"No, others joined in and helped," he said, "but you got it started. Noya has often spoken to me of how she loves you as a friend and a sister."

I looked at him and smiled at the statement, but had to wipe yet another tear from my eyes. Edward looked up toward his wagon, then back at me.

"And now, you seem to have done it again," he said.

"What do you mean?"

"You suggested that Peter and Clara play together in our wagon instead of your own."

We listened for a moment to the sound of the children playing and laughing within their wagon, and I could hear Noya speaking

247

softly to them. Edward and I looked back at each other, and he smiled at me.

"You knew it would help Noya," he said.

"I thought it might."

"Thank you." He stood up and seemed to shiver slightly, then turned and went back to his wagon.

Darkness was descending and so was the already piercing cold. I had wanted some time alone, but now, finishing my lonely sojourn outside, I decided that it was time to seek shelter once again.

We remained where we were for about two weeks, waiting for the weather to ease and for the ferry to begin running again. When it finally started, the ferry owner, a Mr. Berry, seeing an opportunity to profit greatly from the misfortune of others, charged each person a dollar to cross.

The regular price was twelve cents.

With at least one group ahead of us, it took us a few weeks to make it across the southern extremity of Illinois. Once we reached the Mississippi River, we had to wait again, due to ice and bad weather.

While camped in southern Illinois, we sometimes saw a few surly looking white people, watching from a distance. In fact, even though we were unable to make any progress during the weeks when we were here, we often had to break camp and move anyway because angry or unsympathetic landowners did not want us on their lands.

"Several Cherokee were murdered by locals right around here," said Jimmy. He saw me sitting by the fire and had come to join me. I was happy to see him. He and Alice had been keeping to themselves for much of the journey.

"How do you know that?" I asked.

"I was talking to Reverend Butrick. He said it happened to some earlier groups that passed by here."

I looked back at the local people who were watching and felt a shiver that was not related to the cold. I hated them, and I struggled with that knowledge. I knew that it was illogical. I had no way of knowing if those particular people in the distance had ill feelings toward the Indians, but they were white. Despite being white myself, I did not trust them, because so few white people had given me any reason to.

"How are you and Alice faring?" I asked, attempting to change the subject. Jimmy was wearing a heavy coat and was wrapped in a blanket but, as was the case with all of us, it just did not seem to be enough.

"We're doing fine," he replied. "The tents don't keep out the cold, but it blocks the wind anyways." I nodded and adjusted my blanket around my ears.

"Miss Isadora," he said, "Alice and me, well we just wanted to tell you that we appreciate what you're doing for us. I know you wasn't planning on taking no Negroes with you, but Mr Quentin explained to us what he asked you to do."

"Jimmy, I'm very happy that I could do this. I hope you and Alice are able to make a happy life for yourselves." The wind seemed to pick up, blowing the blanket away from my ears. But I was glad to see that the local people in the distance seemed to be dispersing. "If only we can get moving again."

Squinting his eyes against the cold wind, Jimmy nodded and stood up to head back to the relative shelter of his tent. "Thank you," he said, and he walked away.

That night, I heard footsteps crunching in the snow outside our wagon. Clara was asleep in my arms and we had all the blankets we owned covering us. Edward and Noya's wagon was next to ours, and the wind had died down enough that I could hear the steady breathing of their family as they slept.

Again, I heard shuffling in the snow, and quiet whispering. I slowly reached into one of the secret compartments that Quentin had fashioned and pulled out a pistol. Trying not to wake Clara, I moved to the back of the wagon and gently pulled the canvas aside, just enough to peek outside.

The moon was out, and the sky had cleared enough that a pale bluish light reflected off the snow to illuminate the camp. There, I saw three people, white men, approaching the Hodges' wagon. One of them was carrying a burlap bag, and from the apparent weight of it, there were some items already in it.

As one of the men reached for the canvas of the Hodges' wagon, I spoke up.

"What are you doing?" All three of them were startled and turned in my direction. They could not see me, as the canvas was still only slightly parted, but they started in my direction, and I was disconcerted to see that one of them was holding a knife. "What do you want?" I asked, raising my voice.

"We're just having a look around," one of them said.

As they approached, I pulled the canvas apart and, pointing the pistol at them, I raised my voice even more. "Give me a reason to shoot you."

Seeing the pistol, they stopped. "Easy there, ma'am," the man said quietly. "We was just –"

Having heard my voice, a few Cherokee men emerged from their tents to investigate. The white men, seeing now that they were outnumbered and outgunned, and very nearly surrounded, dropped the bag and fled. A Cherokee man who was closest to the bag picked it up and looked inside.

"It's full of jewelry," he said. Several Cherokee were gathered around and looking into the bag as I climbed down from my wagon.

"This belongs to my wife," said another man, as he pulled a beaded necklace out of the bag.

As others crowded around, they found things that belonged to them or to someone they knew. Suddenly, a scream cut through the night air and everyone rushed to the tent where it originated. An Indian woman I had met on a couple of occasions backed out of her tent on her knees, crying. As she sobbed, the flaps of the tent were thrown back to reveal her husband, his throat cut. A friend

251

standing nearby took the woman in her arms and held her as she cried. Someone who knew her recognised some of her jewelry in the bag.

"Check all the tents," said Adalonige'i, a tribal elder. "Look for the footprints of those men and see if you can tell what tents they went to."

The scream and all the subsequent activity had caused others to stir, so most of the camp was awake. I went back to the wagon and found that Clara, thankfully, was still asleep, but Noya, Edward and Peter were up.

"What happened?" asked Edward, rubbing his eyes.

"Some white men came into the camp to rob us," I explained. Then, gesturing toward the woman who was crying, "She had some items stolen, and her husband's throat has been cut."

"Oh, how awful!" said Noya.

"Poor fellow," said Edward.

"He probably stirred when the men were in his tent and they killed him to keep him quiet," I said.

After a quick search of the camp, everybody reported back to Adalonige'i.

"We found two more dead, but from illness," declared one who seemed to have taken charge of the search.

"You are certain they were not murdered?" the elder asked them.

"No, they both had been suffering from the bowel complaint."

"All right. That is little comfort to their families, but at least there was no further violence."

Everyone was shaken and seemed hesitant to go back to their tents. But as it was so cold, and there was little more to be done, eventually the crowd dispersed and we all tried to get some more sleep.

The dead were buried in the morning. Soon afterward we were informed that it looked as if we would be breaking camp in the next day or so.

During the next few days, the weather improved enough that we were able to start moving closer to the Mississippi River. But another lengthy operation still awaited us as the ferry moved the group ahead of us across. All told, it was not until the middle of February that we were able to start making any real progress again.

The weather in Missouri for the rest of February and into March alternated between cold and snowy and cold and rainy. As with all the previous months of our journey, Edward was kept busy as almost every family had someone who was ill. He often lamented that there was little he could do for them aside from offering comfort and occasionally bleeding them. Victims who succumbed to their illnesses were buried in hastily scraped graves at almost every stop.

In the middle of March, in southwestern Missouri, there was an accident. Somehow a wagon had run over a little boy's head and neck, and the poor child was in severe pain. The ground had been soft and absorbed a good deal of the impact, and fortunately there were no broken bones.

Edward tried to make him as comfortable as possible, but decided that there was little that he could do for him. Dr Morrow was even called from wherever he was staying that particular evening, and he found that he could do nothing for him either. Edward said that that was the first night that he had seen Morrow actually stay in the camp.

Happily, the next day, the little boy was found to be doing much better.

Our march across Missouri and the northwestern portion of Arkansas continued with a grim monotony, and finally at the end of March, 1839, we arrived in the Indian Territory. All told, our journey had taken about five months, and although fifteen babies were born during those months, at least fifty-five people had died. From what I heard later, the other detachments reported similar results.

253

John Ross and his family traveled with a group that left after us, and sadly his wife died on the way. Based on the official reports that were compiled from all the detachments, at least a thousand Cherokee died on this forced march, although some estimate that the actual number was at least four times that number. There was not a single person who made the march who had not lost at least one loved one on the way.

Our journey ended at Tahlequah, a new town that was now the capital of the Cherokee nation. We were met by mounted soldiers in uniform, posted at Fort Gibson. I must admit that I felt an initial disquietude at seeing them approach. But apparently it was simply a formality since, after the leaders of our group reported to them, they directed us to the settlements and then left us alone. I was very happy to see the white soldiers ride away.

The town was settled in forested land in the hills near the base of the Missouri and Arkansas mountains we had just descended. Under different circumstances, we might have appreciated the beauty of the area. Initially, though, the feeling that most of us experienced was simply relief that the long march was finally over.

We camped for a while near the banks of the Illinois River, but we soon discovered that we were not so welcome here in the Indian Territory either.

ora sighed, and Shawn looked at her. There was sadness in her eyes.

"What's wrong?" asked Shawn. "Mahaley?"

"No. Well partly, yes, the poor thing. She was such a sweet lady."

"I know. I'm going to miss her in Isadora's narrative."

"But not just her," Dora said. "All of them. We put them through such hell."

Shawn nodded and they were silent for a few moments.

"Isadora's description of Mahaley when she died reminded me of my own mother," Dora said. "I mean the circumstances were completely different, obviously. But when I found her that morning, I noticed how gaunt and emaciated she was."

"You're the one who found your mother dead?" Shawn asked with sympathetic disbelief.

"Yes. She was deeply depressed and taking medication, but apparently it wasn't enough. So one evening, she got undressed and climbed in the bathtub, filled it with water and sliced open her wrists."

"Oh my God."

"Her mood had been so dark and hopeless. I had tried to convince her to get some counseling, but she would never agree to it, so I just made it a point to call her two or three times a day and visit her every day after work.

"I had just left her place and had gone home for the night. I tried calling her before I went to bed, but there was no answer, so

I assumed she had gone to bed herself. When I still couldn't reach her by phone the next morning I went to her apartment.

"I hadn't realized before that morning, seeing her naked and small in that tub, how thin she had become. Her face was partly under the bloody water and her eyes were still open, but blank." Dora shuddered and shook her head at the memory.

"I'm so sorry!" Shawn said, his arm around her shoulders. "How long ago was that?"

"About six years ago. But there's not a day that goes by that I don't see that image in my mind."

"I can't even imagine how horrible that must have been. Your father was gone by then?"

"Yes, he had left the year before. Haven't heard from him ever since. He was a mess himself, so it wouldn't surprise me if he was dead too."

"So you're basically an orphan like Isadora and Noya." Dora nodded and leaned her head against Shawn's shoulder.

"These are Cherokee people!" Noya barked as she brushed dirt off of her clothing. Dirt and debris were clinging to her hair and she started combing her fingers through it. She and I had gone into Tahlequah for supplies and had met with hostility. "They are acting like the white people in Georgia who took our land from us."

"I don't understand," said Edward. "They threw dirt at you?"

"The children threw dirt," I explained. "The adults only sneered with contempt. The owner of the store ignored us for as long as he could, making it a point to serve people who came in after us."

"Why would they do that?"

"I've been hearing about feelings of animosity and bitterness between the ones who moved out here earlier and those who waited," I answered. "Many of those in our group have said that they have experienced the same."

"It is as if the rivalry between the Ridge and the Ross factions has followed us and resumed out here," Noya said bitterly.

Edward sighed. "I had hoped that this experience would have united all the Cherokee."

"Well," I observed, "they seem to be as polarised as before, if not more so."

"And," added Noya, "the Old Settlers want to hold on to the old ways of the Cherokee, which is partly what moved them to come out here in the first place, and they resent those who chose to adopt the ways of the white man."

257

I remembered Atsila talking about his father's desire to con-
tinue the traditional Cherokee ways, and the memory brought a
brief pang to my heart. I could certainly understand the desire, but
I did not agree with the idea of hating or mistreating those who do
not believe the same way.

It was May, 1839, and though we had been in Indian Territory
for two months, we had not begun setting down roots yet. We
moved camp a few times, looking over the area, but we often en-
countered the hostility of the Old Settlers.

Of our immediate party, Jimmy and Alice seemed to be the only
ones who felt accepted. Along the trail, Jimmy had met and be-
come friends with Amonida, a young Cherokee girl who had rela-
tives who had moved to Indian Territory earlier. Being free Ne-
groes now, he and Alice were often invited to the home of
Amonida's relatives, and over the course of the last two months, a
romance seemed to be growing.

But Noya was becoming very disillusioned about life here, and
truth be told, I was too. Then, in June, more blood was shed.

In an apparently well-orchestrated plan, Major Ridge was shot
and killed by multiple gunmen. At almost the same moment, his
son John was dragged from his home by several Cherokee and
stabbed over forty times in front of his wife and children. And, also
at the same time, another group of Cherokee killed Elias Boudinot
with several tomahawk blows to the head. Those investigating the
murders determined that all three of these men were assassinated,
without the backing of the Cherokee Nation as a whole, for their
role as leaders in signing the unsupported treaty of New Echota.
The killings were carried out by supporters of John Ross, though
Ross himself was not implicated.

These murders, closely following the personal hostility we had
been receiving, prompted a family discussion.

"I do not want to live here," Noya said.

"I know, honey," Edward said. "But where can we go? The
Cherokee were forced out of their homeland. We can't go back."

"I don't want to go back," she said. "I am not feeling homesick for Georgia. I want to be away from the enmity and animosity. I want to be able to raise Peter among people who don't hate each other."

"I had hoped that getting away from the white man would accomplish that," I said. "Perhaps these Cherokee have been too influenced by them."

"Yes, perhaps," Edward agreed.

"Well, I do not want to live among people who act like this," Noya said with determination.

"Again, honey, where could we go?"

"I don't know!" she answered, shaking her head and throwing her hands in the air, clearly frustrated.

"Maybe I can help," I offered. "I have been experiencing similar feelings, and I remembered my original plan when I came to America." I produced the map that Danny O'Riordan had sent to Liam so many years ago. "It would mean another long journey, but if we were to get started soon, I am certain that we can finish it before winter and it would not be so difficult."

I explained to them how I had come to America with the plan to make my way to the Rocky Mountains, and I opened the map which clearly delineated the states to the east, and the Louisiana Purchase to the west. In this area, it showed very little detail, although there were some hand-scrawled notes and markings which Danny had made. I told them of Danny's description of life in the Rocky Mountains, at the extreme western end of the territory, and I could see a light forming in Noya's eyes. As Edward had no personal ties to anyone in Indian Territory outside of his family, he was also willing to explore this option.

So the next day, I saddled my horse. Donning a pair of trousers which I am not ashamed to say I sometimes used to be better able to ride astride a horse, I rode west toward Fort Gibson in hopes that I could find and hire a guide to lead us westward. I felt a severe inner discomfort at purposely approaching and talking to so many white people, but I must admit that they were kind enough and helpful.

I did not find a guide right away, but after a couple of suggestions from soldiers in the area, I was directed in short order to Florian MacTavish, a Scotsman of rough demeanour and colourful character who was soon to be going back west. He had quite an impressive tangle of hair and beard. He also had a savage looking scar up the right side of his face, terminating at an eye patch – injuries sustained, he said, in a fight with a grizzly bear.

Forty dollars in gold, with the promise of another forty when we reached the Rocky Mountains, secured his services as guide. I spent several more dollars on supplies we would need, including tools for building our home when we arrived at our destination. We left a week later.

MacTavish rode ahead of us on his sure-footed mount, followed by the packhorse tethered to his saddle. Beginning our journey out of Indian Territory, we saw many expressions of disbelief and derision on the faces of those we left behind. Perhaps we were a bit daft to be going on a lengthy journey so quickly on the heels of the last one, but we felt good to be on the way, on an excursion of our own choosing to a destination that we all desired.

Florian MacTavish was a blustery man, clothed entirely in animal skins. He spoke loudly regardless of the close proximity of his audience. His utterances were often punctuated with oaths of a very coarse nature, though he did seem to tame his vocabulary a bit when we were nearby. And I hesitate to speak of it, but his presence was accompanied by a pungent odour, as if he had not yet found the opportunity to bathe this year. However, he did seem well-informed of routes and people, so we let him lead the way and always attempted to keep a discreet distance from him.

Undertaking this endeavour during the hot and humid summer months made travel uncomfortable, though we all agreed that it was more pleasant than the freezing temperatures in the winter we had endured a few months before. Again, each day was a monotony of hardship, but the children seemed to enjoy the adventure, and when they became bored, they distracted themselves with play in one of the wagons.

For many days, we traversed great, expansive plains, and several times, we saw Indian villages consisting primarily of what MacTavish called 'teepees,' structures made of long poles arranged in a cone shape and covered with animal skins. These people were friendly enough, either waving a greeting to us or leaving us alone altogether.

We had been traveling for about a month and half, and the terrain was gradually changing, becoming more undulating than the flat plains that characterised the earlier portion of the journey. There were times when we crested a hill and we could see the tops of great mountains in the distance far ahead of us, and we began to foster a bit of excitement at the prospect of reaching our destination.

Sometime in August, three Indians approached us. They were on horseback and came riding toward us from the north. I had seen them advancing for about a minute as they made no attempt to hide themselves. But MacTavish, perhaps because that was the side of his missing eye, had not seen them as readily. When he did see them, he seemed startled by their presence and he unsheathed his musket.

"Arapaho!" he shouted back to us, but we did not understand the significance of his exclamation. Before the rest of us knew what was happening, he had turned in his saddle and fired towards them.

The Indians had seen what he was doing and in what seemed to me to be purely an act of self defence had fitted arrows to their bows, but one of their number was not so fortunate – MacTavish's shot had pierced his chest and he fell from his horse. One of the other Indians was letting loose his arrow toward MacTavish, but the dead Indian's horse collided with his and his shot went wild.

261

The arrow embedded itself into my wagon, inches from my right foot.

Before MacTavish could pull his pistol out to fire another round, I had mine pointed at him.

"MacTavish!" I shouted. He looked back at me and appeared to be shocked that I was threatening him in such a situation. I noticed that the Indians had stopped in their tracks as well, surprised, I think, that his attack should be thwarted by a white woman wearing Indian clothing and ornaments. "They did nothing to us," I said angrily.

"But they're God damned stinkin' Arapahos," he said, as if that should explain everything. "It's an Arapaho war party."

Looking at the two remaining Indians, I saw that they were still watching curiously. "You shot first," I said. "They do not seem warlike to me, and there were only three of them."

"Ma'am, beggin' your pardon, but if we don't kill the damn savages, they'll kill us all."

"Are you forgetting who is in your party?" Noya asked coldly as their wagon was now alongside mine.

"No ma'am," he said. "You're Cherokee! The Cherokee are civilised. The Arapaho ain't like you."

During this exchange, the two remaining Arapaho had slowly come closer, and while I was wary, I noticed that they had relaxed their bowstrings.

"Mr. MacTavish, we shan't be needing your services any longer," I said.

"Ma'am," he said, his voice quieter than I had ever heard it, "you can't go on alone. I ain't gonna leave you folks to go on by yourselves through hostile country. Besides, I'm goin' west anyways. We oughta stay together."

"We can't stop you from going the same way we're going, but we will not be party to your hostility against these people."

"People?" he said in disbelief. "These ain't people! They're animals!"

262

"Be on your way," I said through clenched teeth, my pistol still aimed at his face.

Glancing toward the Indians, he shook his head. "Damn stupid woman!" he ranted as he turned his horse and rode away. "Got no more sense in 'er damn fool head than a God damn pile o' festerin' sun-baked horse shit." Frequently looking over his right shoulder, he soon disappeared over the next rise, no longer inhibited by the slowness of our wagons.

Lowering my pistol, I raised my left hand in a wave toward the Arapaho, hoping to God that I had not been completely stupid and mistaken. The two of them looked at each other. With expressions of puzzlement on their faces, they looked back towards me and waved. They turned and rode back toward their fallen friend, and as they placed his body on his horse and rode away, we continued on our journey.

The next day, we came upon a body with seven arrows in it, similar to the one I had pulled from my wagon. The body had apparently been beaten and had a portion of the top of his head taken off. It was Florian MacTavish.

We had seen mountains in the distance ahead of us for a few days as we continued northwest on our journey. On numerous occasions after the incident with the Arapaho, we saw mounted Indians in the distance, but they never molested us. The remainder of our passage was completed without violence.

We traveled on average, if my estimates are accurate, approximately twelve miles per day on this journey. By early September, we arrived at a seemingly insurmountable stone barrier. We agreed that the Rocky Mountains had indeed been aptly named, and we decided to make camp.

That evening, I opened the valise that Liam had given me. Inside it was the gold I had brought with me from Georgia, and the etched silver artifact with the Celtic designs on it. I caressed the block, feeling the texture of the design under my fingers, as Atsila had done on our last night together. Sighing, I finally pushed the artifact aside and pulled out all the papers I had from Danny O'Riordan. I scrutinised them mercilessly, looking for clues about locations of settlements, water, shelter, anything that could help us to decide which direction to go. In one of his letters to Liam, I found the following passage.

> The Indians call this place Manitou. It is on the eastern side of a colossal dome shaped mountain discovered over twenty years ago by a United States Army captain named Zebulon Pike. The massive peak stands somewhat apart from others of its size, and is variously called Pikes Peak and James Peak, after Edwin James, the first white man to climb it.
>
> This place is possessed of a wild and savage beauty unlike anything you or I have ever encountered in Ireland or England, and abundant game can be found here. Near the base of this mountain is a verdant valley, watered by springs that boil, not with heat but with healing power. French trappers in this area, of whom there are actually many, call it Fontaine qui Bouille, or Boiling Fountain, but as stated earlier, the Indians call it Manitou.
>
> Manitou is an Indian name referring to a Great Spirit or deity, and indeed these natives consider the place to be sacred. The natives here in America are divided up into different tribes, and some of them war against the others. But at Manitou, they shed their hostilities and drink of the springs in peace, as brothers and without fear of violence. All are welcome to partake of the healing waters.

He went on to insist that Liam come to America, and I briefly wondered if he was still writing to Liam, as I thought it rather unlikely that he had heard anything about Liam's death. Then I realised that, living in such a wild and savage land as this, it was quite likely that Danny himself had met his end by now.

Drawing my attention back to the matter at hand, I opened the map and carefully examined all of the hand-written notes that Danny had made. Some of them were inscrutable, but there next to a little "x" was written "Pike," and directly east of it was writ-ten "Manitou." Unfortunately, the map was in no way detailed. I knew we had been heading in this general direction throughout our trip here. But lacking now a guide or sensitive navigational apparatus, I had no way of ascertaining the accuracy of our course.

Danny's description of the mountain was indeed similar to the mountain which stood just to the west of where we were camped. But given the unimaginable size of the mountain and the insuffi-ciency of directional and distance notations in Danny's papers, it seemed likely that we could wander for days or even weeks and not find the magical place of which he spoke in such colourful and enticing terms.

The next morning, I revealed my findings and my apprehen-sions to Noya and Edward. They agreed that it could take a very long time to find this Manitou, but lacking any other options, we began discussing a methodical way to cover ground. Edward vol-unteered to ride one of his horses to more quickly scout the area.

As we were finishing our breakfast, we saw four mounted In-dians in the distance to the north, apparently watching us, and a wild idea occurred to me. Pressing Clara closer to Noya, I stood up and began walking toward the Indians.

"Isadora, what are you doing?" Noya asked urgently. I ig-nored her, lest I lose my resolve. I raised my right hand as a greet-ing to the Indians, and as I continued walking toward them, one of them began riding slowly toward me. We finally met, and I saw

that he was one of the Arapaho warriors we had encountered several days before. He was a fine specimen, well-proportioned and very handsome. Of clothing, he wore very little, but he seemed not at all embarrassed nor uncomfortable, and he looked at me with a very great curiosity.

"Good morning, sir," I said. "I do not know if you understand what I am saying," and as I spoke, I determined from his blank facial expression that he most likely did not. "But we have been traveling for quite a long time and are not entirely sure where we need to go."

He threw a quick glance over his shoulder toward his companions some distance away, and looked back at me with no expression.

"Do you know if this is Pikes Peak?" I asked, pointing toward the great mountain to my left. He looked where I pointed, then looked back at me. "Or perhaps James Peak? We are trying to find a place called Fontaine qui Bouille. Or maybe you know it as Manitou?" At that, I finally received an expression of recognition.

"Manitou?" he said.

"Yes, Manitou," I repeated with growing excitement, nodding my head enthusiastically. "Is Manitou in this direction?" I asked, pointing again. He held up his hand in a gesture that suggested that I wait, and he rode toward his friends.

I stood there waiting while he conversed with them, and looking back, I could see Noya and Edward, watching me quite anxiously, holding Clara and Peter tightly. I turned as I heard hoof beats, and I saw all of the Indians approaching me. The one I had spoken with earlier uttered some words which I did not understand. But in the midst of his expression, I clearly discerned the word "Manitou." He motioned for us to follow.

"Thank you so much! Please wait," I exclaimed. "We shan't be but a few moments. Thank you!"

I made haste back to my family and quickly explained what was happening. As we broke camp, Noya and Edward repeatedly cast

266

*disbelieving glances toward me. In just a few minutes, we had be-
gun, with our new guides leading the way.*

*Edward's horses had been struggling over the rough ground,
so he, Noya and Peter had dismounted, continuing on foot, to
lighten their load. We were heading west and a bit south, going
straight toward the great bulk of the mountain, the like of which I
had never seen in my life.*

*But more wonders awaited my eyes as we approached a for-
ested area clinging to the base of the crag. Soaring out of the ev-
ergreen timber were red, rocky formations of the most fanciful
shapes and sizes. Arches and spires, large rocks balanced upon
small ones – it appeared to me as if an artist's depiction of a fairy
story had somehow come to life.*

*I saw a few thin columns of smoke rising from the forest in var-
ious locations amid these rock structures, and I assumed that there
must likely be Indians camping among the forest and rocks. We
did not stop, though, nor were we molested by anybody from
within those woods.*

*Clara was beside me, quietly staring, as I was, at the beautiful,
almost whimsical panorama. Looking to my left, I could see that
Noya, Edward and Peter were engaged in a similar pastime. Seeing me looking at her, Noya glanced at me and smiled, slowly
shaking her head in wonder.*

*Apparently this magical place was not our destination, how-
ever, as we continued following our guides to the south of this ar-
rangement of rocky figures. I believe it must be stated that the
Arapaho braves who were guiding us were most considerate and
adjusted their speed to the slower speed of our wagons and draft
animals.*

*At about noon, we rounded a rocky precipice on our right and
came to a crystal clear stream where we stopped to rest and water
our animals. The water was cold and sweet, but with a slight flavour that I could not readily identify.*

In short order, we were all very refreshed and, nibbling on a piece of salt pork, I seized upon the opportunity to become friends with our guides. Taking four additional cuts of salt pork from my store, I approached them, slowly but steadily with the meat presented in my hands, to show them that I meant no harm.

The Indians stood up from their place beside the stream and faced me warily but with some curiosity, and they accepted the victuals from me. Each of them looked at it curiously, sniffed it cautiously, and finally tasted it. They initially appeared to be somewhat surprised by the saltiness of the meat, but they all seemed to enjoy it.

I attempted to introduce myself, and I think that I was successful in making them understand. The young man who had taken the lead among them repeated a very close approximation of 'Isadora.' He placed his hand upon his chest and said what sounded to me like 'Gohohok,' which I in turn attempted to repeat. They all smiled and, after a brief pause, he nodded his head. I'm not sure I got it right, but they seemed to shed their suspicion of us at that point as I introduced each member of our party.

After our brief and pleasant repast, we got under way again, following the stream on our left. Perhaps an hour later, we came into a lovely green canyon. On several occasions, I saw deer with black-tipped tails and very large ears, usually disappearing into the forest as we approached, although there were a couple who watched curiously from a distance. There were plentiful signs of other game as well, and I decided that obtaining meat would not be a problem.

Now in the afternoon shadow of the mountain, our guides stopped a short distance ahead of us, and as we approached, I heard a curious rumbling sound. There in front of us was the spring of which Danny O'Riordan had written. A stone basin perhaps six feet across had been naturally formed by the mineral deposits and the erosion of the water issuing forth from the center of it.

The Arapaho braves knelt before it, and out of respect, we kept our distance as 'Gohohok' took an arrow and placed it in the water. After this, the Indians drank from the spring. Gohohok motioned for us to come, and as we drew near, I saw several more arrows, bits of cloth weighted with stones and other items left in the spring, I assumed as offerings to their deity. The Indians stood back and as I dipped my hands in the water, I watched their faces to make certain I did nothing to offend them. Then we all drank.

The water had an unusual soda flavour, and I realised that it was similar to the water I tasted from the stream, only more concentrated, and it was effervescent. We found it to be not at all unpleasant, and in fact the children took great delight in the bubbles.

"Is this Manitou?" I asked Gohohok, pointing to the spring.

He shook his head and uttered a string of unintelligible words, among which I did recognise 'Manitou.' As he spoke, he motioned toward the ground, the mountain, the forest and the sky. He followed that by waving his hands, palms downward, toward the ground surrounding us, again repeating 'Manitou.' If I understood him correctly, I assume that they believe that Manitou was all around, in all aspects of nature, but particularly manifest in this area.

I smiled and nodded, extending my hand toward him, hoping I was not overstepping any gender boundaries among his people. He hesitated for a moment, then extended his hand which I took and shook firmly. "Thank you so very much," I said.

He seemed amused by my hand shake, and when I let go, he responded in his language, smiled and nodded. He waved at Edward and Noya, then he and his friends mounted their horses and rode away.

As we did not want to appear to be taking over the spring, we moved a few hundred yards away and set up camp in the shelter of a rocky overhang. During the course of that afternoon and evening, we saw other Indians as they made their way to the spring. Although none of them approached us, they did return our waves.

Edward went hunting that first evening and even though I heard a couple of shots fired, he came back empty-handed. Noya, being familiar with my marksmanship, suggested that I try my hand at it. I hesitated at first as I did not want to outshine   Edward, but when he heartily agreed, I assented. Early the next morning I went out, armed with a musket, and found that Danny O'Riordan was right in his description of the area. Game was quite abundant – within ten minutes I had shot a stag.

I did not have to go very far away, so it did not take long for Edward to follow me to the kill and help me drag the deer back to camp. We spent the rest of the day butchering the deer and pre-serving the meat, some with salt, and some by drying, and Noya showed me how to tan the hide.

The children were initially fascinated by the process, but they lost interest after a short time. They went on to occupy their atten-tion with other things.

On the third day, knowing that we would eventually have to build a more permanent shelter, Edward mounted one of his horses and went exploring farther up in the hills. Based on his report, we decided to move camp upstream. Though we did not travel a long distance, the ground was rough, our trek was uphill, and the trip took us almost the entire day. But we arrived at the spot he had in mind and knew immediately that it was the place for us.

The area was surrounded on three sides by a mixed forest of evergreens and some form of poplar, and on the fourth side by the river. The grassy meadow was relatively level and free of rocks, attributes which we felt would serve us well when we began to build. Dappled sunlight played on the grass and a gentle breeze whispered through the forest, and we all felt as if we had found our new home.

"Bonjour, mes amis!"

Looking up from my work of preparing several trout for breakfast, I saw someone who brought to my mind the memory of Florian MacTavish. Dressed in animal skins, his head and face mostly covered with quite a lot of hair, a white man, his skin brown from living out of doors, was leading a horse toward our camp from the northwest. The horse was loaded down with layers of some form of animal skins, and though the man was younger than MacTavish and did not have an eye patch, still the superficial resemblance was quite similar.

"Good morning," I replied with some trepidation, as the children played nearby.

"Ah, English," he said with a smile and a very strong French accent. "You are quite a long way from home, no?"

"And you, it would seem," I said, attempting to return the smile. He did seem a friendly sort.

"No, but this is my home," he said, opening his arms wide as if he were ready to embrace his surroundings. "I am Emile Broussard."

"Isadora Byrnes," I returned. "It's very nice to meet someone of such an amiable disposition here in the wilderness."

"Pleased to meet you, mademoiselle."

272

Noya and Edward emerged from their wagon, seemingly confused at hearing a conversation in English, and introduced themselves as well.

"Where are you headed, Monsieur Broussard?" Edward asked.

"I am on my way to trade these beaver pelts before my horse, Souffle Mauvais, stages a mutiny." Despite his rough exterior, Monsieur Broussard had quite a pleasing sense of humour and a delightful temperament.

"Will you join us for breakfast?" Noya asked.

"Oui, merci!"

Broussard pitched in and assisted with the preparation of breakfast. He also contributed some kind of dry but tasty biscuit which he quickly mixed and cooked over the fire.

We enjoyed our breakfast in a leisurely fashion, getting to know each other. We briefly related about my move to America, the forced removal of the Cherokee from Georgia, and our overall dissatisfaction with life in the Indian Territory.

"In all," I said, "we have been living in these wagons for about a year now."

"Oh, mon seigneur! I do not envy you."

"Well what about you?" asked Edward. "Don't you live out of doors? Constantly on the move?"

"I move for the trapping and trading," Broussard said, "but I live in a cabin that I built a few miles west of here."

"We have been thinking of building a home here," I said, "but we do not wish to do so without the permission of the local Indians."

"The Indians are welcoming. You are far enough away from their sacred areas that they would not mind you making your home here."

"Perhaps," said Edward. "But considering what we've been through recently, we'd like to respect them and have their blessing. You understand."

273

"Oui, naturellement!"

"The problem is," added Noya, *"we don't understand their language, and so far we have not found anyone who understands ours."*

"Well, you have now, mademoiselle. I would be happy to introduce you."

"How very kind of you!" I said.

"Ce n'est rien."

"This is Ute country," Broussard said. He was leading the five of us down toward the spring to meet the local Indians. *"The Utes are a warlike people, but in this area, near the Fontaine qui Bouille, they are generally peaceful. The Utes around here do not really live in villages but as extended families. They move around sometimes, but several of them always seem to end up back here.*

"Other Indian tribes come around and everyone seems to get along fine here. The Arapaho are also nearby. They are a nomadic tribe and they live on the plains, following the buffalo, but they consider this area sacred too and come here for the waters. But they are peaceful Indians."

"Our guide did not think so highly of them," I replied. I related to him our experience with MacTavish and the Arapaho Indians.

"Ah, MacTavish. I knew him a little. He had a —" Broussard seemed to be searching for a word. *"Ressentiment, how do you say? A grudge. He had a grudge with the Arapaho since they ate his dog."*

"They ate his dog?" Edward asked incredulously.

"Oui. The Arapaho do eat dog. Really, though, it was nothing more than a misunderstanding. They did not realise that the dog was his pet." He paused in thought for a moment as we walked. *"He was a filthy mongrel, but I will miss him."* He looked up at us and smiled. *"And his dog."*

"It just occurred to me," I said, *"that you may know a person I am looking for. Do you know Danny O'Riordan?"*

"Danny O'Riordan," he repeated, pondering. "No, that name does not sound familiar to me. I am sorry."

"It's all right," I said, trying not to show my disappointment. "I do not know if he is still around here, or if he is even still alive. The last information I have from him is over ten years old."

Peter and Clara were gathering wildflowers as we walked along beside the river, and pointing with delight at the plentiful fish they could see through the water. I looked from them to the others in our party. Judging by the smiles, we all seemed to be quite happy in our idyllic surroundings.

We followed a path that entered the woods to our left and after a while, we came to a clearing with a few teepees scattered about. Several Indians were working at various duties as we approached, and they looked up at us curiously but without any apparent fear. A few of them smiled at Broussard.

Broussard called out as we came near one of the teepees. There was the sound of stirring within, the flap was flung open and an Indian man, whose age I was unable to determine, emerged. He was well-built, and his face was relatively unlined, but he had long, beautiful silver hair.

Broussard put his right hand out and they clasped forearms. He and the Indian exchanged some conversation which none of the rest of us understood. Then they looked at us.

"Hissing Snake is the patriarch of his family. He welcomes you," Broussard said.

The Indian looked at me with what I can only describe as a stern smile and said something else.

"He said they heard about your experience with the Arapaho scouts and your guide," Broussard continued. "Your reputation has preceded you. You have become something of a legend among them. He knows that you are a friend of the Indians."

"Hissing Snake," I said, and I extended my hand. "I am very pleased to meet you. I am Isadora Byrnes." Broussard translated my greeting to him. Hissing Snake looked at my hand briefly, as

275

Gohohok had, then extended his and I clasped his forearm as I had seen Broussard do.

After a brief exchange with Hissing Snake, Broussard turned to me with a smile.

"Hissing Snake is happy to have new friends in the area," he said. "You are welcome to make your home here."

ora and Shawn were in the sunroom at the back of the house as the afternoon rain fell outside. His arm around her shoulders, they each were enjoying the closeness.

"Do you realize that this is the second time we've been in the sunroom," Dora asked, "and both times, it was raining?"

"Must be a misnomer," Shawn smiled. "I've always loved that word."

"You really *are* a nerd, aren't you?" Dora smiled back. "Did you notice Isadora's description of her approach to Manitou? It seemed as if she was describing the Garden of the Gods."

"Yes, I noticed that too. And apparently Indians lived or camped in there, at least before white people took it over.

"Hey, I just thought of something!" Dora exclaimed and sat up excitedly. "I hadn't thought about whether Isadora or her descendants moved around in the last two hundred years. Do you think where we are now is the clearing where Isadora settled?"

"It's possible," Shawn replied, looking back at earlier pages. "Based on her descriptions of the area, the distance and directions they went, I think it's very likely. I'm amazed, though. Manitou Springs was not settled as a town until two or three decades later. They must have been a hardy breed, living alone here in the Rocky Mountains all those years."

"They weren't alone. The Indians were around and helped them."

"But you know what I mean. Away from civilization, and the conveniences of their day."

"Yeah, people back then were so different from us in a lot of ways," Dora said thoughtfully. "We've gotten so soft. We think it's a tragedy if we can't see what our Facebook friends are up to."

Shawn smiled and squeezed her a little closer. Dora looked up at him, their faces only a couple of inches apart, and she reached up around his neck to pull his face nearer until their lips met. Shawn leaned into the kiss, wrapping his other arm around her, as Isadora's book slid off of Dora's lap and onto the floor.

Dora woke up in her room on the second floor, the room she had been using since coming to Manitou Springs. It was dimly lit by the early evening light seeping through the curtains. Completely relaxed, she had fallen asleep in Shawn's arms. She looked up at him and saw that he was asleep too, and she smiled, snuggling closer to him under the sheet.

She had never gone to bed with someone she had met just three and half days earlier. And yet, as uncharacteristic as it was for her, it felt right. There was obviously a mutual attraction between them. But beyond that, she felt a connection with him, not just physical but intellectual. She felt as if she had known him for much longer, 'at least four and a half days,' as he had said after the funeral, and she smiled at the memory.

Their lovemaking had been wonderful. Shawn was responsive to her needs, as if they had been lovers for years. He had delayed his own gratification long enough for her to be able to join him, as if he felt that her pleasure was just as important as his.

And once he had gotten his jollies, he didn't just roll over. They had lain in each other's arms, holding each other tightly, until they both fell asleep. Dora was unwilling to say this early that he was 'the one,' but she admitted that, at this early date, he certainly had long-term potential.

Her stomach growled and she decided that she was hungry. She realized that they had not eaten lunch, so she turned and quietly slipped out of bed. She tiptoed toward the bathroom where she kept her robe, then headed downstairs to think of what to do for dinner.

She went into the sunroom where their lovemaking had begun, and she saw Isadora's book on the floor. Bending down to pick it up, she saw a loose piece of paper sticking out from the back of the book. Being almost two hundred years old, she was afraid that the book had been damaged when it fell on the floor. As she picked it up, though, she could see that it was not a loose page that had fallen out but rather a separate sheet of paper. Dora looked at it curiously.

The paper had a couple of lines of handwritten text, but it was not Isadora's handwriting. And it made no sense. It was just combinations of letters and numbers. She had the feeling it was important, but she didn't know what to make of it.

Was it some kind of code? She hoped it wasn't. She had never been good at code breaking or solving mysteries. She almost never figured out "whodunit" before the end of a mystery. She had little confidence that she would be able to figure out who did this, or why they did it.

On the other hand, it could be something completely unrelated to Isadora's story. Just mundane notes or meaningless scribbles that had, at some point in time, gotten stuck into the book for safe keeping. She slipped the paper into the back of the book and placed it on the coffee table. Feeling her stomach growl again, she went into the kitchen.

Shawn stirred when he felt Dora get out of bed, and he surreptitiously peeked at her. He admired the curves of her naked tanned body as she moved quietly toward the bathroom.

"Damn!" he thought. "What a beautiful woman." She was wonderful. He had never known a woman who appealed to him so deeply, on so many levels. She had been responsive when they were making love, and seemed to really appreciate his efforts to please her.

Annie, his ex-wife, even in the early heat of their relationship, had never touched him so deeply. He had spent a couple of pleasant years with her. She was pretty, and they had had a few common interests. Having met in college, they married right after he graduated. But they gradually realized that there were fewer common interests than they had originally thought. They had eventually drifted far enough apart that pleasantness alone wasn't enough to hold the marriage together.

Finally, it got to the point where their interactions consisted of just the sharing of mundane facts, if they were lucky. If they were not so lucky, their interactions were more antagonistic, and the resulting coldness and silence would last for days. They divorced ten years ago.

Meeting Dora had been just what he needed. She seemed perfect, at least perfect for him. But something was bothering him. He knew what it was, but he didn't want to think about Nicole. Not now. This was too nice, too perfect. Too easy, he thought. Easy in the sense of being completely comfortable with someone, and he didn't want to spoil it with disturbing thoughts. So he pushed Nicole from his mind.

He could hear the distant sound of Dora puttering in the kitchen and, feeling hungry, he got up to go downstairs and join her.

Edward, as it turned out, was quite handy in our building ventures. He had helped his father build their home, and later helped his brother build his. He was quite familiar with the use of the tools that I had had the foresight to purchase before leaving the Indian Territory.

The first thing we built was a fence enclosing a large portion of the meadow for our animals, so that they would not need to remain tied up in one place. They seemed to relish the relative freedom they gained on the day when we untied them and let them loose within their respective fenced areas.

The next thing we focused on was a shelter for ourselves, and we did not spend a great deal of time designing it. We knew that winter was coming, and Broussard had told us that winter can come early and be quite cold and snowy in this area.

So we simply wanted to be sheltered from the weather by more than just our wagons which, after a year in the elements and on the move, were quite ragged and nearly spent. We decided that we would create a larger and better home next year, but for now, we built a functional cabin from trees which we cut down around our clearing.

Even though it was small, it was very difficult and time-consuming work. Edward instructed us and demonstrated well how to strip the bark from the logs, how to cut notches in the ends for the logs to fit together in an overlapping pattern, how to build a fireplace and chimney from the smooth river rocks which were in such abundance.

We all pitched in, including the children who were now seven years old. Many mornings, I awoke feeling sore from having used muscles which I was not accustomed to using, but in time, I felt myself growing stronger and developing a greater stamina.

As I was gaining that strength and stamina, with the focus of my attention on the physical needs at hand, I found that I no longer kept track of the date. We conducted our daily business based on the rising and setting of the sun, and perhaps a month after our arriving in the area, I realised that I did not know the date or day of the week. And I found that it did not matter.

The Indians in the area were quite friendly and helpful to us, particularly after Hissing Snake had issued his welcome. There were some days when Indians would show up as we were building our cabin and help us with the work. At first, we did not know each other's language, but we were able to show them what we were trying to accomplish, and indeed they proved to be helpful in our endeavour.

Thus, as the temperature began dropping, our log cabin was complete and we began to make ourselves comfortable in our new home. The idyllic qualities of the area passed as we settled into the work of living each day, but the hard work was satisfying and was not tainted by hatred or prejudice. Some of the Indians became great friends of ours, and little by little, we learned bits of their language and they learned bits of ours.

We met several other white trappers who sometimes passed by, following the river, and I found that I did not feel uncomfortable with them as I had with the "civilised" white people, but rather felt completely at ease with them as I did with the Indians. Though I made it a point to ask about Danny O'Riordan, nobody had heard of him.

Sometime in the early spring of 1840, we began cutting down trees for our permanent home. During the winter, Edward had designed a lovely house, incorporating ideas and suggestions from

Noya and myself, and we were anxious to get started on it and move out of our cramped quarters.

The sky was a brilliant crystal blue, which early on I realised was common for the area, and the air still had a crisp quality to it. I will not devote time and pages to the monotonous work we put into building our home. Suffice to say, many long days and weeks were spent, often on the same repetitious task, and   Edward's medical skills were frequently put to the test by such mundane complaints as splinters, blisters and scrapes.

The animals were not excused from the work, as we utilised their strength in dragging logs and stones to the building site, and Edward devised some complex pulley systems to help us to lift them into place. He insisted that he did not invent them, but this did not detract from our admiration of his ingenuity.

Some of the work was, of course, too heavy or complicated for the children to help with, and we did not want to continually keep them busy at it anyway, as we knew that children need their play-time. So this was allowed with the qualification that they not play near the river.

But one morning, we very nearly lost them both.

Peter and Clara seemed to greatly admire the Indians we had met. They were playing at being Indians themselves and had set up a make-believe camp near the edge of the woods, several yards from where we were working. Though we often glanced up to make sure they were in sight, our attention was focused on laying the second row of logs on the stone foundation for the house, when we heard Clara scream.

Looking up, we were horrified to see Peter bravely standing between Clara and an advancing panther. The great cat was scrawny, his ribs clearly showing through his tawny fur, but knowing he was hungry made the situation all the more terrifying. Peter had a long stick in his hand and was holding it in front of himself like a spear, though the puny weapon was no match for the wild beast.

283

The moment we looked up, we all shouted as we jumped down from the scaffold on which we stood and started running toward the children. The only weapon we had was a mallet that Edward had been using, certainly of no use against the panther, but our first thought was for the children.

The animal was momentarily distracted by our calls, but had turned his attention back toward Peter, apparently considering us no immediate threat. He was tensing his muscles in preparation for his jump when suddenly three arrows buried themselves in quick succession in his side, and the beast fell dead.

We were briefly stunned, but we made it to the children, holding them tightly in our arms, as two Indians emerged from the forest, both of whom we had met before. Hissing Snake said something too fast for me to understand, but I was not concerned at the moment.

"Hissing Snake!" I exclaimed, tears filling my eyes. "Thank you so much!"

"Welcome," he said slowly, as he switched to English in response. Accompanying him was his son, Bear Killer, a man who had helped us with our building project on many occasions, and whose English vocabulary was considerably larger than Hissing Snake's.

"Mighty brave," Bear Killer said as he placed his hand on Peter's head. I could see great admiration, not only on his face, but on Noya's and Edward's as well.

"I am so glad you were there," Noya said.

"Is good we were," he agreed. Peter and Clara had, by now, pulled out of our arms and were curiously poking at the panther's carcass.

"Please join us for our lunch," I offered. It was about mid-day and I knew that, with our hearts pounding after this scare, it would be a while before we were ready to get back to our construction work.

"Thank you," they both said with a nod.

After we finished our meal, they stayed and helped us build our home.

By the time the foliage of the forest around us was turning many vibrant hues of gold and red, we had, with much welcome help from many of our new neighbours, completed our home. We all felt a great deal of pride in looking at the house, for we all had a hand in building it.

Edward admitted that he had been over-confident in his design and that we had taken on more than we could have accomplished on our own. If not for all of the help we received from our new friends and neighbours, we never would have completed the house before winter.

The house really was a thing of beauty. Having applied and perfected skills we developed while building the cabin, the house was, if I may be allowed to boast a bit, very well-made. The thick foundation of smooth river rocks rose five feet from the ground at the front, allowing for a cellar which nestled into the ground which rose toward the back of the house. Above that, great golden logs formed the walls which soared two storeys high.

The house was not large, but it did have four bedrooms, all upstairs, so that Clara, Peter and I each had our own rooms, and Noya and Edward had a room for themselves. After a year in our wagons, followed by a year in the small cabin, it seemed like a mansion. Some portions of the interior were still incomplete, but they were things that we would be able to work on while living there, during the coming winter months.

As for the cabin, we turned it into a stable for the animals. In the previous year, we had erected a flat roof over part of the fenced area to provide the animals some shelter from the elements, but it was still open around the sides. So we were happy to now have a stable, to be able to provide better protection to them from the more severe weather, and for storage of our tools and other supplies.

While we were working on the house, Noya and I had also planted a garden in back, with seeds that we had brought with us, so we had fresh vegetables to serve with our fresh meat.

"Looking back at my sheltered existence in England eleven years ago," I commented as Noya and I surveyed our home, "I never would have seen myself being so self-sufficient."

"And now you've built your own home, you grow your own vegetables, you kill your own meat."

"Yes," I replied. "I wish my family was still alive. I think they would be quite proud of me."

"I'm sure they are," Noya smiled, and she put her arm around me. I remembered belatedly that her parents were dead too, and I put my arm around her waist and leaned my head on her shoulder.

As the sun sank behind the great mountain, we felt the chill of autumn and went into the welcoming warmth of our home.

am so excited!" Dora exclaimed. She pointed to the open page in Isadora's book. "That is this house, or at least the beginnings of it."

"Yeah," Shawn agreed, "I'd say it's been added on to at least once over the years, but based on Isadora's description, it's obviously the same original structure."

Being unable to think much about food, Dora had opted for sandwiches, and their empty plates sat on the coffee table in front of them now. Dora was still in her robe, which Shawn found strangely sexy, as it clung intriguingly to the curves of her body, curves which he fondly remembered holding in his arms a short time before. Having no loungewear here, Shawn had put his clothes back on, but he still felt very comfortable with Dora.

Looking at his watch, Shawn leaned forward. "Will you be alright here alone tonight?" he asked.

"I suppose so," she responded. "Why?"

"I have an early appointment tomorrow. I can't have Colin cover for me all the time, I'm afraid."

"Tomorrow's Tuesday, isn't it?" Dora asked. "Without having to go to work, I lose track of the days, just like Isadora."

"Yeah, but some of us poor slobs still have to work to support ourselves," Shawn smiled.

"That's fine," she said. "Having the burglar alarm helps. I feel a little more secure now."

"Good. Then with that, I'll tell you good night." They both stood and began walking toward the front door.

"Good night," she said, and they held each other for several wonderful moments. Dora pressed her body against his, pulling him tightly against her. She thought she could feel the contours of his body changing a bit under his clothes, and she was certain of it when Shawn pushed her away.

"Okay, you're going to have to stop that," he said a little breathlessly, "or we're going to end up in bed again."

"Oh, wouldn't that be awful!" Dora said teasingly.

Shawn smiled at her and kissed her again. Then he pulled away and went out the door as Dora watched.

After Shawn got in his car and drove away, the feel of his kiss still lingering on her lips, Dora closed the door and set the alarm.

Dora had passed the night without incident, and awoke feeling rested and refreshed. She was also missing Shawn, knowing that he would not be coming over until the afternoon. And though she wanted to continue reading Isadora's book, she waited until Shawn could join her.

Instead, she decided to look into what would be necessary to turn the house into a bed and breakfast. As she knew little about starting a business, she looked in the phone book and found the Manitou Springs Chamber of Commerce. A quick call to them and she knew where they were located. A small building with a big green question mark standing out in front. That should make them easy to find. She decided to drive there and get copies of everything that they had about starting a small business.

Shawn was occupying her thoughts extensively as she got ready to go, and she thought again about their unlikely liaison the evening before. She knew it was too soon to start thinking about love, but they quite obviously had something fairly serious. She wondered if he was feeling the same way. She admitted to herself that she was shocked at the way she had been able to so easily overcome her over-analytical approach to romance.

Madeline would be proud of her.

It did not take her long to drive into town and to find the Chamber of Commerce on Manitou Avenue, just down the street from the Police Department. The big green question mark sculpture did indeed stand out. The people had been quite helpful and encouraging, and had given her much literature on the subject. As she was leaving, Dora actually found herself seriously considering the venture.

As she came out the door from the Chamber of Commerce, she noticed Shawn's easily-recognizable bright blue Malibu parked across the street. She looked around at the row of businesses and saw "Estate of Mind" on a little sign over a door. Realizing that his office was right there, she thought she might drop in and see if he wanted to go to lunch.

As she was thinking this, she saw the door open and a beautiful blonde woman came out, followed by Shawn. They were both laughing and Dora thought in that brief moment that they seemed close.

The woman said something and placed her hand on the front of Shawn's shoulder in an intimate way. He smiled, put his arm around her waist and opened the passenger door to his car, and the woman, kissing him on the way past, got in. He went around and got behind the wheel and started the car, and as they drove away, the top down, Dora could see the woman lean toward him and kiss him again.

That bastard!

Feeling restless, Dora paced around the house, not knowing what to do.

We've only known each other for four days, she thought. *How can I be feeling so strongly about this?*

She remembered the intimacy of the night before. Had she just imagined the intimacy, or was it more carnal?

I know it's not just a casual thing. We didn't just fuck. We made love.

Her heart was racing and she knew she needed to calm down. To think clearly.

This wouldn't have happened if I had just been more careful and followed my usual tried and true approach. God, why did I have to listen to Madeline?

She went into the kitchen, got a bottle of Sauvignon Blanc out of the refrigerator, and poured herself a glass. Feeling its cool sweetness course down her throat, she took a deep breath and walked into the sunroom. She saw Isadora's book on the table where they had left it the night before.

To hell with him. I'm not going to wait for him. He's out with his little blonde slut. We're through!

She threw herself down on the sofa and started reading, trying to ignore how silly and immature it was that she was thinking, *This will show him!*

After lunch, Nicole was not too happy, but Shawn was glad to have gotten that nasty business out of the way. Without a word, she got out of his car, slammed the door and went straight to her own car, squealing her tires as she drove away. Shawn sighed as he watched her disappear down the road, then he went into the office.

"Well, she seemed a little peeved," said Colin from the front desk as Shawn walked in.

"Yeah thanks, Captain Obvious." He sighed. "Well it's for the best."

"I suppose. You got company," Colin said, quickly changing the subject. "I knew you were going to be back soon, so I told them they could wait in your office." Shawn wasn't expecting anybody else.

"Who is it?"

"Don't know. Couple of Micks."

"Very PC of you," Shawn said sardonically, making his way toward his cubbyhole of an office. He walked through the door and saw two men sitting in the vinyl-covered chairs in front of his desk.

"Can I help you?" he asked.

"Aye, lad, you can," replied one of the men with a strong Irish accent. "Me name's Brian," he said, putting his hand out for Shawn to shake. Brian had a diamond stud in his ear and was wearing large shades. Shawn noticed a resemblance to Bono, and realized that it was probably intentional. The other man was large. He just sat quietly and seemed hard and bulky, tight, as if he were trying very hard to keep something inside him that desperately wanted out.

As Shawn went around his desk, Brian reached over and pushed the door closed. "We need your help."

"With what?" Shawn asked. "Do you have some property you want liquidated?"

"No, actually *you* have some property; or rather your little friend does. We want you to get it for us, or *you* will be the ones to be liquidated." The man smiled grimly at his joke and looked over at his friend who remained impassive.

"What is this?" Shawn asked, feeling a prickly sensation on the back of his neck.

"This is just a simple business proposition, lad," Brian replied easily. He sat back in his chair as he began to expound on his reason for being there. "There's an item that was taken from us quite a long time ago. We've been trying to get it from little Dora's house, but we've been surprisingly unsuccessful. One o' our boys even got himself killed a few days ago an' come out with nothin' to show for it."

Perspiration was beginning to form and run down Shawn's back, and he was starting to feel particularly uncomfortable. He had never had any dealings with crime figures before. His knowledge of them consisted of little more than what he saw in movies and TV shows. But these men before him were very real and did not seem to be too hesitant to do violence to him. In fact, judging by the look on his face, the big, quiet one seemed to want to get to it as soon as possible.

"What is it you want?" Shawn asked quietly, trying to keep his voice steady.

"Somewhere in that big house o' hers is something called a pyxis, a silver box with a Celtic design on the outside. We want you to find it and give it to us. You do that, and we'll pay you handsomely."

"Why do you want this pyxis?" Shawn asked, trying to buy himself some time as he thought of his options. "Why is it so valuable?"

"You needn't worry about that," Brian said. "Just get it and you'll be a rich man. Don't, and you'll be a dead man. Oh, and you can rest assured that little Dora will be dead too."

"Why are you coming to *me* about this?"

"We figure you have more to lose than little Dora. You got your brother and his family. You got your parents down in   Pueblo. And of course you got Dora. I figure that gives you quite a lot of incentive."

"You're threatening them?" Shawn asked, feeling an icy chill down his spine.

"Let's just call them leverage."

"How do you know the pyxis is still there?" Shawn struggled to suppress a shiver. "Dora said she hasn't seen anything resembling that."

"It's still there. We been watchin' for it for quite a long time, and we know it's still part of the estate, most likely still in the house."

"How am I supposed to get it out of there?" Shawn countered. "She'll never let me just walk out of her house with it."

"I don't give a shite how you get it. Just get it," Brian snapped. Then he seemed to try to calm himself, and he thought for a moment. "Alright, tell you what: You find it and leave it. Get her out o' the house, but before you get in your car, give us a sign. Give us a big stretch. Stretch your arms out to the side. Try to act like you're relaxed," he said with another one of his grim smiles. "We'll go in and get it." That chilled Shawn as he pictured these goons – and probably more – outside Dora's house watching them closely. "Oh, and don't bother callin' the police. That'll just get you killed sooner."

"What if we can't find it?"

"Find it," Brian said quietly.

As the years passed, I fear that I became somewhat delinquent in my writing, though I must admit that little of a truly dramatic nature happened as we settled into our lives in our new home. We had become friends, as reported earlier, with many of the local Indians, and with several white trappers, although by 1850, several of the trappers had moved on due to diminishing beaver populations and difficulties in the fur trade.

We had made it clear to trappers we had befriended that they were welcome to spend the night with us at any time, and occasionally some did in the course of their travels. When they did, it caused a feeling of nostalgia within me as it made me remember the years of the boarding house in Georgia, of living and working with Mahaley, and of the friends we had left behind and lost along the way.

I was happy to find that our new isolated lifestyle in the forest had a calming effect on me. I did not necessarily desire to be a hermit, but living in partial seclusion as we did, with occasional visits from Indians and trappers, seemed very nearly like paradise. I felt truly happy again, despite the losses I had experienced in recent years.

After we had been in the area for a while, Edward and Noya took several days and made a trip to the trading post at Fort Pueblo, a new establishment approximately fifty miles south, for supplies. Peter, Clara and I stayed at home. I had written a letter to Quentin and Betsy, and Noya and Edward took it with them to post from Fort Pueblo.

We made arrangements with Emile Broussard and a couple of other trappers who regularly went there to pick up any mail that might come for us. Thus, a few months later, we received a reply from Quentin. He and Betsy were doing well, though they said they missed us. He also said that, shortly after we left, he found some white men prowling around our old house.

When I confronted them about it, they tried to come up with a story but didn't do a very good job. It was hard to understand them, though. They spoke with some kind of accent, kind of similar to yours, but different. Maybe Irish.

"What are you doing here?" I asked them.

"We're good friends of the English lass who lives here," one of them said.

"There's no English lass living here," I said. "I own this house. She moved away a few years back."

"Oh, dear," he replied. "And would you mind telling us where she went?"

"If you were such good friends," said I, "wouldn't she have told you?"

They had nothing more to say after that, and they left displaying a certain belligerence.

I admit I felt a bit of consternation at this, remembering the confrontations that I had had with Irishmen in the past. These men, from the short conversation Quentin related, did indeed sound Irish. I also experienced some curiosity as well, assuming that, as before, they were after the silver artifact that Liam had left with me. Could it really be that valuable?

Back at our home, Clara, now eighteen years old, was quite simply the most beautiful young woman I had ever seen, with her

296

perfect brown skin, deep umber eyes and luminous golden hair. And unspoiled by the petty traits and influences of modern civilisation, her character was equally beautiful. She seemed to possess the best qualities of both myself and Atsila, and I could also see certain gentle and mild qualities of Noya reflected in Clara's personality as well.

She was a hard worker and took great pride in completing her chores, and I knew that she would one day make someone a fine wife. There were times, though, when I felt guilty about bringing her out to the Rocky Mountains, since the remoteness of our home made a normal social life quite impossible for her. However, I was not plagued with this guilt for very long.

Clara's qualities did not go unnoticed by Peter who seemed to relish his time spent with her. As they grew together, I could see that their developing relationship was becoming much deeper than mere friendship.

My appearance, in time, began to resemble the Indians even more as the fabric of my clothing wore out. I began making my clothing entirely from deer skin, which I admit better corresponded with the ornamentation I had become accustomed to wear. I also found it to be very comfortable and wondered that I had taken so long to try it.

As time went by and people visited the area, word got out about the springs and its therapeutic effects. Though white visitors to the area were somewhat rare, still they were increasing. Edward, Noya and I recognised that, with the word-of-mouth advertisement taking place, at some point in the future, this would become a popular destination.

So early in 1848, Edward started working on designs for an addition to the house. Whenever we had guests, I would sleep with Clara and give my room to the visitor, so this addition would create more rooms to use as an inn. With the nostalgia I had been feeling, I was anxiously looking forward to the completion of this addition.

Since there was no urgency with this, as there had been for the original house, we took our time with it. Edward was patient with us and in two years, ten years after the house was built, we had completed the addition which added two rooms each on the first and second storeys, and also added a third storey with two small rooms. In this venture, as before, we received much voluntary help from our friends and neighbours.

One of the rooms on the first storey, Edward began using as a clinic, as word had gotten out that he was a doctor. When people, particularly Indians, first started seeking treatment for injuries or illnesses, he was initially reluctant as it had been quite a long time since he had practiced medicine, but he found that it came back to him quite quickly.

However, he soon realised that the kitchen was not a good place to practice medicine, particularly when we were attempting to prepare a meal. Thus, he began using one new room at the back of the house as a medical clinic, and while it was not used nearly as much as the clinic in Georgia, Edward seemed to feel much more useful.

"Peter's asked me to marry him," Clara said with a bit of the shyness which was one of the qualities that seemed to make her personality so endearing.

"Oh, darling," I said, feeling a combination of mother's pride and the fear of losing one's daughter to someone else. Of course, I knew the second feeling was entirely irrational. Nevertheless, it was there. "That's wonderful. How did you answer him?"

"I love him, mother. Of course, I said yes," she answered as if any other notion would be entirely inconceivable. I smiled as I took her into my arms, and we held each other tightly. I felt tears welling up in my eyes, but I admit that they were mainly tears of happiness.

"Have you discussed the manner in which it will be accomplished?"

"We were thinking that we could go to Fort Pueblo and be married there. There are not so many clergymen here," she said with a gently mocking smile.

"You're right," I smiled back. "I think that is a wonderful idea."

"We want to go to Georgia after we are married. Not to stay, but we want to revisit where we started out."

"What a splendid notion!" I said, trying to mask the feeling of missing my little girl already.

"I can't believe that I'm forty years old and that my daughter is now grown and married," I said. In the summer of 1850, Noya, Edward and I were on our way back home from Fort Pueblo.

"They do grow fast, don't they?" replied Edward. The five of us had gone to Fort Pueblo in two wagons, and we parents were going back home in one, feeling lonely despite the company of each other.

"A lot has happened since they were born," contributed Noya. "Our lives have changed much more than I would have ever thought."

We all nodded silently, as we each privately recounted the memories, both good and bad, of the lives we had led. And as I write this, I wonder if my narrative has come to an end. I have created a happy life, but it was created at great cost.

The memories occupying my mind included the loss of two men whom I dearly loved romantically, as well as the loss of my mother, father and sister, followed a few years later by the death of my 'other mother,' Mahaley. I realised that I had already recounted these losses before in this narrative, and not wanting to bore whoever may eventually read this, I will end it, for now at least.

ora could see that it was not, in fact, the end. There were more handwritten pages, although some of them seemed to be pages torn from a different book, slightly smaller, that had been inserted at a later time. But Dora was feeling what she thought of as a feeling of loss. She was certain it was related to more than just the approaching end of the book, but rather to Shawn's betrayal. She missed him, but she could no longer trust him and did not want him around.

She finished off her second glass of wine and, since she had not had any lunch, she was feeling the alcohol more than she usually would have. She placed the book on the table, stood up and stretched. But she still felt aimless and without purpose. She knew that this was dangerous as she was aware that she had inherited some of her mother's tendency toward depression.

By now, it was mid-afternoon, and she knew that Shawn was planning on coming over soon.

Probably hoping to fornicate some more!

She also knew that she did not want to see him. Putting forth a concerted effort, she recognized that she needed to focus her attention on something positive. So she picked up Isadora's book and went upstairs to her bedroom.

Even if she did not read much, a nap sounded good!

Shawn was terrified. Fortunately Colin had left earlier. When Brian and his sidekick finally left, Shawn was alone, and he was glad. He didn't think he could cover over the fear he was feeling.

But he was going to have to do just that when he was with Dora. Act like nothing is wrong.

He sat at his desk, trying to think of ways to protect Dora. But his mind was too jumbled. He couldn't think clearly.

Brian had said that they would pay handsomely for the pyxis. Shawn did not really believe that. Honor among thieves? No. But on the chance that they did pay for it, at least that would be better than nothing. It would not be a total loss.

What the hell am I thinking? They won't pay for it. But at least letting them take it is better than being dead!

He got up and went to the back of the office, into the little restroom. He splashed cold water on his face. He needed to pull himself together. He pulled a couple of paper towels from the dispenser. He pressed them to his face, then rubbed them on the back of his neck.

Drying his face, he took a deep breath and looked in the mirror. The fear was showing very clearly, and he knew that Dora would see that.

He tried to take another deep breath and realized that he hadn't exhaled the last one yet. He forced himself to exhale, and he paced around the office for a few minutes, trying to think of any ideas he might have missed.

He sat down at his desk, feeling the chill of the air conditioner on his wet shirt.

In imitation of my mother's wonderful example, I shall attempt to document my travels and adventures, the sweetest and greatest of which, I believe, I am now embarking upon.

My name is Clara Hodges, at least as of four days ago, when I married my best friend Peter. We were married by a little "Padre" whom, I fear, I cannot avoid thinking of as adorable.

I, like my mother, am not tall, yet I was at least two inches taller than this little clergyman who had a tendency to smile easily, sometimes in embarrassment, such as when he forgot my name and almost married Peter to someone named Carlotta.

The marriage was performed at Fort Pueblo, an adobe outpost near the eastern "foot-hills" of the Rocky Mountains, and was witnessed by the three other people to whom I am closest: my sweet mother, Isadora Byrnes, and my husband's parents, Edward and Noya Hodges.

Having spent my entire life so far with my dear mother, it was a bittersweet moment when we said good-bye and my husband and I mounted our wagon and headed toward the east, to visit the place of our birth and early childhood. Peter and I were both quite young when we left there, but I do have some memories of the place and of a few people.

I especially look forward to seeing Betsy Fairfax again, a woman I seem to remember rather vividly, despite my tender age at the time. She and her husband, Quentin, proved to be quite a great help to my mother during our last few difficult years in Georgia.

Following existing trails whenever possible, my husband and I made rapid progress on our journey, and we were both anxious to reach our destination.

Arriving in Gainesville from the west, Peter and I had come through town and we stopped at the old mission first, to look around. The building was still divided much as it had been, part of which was now occupied by a doctor and the other by a feed store.

Peter spoke briefly to the doctor, Myron Asherton, and found that after the "Trail of Tears," which is what some were calling the forced removal of the Indians, Quentin Fairfax fought hard to keep the clinic running as a free service, and particularly for the Negroes and any Indians who might have still been in the area. However, he was opposed so fiercely on this matter by the local townspeople that he ultimately saw no other course than to let the town decide and hire their own doctor.

While in town, we drove by Peter's old house. We remembered it being a small place, but in the last several years, it had been enlarged with an addition. The flower garden in front was pretty, though not as well-kept as we remembered it when Noya tended it.

From there, we headed out of town, first passing by my old house which, from the road, looked much the same as I recalled, though Quentin had sold it to a nice large family a few years ago. The grounds were well-tended as they were at the Fairfax home, where we arrived moments later. They had been warmly welcoming, though initially a bit embarrassing. But as we sat down and visited with them, we found them to be as comfortable as family.

"Now I really feel old!" said Quentin. "You kids were practically babies the last time I saw you." I remembered Quentin Fairfax as being quite tall when I was a little girl, but now, at about seventy-five years old, he was hunched over a little. He still used a cane, but instead of limping, he now hobbled as if both legs gave him trouble.

"You're both so adorable!" said Betsy, pinching my cheek, and I began to wonder if coming here might not have been a good idea. Betsy was older too, in her sixties now, but still looked much the same as I remember her, though I don't remember her being so embarrassing. Perhaps as a child I was not as affected by such things.

Peter commented briefly on his conversation with the doctor, and about Quentin's valiant but ultimately failed attempts with regard to the clinic.

"These are turbulent times," Quentin said. "It's been about twelve years now since folks around here resolved what they called the 'Indian problem,' but things haven't really settled down yet."

"What's the problem now?" Peter asked in his characteristic soft-spoken voice.

"Slavery, son. It's such a hot topic now that Georgia is even considering the possibility of seceding from the Union."

"Which side of the issue has Georgia taken?" I asked.

"Oh, they're in favor of it. Georgia's definitely in favor of slavery. I don't know if it will ever come to the point of actually seceding from the Union, but there are a lot of boys discussing it right now over in Milledgeville."

"I'm so glad Jimmy and Alice were able to get out of here," Betsy said.

"Yes," Quentin said, brightening up a bit. "I got a letter from Jimmy a few months ago. You know he married his Indian girl, Amonida, a few years back. Well, they just had their second child, a boy. And Alice is getting close to getting married to a young Negro man she met in the Indian Territory. I guess he's still a slave, so I'm not sure how that will affect Alice. But she and Jimmy both seem to be very happy."

"I'm so glad," I said, always a fool for a happy ending.

We spent some time seeing the sights in the area, places that we vaguely remembered. But few of the people we knew when we lived here were still around, so the visit was bittersweet. Especially when we visited the graves of my father and Peter's grandfather, both of whom were buried in the town cemetery. Neither of us had known Yancey Franklin, but he was family.

We stayed with Quentin and Betsy for a few days, then we left to make our way back home. Our wagon was full of things that Quentin had saved for Mother, things that she had not been able to take with her on the "Trail of Tears." This included paintings that I remembered from our home, and one especially caused a lump in my throat – a family portrait that included my father, dead now for about fourteen years. This precious cargo was carefully wrapped in blankets to protect them, and I looked forward to seeing the expression on Mother's face when we got them home.

Again, we made good progress, but when we were a few days out from Gainesville, I noticed that Peter had slowed a bit and kept glancing over his shoulder.

"What is it, Dear?" I asked.

"I'm not sure," he said, a troubled expression on his face. "I've had the impression that someone was behind us several times, but whenever I look, it seems as if they duck out of sight." The road we were on was winding and tree-lined, so it would have been an easy matter for someone to do that. I turned but did not see anyone.

Peter reached under the seat and laid a pistol on his lap. Then as we rounded another curve in the road, he quickly reined the horses to the left and into the cover of the trees and stopped.

"Stay here," he simply said, then jumped down, the pistol in his hand, and crept near the road and waited. After perhaps half a minute, I could hear approaching hoof beats. As the rider came into view, Peter stepped out into the road, the pistol pointing at the man's chest. It was a white man, and he seemed quite surprised when he saw Peter. He pulled back on the reins and the horse reared up, but the man remained mounted, raising his hands in front of himself.

306

"Why are you following us?" Peter asked.

"I'm not followin' you, lad," he said with an unusual accent. "I'm just ridin' me horse, mindin' me own business."

"You've been matching our speed," Peter said, "ducking out of sight when I looked back."

"No, lad. I don' want any trouble." Peter thought for a moment, keeping his eye and his gun on the man.

"All right," he finally said. "Be on your way." And without waiting to be told twice, the man slapped the reins and quickly rode away, while Peter watched him. He waited till the man was out of sight, then came and got back up on the wagon. His face was tense and he said nothing as he worked the wagon back onto the road.

From that moment on, we were very alert to our surroundings, but fortunately we had no further trouble the rest of the way home. It was a long trip, but we started feeling more at home, though our destination was still a long distance away, when we saw the first of the Indian settlements.

Mother was curious as Peter unloaded the paintings. There was a chill in the air, but Peter took his time, being very careful not to damage any of them. When he put the first one down on the floor inside the house and unwrapped the blanket from around it, Mother saw the family portrait of the three of us, and her eyes immediately filled with tears. She was still looking at it when Peter produced the next one, unwrapping the portrait of Mahaley, and Noya joined her with a similar reaction.

The third painting that Peter brought in was one that Quentin and Betsy had had painted especially for mother. It was a portrait of the two of them, standing in front of their fireplace. Betsy was dressed in her usual fashion, with a brightly colored dress which did not quite fit her, but it was Betsy, and Mother seemed to appreciate it too. She wrapped her arms around Peter and me and hugged us both at the same time.

There were other smaller paintings too that had been hung in various places in the boarding house, and a few from Noya and Edward's house. Mother and Noya engaged Edward in hanging them all immediately.

I also presented Mother with a gift of my own. When we were in Georgia, I had found a store that sold tea, the lack of which I had often heard my Mother lament. Apparently it was quite a common drink in England and she missed it terribly upon coming to America where coffee was the more popular beverage, so I purchased three tins of it. When I presented it to her, once again, she threw her arms around me, then rushed to the kitchen to prepare some. A few minutes later, she came out carrying a tray with five cups on it and we all had some.

Taking a few sips, Mother was looking at it, apparently deep in thought. She tasted it again, then looked around at the rest of us with a puzzled look on her face.

"I can't imagine what all the fuss was about," she said.

We had a surprise ourselves upon our return – a house a bit farther upstream. It was little more than a cabin, and it was not yet complete, but Edward, Noya and Mother had worked tirelessly upon it the whole time we were gone, with much help from our Indian friends, hoping to have it finished upon our return. Even though it was not finished yet, we were overwhelmed and threw ourselves into the work with them, to complete it and move in before the arrival of winter.

Dora was lying on her bed. She had barely finished reading these few loose pages that had been inserted into Isadora's book when she dozed off, and she had slept fitfully for about an hour. She awoke to the sound of knocking on the front door. From her room upstairs, it was a distant sound. For that to have woken her, she knew that she had not slept deeply. She felt groggy, but she still acutely felt Shawn's betrayal, so she didn't move. She was not going to let him in.

She rolled over on her side, remembering the feel of his arms around her in this very bed. She struggled to wipe the thought from her mind, but it was maddeningly persistent. She felt her eyes filling with tears.

God! What the hell's wrong with me? The guy's an asshole! Don't waste your emotions on him!

She heard him knock again, and harder this time. A minute later, she heard her cell phone ring somewhere downstairs. She sat up and shook her head. She knew she had to face him, but she was not ready yet. She got up and walked into the bathroom to splash cold water on her face.

She came back into the bedroom and lay down on her bed again. She knew that she was in danger of sinking into a deep depression – she had seen it often enough in her mother – but she felt powerless to stop it. She felt a great fatigue throughout her body, and she just wanted to rest.

She kept seeing Shawn and his little blonde slut, and she kept seeing her kiss him, his arm around her waist. The thing was, she didn't look like a slut. She was just a pretty young lady, who prob-ably didn't have any idea that Shawn was a two-timing son of a bitch.

Forget it! He's not worth it.

She opened the book again and tried to focus her mind on what she was reading.

Though I stated in my last entry that I had little more to write, I now find that I was mistaken. Clara and Peter, having related to me the account of their encounter with the Irishman on their way back home, assured me that they had seen no further sign of him on the rest of their trip. Yet I admit that the story did give me pause. Having experienced several years of peace in our wilderness home, with Indians for neighbours, and only occasional contact with passing trappers, the return of this feeling of apprehension was an uncomfortable reminder of the tension we experienced so often back in Georgia.

But I accepted their assurance that there was nothing more to worry about, and indeed, in a few days, the apprehension had passed. Clara and Peter were living in their new home upstream from us and were blissfully engaged in their daily life together, though happily their life still often overlapped with ours.

In recent years, white people had been coming a bit more frequently to partake of the healthful waters of Manitou, and though our house was not yet officially an inn, many times we found that we had guests staying with us, more than just the occasional trapper. Usually these people had endured difficult circumstances to get here and were happy to find once they arrived that they would not have to camp out of doors during their stay.

I often found these people to be of quite a hardy constitution and somewhat adventurous personality. In time, I found that the disquietude around white people that had developed in me in the past to be, finally, greatly reduced.

Thus, late one cold afternoon in October, 1851, as an early snow was falling, there was a knock at the front door. Opening it, I found a young white man, wrapped in furs against the cold, but he did not look like a trapper. He was clean-shaven and wore spectacles.

"Good morning, ma'am," he said. "I was told you put people up who wish to rent a room for a day or two." I noticed that he spoke very clearly, with a very precise manner of pronunciation.

"Yes, that is correct," I replied.

"Wonderful! I have come from New York for the waters and would like to remain here during my stay."

"Please come in," I said as I held the door open for him. "I'm Isadora Byrnes."

"John Smith," he said. We briefly discussed the terms for his stay and he paid me in advance for three nights. "I noticed your accent," he said as I led him upstairs to see the room. "Are you from England?"

"Yes, I am," I answered. "I came to America nearly twenty-two years ago."

"A wonderful place, England," he replied. "Or so I have been told. I have never been there."

Opening the door to his room, he looked inside and found it to be to his liking, so I took my leave from him.

Mr Smith left after breakfast the next morning, to sample the spring's water as treatment for a stomach ailment. Edward went out back to chop wood, to replenish our store, while Noya and I cleaned up the kitchen and dining room from breakfast. It was mid-morning when the front door opened and Mr. Smith walked back in.

"Mr Smith, back so soon?" I asked.

"Yes, I am," he said. Somehow his speech seemed a little different. "I've not come for water. I've come, rather, to reclaim stolen property." I noticed there was a bit of an accent. An Irish accent.

"I don't understand," Noya said as I tried to mentally locate the nearest gun.

"You've led us on quite a chase," he continued, "but we feel very fortunate to have stumbled upon your children in Georgia. The Fian Rúnda are quite happy to renew our acquaintance with you, lass. So now, why don't you just hand it over and be done with it?"

"What are we to hand over?" I asked bitterly, feeling that old anger returning.

"You know very well what I've come for," he said impatiently. "The silver pyxis. Where is it?"

He placed his right hand in the pocket of his coat and pulled out a gun. I raised my hands up in front of me, to attempt to keep him calm and placated. "All right," I said, "I'll go get it." I walked into the front parlour and he moved to keep his eyes on me. I opened a drawer in a small cabinet, and started to reach for the pistol that we kept inside.

"Hold on there, lass," he said. "Step back." I sighed and did as I was told, and he advanced toward the cabinet until he saw the gun. He looked back at me and smiled a grim smile, then pointed his gun at Noya. Still looking at me, he asked, "Where is the pyxis?"

"It's upstairs," I replied in fear. It was certainly not worth Noya's life.

"You go get it, but don't try to get brave or stupid again." He spread the fingers of his left hand and inserted them into Noya's long hair and grasped it tight, pulling her head back against the pistol. "You try anything stupid and your friend dies."

I nodded, eager to placate him, and walked out of the parlour. Pushing Noya ahead of himself, he followed me into the entryway. I went upstairs to my bedroom where the artifact of silver sat on top of a chest of drawers. I lifted the heavy block from its place, trying to think of anything else I could do, but not wanting to take too long.

313

I could not imagine why this "pyxis" was being sought after with such fervour. Even if it was solid silver, could it really be worth enough to bring people all the way from Ireland to find it? But Noya's life hung in the balance, and this was the ransom, so I went back downstairs. Mr Smith's eyes lit up the moment he saw the block of etched silver in my hands.

"Set it down on that table and step away," he instructed, and for emphasis, he pulled Noya's hair tighter, causing her to wince with pain and fear as she felt the gun pressed hard against her skull. I placed the artifact on the side table and stepped away. Mr Smith pushed Noya toward me and picked up the silver block, an expression of apparent awe on his face.

"That was a wise choice," he said. "My friends wanted to assail your home and tear it apart until we found this. Now, you ladies just stay here and nobody will get hurt." With that, he backed away with the gun still pointed at us. He opened the front door and slipped out, and as he did, we could see another man waiting for him, holding a rifle.

"You got it!" he said.

"Aye, lad," said Mr Smith. "I got it." At that moment, Smith's friend was impaled through the neck by an arrow, and he fell on the porch, kicking momentarily as the lifeblood pumped out of his throat. Smith looked for just a moment at the corpse then, in a panic, stepped quickly back into the house and pushed the door almost closed, trying to see out the crack.

We heard a couple of gunshots outside and knew that he did indeed have other friends with him. When Smith stepped back into the house, I slipped into the parlour to retrieve the pistol from the cabinet, and as I picked it up, I heard the back door open and slam closed.

"Noya!" Edward called, and as he ran into the entryway, Smith fired. A half second later, as I heard Noya scream, with an angry shout I fired my pistol and Smith fell dead with a lead ball through his face.

I ran past Smith and saw Noya weeping over Edward's body. My heart fell at the sight, but I pulled myself together as I heard soft footsteps on the porch. Edward's musket had fallen to the floor and I picked it up, pointing it at the front door as it eased open. I pulled the hammer back, prepared to put a bullet through the next white face I saw. But I breathed a sigh of relief as I saw Gohohok peek around the door.

Over the years, he had learned a little English, so he was able to briefly explain. He and two companions had ridden out from their camp and had seen a group of six white men on horseback approaching our house. White people were not an entirely uncommon sight at our house, but these had guns at the ready, so the Indians were wary.

They followed the white men slowly, closely watching them from the concealment of the forest and saw four of them dismount and spread out around the house as Smith entered the front door. They knew something was wrong when they saw Smith back out of our door with his gun pointed in at us, and that was when Gohohok's arrow found the neck of the other man on the porch.

In response, a couple of their number loosed shots toward the forest, but none of the shots found their marks, and within seconds, the remaining three white men lay dead and bleeding in the snow. The sixth one who had remained on his horse had wheeled and galloped away with an arrow in his shoulder, but apparently still alive.

The Indians had taken it upon themselves to dispose of the dead bodies for us, though we buried Edward ourselves. Clara and Peter had come when they heard the gunshots, and Peter helped a great deal in comforting Noya.

A few months later, in 1852, troops came from newly-formed Fort Massachusetts, several miles south of us, and wiped out the Arapaho camped near the springs. Gohohok and others that we had come to know were killed as punishment for the "murder" of the white men at our house. The man who escaped had reported that his party was ambushed and massacred by Arapaho savages. No investigation was conducted to determine that it was a matter of self-defence.

In the wake of this massacre, we gave some of our guns to the Ute Indians camped nearby and taught them how to use them. Even though they could shoot arrows much faster than we could shoot and reload guns, we hoped to remove the danger of them being implicated if they had to be involved in any other battles. We did not want our remaining friends endangered by the prejudice and animosity that seemed so prevalent among white people.

But there was some good news at that time as well. Clara and Peter had come in the late summer and, just before dinner, Clara smiled and announced that Noya and I were going to be grandmothers. I was overjoyed, and Noya seemed to appreciate the news as well. It was the first time I had seen her laugh in several months.

"Do you recall my mother's wish to compile a collection of Cherokee stories?" Noya asked. We were in the kitchen, working together on dinner. We usually did not put much effort into dinner for just the two of us any longer, but Clara and Peter were joining us again tonight.

"Yes, of course," I answered.

"I want to start working on that, for her." Noya had become quiet and withdrawn since Edward's death nearly a year ago, and I was happy to see her becoming interested in something again.

"Yes, by all means," I said enthusiastically. "That would be wonderful."

That was all that was said about it at the time, and I did not press it any further. At that moment, there was a knock at the front door, and Noya went to answer it. We had gotten back into the habit of keeping guns within easy reach, so I was not overly worried about her.

While I could not hear much that was being said, I could tell that it was a man. Then, I heard occasional words, and realised that there was an Irish accent, and suddenly my suspicions were aroused.

I went to the doorway of the kitchen where I could hear a little better, and my breath caught in my throat as I heard Liam speaking. I knew that was impossible, of course. Nevertheless, though it had been twenty-three years since I had last spoken with him, I recognised his voice.

Walking cautiously into the front entryway, I saw Noya speaking with a man who had a short beard and reddish hair, graying at the temples. He was dressed in animal skins and, like   myself, wore feathers and beads and a great deal of other Indian ornamentation. He looked up at me and smiled as I came into the entryway, and he acknowledged my presence with a slight bow of his head.

"Afternoon, ma'am," he said. "How d'you do?"

"Danny O'Riordan?" I asked. He seemed very surprised and, after a brief hesitation, nodded his head.

"Aye, lass, that's me name, though I've not heard it spoken in many years," he said. "How is it that you happened to come across it?"

"I was engaged to marry Liam twenty-three years ago."

"You're Isadora?" he asked incredulously. I nodded. "That's – that's about when I stopped hearing from Liam."

"I'm sorry, Danny. Liam's dead. He was killed moments before the ship set sail that brought me to America."

He nodded, silent for a few moments. "After all this time, that's what I feared," he said quietly.

Having rented a room, Danny joined us for dinner that evening, and after I recounted many of our experiences from the last couple of decades, I finally implored him to tell some stories of his own.

"It was about twenty years ago. It was a hard winter and times were hard, not just for me but for all o' God's creatures. I was

317

hunting for deer, just a little ways north of here. I had been fol-
lowing a trail in the snow and was almost upon the buck I was
after. I was keeping meself hidden in the trees when a bobcat
jumped me.

"He clung to me back, diggin' his claws into me shoulders and
sides. I was swingin' me musket round, tryin' to knock him off me,
but he wouldna let go. Before he had a chance to sink his fangs in
me neck, I threw meself back against a tree. Well, that did the trick.
He grunted and fell off me to the ground, stunned, and I spun
round and shot him." He fingered a short, black-tipped tail hang-
ing from a leather thong around his neck.

"Folks started calling me Bobcat Éamonn after that, and it
stuck."

"Éamonn?" I asked.

"Éamonn Daniel O'Riordan," he said, and bowed as if he were
introducing himself for the first time.

Dora sighed as she placed the feather bookmark in the book and closed it. Still lying on her bed, she turned on her side and something caught her eye on the bedside table, something shiny and silver. It was Shawn's pendant, and she remembered how it got there.

When Dora and Shawn had been making love the night before, the little pendant kept hitting her in the face.

Shawn had been caressing and thrusting into her, concentrating on bringing her to climax, unaware at first that she was distracted by this pendant bumping into her face. They laughed about it and he slipped it off and placed it on the table. He must have forgotten it when he got dressed.

She picked it up and looked at it, admiring the engraving on its surface. The Celtic knot. An Irish design. Suddenly she remembered other things. She realized that Shawn Murphy was an Irish name. In fact, he had said, when they were talking about genealogy, that he was mostly Irish. She went downstairs and found her cell phone and her purse. In the purse was the business card of Sergeant Jerry Devlin, the police officer she had spoken to about her grandmother's death. He picked up on the second ring.

"Devlin," he simply said.

"Sergeant, it's Dora Baskin."

"Yes, Ms. Baskin. How are you?"

"I'm fine thanks. Listen, I wonder if you could tell me again the name of the man who killed my grandmother."

"Sure. Finn Gallagher. Does it ring a bell?"

"No. No, I'm sorry. I was just wondering. Thank you." She disconnected and added that detail to the list that she was compiling in her head. The man who killed her grandmother also had an Irish name.

Was it all just a coincidence? She didn't know what it meant, but her thoughts kept going back to these accounts of Isadora's and Clara's lives nearly two centuries ago, and the part that a group of Irish men called *Fian Rúnda* played at various distressing times.

She picked up her phone again and clicked on the internet app. She entered *Fian Rúnda* in the search window and found several pages which were apparently in Gaelic and meant nothing to her. Scrolling down through the list, she found one entry from Wikipedia that she could read and she selected it.

Apparently *Fian Rúnda* was an organization in Ireland with the revolutionary objective of gaining independence from   England. *Rúnda* was the Gaelic word for "secret" and indeed the legendary organization had been known for both its secrecy and for the loyalty of its members. No suspected member who was captured ever revealed anything that could endanger the group as a whole.

The other part of the name, *Fian,* was a mythological reference. The *Fianna* were small, semi-independent warrior bands in Irish mythology, though some experts claimed that they were based on actual historical fact.

The *Fian Rúnda,* or Secret Warriors, was rumored to have formed sometime in the late sixteenth or early seventeenth century, after the Tudor conquest of Ireland. Little is known for certain about the secret group, but it was thought that they purposely kept the size of the group small. The fewer their number, the less likely that they would attract attention.

They were suspected to have been behind many acts of violence that some categorized as terrorism, with the goal of gaining independence from England, and funded by numerous other illegal activities. Most consider these attempts as having been unsuccessful, though there has been some disagreement as to whether or not they ultimately contributed to the start of the revolution.

Their activity seemed to have been curtailed in the mid-nineteenth century, and while some historians have offered speculations on the reasons for this, none could ever provide concrete evidence to back up their theories. Some feel that economic hardships affected them and that with a decrease in funds, *Fian Rúnda* lost a great deal of their power. Others have supposed that they were eventually put out of business by British forces, though if this were the case, there would likely be evidence to prove it. Whatever the reason, *Fian Rúnda* ceased to be a truly menacing entity at this time.

After the Irish revolution in the 1920s, the Republic of Ireland was formed, and though their goal of freedom was finally realized, the *Fian Rúnda* is believed by some to still exist as simply a criminal organization, a sort of Irish mafia. Others think the group has dwindled away to little more than a group of thugs, if indeed it has survived at all.

Though the group's existence still cannot be proven, a few suspect them of having been behind several high-profile murders in past decades, and in the theft of numerous valuable items. But without solid evidence, for the most part they have been cast aside as mythical fabrications or as fodder for conspiracy theorists.

Could they have been trying to steal something in particular from her grandmother? Did they think that that silver "pyxis" was still here? The whole case had the appearance of an amateur break-in – Devlin had said that Gallagher apparently had not found anything worth taking before he was discovered.

Dora knew there were many things on the first floor, and in Gramma's room on the second floor, right out in the open, that would have been considered quite valuable, yet none of them had been taken. But Gallagher had been going through boxes in the room on the second floor that had been used for storage when he was interrupted.

An amateur break-in could support one of the theories in the Wikipedia article that *Fian Rúnda* had dwindled away to a group of unorganized thugs. But the coincidences were piling up, and Manitou Springs, Colorado was a long way from Ireland.

As I have stated earlier, spring was my favourite time of year, as it always brought new life. 1853 was no exception, as Ross Hodges was born to Clara and Peter. They chose his name after John Ross, Principal Chief of the Cherokee Nation, and I felt a measure of pride in the honour they were bestowing upon him.

Noya and I found ourselves competing with each other for his time. We were good enough friends that we often stepped back to allow the other time with the baby, though I am certain that I was more fair than she.

The boy was lovely, possessing features of both his parents. I recalled my dear Clara at that age and felt a mixture of nostalgia for the time I was able to hold her, as well as an appreciation of the present, new generation. Ross' hair, though, unlike that of his parents, was dark, perhaps drawing from the features of Noya or Atsila.

Beginning at this time, Noya was happier than I had seen her in the last year and a half, since Edward's death.

"You're a mighty fair lass, Isadora Byrnes," Danny said, and I felt my face flush with the compliment.

"Thank you, Danny," I said, "but I'm no lass. I'm a forty-three year old grandmother."

"I'd say you're holdin' up quite well."

Danny had begun coming around more and more often, staying for at least one night at a time. Despite his wide-range wandering in previous years, he seemed now to stay nearby. At first, I tried

323

not to flatter myself that it was because of me, yet I did admit to feeling a certain attraction myself to this wild Irish mountain man.

We were walking on the road that, over the years, we had cut alongside the river, enjoying the early autumn day, though the heat of the afternoon was becoming a bit stifling. The deerskin dress I wore was sticking to the perspiration, and Danny noticed me fanning myself with my hand.

"Come with me," he said, and he turned away from the river and into the forest. There seemed to be a bit of a trail, but it looked to be little more than a path frequented by animals. I was immediately more comfortable as we were engulfed in the shade of the forest, but Danny seemed to have a specific destination in mind.

"Where are you taking me?" I asked as we continued tramping through the forest.

"You'll see soon enough, lass," he said, and indeed I did after we had walked another five minutes or so, when we came into an unspoiled, picturesque clearing.

The setting was beautiful with a pond fed by a small stream that trickled lazily over smooth rocks. The pond was surrounded by the last of the late summer wildflowers, and shafts of sunlight pierced through the foliage of the surrounding trees, dappling the grass of the forest floor.

"Oh, Danny, it's beautiful!" I said.

"Aye, that it is."

We slowly walked around the little meadow, enjoying the melodic sound of the water, and we found a large relatively flat rock to sit on. "Have you ever seen anything like this land?" Danny asked in awe.

"It is a wonderful place," I answered. "But I admit that I do miss the moors and the rocky coast of England sometimes."

"Mm," Danny said ambiguously. "I miss colcannon and real Irish bacon."

"I miss Yorkshire pudding, though I must say that I have accomplished a rather savoury substitute with venison."

"A nice cool pint of Guinness stout," Danny said, with a wistful tone of voice.

"I used to miss tea," I said with a smile, "but apparently I've come to appreciate coffee to a greater degree than I realised." We sat there, quietly salivating for a while.

Finally, Danny turned to me and broke our silent reverie.

"Do you think you'll ever go back?" he asked.

"I don't know. Probably not. All the family I have any more is right here. It takes so long to travel very far, during which time, I would miss out on what I have now."

"Mm," he replied again. I smiled, as I had become accustomed over the last few months to his sparse and unembellished responses. I felt him move slightly and I turned to see his dark eyes looking at me.

"What is it?" I asked.

"You're a fine lass, Izzy," he said. He inclined his head toward me and, feeling powerless to resist, I leaned closer to him until our lips met. In a moment, his arms were around me and I melted against him, pulling him tighter against me as our mouths hungrily sought each other.

Almost without a thought, I reached up and untied the leather thong which held the neck of my dress together. Never in my life had I known myself to be so brazen. Even with my new husband on our wedding night, I had felt shy and embarrassed. But with Danny, I felt so comfortable that it seemed perfectly reasonable and unpremeditated.

Danny, while still kissing me, spread the top of my dress open and quickly found my breast, cupping it ever so gently in his hand. His lips moved down my throat, then my chest, and closed over my nipple, causing the most exquisite shiver to course through my body. It had been fourteen years since I had exposed my body to a man, but it seemed now to be the most natural thing.

We made love in the dappled sunlight, accompanied by the songs of birds and the gentle trickle of the stream.

The water in the stream was rather cold, but the pond had been warmed by the sunlight and was quite comfortable as we floated on its surface in the wake of our lovemaking, and I felt more at peace than I had felt in years. When we finished our swim, we climbed out of the pond, not attempting to hide our bodies from each other, and we found ourselves in each other's arms again.

But the sun had slipped behind the mountain and there was a bit of a chill in the air. In each other's arms, we attempted to warm ourselves, but after only a brief episode of kissing and caressing, we got dressed and began our journey back home.

During the next few weeks, we made love at our pond several times, but I hesitated to let it be known to anyone else. I was surprised, therefore, when we returned to the house one afternoon and Noya smirked at me.

"What are you grinning about?" I asked.

"It's going to get cold pretty soon," she replied. "You two will be much warmer in your room." Having thought that we were being so discreet, I did not know how to respond and only gave a slight embarrassed smile.

As it turned out, though, she was right. It was much warmer in my room. And softer.

I was lounging in bed early one morning. At first I had thought that it was quite late and that I had overslept, considering the light in the room. Instead I found that it had snowed and I got back in bed.

"I've heard," I said, "that marriage among the Ute Indians consists of the man simply engaging in intercourse with the woman in her home."

"I guess that makes you me wife," Danny said. I was happy to hear how easily he said it. I snuggled against him, attempting to drive out the cold that had quickly entered my body when I had gotten out from under the covers, but it was not going away so easily.

"Danny, dear," I said in my best pleading tone of voice, "would you get another blanket, please?"

"I'd be happy to, me darlin'. Where are they?" I pointed to the wardrobe that stood on his side of the bed. Edward had built it for me a few years before.

Danny got out of bed and opened the door. I lay there appreciating his naked body as it was contrasted against the dark wood. He saw a blanket on the top shelf and pulled it down, but something caught his eye at the back of the shelf, and he seemed to forget about the cold. Reaching back into the wardrobe, he pulled out the silver artifact, the so-called "pyxis."

"Where did you get this, lass?"

"It was in a bag that Liam left with me just before he was killed."

Danny seemed transfixed by the artifact. He had not even looked at me when I answered him. Watching him considering it so closely, I felt a great curiosity, almost a feeling of apprehension. "Danny, what's wrong? Do you know what it is?"

"Aye, Izzy," he said quietly. "This is the O'Riordan family fortune."

"What?" Liam had never spoken to me of a family fortune. To my knowledge, he and his family had always been poor. Danny got back into bed, pulling the covers up, and I spread out the new blanket on top.

"Years ago," he related, his eyes still focused on the silver artifact, "so the story goes, we were, not wealthy, but quite comfortably situated. Me granddad, like his father before him, was a silversmith near Dublin, but he had other interests too.

"Apparently he was not quite right in the head, at least later in his life. At least that's what the family related. He had an eye for fine things, which was all right because he could afford them. But he shocked the family when, after he had scraped together all his means, including real estate holdings, he sunk it into a couple of collections that had caught his eye.

327

"He had some knowledge of old coins, but had never really pursued it until then. He found two coin collections that, as luck would have it, were up for sale by two different people at the same time. Separately, each collection was quite valuable, but when combined, their value increased exponentially. But Granddad was reviled by the family for placing all his financial eggs in one basket.

"He knew the value of what he had, though, and constructed a silver case to hold them, to keep them safe. His craftsmanship was impeccable and any who inspected the case could never discover how to open it, or indeed that it even did open."

With that, holding the artifact horizontally, he pressed his right thumb against a depression in the etched design on the lower right side, and simultaneously pressed his left thumb against a corresponding depression on the left. There was a solid-sounding click. Then the block, with a concealed hinge down one corner, opened into two triangular shaped halves.

The opening revealed many velvet-lined trays with indentations, and each indentation snugly held one ancient Roman coin. Each coin bore the likeness of a different Caesar, and I could only imagine the value of such a collection. The construction of the box was such that each velvet-lined tray slid tightly against and overlapped the next, in an interlocking fashion. This allowed no movement and no noise, giving the impression, when closed, of a solid block of metal.

"Danny, it's incredible!" I said. *"I've had that box with me for twenty-four years and never knew it opened."*

"That was the effect Granddad wanted it to give. He thought that if few people knew what it was, it would remain safer."

"Apparently some know of its value, though," I said. *"There's a group called* Fian Rúnda *that keeps trying to get it from me."*

"They've been here?" he asked with some alarm, looking up at me for the first time. I nodded. He looked down at the coins, then back up at me.

"Sometime after Granddad devised this case, the previous owner of one of the collections got wind of the new, combined collection and of its value. He evidently regretted selling his collection, but Granddad was not interested in letting it go. The bounder was quite persistent and finally Granddad ran him off at gunpoint.

"But the fellow didna give up so easily. Either he was a member, or had friends who were members of Fian Rúnda, and a couple of days later, Granddad's home was broken into and this box, or pyxis as he called it, was stolen, thus wiping out the family fortune."

"I wonder how Liam came to have it," I said.

"Well," Danny continued, "Liam had been involved in somewhat questionable activities, although, to my knowledge, never anything truly illegal. But some of his cronies were less concerned about propriety than he. One of them, in the course of his criminal activities, had discovered this box that Liam had described.

"So, against my advice, Liam started discreetly asking around and eventually became accepted into Fian Rúnda. I left for America at about that time. I tried to convince him to come with me, but he was determined.

"Obviously he found the pyxis and made away with it, but it wasn't a clean job. Apparently they knew he took it and went after him, but he left it with you before they caught up to him."

"How much is this worth?" I asked.

"I couldna say," Danny answered with a slight shake of his head. "But fifty years ago or so, it was rumoured to be worth several million pounds."

And I had thought that the few stacks of gold coins in the valise had been the fortune!

It was not long after this that the pyxis became my own family fortune when Danny O'Riordan and I were officially married in Fort Pueblo.

The sun was behind Pikes Peak now and, though it was still a little while before sunset, the light was growing dimmer. Dora had impatiently switched on a lamp, anxious to continue reading to the end of the chapter.

She sat back in the sofa when she realized that she had been leaning forward tensely as she was reading. She was fascinated by the account, having finally found out what the mysterious pyxis was, and felt even more curious about where it had finally ended up.

But Dora had skipped lunch and was feeling a little hungry, so she reluctantly took a necessary break from reading. She went into the kitchen and cut a few slices of cheese and placed them and some crackers on a plate. She poured a glass of Cabernet, but she jumped as she detected unexpected movement out the kitchen window.

She had the impression that someone had been watching her from the back yard, but as she peered out the window, she realized that it was windy outside. Foliage on the linden tree was whipping back and forth. That must have been what caught her eye, and she breathed a sigh of relief.

She took the wine and the crackers and cheese back into the living room and opened the book again.

Shawn pressed a button on his phone and it lit up. He just wanted to be sure it was still on. He didn't understand why Dora had not called back yet.

From Dora's house, he had gone back to his office. He was pacing again, attempting rather unsuccessfully to just breathe normally.

As long as he had his phone in his hand, he thought about calling her again, but he decided to wait. He was anxious to find that curious pyxis, but he didn't want to seem like a pest and have her turned off toward him. That could be fatal. He would wait a little while longer.

He needed to be with Dora. Their time together these past few days had awakened something inside him that had been asleep or dormant for years. When he was away from her, he could only think of her. And when he was with her, he only wanted to stay. He could not see a future without her.

He knew how ridiculous it was to be thinking this way. He had only met her just a few days ago. He had never fallen for someone so quickly. He was always much too practical for that.

Dora was obviously special.

He pictured her face in his mind, and he noticed himself calming down. Just thinking of her features, of her gentle qualities, actually made him feel more peaceful. Seeing her smile brought a smile to his own face.

But then, the image in his mind changed. Dora was lying on the floor with a bullet hole in her face, her eyes lifeless and locked in a vacant stare, a glistening pool of blood under her head, and Shawn felt a violent shudder heave through his body.

If they didn't find that damn pyxis, there would not be a future. For either of them.

Early in 1854, Danny conceived of a better hiding place for the pyxis than I had come up with. Placing it behind a blanket on a shelf, he said, would confound none but the dimmest of criminals. He spent a month or so devising it, using Edward's tools with Noya's permission, and I admit to being quite proud of his inge-nuity after it was completed. The hiding place was very clever, though for safety's sake, I will not provide any details or descrip-tions here.

It was not a moment too soon, as we were again paid a visit by the Fian Rúnda. *I must say that I was finding these people to be most tiresome.*

This time, they did not bother to attempt a ruse as they had last time. Clara and Peter were visiting for dinner, and ultimately, that was fortunate for us, though it was quite a stressful time for poor little Ross.

We were busy setting the table for dinner when we heard the sound of approaching thunder. Danny looked out the front door and counted at least twenty armed men on horseback, one of them carrying a flaming torch. They stopped about a hundred yards from the house and just sat there, observing and apparently dis-cussing plans. After a few moments, they dismounted and spread out.

Knowing they were up to no good, Danny told Clara to take Ross to the cellar where he would be safe, and he grabbed two rifles from a cabinet near the front door. The year before, Danny had acquired two Smith-Jennings rifles which could fire multiple shots without having to reload each time. He kept one for himself and handed the other one to me.

We also had a collection of older guns so, seeing what was happening, Peter and Noya each selected muskets, and the four of us sought vantage points at various locations around the house. In passing Noya, I saw the hard and determined expression on her face – she knew that this was the same group that was responsible for killing her husband.

By comparing our experiences later, I was able to compile a fairly accurate account of what happened. Danny stayed at the front door, watching the movements of the men within the range of his view. Peter went to the back door and Noya looked out various windows until she found one that gave her a good view of several of the men. They were in hiding, on the fringe of the forest, but we could occasionally see a head here and there as they were waiting for all of their number to take their positions. After securing Ross in the cellar, Clara came back up and took a musket as well.

I went up to the third storey and into the bedroom that faced east, which was roughly the direction from which they came. I had barely gotten into position when the man carrying a torch attempted a run at the house, while others near him fired a barrage of shots toward us to provide cover for him. Danny had lain down on the floor just inside the front door, and as high as the porch was, he was nearly invisible to them. As the rest of us stayed hidden from the oncoming shots, Danny took aim and fired just as the man flung the torch onto the roof over the porch. The man fell dead, but the torch found its mark.

Looking out my window from an angle, I could see the torch as the flames were beginning to spread to the roof. I hesitated to waste a shot on anything other than our enemies. But in order to save the house, I took careful aim and fired, hitting the torch at its widest part. The torch splintered and flew off the roof, leaving it mostly unscathed.

Turning my attention back to the men surrounding us, I saw a cloud of smoke from behind a tree followed quickly by the sound of a shot. From my vantage point up high, I could see the head and one shoulder of the assailant as he had turned his back to a tree to reload. I raised my rifle, bracing it on the window sill, took quick aim and fired, and the man fell to the side and was still.

Shots were coming quickly now, too quickly to discern and narrate, but my vantage point nearly twenty-five feet up gave me an advantage. I could fire upon them while remaining almost entirely hidden, but they could not fire up at me without exposing a good portion of their bodies. To increase my advantage, I moved from one third storey room to the other, keeping an eye on both sides of the house that were visible from there.

At the back door, Peter and Clara were working together as a team. They had three muskets between them, so after Peter fired one, he handed it to Clara who reloaded it. She could almost keep up with him, but there were so many men attacking the house that Peter was able to take plenty of shots in quick succession, so occasionally he would have to reload one of the muskets himself.

It was during one of these times that one of our attackers rushed the back door. Peter was just beginning to reload when the man appeared at the door. Seeing Peter, he raised his gun. Clara, sitting on the floor partly hidden behind the door, was just ramming the shot home in her gun. When she saw the man about to shoot Peter, she raised her musket in a panic and fired at the man's chest from about two feet away. The ramrod went in the left side of the man's ribs, up and out the back of his right shoulder and he fell dead.

Noya was at a window in our small library on the east side of the house and was fighting valiantly. Though we were surrounded, we had more protection than our attackers did. They were staying behind trees at the edge of the forest, but some of them were getting closer, working their way up behind clumps of trees that remained in the clearing.

One man was making a run for one of these clusters of trees when Noya's shot hit him in the stomach. The man fell to the ground, writhing in pain. She rose slightly from her position, torn by a combination of the desire to dispense justice for her slain husband, and fellow feeling for a human being in pain. The man saw her and, despite the pain he was in, raised his gun and fired, but his aim was bad. Noya picked up the other musket she had and killed him.

From my position on the third storey, I saw, like before, a puff of smoke from a shot at the edge of the forest. Locating the man behind the gun, I fired and he fell dead. I did not realise, though, that I had exposed myself to one of the men to my right, and I felt a sudden searing pain as a lead ball smashed into my shoulder with surprising force. I fell to the floor, glad in that instant that the angle at which I was hit prevented the ball from entering my chest. Nevertheless, I was in excruciating pain.

I gritted my teeth and, fighting back the tears, rose to the window again, watching for any movement that I could exploit. Soon after this, I saw the smoke from the report of a gun, sighted and fired. I nearly cried out in pain as the recoil of the shot caused the butt of the rifle to impact against my right shoulder. But I hit my target and one more attacker was eliminated.

Meanwhile Danny, still shooting from the floor behind the partly opened front door, had shot three or four of the men, but several of them were attempting to get closer, behind those clusters of trees. As they came nearer, their shots were more accurate, and one of them smashed into the door frame an inch from Danny's head.

Taking aim at where he supposed the chest of a man was through the foliage, Danny squeezed the trigger, but his rifle was empty. He rolled over out of view to reload, and the men made a run for the front porch.

It was at this time that Hissing Snake, Bear Killer and others who had heard the gun battle, had rushed to our assistance. Using *the muskets that we had given them, they opened fire from concealment in the forest.*

With shots coming from both sides of the men, our attackers were unable to remain concealed. They had to divide their attention between two groups of enemies, and in a matter of a few minutes, the last one fell. This time, there were no survivors left to report to the soldiers.

As soon as the conflict was over, Danny ran up the stairs and found me leaning weakly against the window.

"Oh, dear Lord," he said, seeing all the blood.

"It's all right, Danny," I reassured him. "I'll be fine." Gathering my small frame easily in his arms, he carried me down to the main floor. Clara was there, trying to comfort little Ross who, neglected but safe in the cellar for the duration of the battle, was understandably upset.

Noya and Peter had greeted the Indians in front of the house and offered profuse thanks for their help. Noya offered to share our dinner with them, which they declined, but they wanted to check on Danny and me. I persuaded Danny that I could stand, so he put me down and we went outside to offer our own thanks to our friends.

Bear Killer and Hissing Snake were concerned about my wound, but I assured them that I would be fine. After removing guns, ammunition, and other useful items from the corpses strewn about the property, the Indians removed the bodies and disposed of them in a rather large fire deep in the forest.

My wound, it turned out, though quite painful, was not as bad as I had thought. The ball had passed through my shoulder, so we did not have to worry about getting it out. Noya took great care in treating the wound, but my arm remained somewhat useless for a while afterwards.

We walked around the house in a daze, surveying the damage. There were bullet holes inside and out, and we knew that there would be a good deal of repair work required. After we had taken some time to relax a bit, Noya reheated the dinner and we sat down to eat, very quiet, but all thankful that we had survived.

We spent the summer repairing damage to the house and we heard nothing more from Fian Rúnda *for the rest of the year. I knew very little about the organisation, including how large it was. But I hoped that we had crippled it extensively.*

The Indians continued watching out for us, particularly when white people approached. Bear Killer was especially attentive after that battle. I thought at first that his concern was for all of us, and indeed it was, but I noticed that he paid special attention to Noya.

Bear Killer's wife had been killed some years before during a raid by a small band of Navajo warriors, and I think that he was now noticing that Noya would make a good wife – hard-working, brave, and still quite attractive. In time, she began to respond to his attention.

They were married before the snows came that year.

ora's phone rang and she picked it up and looked at the display. It was Shawn calling again. She sighed and was about to put the phone back down when she noticed the icon indicating that a voice mail message had already been left. She touched the icon and entered her password. The message had been left earlier in the afternoon.

"Hey Dora, it's me," Shawn said in the message. Dora thought his voice sounded a little unnaturally cheerful. "I'm standing outside your house, and I see your car's here. I don't know. Maybe you went for a walk or something. Anyway, I wanted to see if we could get together and read some more of Isadora's book, maybe figure out what that mysterious pyxis is. Give me a call."

Dora sneered at the phone and deleted the message without hesitation, but she noticed that the voice mail icon was still there, indicating that there was another message. She looked at the information for this one and saw that the message was left just now, with his most recent call.

"Dora, it's Shawn." His voice sounded almost desperate. "I really hope you're okay. I'm not sure if you got my earlier message or not. We need to get together as soon as possible. I don't want to alarm you but it's pretty imperative. I can't really tell you much over the phone. Please, call me!"

Confused by this tactic, Dora decided that it did not sound like a ploy for another roll in the hay. Reluctantly, she called him back. He picked up on the first ring.

"Dora, hi!" he said sounding very relieved.

"What do you want?" she asked, clearly irritated.

"What – what's wrong?"

"What's wrong? I saw you and your little Barbie doll."

"What are you talking about?"

"The pretty blonde you went out to lunch with."

"How do you know about her?"

"I was just coming out of the Chamber of Commerce and saw you and Barbie getting into your car. You both seemed very intimate, pretty touchy-feely, considering that you fucked me just last night."

"Oh, God!" Shawn said. "Dora, I'm so sorry you saw that. It was Nicole, my girlfriend. Or at least she was."

"She *was?*"

"We were together for a couple of years, but it wasn't really going anywhere. Not from my standpoint, anyway. She was out of town for a few days on business and I decided to break it off with her.

"Then I met you and I was even more determined. Today was her first day back and we already had plans for lunch. I broke up with her."

Dora had not expected a logical explanation such as this, and she hesitated as she thought about what he said.

"What about all the Irish shit?"

"What Irish shit?" he asked with a quiet note of fear in his voice.

"I put some things together. The man who killed my grandmother was Irish. You're Irish, your name is Irish, you wear a Celtic knot around your neck. And you are particularly interested in finding that pyxis."

She heard him sigh.

"Well, clearly you've done some thinking about this, but I can assure you that I care more about you than about that damn pyxis. And that's exactly why we need to get together."

"Why?"

"Let me come over and explain."

"That's a pretty unbelievable story," Dora said. She was not sure whether she should believe him and be frightened or if she should toss him out on his ass.

"Yeah, tell me about it."

"You said you didn't want to worry me. So why are you telling me now?"

"Because I'd rather have you worried than dead. When you didn't answer the door or return my call, I started to worry that the *Fian Rúnda* goons might get tired of waiting for us and take matters into their own hands. Again. Don't forget, these are the same people who killed your grandmother. It wasn't just a random Irishman."

"I know," Dora said with a sigh. She decided that she believed him, and she was frightened.

"We have to find that thing," Shawn said, "whatever it is."

"I know what it is. When I saw you and Barbie – sorry – Nicole, I didn't wait for you. I kept reading."

"And?"

"And it was a collection of ancient Roman coins which, two hundred years ago, was worth several million pounds."

"Well, that makes more sense," Shawn said thoughtfully. "I didn't think a block of solid silver alone would be valuable enough to draw the sustained attention of a criminal group all the way over in Ireland."

It was early evening and Dora was feeling hungry again. The cheese and crackers hadn't lasted very long.

"Are you hungry?" she asked. She remembered bringing home a few slices of leftover pizza from the restaurant Sunday evening.

"I don't know. I guess." He hadn't thought about food for a while.

"Why don't you skim through the book and catch up with me, and I'll heat up that pizza from the other night."

341

"Okay," he agreed. "That's a good idea."

"Well, that's frustrating!" Shawn said, as he put the book down.

"What?"

"Isadora mentions the clever hiding place of the pyxis, but doesn't give any details. Understandable, of course, but still maddening."

"I know. I was hoping for more too." Dora looked nervously toward the window. It was dark now, and she got up to close the curtains. "Do you suppose they're watching us now?"

"I'm sure they are," Shawn said, feeling the nervous tightness in his lungs again.

"What if we can't find the pyxis? What if Isadora and Danny sold it or it was stolen or something like that?"

"I broached that possibility to Brian. He replied that he was certain it's still around. Apparently they've been watching for it. Something that valuable can't be put on the market, even underground, without raising some flags."

"What if a coin collector got it for his own collection? Maybe it wasn't put on the market."

"I don't know," Shawn said with some irritation. "We just have to keep looking until we find the pyxis, or we find the empty spot where it was. And just hope it's not the latter."

Dora looked up at him when she heard the chilled tone of his voice.

My mother wrote nothing more in this book for the rest of her life so, for the sake of anyone who may, for whatever reason, find this account interesting, I have taken it upon myself to provide a conclusion to her history.

Peter and I found it necessary to enlarge our home, particularly when Ross' sister Betsy was born. Eventually, Peter and I had four children when we added Edward and Quentin to our family. Mother lived to see all four of them grown and married.

After Noya and Bear Killer were married, she moved with him into his teepee. While we all expected that she would not last long in a primitive Indian camp, she actually seemed very happy. Bear Killer (or just "Bear" as many of us started calling him) was very attentive to her and they were very much in love. They were somewhat nomadic and moved around at times, but Bear's family did seem to spend most of their time near us.

In 1861, the War Between the States began and went on for four years, though thankfully, it did not affect us much in our remote area. What did affect us during this time, however, was what became known as the Colorado War, fought between the American government and several Indian tribes in our area.

We heard many reports that disturbed us greatly. Indians were shot and killed on sight, and one particularly horrifying account told of American troops slaughtering and mutilating an entire Cheyenne village camped at Sand Creek about 150 miles east of here. Most of the victims were women and children since the able-bodied men were away on a buffalo hunt.

Frankly, we refused to believe many of these stories until they were finally confirmed to us by several visitors. Colonel John Chivington, who was in charge of this particular massacre was quoted as saying, "Damn any man who sympathizes with Indians! I have come to kill Indians, and believe it is right and honorable to use any means under God's heaven to kill Indians."

However, our little area was generally peaceful, though it did not remain remote for much longer. People had heard of the healing waters of Manitou, and over the years, many journeyed here. With Mother and Danny living alone in their large house, they turned it into an inn and in later years, they almost always entertained visitors.

Danny seemed to have a very good, calming effect on Mother. All my years growing up, I remember her occasional episodes of depression, or her anxiety when white people were around. But after Danny came along, she had very few episodes of depression, and she was able to deal well enough with white people, individually and in groups, that their inn was a great success.

Mother and Noya spent much time together, when their own domestic duties allowed, and over the course of about five years, finally realized Mahaley's dream of compiling a collection of Cherokee folklore. Working together, they remembered many of the stories she used to tell, writing them down and adding details as they recalled them, eventually publishing them in a small volume. It never went into a second printing, and most of the copies that did sell were in the Indian Territory, or Oklahoma as it later came to be called. But Wisdom of the Principal People *was greatly appreciated and treasured by those who purchased it and wanted to preserve the legacy of the Cherokee.*

In August of 1876, Colorado became the thirty-eighth state of the Union. A year and half later, the town of Manitou was officially founded a few miles from our home. Sadly, this was after the Cheyenne and Arapaho Indians were removed from the area and relocated to reservations. The Ute Indians were finally removed in

1879, and though Bear and Noya were quite old, they made the move together. We never saw them again after that.

Over the years, the people that Mother called Fian Rúnda made a few more attempts at getting the fabled pyxis, though none of those attempts had anywhere near the fervor of the attack in 1854. It seemed as if they had lost a great deal of steam, so the combined forces of our family, white and Indian, repelled them fairly easily.

Danny died in December of 1881 at the age of seventy-five. A couple of weeks before, he had been hunting and, as his hearing was not as good as it used to be, he surprised a bull elk and was gored by an antler. He survived the attack, but eventually succumbed to an infection that followed. Mother mourned his passing stoically, and though I did see tears in her eyes on numerous occasions, she more often smiled when she remembered her time spent with him.

Mother lived to see the new century and died in 1901. She was ninety-one years old, and ran her inn, with my help, almost up to the day she died. Aside from spending time with her grandchildren, nothing made her happier than visiting with her guests, and making their stay a happy one. She could often be found in the kitchen preparing meals, and the menu often featured the fare to which she was originally introduced when she first came to America, including biscuits and gravy, ham and grits.

Though tea was always available at her inn, Mother never developed a taste for it again.

W ell, it's a fairly happy ending," Shawn said. "But I'm afraid it doesn't help us a bit!"

"I know," said Dora. She had a tight feeling in her gut that would not go away as she thought of the *Fian Rúnda*.

"There's nothing more?" Shawn asked as he flipped through the last few blank pages.

"Nothing except a loose piece of paper I found in there," Dora replied. "I stuck it back in there near the back." Shawn flipped the pages again, more carefully until he saw the loose leaf. He pulled it out and looked at it, frowning as he tried to decipher the cryptic lines of letters and numbers.

"Do you know what this means?" he asked.

"Not a clue."

"a-4-2 b-2-6 c-9-5 – I don't get it."

"I know. It's not Isadora's or Clara's handwriting. I'm not even sure it means anything at all." But then, as she was looking at the paper in his hand, she felt as if at least one piece of the puzzle fell into place. "Wait a minute!" she said and snatched it out of his hand.

She sprinted up the stairs with Shawn close behind her. On the third floor, she knelt before the still open trunk and the items that were arranged on the floor around it.

"What is it?" Shawn asked, as Dora carefully picked up the short stack of old documents.

"I thought I recognized the handwriting," she said as she held out the papers. The bill of sale for Jimmy and Alice was on top.

Shawn didn't see the connection until Dora pointed to the small letters handwritten in the top margins of some of the pages. The handwriting matched that on the loose slip of paper. "I still don't know what it means, though."

"Let me see those," Shawn said as a thought occurred to him. He laid them out on the floor and arranged them in order based on the letters in the top margins. "Now, let's see that piece of paper from the book." Dora handed it to him and he looked back and forth from the two short lines of figures and the documents. Gradually a smile spread across his face.

"What?" Dora asked curiously, as Shawn took out his phone. He touched the icon for a text app and started typing.

"It's a fairly simple code," he said. "The letter corresponds with the letter at the top of the page, the first number refers to the line on the page, and the second number refers to a word in that line. 'a-4-2' means page 'a,' line 4, word 2." He kept typing until he had gathered every word referenced in the lines of code, then read it aloud.

"Main fire place push mantel left pull." They looked at each other, then quickly stood up and raced down the stairs and into the living room. The mantel on the fireplace was a huge slab of polished yellow pine, displaying several pictures and other heirlooms. Dora carefully removed the items and placed them on an end table.

Shawn tried to jiggle the mantel, but it seemed solid. He applied more force, pushing to the left, and he felt it budge just a bit.

"Shall we?" he asked, and Dora grabbed the mantel tightly, pulling to the left as Shawn pushed hard from the right side. There was a solid, wooden thud from inside the slab and they pulled out towards themselves. "Be careful," Shawn said. "This is probably pretty heavy."

But nothing happened. The mantel still seemed solid. However, as Dora felt around it, she noticed that there was a little space now between the slab of pine and the rocks of the fireplace. She could just barely get her fingertips inserted in the space.

"Pull harder," she said. Getting as much leverage as they could, they strained out away from the wall, and the mantel slowly produced a wood-on-wood creaking sound as it finally came free, sliding off the four notched wooden support pegs protruding from the fireplace.

They set the mantel down on the floor and saw the carving on the back side of it. An area about six by fourteen inches had been hewn out of it, and fitting snugly in the cavity was a tarnished silver box, embellished with a profusion of Celtic designs. Shawn pried it loose, looked up at Dora and handed it to her.

It was quite heavy, and examining the surface, Dora could understand why Isadora had thought it was a solid block of silver. Remembering her account of Danny opening it, Dora located the points that Isadora had referred to, pressed her thumbs against them simultaneously and heard a dull, reluctant click, as the artifact opened, revealing the interlocking velvet-lined trays that Isadora had referred to.

"Oh my God!" they both said, as they saw the coins, millennia-old currency of various denominations, each bearing the figure of a Caesar. It was just as Isadora had described it – the trays rotated out from each half, with a space between them exactly the thickness of the tray on the other half to fit into. Dora started silently counting.

"Eighty coins," she finally said, "probably reflecting the entire history of the Roman Empire!"

"It's got to be worth millions."

"I can't believe we have to just give it to a bunch of thugs!"

"Maybe we don't," said Shawn.

"I'd rather not die," Dora said sarcastically.

"Living is pretty high on my 'to do list' too," Shawn said. "But you know they weren't just going to leave us alone once they got this."

"Yeah, that's what I figured," Dora said, feeling that tight sensation in her gut again.

"But I think we still have a trick left up our sleeve," Shawn said with some confidence.

With the coins wrapped tightly in a cloth as Isadora had done, and placed snugly in Dora's purse, they walked out the door into the cool night. The pyxis was where they had left it on the mantel, though not in its original condition. Dora had looked at Shawn as if he had quietly gone crazy when he was sealing it with Super Glue.

"If any of those goons know how to open it," he had explained, "I don't want them doing it here. I want them to take it with them and leave, and not realize that the coins aren't in it until they're away." Even without the coins, the silver pyxis was fairly heavy, and Shawn hoped that it wouldn't register with them that it might be empty.

As Dora closed the door, Shawn stretched his arms out to the side and feigned a yawn, giving the signal that Brian had suggested to him. Feeling nervous, a real yawn followed naturally. He tried not to look around. He was certain they were being watched, but he didn't really want to see Brian or any of his cronies. They descended the steps from the porch, got into Shawn's car and drove away.

Waiting a minute or two after they disappeared down the road, two men got out of a black SUV parked up the road a short distance. Keeping to the shadows, they approached the front door and within a couple of minutes, were inside.

Once in the door, they looked around, first in the entryway, then in adjoining rooms. When they entered the living room, they saw the pyxis on the mantel. One of them picked it up while the other one pressed a speed dial number on his phone.

"Brian, we've got it," was all he said, and they left.

They went back out the door and walked up the road toward the SUV. They were just about to get in when FBI agents appeared

350

from out of the shadows and swarmed around them with guns drawn.

Dora and Shawn had just sat down at a table on the outdoor patio at Adam's Mountain Café, a restaurant on Manitou Avenue in the old Manitou Springs Spa building. Listening to the sound of Fountain Creek which flowed alongside the patio, they each ordered a glass of Orange Spice iced tea.

After Brian and his friend the gorilla had left his office early this afternoon, Shawn had agonized over whether he should call the Police, despite the warning that Brian had given. Then he realized that, given the fact that this was an international crime, this might actually fall in the jurisdiction of the FBI. He looked up the number for the FBI office in Denver and told them everything he knew about *Fian Rúnda,* including what he knew about the murder of Dora's grandmother and his impromptu meeting with Brian.

Even while he was still on the phone with Agent Munson, some of the things he told them were able to be verified. Munson told him that a quick search of the Interpol database returned information about a suspect that resembled Shawn's description of Brian.

The FBI quickly assembled a team and put them in place in a wide radius around Dora's house, while they waited for Shawn to let them know of the progress in the search for the pyxis. As soon as he and Dora had found it, Shawn called Agent Munson and told him that they would be leaving soon, as previously arranged. Munson would contact him when the operation was completed.

"So, what are we supposed to do now?" Dora asked.

"Agent Munson said that we don't have to do anything except stay out of the way. It should be over pretty quickly."

The waitress had just put down their glasses of tea when Brian approached their table and sat down, the hostess following close behind. He was still wearing his shades even though it was dark outside.

"See, I told you me friends were here," he said to her. Shawn and Dora glanced at each other with a look of panic in their eyes. After the hostess left, Brian turned to Shawn. "You two have done very well. I just wanted to come and thank you personally." He obviously did not know about the FBI.

"You're welcome," Shawn managed to say.

"Why don't we leave here, so I can thank you properly."

"We're fine right here."

"You don't understand," Brian said icily. "It was not a suggestion."

"You're not going to thank us," Dora said.

"I don't think we've had the pleasure, lass," Brian said to her, extending his hand. "It's Dora, isn't it?" Dora looked at his hand but sat perfectly still.

"She's a bright one, she is," Brian said to Shawn. "And I'm afraid you're right, miss. You're a couple of loose ends. Can't leave any of those untied."

"We won't be going anywhere with you," Shawn said resolutely.

"Oh, I think you will. Don't think I won't shoot you here. Believe me, I've no compunctions about shooting you both right here in front of other people, but if I do, it'll just make it a bit more complicated for me. And there's always the possibility that somebody else could get hurt too. And I know you're a couple of conscientious people. You don't want to endanger anyone else. Including family."

Shawn stiffened at the mention of his family members and was reminded of the threat that Brian had made against them. He looked around the patio. It was late, but there were a few other people there, at a couple of tables toward the back.

Shawn found himself making calculations in his head. He had found a parking space on the street just a short distance to the east. But he could not think of how they could get away from Brian, to make a run for his car.

352

"Stop lookin' around," Brian warned. "Just stand and come quietly."

Hoping he could think of something before it was too late, Shawn gave a slight nod toward Dora. The three of them stood up and as Dora took her purse from where it hung on the back of the metal chair, she felt the weight of it, remembering the eighty coins wrapped tightly inside it. Before she could talk herself out of it, she swung the purse with all her might toward Brian's head. Catching him squarely on his right temple, Brian fell across another metal table and lay on the ground unconscious.

"Nice!" Shawn said admiringly. Then, grabbing Dora's hand, he headed toward the front of the metal fence surrounding the patio. He had just helped her over it and they were running toward his car when they saw Brian's giant sidekick coming toward them up the sidewalk. Doing a quick glance at their surroundings, Dora pulled Shawn to the left, into the maze of scattered buildings that made up the Manitou Springs Arcade.

There were still a lot of people here as Dora and Shawn tried to blend in, past the kids playing skeeball, pinball and electronic video games. Turning down an alley to their left, they ran past gift shops and the old fashioned Penny Arcade. Their feet and hearts pounding, they were nearly at the end of the buildings when Shawn stole a glance behind them. The musclebound man was, as Shawn had hoped, not able to run fast, but he was still there, and to Shawn's terror, he was aiming a pistol at them. Just as he heard the shot, they swerved left onto the sidewalk on Cañon Avenue and the bullet slammed harmlessly into the stone wall that, a moment before, had been right beside them.

Running northwest on Cañon Avenue, Dora panted, "I don't know where to go!"

"That's the Cliff House Hotel across the street," Shawn replied, feeling his breath burning his throat. The beautiful historic building was lit up with a welcoming glow coming from all the windows. "Maybe we can hide in there."

Just then, they saw someone running in their direction from the hotel. They could not make out any features as he was backlit by the hotel. It could just as easily be someone rushing to the Arcade, but they didn't wait to find out his intentions.

They ran to the corner and turned left again toward Manitou, and soon found themselves at the back end of the Adam's Mountain Café patio, where they had started. A quick glimpse of the seating area and they could see the restaurant staff righting and repositioning the fallen table. They also saw that Brian was not there.

Taking the walkway that crossed Fountain Creek, Shawn wanted to turn left to try to get to his car, but he heard heavy running footsteps in that direction. Rather than waiting to see who it was, they turned to the right.

They ran in front of more shops, including the Sahara Café where they had eaten lunch just a few days before. They both wanted to slip into one of the stores and catch their breath, but another gunshot spurred them on.

Coming to the roundabout at the junction of Manitou and Ruxton Avenues, a third gunshot sounded and Shawn stumbled as he felt a sudden burning in his left thigh. Dora was still holding his hand and felt him jerk. Her heart nearly stopped, thinking the worst, until she saw him grip his thigh. She grabbed him and pulled his right arm over her shoulders and helped to support him.

"Over there!" Shawn pointed across the roundabout to a store that stood on the corner, The Mountain Man. Hampered now by a bullet wound, the two were moving too slowly. Shawn was certain the Irish gorilla was catching up with them by now.

And in fact, he was. He did not wait for the roundabout though. Seeing his quarry heading away from the well-lit tourist area, he hoped to stop them before they were concealed in the darkness of a side street. He stepped out from behind a parked car with his gun raised, singlemindedly focused on his prey, and was struck from behind by a pickup.

On the narrow downtown street, the truck was not going fast enough to throw the man's body ahead of it. Rather, the impact knocked him down on the pavement and rolled him over so that the front left wheel of the truck ended up resting on his chest.

The collision broke his left leg and his lower back. Though he was conscious of what happened to him, the weight of the truck on his chest squeezed the air out of his lungs and prevented him from being able to take another breath.

The traumatized driver got out of his pickup, saw the man under the wheel and struggled to keep from vomiting. He immediately got back in the truck and carefully backed up to get the wheel off of the man, but by that time, the man was dead.

Shawn and Dora were aware of a commotion behind them, but they did not stop to look. They made it to the door of The Mountain Man, under a sign that said, "Muzzleloading Outfitters." They pulled the door open and ran inside, and together, they hobbled around racks toward the back of the store. Shawn pulled out his phone and quickly called Agent Munson, while a bearded man watched with surprise from behind a counter.

"Munson here," he heard on the other end.

"Agent Munson, it's Shawn. They're after us! I've been shot!"

"Where are you?"

"We're at The Mountain Man, Manitou and Ruxton."

Just then, the front door burst open and there stood Brian, a trickle of blood on his left temple where he hit his head on the metal table at the cafe.

Hearing the door, Shawn and Dora shrunk down behind racks of outdoor gear, fearing that this was the end. Dora tried to pull Shawn behind one of the counters, knowing it would only be temporary concealment. Brian, pistol in hand, slowly began weaving through the free standing racks in the store, his eyes darting back and forth looking for them.

As he moved from behind one of the racks, he saw the bearded proprietor of the store on his left, behind the other counter, with an old fashioned musket in his hands. Before the musket could be raised to point at him, Brian coldly fired and the man fell, dropping the musket beside him. That obstacle removed, Brian resumed scanning the store for Shawn and Dora.

He moved toward the right where he thought he had detected movement when he first entered the store. Cautious, but anticipating the end of his search, he came around the final rack and saw Shawn on the floor, his back against the wall. He did not see Dora, but figured he would find her soon enough – it was a small store.

Dora had worked her way behind the counter, and around the corner. She saw the proprietor of the store, lying on the floor bleeding behind the other counter. But she saw that he was conscious, the bullet having gone into his left shoulder. She quietly picked up the musket and the proprietor reached over with his right hand and carefully pulled the hammer back, hoping the click could not be heard. Then he nodded to Dora who lifted her head just above the top of the counter.

Her heart pounding, she stood up and pointed the musket at Brian, but she only had a shot of his left side and arm. Never having fired a gun before, she wanted as large a target as possible. She could see that he had found Shawn and was smiling as he pointed the pistol at him.

"Hey asshole!" she said, spurred on by adrenalin and fear for Shawn. Brian was surprised to see her pointing the musket at him and was just turning his pistol toward her, giving her the larger target she wanted. As Dora squeezed the trigger, Brian heard the sound of two explosions in quick succession as the musket's hammer struck the cap, the ignition of which then ignited the powder in the gun.

The last thing that Brian experienced was the sensation of the lead ball smashing through his sternum and sending fragments of bone and lead through his heart. He was dead when he hit the floor.

Realizing that she had been holding her breath, Dora exhaled and placed the musket on the glass counter as the proprietor pulled himself up. Seeing that he was not critically injured, Dora retraced her route behind the counters to where Shawn lay against the wall, a glistening splash of crimson on the floor under his thigh. She smiled at him as he gradually realized that Brian was no longer a threat.

"Shawn! Shawn, are you there?" Shawn picked up his phone when he heard Munson's voice.

"Yes, Agent Munson, I'm here," he replied, his voice becoming calmer. "Brian's dead. Dora shot him."

"We're almost there!" Munson said. "We'll have an ambulance meet us." Shawn disconnected and, throwing his arm over Dora's shoulders, struggled to his feet.

"Tommy, are you alright?" he asked the proprietor when he saw him bleeding.

"I will be," Tommy said through clenched teeth as he endured the pain in his shoulder. "You must have really pissed him off. He didn't seem too happy with you."

"Yeah, you could say that."

"Your girl's a crack shot," Tommy said, turning his attention to Dora, and she flushed at the compliment.

"Must be genetic," Shawn said, and he glanced at Dora with a smile, recalling Isadora's marksmanship.

He reached out and shook Tommy's hand.

"Colin and I took care of Tommy's father's estate a couple of years ago," Shawn explained to Dora. She shook his hand as well.

"Sorry to have involved you in this, but I sure appreciate your help," she said.

"I'm glad I could help." Dora noticed the musket on the counter, and other previously owned muskets hanging on the wall behind the counter.

"You don't suppose," she said to Shawn, "that this could be one of Isadora's old muskets, do you?"

"I think that might be a little too much of a coincidence," Shawn replied, though he clearly liked the idea.

It was determined, once the FBI started making their arrests at Dora's house and interrogating those in custody, that they didn't have Brian Doyle, or Ryan Walsh, his muscle. Agent Munson was just about to call Shawn when Shawn called him from The Mountain Man.

The three men they arrested at Dora's house would eventually be arraigned on multiple counts of breaking and entering, grand larceny, conspiracy to commit murder, and a handful of other charges. Unlike their predecessors of earlier days, their loyalty toward *Fian Rúnda* was not unbreakable.

The bullet in Shawn's thigh was lodged in soft tissue and was removed at the hospital without any complications. Though it was initially painful, there would be no permanent damage. He was kept for a day and then released.

Tommy was equally fortunate, as the bullet had passed through his shoulder and lodged in the wood paneled wall behind him. He proudly drew a circle around the hole with a marker and, beneath it, hung the musket that had killed Brian.

Local Woman Helps Topple Crime Organization

Coin Collection One of the Richest Finds in Numismatic History

Denver Post, September 9, 2012

Dora Baskin did not know, when she drove to Manitou Springs after the death of her grandmother last month, that she would be a central figure in bringing down a legendary criminal organization. The former Denver social worker found that she had inherited the bulk of her grandmother's estate, including an expansive 172-year-old log house now listed in the National Register of Historic Places. She also inherited a family fortune that has been the target of treasure hunters for the last two centuries.

Ms. Baskin's nineteenth century ancestor, Isadora O'Riordan, left a handwritten history of her colorful life after emigrating from England to America. Her tale included her life among the Cherokee Indians of northern Georgia and their subsequent ousting by way of the Trail of Tears, and ultimately her settlement near Manitou

Springs. Mrs. O'Riordan was known in her time for her sympathy toward the Native Americans, and for her native-styled mode of dress. Her writings alluded to a treasure, a coin collection of almost mythical value which, as Ms. Baskin found, was hidden in the house.

Fabled Irish crime syndicate *Fian Rúnda*, the existence of which was finally confirmed by a spokesman for the FBI, has allegedly made numerous attempts to steal the coin collection since it was assembled more than two centuries ago. This campaign resulted in a deadly showdown in Manitou Springs last month, culminating with the arrest of several Irish crime figures formerly considered out of reach.

Ms. Baskin's grandmother, Isadora Baskin, was killed in her home on August 14 when she apparently surprised a burglar. The break-in, investigators later found, was a part of the latest attempt to find and steal the coin collection.

The burglar, Finn Gallagher, suspected member of *Fian Rúnda*, was then killed by neighbor Robert Johnson during an attempted escape. Brian Doyle and Ryan Walsh, both suspected members of *Fian Rúnda*, were later killed while in pursuit of Ms. Baskin and her friend, Shawn Murphy, after they had found the coin collection. Their accomplices who were arrested in Manitou, in exchange for lesser charges divulged information about several persons in authority within the secretive organization.

Irish law enforcement, in cooperation with the FBI and Interpol, was finally able to level specific charges against suspected key players in the criminal organization which, until now, were considered almost untouchable. *Fian Rúnda,* according to certain authorities, had previously been recognized for the fierce loyalty of its members and their refusal to divulge any incriminating information concerning the organization, its structure, and its operation.

"This is a real coup for the Garda Síochána, the police force of the Republic of Ireland," said FBI Agent Terry Munson, one of the arresting agents, "and for law enforcement in general. I've been in communication with a couple of officers over there, and they have made numerous arrests for crimes that had remained on their books for several years." When asked what changed concerning the devotion of *Fian Rúnda* members, Agent Munson replied, "*Fian Rúnda* changed. It's not the elite organization it was back in the nineteenth century. Now it's just a disorganized mess, little more than a group of thugs. I think that getting that coin collection back was one of the only things driving them now, and when that fell through, it was pretty much every man for himself."

The coin collection traces the history of the Roman Empire from Caesar Augustus to the lesser known Julius Nepos, considered by many historians to be the last emperor of the Western Roman Empire. While the Roman Senate had authority to mint bronze coins, the O'Riordan collection contains only gold and silver coins, eighty in all, minted by decree of the Caesars themselves. At least two of the coins are the only known ones of their kind in existence. According to a spokesman for the Professional Numismatists Guild, "this is without a doubt the most valuable single private collection I have ever seen. I don't know that it's necessarily the most valuable ever, but in terms of monetary worth combined with historical value, it's certainly one of the most important finds of the last century or two."

Several experts have examined the collection since the story hit the wire last month and have deemed it to be worth in excess of ten million dollars, and likely much more. After a careful examination of the collection, and of Isadora O'Riordan's history, provenance has been established and Ms. Baskin is considered to be the rightful owner of the collection. She has since employed Sotheby's to auction the collection.

"I don't want to be rich," she said. "Whatever I get from the sale of the coin collection will go into a trust fund. I still want to help underprivileged people and I have a lawyer and a financial advisor who are looking into various options for me."

Ms. Baskin has left her job as a social worker for Looking Up, a Denver-based organization primarily devoted to helping the city's homeless get back on their feet. She is now living in Manitou Springs in the house she inherited from her grandmother, with the intent of opening a bed and breakfast.

ere's the tally so far," Shawn said proudly as Dora walked into the room. He looked back down at the computer screen. "I've found four living descendants of Mahaley's sister and two descendants of her brother."

He had started tracing Dora's ancestry on his laptop while his leg healed, and now that he had regained his strength, he still found the occupation to be fascinating enough to keep going. He was sprawled out on the sofa in Dora's living room, soon to be the common sitting room for "Isadora's Bed and Breakfast." The B&B was scheduled to open in a month, and Shawn's sister-in-law, Robin, was making good on her offer to help. She and Dora were becoming good friends.

"I've also found five descendants of Clara and Peter's children. By the way, you're descended from Quentin Hodges."

"Well, you've certainly been busy," Dora replied. "So, where are they?"

"Interestingly, almost all of them live in a small town in northern New Mexico."

"Not Oklahoma?" Dora asked. She had expected that they might still be on or near the Cherokee reservation. She sat down on the sofa next to him.

"A couple of them are, but most of them lost their farms in the 1930s."

"Because of the depression?"

"Actually, it was during the dustbowl in the midwest," Shawn explained. "Due to a number of compounded reasons, including over-cultivation and other generally poor farming techniques, erosion became a major problem. When the drought struck, there was nothing to hold the topsoil down.

"Then the winds came and people quite literally lost their farms when the topsoil blew away. When that happened, a lot of Cherokee people relocated to New Mexico and southern   Colorado."

"Do you know anything about them?" Dora asked.

"Nothing specific. There are several scattered Cherokee communities – one is even an actual township near Albuquerque. But the one where your relatives live seems to be a fairly poor unincorporated community. No police force or fire department. Nearest hospital is about forty miles away in Taos."

"Sounds like the perfect place to establish my Cherokee Trust Fund."

Shawn looked at Dora with wonder. "You got nearly thirty million dollars from the sale of that coin collection. I've never known anybody who had that much money, to do with as they pleased. And you're giving it away to help others."

"I don't want to be a millionaire," Dora replied with a shrug. "I barely know what to do with the stocks and bonds Gramma left me. That's why I hired a financial advisor to help me with that. But even that's more than I need, especially with the B&B."

"Have I ever told you that I think you're awesome?" Shawn asked.

"You have," Dora replied. "Please continue." Shawn smiled at her and, putting his computer aside, pulled her closer to him and wrapped his arms around her.

"Dora Baskin, you're an amazing woman."

"Thank you," she said with a mischievous smile. "But my name is Isadora."